Season of the Jew

By the Same Author

FICTION

The New Zealanders (stories)

Summer Fires and Winter Country (stories)

Among the Cinders

The Presence of Music (stories)

The Summer's Dolphin

An Ear of the Dragon

Strangers and Journeys

A Touch of Clay

Danger Zone

Figures in Light (Stories)

The Lovelock Version

DRAMA

Once on a Chunuk Bair

NONFICTION

New Zealand: Gift of the Sea

The Shell Guide of New Zealand

Love & Legend

Season of the Jew

◂◂◂◂ *a novel by* ▸▸▸▸

Maurice Shadbolt

A Nonpareil Book

David R. Godine, Publisher

Boston

This is a *Nonpareil Book* published in 1990 by
David R. Godine, Publisher, Inc.
Horticultural Hall
300 Massachusetts Avenue
Boston, Massachusetts 02115

First U.S. edition published by W. W. Norton & Company, Inc.

Library of Congress Cataloging in Publication Data
Shadbolt, Maurice.
Season of the Jew.
(Nonpareil books; 55)
1. New Zealand—History—1843–1870—Fiction.
I. Title. II. Series
PR9639.3.S5S4 1990 823 88-45293
ISBN 0-87923-753-8 (pbk.)

PHOTO CREDITS

Grateful acknowledgment for use of photographs is given in the order in which the photos appear, as follows: 1-2: The Gisborne Museum Collection, New Zealand; 3-7: Alexander Turnbull Library, New Zealand; 8: Hawkes Bay Art Gallery; 9: The Cornell Collection, Alexander Turnbull Library; 10: Alexander Turnbull Library; 11: Gisborne Museum Collection; 12-13: Alexander Turnbull Library; 14: Gisborne Museum Collection; 15: Cowan Collection, Alexander Turnbull Library; 16: Defenders of New Zealand, Alexander Turnbull Library; 17: Gisborne Museum Collection; 18-20: Alexander Turnbull Library; 21: Gisborne Museum Collection.

First printing

PRINTED IN THE UNITED STATES OF AMERICA

SHYLOCK: If you prick us, do we not bleed? If you poison us, do we not die? And if you wrong us, shall we not revenge? If we are like you in the rest, we will resemble you in that. If a Jew wrong a Christian, what is his humility? Revenge. If a Christian wrong a Jew, what should his suffrance be by Christian example? Why, revenge. The villainy you teach me I will execute; and it shall go hard but I will better the instruction.
SOLANIO: Here comes another of the tribe; a third cannot be match'd, unless the devil himself turn Jew.

William Shakespeare, *The Merchant of Venice*

Author's Note

The greater part of this novel derives from events on a remote coast of the then British colony of New Zealand during the years 1868 and 1869. The few people familiar with these events (which are still in search of an historian) may note some highlighting of essentials, condensation of incident and fusing of historical dramatis personae. Others need only know that most of this happened, and much in the manner described.

Poverty Bay, c. 1870

Church at Manutuke, Poverty Bay, built 1889

Thought to be the most likely portrait of Rikirangi Te Turaki Te Kooti (lithograph)

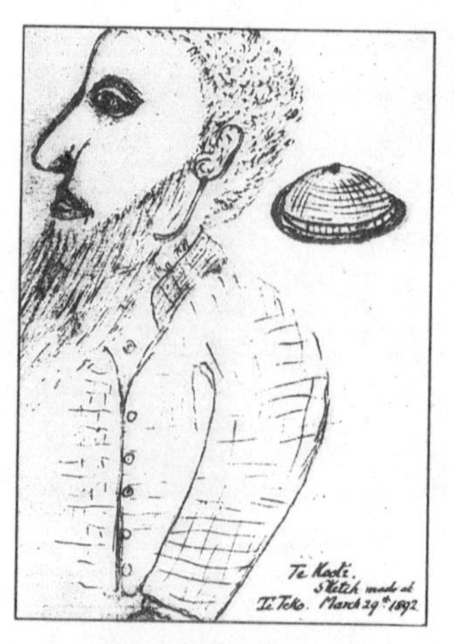

Sketch of Te Kooti, March 29, 1892, by Mr. T.H. Mill, Inspector of Native Schools

(opposite page)
Maori Prisoners, Napier Jail, 1866. Te Kooti rumored to be among this group.

Major-General Sir George Stoddard Whitmore, 1830-1903.
(opposite page) *Hauhaus captured at Napier, November, 1865.*

Hemi Kumekume, wife of Te Kooti. Escaped with him to the King Country in 1872. Probably not his wife at the time of the events of this book.

"Encampment of the Forest Rangers near Te Putahi Pa on the Whenuakura River, 7 January 1866," by Gustavus Ferdinand von Tempsky (1828-1868)

Pioneer huts, Makauri bush near Gisborne

Gilbert Mair's camp at Kaiteriria, Rotorua with his Arawa flying column. Mair second from left leaning on house to right of spades.

Ropata Wahawaha, later photograph

Major Ropata Wahawaha c. 1865

Captain Porter (far right) and a party of Ngatai Maori auxiliaries at Opotiki 1870

Major Reginald Newton Briggs

East Coast Hussars cross the Waipaoa River, c. 1885

Illustration from N.Z. Herald December 1, 1868: "War in New Zealand – Volunteers surprised by Maoris at To Ngutu-ote-manu"

"Forest Rangers camp in the bush during Chutes march around Mt. Taranaki," by von Tempsky, who stands at left

A unit of the New Zealand Armed Constabulary seeking Te Kooti

Volunteers in camp Poverty Bay

Season of the Jew

1

There was once a man called George Fairweather, who might have been many things, but was most singly a soldier. In November of 1863, still on the supple side of his fortieth year, he was amiably and muddily resident in the uniform of a British imperial officer. Lieutenant George Fairweather of the 65th Foot (alias The Royal Tigers, The Young and Lovelies, and lately and locally the *Ickety Pips*) stood on a scrubby antipodean ridge and watched three efficient Armstrong guns drop shells into a Maori hilltop fortress. To the right was a wide river in which two British gunboats struggled to make themselves useful in a fast current. To the left was a fat lake, fitfully sunlit, above which startled birdlife circled. Beyond were ferny river flats and then misted mountain ranges of the New Zealand interior. With high parapets, robust palisades and large outer earthworks, the Maori fort bulked on the approach to that interior.

For the most part the Armstrong guns made their point. The anguish of the defenders became more evident, their cries and curses carried three hundred yards on unruly wind. Sometimes artillery was answered weakly by shotgun and musket. Otherwise, with eight hundred soldiers assembled as witness, and half as many sailors and marines, the spectacle was more one of formal execution than battle.

'A damned comfortable way to win a war,' Captain Duke said.

'More to my taste, sir,' Fairweather agreed.

'Astonishing,' Duke mused, and lit his pipe. 'They give us a run for our money in the forest. Yet they doom themselves with a hopeless site.'

'Anything for glory,' Fairweather suggested.

'Or land,' Duke said.

'If despair is the sum of it.'

'Or pride. My understanding is that such hilltop forts are traditional. From the days of spear and club. One supposes they dig deeper now.'

An Armstrong gun scored beyond the Maori defences. Scraps of earth rose. Smoke. A lengthening scream.

'Thank God, then, for tradition,' Fairweather said. 'It makes no inconvenience for imperial artillery.'

'Tomorrow,' Duke predicted, 'most should be disclosing much anxiety to swear themselves loyal subjects of the Queen.'

'I understand there is more to it now, sir. In the matter of land.'

'Ah,' Duke said, and relit his pipe. 'It can be argued that confiscation of rebel land is in conformity with Maori custom. They refuse to comprehend defeat until their lands are lost.'

'It can be argued?'

'Rather rhapsodically.'

'By the colonists.'

'Who else?'

'If this campaign is one for land, rather than the peace of the realm, desirably colonists should be fighting their own battles.'

'Colonial militia is currently being recruited on the basis of four hundred confiscated acres for officers, an even fifty for men. The inducement has produced miracle cures among colonists hitherto thought too lame and blind for military service. You and I, Fairweather, are in the wrong army. We could be landed gentry.'

'Aristocrats of Oceania, sir.'

'Quite,' Duke said. 'Even General Cameron makes no secret of his distaste. To subdue the Queen's avowed enemies is one thing. To serve colonial avarice is another. What, then, are we?'

'Soldiers, sir,' Fairweather said.

'So General Cameron has likewise been heard lamenting.'

Armstrong guns sounded again. Their shelling was echoed by gunboats now tethered to the riverside. Maori cries rose in pitch.

'They would do well to surrender now,' Fairweather observed. 'If not with their land, at least with their lives.'

'It is reliably said they are a dying race. They show much resolve to hasten the process.'

'Or to show life is worth little without land.'

'Perhaps,' Duke allowed.

A flustered subaltern arrived with a written order. Maori muskets conveyed another message; shot hummed about. Fairweather and the subaltern made themselves small. Duke, never conspicuously in love with life, took no cover. He finished reading the order, disbelief apparent, and sent the subaltern on his way.

'It seems we are now given our chance too,' he disclosed.

'Sir?'

'To show what we are worth, Fairweather. I must presume General Cameron feels the affray ignoble this far.'

'We are winning, surely, with magically few tears.'

'We must be seen to have won. A commander who led Scottish infantry up

Crimean heights cannot let it be said that this war was won with artillery.'

'The natives will soon be starved out, sir.'

'Untidy. Also conducive to colonial scorn.'

'So what is the word, sir?'

'Three companies of the 65th are to advance. Ours first with bayonets fixed. To us falls the privilege of clearing the foe.'

'From that fort, sir?'

'We appear to have no other in view,' Duke said calmly.

'Quite so, sir,'

'General Cameron appears to feel the artillery has sufficiently prepared the path to glory. Desirably the Maoris will have no muscle left to repel British bayonets. First we take the outer trenches. Then we gallantly scale the parapets.'

'For appearances, sir?'

'Think on the bright side, Fairweather. No further lashing from colonists' tongues. Tomorrow we shall be accredited conquerors.'

Engineers stood ready with ropes, scaling-ladders and planks. Duke saw fit to shake Fairweather's hand. A bugle announced their advance. They moved forward in skirmishing order, at first across dead ground, then unsteadily down a steep slope where vegetation rose to the chest; arms had to be held high. In their elevated rifle pits, and perches above their central redoubt, Maori warriors watched the bobbing heads of Her Majesty's 65th Foot Regiment with elation apparent. Their first volley was ragged, mostly harmless. The second, at a hundred yards, had more teeth. Here and there men of the 65th spun and cursed, or quietly sank. Duke felt for his moment. With no marksmen in reserve, the vulnerable Maoris in the outer trenches were busy reloading.

'Forward,' he shouted. 'Charge!'

Clearing the scrub, his men fanned into a staggering run. The ground lifted. With mounting yells they met the first Maori trenches. Many defenders saw no wisdom in warring against bayonets; they fled minus firearms. Fairweather's men spent much lethal energy in spearing bulky Maoris too slow to shift.

Duke dropped into a pit beside Fairweather. 'First blood,' he said. 'Now we tease out another volley.'

'There are their parapets still.'

'Patience, Fairweather. It isn't incumbent upon you to take this fort alone.'

Duke, with pistol cocked persuasively, directed an adjoining platoon forward; they drew fire. Fairweather's platoon raced through in support. Soon, and with no excess of savagery, all the outer Maori entrenchments were taken. Here and there men moaned, but no Maori for long. Duke and

Fairweather crawled to an elevation from which they could consider the substance of the fort. There was a wide, waterless and dismayingly deep moat. Then parapets surely twenty feet tall, trimmed with palisades, and defended by industrious Maori guns. Shot passed intimately overhead.

'We promise to provide much spectacle, sir,' Fairweather decided.

'Just so,' Duke said. 'Order up the scaling-ladders.'

'They will be too short, sir.'

'And they must be seen to be. Bring them up.'

A white flag lifted from the parapet before them. Musketry soon ceased.

'Surrender?' Fairweather asked.

'I think not, Fairweather. Not with the 65th on offer.'

A defender in the feathered cloak of a Maori chief, with ragged European trousers incongruous beneath, rose beside the truce flag. He shouted in Maori.

'What does he ask?' Fairweather said.

Duke, who had made himself familiar with Maori, saw humour. 'He requests a fair fight. In furtherance of which he desires a more ample supply of British gunpowder. Shot they have in plenty. Powder is running low. Food and further water, he says, might also be appreciated if the siege is prolonged.'

'They never disappoint us, sir.'

'He wishes us reminded that thus far in this campaign he has kept our commanders supplied with meat, potatoes and milch goats in accord with the scriptural injunction to give thine enemy meat if he hungers, drink if he thirsts. He feels some reciprocal gesture might now be timely.'

'From Christian gentlemen.'

'If we still pass muster. We have already laboured mightily to convince them that slaughter is no sin on the sabbath. Hope springs eternal in the savage breast.'

'I take it we are to disenchant yet again.'

'Colonel Wyatt appears to have advanced within earshot. Unless I am much mistaken, he will convey the request to General Cameron, who in turn will reject it most solemnly. Meanwhile we have five further minutes to consider fate, and those parapets.' Duke refilled his pipe and lit it with care. 'To think that my greatest fear in this campaign was that I might find myself short of a tolerable tobacco.'

'A droll war,' Fairweather said.

'They all are,' Duke said. 'Never dream of Agincourt or Waterloo.' Perhaps Duke had once. His hair was grey and his smile bitter.

'It is this war I wish to wake from, sir. The theological firepower quite steals our thunder.'

'Alas,' Duke sighed. 'In the meantime you, Lieutenant Fairweather, will direct fire toward the top of the parapets while I confirm the dimension of the scaling-ladders.'

Fairweather understood the order; a reprieve. 'That,' he argued, 'will not be necessary, sir.'

'Covering fire will be,' Duke insisted.

A messenger from General Cameron appeared within their line; and shouted a reply to the Maori. The general, it seemed, regretted his inability to provide the rebels with gunpowder; it was not in his power as commanding officer to offer more than honourable surrender.

'The man has no charity,' Fairweather said. 'Nor humour. He might at least wish them luck with their endeavours today. And the promise of a little water would not go amiss. We have millions of gallons of river.'

'Never haggle with a Scot,' Duke said.

The Maori by the truce flag indicated his disappointment with the British. Duke interpreted, 'He says he fears not British guns. He fears not British bayonets. He fears only God on this sacred day. He trusts General Cameron, as his comrade in Christ, feels no shame.'

More traditionally, the Maori on the parapet turned and bared his buttocks by way of contempt for British commanders; and ducked out of sight. The truce flag was lowered. There was an experimental shot or two from either side. Battle had begun again, if not yet with conviction. That was over to Duke.

'Haere mai,' the Maoris began calling; and jeering. *'Haere mai, te Ickety Pips.'*

Welcome. Welcome the 65th.

To Fairweather Duke said, 'Remain in reserve unless extremity is apparent.'

'You are a brave man, sir,' Fairweather was impelled to say.

'I shall endeavour not to remember that you have always been a poor judge of character,' Duke said.

Scaling-ladders were at hand, also three silent platoons of the storming party. Captain Duke rose with sword aloft, pistol pointed, and ordered advance. It could be seen that he had lived an unremarkable martial lifetime for this moment; cowardice was no longer within his range. Shouting encouragement, Duke led the platoons down into the moat, where they met overhead fire, then hard up against the foot of the parapet enclosing the central Maori redoubt.

Fairweather's platoon was shooting at will. Some Maoris along the top of the parapet slumped, but not before many of Duke's storming party buckled. Those pressed to the foot of the parapet were out of the Maori field of fire; those struggling to lift scaling-ladders were necessarily exposed. Ladders rose, swayed, dropped. Men staggered, cried out, fell. For every Maori marksman silenced by Fairweather's platoon, there were two more to make themselves murderous. Artillery had done little to dim warrior fancy for British infantry at short range. Duke was still conspicuous in the noisy mêlée below. Eventually and incredibly one scaling ladder, then a second, was mounted against the parapet. They were all of three feet short.

'No,' Fairweather prayed.

Duke, his sword again high, was already climbing the first ladder, calling upon others to follow. To gain the lip of the parapet, and make himself credible there, he would have an awkward leap from the top of the ladder. If appearances were to be provided, Duke was the man to watch.

'Hold fire,' Fairweather ordered his men. 'Don't hit the captain.'

Duke leapt. There was a flash deriving from several detonations along the parapet. Duke seemed suspended in the blast, jiggling, floating, finally falling; his feet never touched the parapet top, and there was a long way to fall. Others ascending the ladders, making the same melancholy leap, offered less arresting imitations. A fellow lieutenant of Fairweather's actually set foot on the parapet and plunged into the fort; tomahawks rose and fell and he could be observed no more. Casualties clustered at the foot of the scaling ladders.

Extremity hardly held worse in reserve. No one could now argue that General Cameron had waged an easy campaign; nor could colonists accuse him of lacking aggression. Fairweather stood and ordered his platoon to advance.

'Us too, sir?' asked a bemused sergeant. 'Up them ladders?'

'When so ordered,' Fairweather said. Discharging his pistol at the most visible Maoris, he skidded down into the moat and arrived at the foot of the parapet. He found Duke among the damaged and dying. Survivors breathlessly hugged the parapet wall.

'You are to retire,' Duke said, just audibly. 'That is an order.'

'I heard,' Fairweather said.

Duke was all but beyond recall. His tunic was shredded and bloody; his groin bled also; his legs seemed shattered.

'I never made much of a soldier,' Duke said feebly.

'Quiet,' Fairweather pleaded. 'We shall soon get you out.'

'There are needy to get out.'

'You qualify.'

'For a prayer.'

'There will be many,' Fairweather promised.

'A prayer from you would mean more than most.'

'In which case I shall put aside principle, sir. You shall have mine also.'

'That is worth dying for,' Duke said with pain. 'A sinner back in the fold.'

'You were loved,' Fairweather protested. 'And are.'

Duke closed his eyes. 'I should have preferred a scene more auspicious. In a cause less indifferent.'

'Good men are good wherever they fall.'

'Pray continue to believe it, Fairweather. Now do what you must.'

Maori fire had slackened; perhaps lack of powder dictated a massacre of modest dimension. Survivors were bearing wounded back over imperilled ground. Fairweather clumsily hoisted Duke on to his shoulders and stumbled across the increasingly vast moat with an even more exposed climb looming; Duke sighed in his ear.

'Look out,' a soldier cried.

To no point. Uncharitable Maori marksmen were obliged to confirm British folly. Fairweather felt shot thud into Duke's spine. Then his left leg, hugely jolted, ceased support; he sagged and sank under Duke's weight. Fairweather tried to rise. He couldn't; his numb left leg refused function. Duke, gone limp, bled stickily. Fairweather heard shouts move away; it seemed he had been abandoned for dead in the moat along with Duke; most men seemed to have escaped. When Duke was finally lifted and rolled to one side, Fairweather saw that this indeed was the case.

It was also the case that a Maori face gazed down on him. Fairweather flinched. But there was no tomahawk upraised. The Maori knelt, examined Duke briefly, then contemplated Fairweather. 'You live,' the Maori diagnosed. 'Not he.'

'Nor you for long, with no white flag,' Fairweather said. He recognized the chief of the parapet.

'I bring regrets,' the Maori explained. 'You were shot while about mercy. This was not my wish.'

'You push scruple too far,' Fairweather argued.

The Maori nevertheless grasped Fairweather under the arms and dragged him away from Duke. Not toward the Maori redoubt; toward British lines.

'Now you push fate,' Fairweather protested.

In confirmation, British shot fell around.

'Go,' Fairweather urged. 'Run. This makes for misunderstanding.'

The Maori was not to be denied. He tumbled Fairweather over the rim of the moat, spilling him among men of his cowering platoon. Perhaps contempt was at work as much as mercy; the one British officer left alive from the assault had been delivered. The unburdened Maori then fled back across the moat.

'Don't shoot,' Fairweather pleaded to men nearby.

They fired all the same.

'Got the cheeky bastard,' someone said. 'Shoulder. We won't see him again.'

'No,' Fairweather sighed. 'We surely will never.'

There was a stretcher, a brutal climb to a hospital tent, and a surgeon. Later he was borne in a slow wagon of wounded back to the settlement of Auckland; a wagon bent on investigating every cruel rut in the military road. The news reached Fairweather on the way. With gunpowder going, the Maoris again wished to talk terms. General Cameron's truce party, made welcome in the fort, took advantage of Maori insistence on preliminary prayers to call up the marines. The Maoris felt it unbefitting as hosts to contest matters further. There had been forty British lives lost; perhaps God kept count of Maori dead. Finally planted in a hospital bed, Fairweather learned that General Cameron had cited him, in warm terms, for his attempted rescue of Captain Duke under enemy fire.

'Nothing like a little valour to sweeten a sullen fiasco,' a fellow officer said. 'It might mean a Victoria Cross.'

Fairweather was silent.

'Well?' the officer said.

'A New Zealand savage merits it more,' Fairweather said. 'If you can't find me a good war, at least locate some good whisky.'

It was a week before surgeons finished mining his leg for splintered bone and Maori metal; a month before he walked again, in irritable fashion. Auckland was a mean and muddy place of confinement. Hobbling along unkempt lanes, he hit out at bellicose dogs with his walking stick and dodged smelly ditches and mouldering horse dung. After two decades the settlement was still no more than a muddled half-moon of wooden frontier habitations about a harbour fretted with tidal waters and greened with mangroves; behind were sheep-filled fields and extinct volcanic cones. Mercantile houses, churches, hotels, shops and a brewery or two rose at its heart. The briskest business on show was war. With fresh troops landing from Sydney and further, the streets often reverberated with drumbeat; landless colonists gathered to cheer. There were silences after the soldiers, behind munition wagons, tramped inland to join issue with Maori belligerents. Then wagons with wounded rumbled back; hotels filled with overnight veterans of the New Zealand war. In the barracks sergeant-majors reasserted authority with large voices and the lash. Fairweather, when he could, put the orchestrated uproar of the barracks behind him; he basked in the sun of the anarchic port.

Maori vessels, often in boisterous armada, were bringing in maize, potato and salt pork to fill British bellies. While Maoris of the interior battled for their lands, these benign coastal tribesmen gave themselves no less passionately to the stratagems of commerce, holding back harvests until prices rose; they tallied their triumphs in pounds and shillings, not British dead and wounded. The fate of their beleaguered fellows did not divert. Disaffected tribesmen, however hungry, paid no bills. The British commissariat had reliable coin.

In the end Fairweather did more than marvel. He dug brushes, pencils and paints from the bottom of his trunk; they had not been deployed since his arrival in New Zealand. He had once read Ruskin with rare emotion, and still considered that sage no fool in matters aesthetic. On the other hand Fairweather had no aspiration to be an antipodean Turner or imperial Millais; at this moment he saw art as no more than remedial. On the Auckland waterside it never permitted tedium. There were always inquisitive Maoris peering over his shoulder; conversation was the price of a pose.

On the fourth day Fairweather had the makings of a magical portrait. A wiry, quick-eyed, flamboyant Maori; jaunty little beard, expensive rings on his fingers, red scarf carelessly knotted about a dark neck; the Polynesian seafarer in well weathered flesh. 'Will I,' this fellow asked Fairweather, 'make your fortune?'

'Fortune?'

'Financial fortune.'

'Alas,' Fairweather said. And drew.

'No?' This Maori was quick to mirth. His laugh was more a nervous neigh; often perilously close to hiccuping out of control. 'Then why?'

'Some would argue,' Fairweather said, 'that my reward is spiritual.'

'Spiritual?' The Maori was baffled.

'Spiritual,' Fairweather insisted.

The Maori considered. 'I am most spiritual also,' he beamed. 'I believe in the redemption of sinful man through the sacrifice of our Lord Jesus Christ.'

'That,' Fairweather argued, 'is a vastly more complicated affair.'

'Might I be,' the Maori asked with fascination, 'the more spiritual for painting your pictures?'

'I think not. Lilies of the field toil not, nor spin.'

'Matthew. Chapter six. Verse twenty-eight.'

'A man so intimate with the scriptures has riches stored elsewhere. And small need to quibble with the work of his Creator.'

'I was a very good mission boy.'

'That seems apparent.'

'First I learn scriptures in Maori, then in English. Also I take my name from a missionary. Coates. From the London chief of all missionaries.'

'Remarkable. I trust Mr Coates was suitably moved.'

'Of course I wished to become missionary too. To give news of Christ's grace to the heathen. To tell them of Satan, temptation and sin.'

Coates was suddenly less genial; he even seemed bruised.

'You have a grievance?' Fairweather said tactfully.

'They did not wish me for a missionary. My family had no mana. You understand that Maori word?'

'Imperfectly. Standing? Prestige?'

'And more,' Coates said.

'A delicate thing,' Fairweather agreed. 'Englishmen have difficulties with mana also.'

'Sons of chiefs were better to serve Christ. Not a *tutua* like me.'

'*Tutua?*'

'A scrub. A nothing, a nobody. That is me, sir.'

'You make, if I may say so, a prosperous picture of frustration.'

Coates' laugh hiccuped again. 'I learned to plough, sir. To break horses. Build boats. Also to buy and sell. Especially to buy and sell.'

'So there is hope for a *tutua* in the temporal world?'

'I captain my own schooner. The cargo I bring to Auckland is remunerative. When the market is good, I think civilization is greatly advantageous. Chiefs and chiefly sons are jealous. Money makes its own mana.'

'I am moderately addicted to it myself,' Fairweather said.

'Mana, sir?'

'Money.'

'It answereth all things. Ecclesiastes. Chapter ten. Verse nineteen.'

'And he that pisseth against the wind wetteth his shirt.'

Coates was puzzled. 'I am far from familiar with that verse, sir.'

'The gospel according to George Fairweather. Chapter one. Verse one.'

'Interesting,' Coates said. 'Please speak your thought further.'

'Maoris with whom I have lately been intimate have been less than circumspect with their urine.'

Coates shrugged. 'War is most inefficacious. Especially against Armstrong guns.'

'There speaks sweet reason. You should travel as a mercantile missionary among the sullenly unconverted.'

'I say that the new sun which rises in the east is the light of Queen Victoria upon the land.'

'The church's loss is Mammon's gain,' Fairweather said. 'You have a talent.'

'But for her gracious majesty I might still be a *tutua*. Now I am somebody.'

'Plainly,' Fairweather agreed.

'Next time you see your Queen, I should be most appreciative if you could convey my gratitude.'

'My audiences with her are infrequent,' Fairweather explained; and fought off a smile.

'I do not presume, sir? I do not say the wrong thing?'

'Never.'

'Good,' Coates said with satisfaction. 'I do not often meet English officers. To speak the truth, sir, you are the first. I see much mana.'

'Conquerors tend to cultivate it. And as we English are greatly given to conquering, it becomes as second nature.' Though Fairweather's hand worked with speed, there seemed too much of Coates to contain; there was a frustrating ebb and flow of expression, not least in the larrikin eyes.

'I think I like you,' Coates disclosed. 'I think you are not so serious.'

'Small thanks to New Zealand.'

'You do not enjoy us here?'

'Men of your race keep us energetically employed. That must be said. We dig an uncommonly large number of graves.'

'You grieve?'

'For good men, and brave. In battle the best are not to be spared.'

'Perhaps I can be of some small assistance in this matter. A merry heart doeth good like a medicine. Proverbs. Chapter seventeen. Verse twenty-two.'

'And from where does this merry heart hail?'

'Poverty Bay.'

'That sounds splendidly desperate.'

'A most beneficial bad joke,' Coates said. 'When the first of you English sailed into our bay, we fought you. Not fed you. Thus we were thought impoverished. Wrong. We have the best riverland in New Zealand. The tallest corn. The finest potato. The fattest pigs. Best of all we have damn few colonists. And no war. Very much no war.'

'That refreshes.'

'I think if we say hello to Queen Victoria, she will look after us. We shall see her settlement in Auckland does not starve.'

'Depending on prices?'

'War prices are most congenial. It is a fast run, sometimes only five days from Poverty Bay. We make quick profit when the wind is well situated.'

'And the war,' Fairweather said.

'Better here than there,' Coates said.

'You have no fears?'

'We do no harm; we give no excuse. Many soldiers would be necessary. Your general is an honourable man.'

'So I have heard said.'

'You say otherwise?'

'It is true that when colonists are out of earshot he declares our business here is unhappy. He would sooner not make war. But be sure he does.'

Coates produced a plausible shiver. 'I trust I never see him in Poverty Bay. No soldier. Not even you, sir.'

'I would drink to that with something in hand.'

'That is not without remedy.'

'Auckland hotels are not to my taste.'

'Also not to mine, sir,' Coates said. 'I find them most crowded with disagreeable colonists and drunken soldiers who think one dead nigger might be as good as another. I am an extremely perceivable nigger.' Coates' laugh neighed vastly again. 'I should delight in entertaining you aboard my schooner. There is rum there in excessive quantity. Truth to tell, it is most of my cargo.'

'For the edification of Poverty Bay?'

'Most urgently. First, however, I have an errand. You could well help me speed it. I wish to purchase a book on English law in commercial matters. It might be to my most considerable advantage.'

'Monetarily, I take it.'

'Most monetarily. I have learned there is more than one gospel; I wish not to be seen lacking. Perhaps you might accompany me to an establishment where my need might be made plain.'

'You are asking me to aid and abet you in embracing the wise man's religion?'

'Quite, sir. If you would.'

In the end, before failure declared itself, Fairweather put the unfinished portrait aside. It lacked life; it lacked Coates. With a vivid Maori in patched nautical garb he proceeded up Auckland's one street of substance; Coates took his elbow to steer him past patches of mud, puddles of rain, and parading whores. They arrived at a dusty and undistinguished outpost of the republic of letters; the window of the bookshop had recent London publications on display. Among them was a biography of Garibaldi; a copy of the book lay open at a competent portrait. Fairweather would rather not so soon have suffered the reminder of his own departure from the field. Nevertheless, for future purposes, he noted the technique.

'Who is this gentleman?' Coates asked.

'An Italian,' Fairweather said. 'A patriot who persuaded other Italians to be themselves; to fight for themselves.'

'A great chief,' Coates concluded.

'Never. A wild man from nowhere. A son of a poor fisherman. A man of the hour.'

'Hour?'

'History's. Such a man cannot be prescribed. It seems the hour makes the man.'

'Would you say Jesus Christ, perhaps, was a man of the hour?'

'True that he was a Jewish carpenter. But there was mana, as I understand it, on his paternal side; and the family vocation.'

'So a man of the hour is best a *tutua*?'

'It would seem. Also such as Garibaldi here feel no obligation to perish on a cross for the sins of men. If he has the wit, he now sits in the Italian sun with a flagon of wine. An irregular Latin rabble rouser in his dotage.'

'I should not find this man instructive?'

'Not in matters mercantile,' Fairweather said.

Inside the bookshop the proprietor watched Coates with suspicion. A flashy native mariner foraging among books left much to be explained, more so with a limping imperial officer in attendance. Fairweather was not disposed to explain; let the man gape. It transpired that there was no primer on mercantile law available; there was, however, a fat treatise. Coates saw this as no problem. 'It is my wish to be thoroughly informed,' he disclosed. 'I have eventualities on hand.' Other volumes soon took his whim and depleted his purse. Not only on law. On theology too. Finally he was to be observed contemplating Darwin.

'What origin?' he asked. 'What species?'

'Come,' Fairweather pleaded. 'Enough.'

'Enough?'

'I think Poverty Bay is best not confused.'

They returned to the waterfront with Coates' erudite booty; and clambered aboard his boat. About were other Maori vessels loading and unloading. Coates' schooner was scrubbed and tidy, larger and visibly more seaworthy than most. 'A *tutua* must never seem so,' he explained. He was quick to broach a flagon of rum. Seagulls gusted noisily around, snapping up flecks of food in the sea.

'It is my impression, sir, that we were to drink to something,' Coates said.

'To my never putting in an appearance at Poverty Bay,' Fairweather recalled.

'Only as soldier, sir,' Coates said, and lifted his glass. He was quick to empty it. He wasn't slow with a second drink either. The third made him lean forward confidentially. 'There are times, sir, when I think I can view that which is yet to be.'

'Liquor on occasion leaves me with visions also,' Fairweather confessed.

'I do not joke. My mission teacher was unhappy when I told him of forthcoming flood. Also of shipwreck with five drowned. These things came to pass.'

'You are trying to tell me something.'

'Quite, sir. I think I have such a far view now. Your face is familiar. It is not in my past. Therefore it is of my future. This must mean you are to arrive in Poverty Bay.'

'See a little further,' Fairweather said amiably. 'In what form?'

A fifth glass of rum appeared to provide Coates with illumination. 'I see you not as now,' he announced. 'I see you with work of peace.'

'Alarm me no more,' Fairweather said. 'I think my talent too meagre.'

'I am sorry, sir,' Coates said.

'On the other hand it suggests that I shall survive the New Zealand war. I drink to compassionate seers.' Fairweather sipped again at the coarse colonial rum. 'It biteth like a serpent and stingeth like an adder,' he pronounced.

'Proverbs, sir. I prefer the verse following. Thine eyes shall behold strange women and thine heart shall utter perverse things.'

A measure of rum later Coates proved to be a prophet of authority. A conspicuously strange woman rose from the cabin of a neighbouring schooner and stood in tall and pleasingly pictorial silhouette against sunlit sea. The wind lifted her long hair as she tried to tame it with a brush. Fairweather's anatomy, if not specifically his heart, was inclined to considerable utterance.

Coates noted his stare. 'She also is of Poverty Bay,' he disclosed.

'I believe all you say. You have a cornucopia.'

'For such a female we say *mehemea ko Kopu.* Like the morning star.'

'We tend to talk of the goddess for whom the star is named.'

'We also say *he pai kai e kore e roa te tirohanga,* Good fare cannot be looked at for long.'

'We say appetite comes from eating.'

'You must be a Maori.'

'It is more to the point whom she is.'

'Her name is Meri,' Coates revealed.

'Merry? There is a name rich with promise.'

'Meri. Much as Mary. In full, Meriana, Meriana Smith.'

'Don't disillusion. And Smith? It cannot be. Too commonplace.'

'Her father was Yankee Smith. A *pakeha* seaman who came among us. Her people are Maori. She is mostly to be seen so.'

'I am not one to let a little Yankee blood confuse matters. From this moment I am mostly Maori too.'

Meriana Smith, hair to satisfaction, allowed her gaze to travel over the vessels around. Her eyes rested frankly on Coates and Fairweather; especially and lengthily on Fairweather.

'Married?' Fairweather asked, rather breathless.

'Not for long. Her man drowned fishing. She thinks herself better without.'

'Men, or a husband?'

'Husband. Even his name.'

'You intrigue,' Fairweather announced.

'You wish to meet her?' Coates asked cheerfully. 'It can be arranged. This minute, perhaps, if urgency prevails.'

'Urgency currently prevails,' Fairweather judged.

'Understand this,' Coates said. 'She is not considered an easy woman.'

'Understand this. I am considered a difficult man.'

'Excellent,' Coates said. 'Follow me, sir.'

Not that there was a liaison of burdening dimension: there were merely most of the requisites, among them a hired Auckland room with curtains drawn against summer sun. Meri Smith's humorous eyes could never be called commonplace. And she manifested as more than the shrinking, wordless beauties of catchpenny Pacific romancers. She was animated, articulate, and in lovemaking equally eloquent; she insisted on slowly and inventively teasing him from tunic, trousers and boots.

'Do you mind?' she eventually asked.

'I find boldness most fetching,' he said. 'All lovers wish to be wanted.'

'When is a lover not?'

'When seducing an Englishwoman. It is often her custom to pretend innocence of the proceedings; to fancy the undertaking as spiritual.'

'You are telling me tales.'

'On my honour. Though I recall a colonel's wife. A less frivolous woman. Her hands had an uncanny life of their own when virile young junior officers were in her vicinity.'

'You,' she said. 'You are a terrible man.'

'When sufficiently encouraged.'

'I am just as that colonel's wife to you.'

'Never,' he said.

With cause. He was soon most exquisitely liberated; her amorous skills permitted no modesty. Surprise never ceased. Nor talented improvization.

'Would your Englishwomen do this?' she asked.

'Never those with lofty thoughts.'

'Good,' she said, and engulfed.

Their lovemaking, once earnest, was abundant, brief, and complete. Fairweather was momentarily unnerved by the volume of sound issuing from his throat. It suggested the collapse of some visceral obstruction. Meri was also far from silent. They grew quieter, tender rather than ferocious; he lay felled.

'Are you a good soldier?' she asked.

'That is an indecent question at this moment.'

'Tell me.'

'Some suggest so. I currently find favour.'

'What made you a soldier?'

'An enterprise much like the one which presently engages us. My lascivious cleric of a father sired a fourth son. Such as we are bred to face the artillery. Had I been the first son, or third, I might have been a scholar or a lawyer. The fourth you contribute to the army, to spare him a long life of dedicated indolence. And buy the beggar a commission. A tithe. A tax. A quaint English custom.'

'Poor you.'

'Perhaps. My impecunious father stumbled absently into his grave before he could purchase me a captaincy. A luckless lieutenant I remained. One who would now never see his innocent daubs hung in the Royal Academy. One shipped off, with his beard barely grown, to deal mercilessly with the Queen's enemies. An ageing apprentice to the priesthood of arms. Always the bridesmaid, never the bride.'

'What might you sooner have been?'

'A person of poor repute. I may yet find a feeble-witted heiress with whom I can lucratively elope; my sense of vocation survives.'

'Yet some think you a good soldier.'

'The man who thinks most things absurd has much advantage. When boredom ends, and guns bite, he is likely to revel.'

'I should not have asked,' she decided.

'You like me less?'

'I think you like yourself less,' she said.

They stood together on an Auckland jetty when Coates sailed for Poverty Bay. Coates was in effervescent mood, having already made enough of mercantile statutes to terrify an Auckland ship chandler, lacking in integrity and the letter of the law, with whom he had a past score to settle; he was pounds to the good and celebration to the worse. Meanwhile he busied his crew, ordered moorings cast off, and supervised the hoisting of sail; finally he turned to farewell Fairweather across the widening water.

'Good wind,' he shouted. 'I shall remember the gospel according to George Fairweather.'

His distinctive laugh lifted; he had only passably sobered.

'What does he mean?' Meri asked Fairweather.

'It means,' Fairweather explained, 'that men often talk much nonsense when without women.'

'Come,' she said. 'I hope you put no ideas in that man's head.'

'Why should that concern?'

'Because he has enough,' she said.

Coates was fast gone.

There was also a night at the theatre. The play was *Romeo and Juliet*, indifferently performed even by colonial measure. She laughed at the prolonged swordplay, which seemed an inefficient way to feud, and considered Romeo extravagantly unrealistic; there were more maidenheads than one in the world. Juliet was altogether out of the question. 'Too *ngoikore*,' she announced. 'Too feeble.'

No one would dare see Meriana Smith as *ngoikore*; that much was clear.

Fairweather argued, 'Perhaps, to serve drama, William Shakespeare found it necessary to make her so. Or he would have no tragedy.'

'Then your Mr Shakespeare is another great English liar. A Juliet born among Montagues and Capulets would be harder. *Kaha*. Strong.'

'What would you know of Montagues and Capulets?'

'Maoris are all Montagues and Capulets. When not fighting, they are finding excuses to fight. Especially Poverty Bay Maoris.'

'My understanding is that Poverty Bay is currently peaceful; your people take no side in the present war.'

'Because you do our work for us. Kill old enemies. Would Montagues help Capulets?'

'Perhaps not,' he said.

'Besides, Poverty Bay Maoris like best to quarrel with each other. Montague against Montague. Why battle the British? Mr Shakespeare knows nothing. Come. See.'

'When the Queen's work is done,' he promised.

'You mean that?'

'Of course,' he said, and possibly did.

Further and more perilous pledges were checked by a Maori schooner's day of departure. She, having made the most of Auckland, and not less of Fairweather, sailed back down the coast again, with replenished wardrobe, and more than a few baubles. His last gift, on parting, was a copy of Shakespeare's mirth-making masterpiece, affectionately inscribed. He, having healed for martial purpose, packed away paints and brushes, shed his walking stick, and rejoined the 65th.

For some months, perhaps even a year, the memory brought him satisfaction, and sometimes a smile. It certainly saw him past the end of the war.

2

Just one end was acceptable. Honour insisted; and General Cameron. 'It is idiotic,' Captain Blewitt said in the garrison mess. 'Ten thousand of Britain's best troops against a few hundred niggers. And no real victory. No more than a few prisoners here, a few there. They taunt us. They lead us on and laugh. When we attack, they are gone.'

'So is their land, nonetheless, sir,' Fairweather observed. 'Colonists can surely count that as triumph.'

'We are not to be made fools of,' Blewitt announced. He was an austere man, devout, a humourless addict of martial virtue. 'Colonists no longer enter into our calculations.'

'Even if we enter into theirs, sir?'

Blewitt ignored the interjection. 'It is time to get this war won. For Britain's sake. For our own. We can all look each other in the eye again.'

Fairweather, having failed to catch Blewitt's eye, reached for more port. Young and sober lieutenants listened with respect as Blewitt laboured on.

'Something of more decisive nature,' he argued, 'might allow us to think of return home.'

'I understand that to be a possibility anyway,' Fairweather said, 'with colonists unwilling to foot the bills for this campaign. Is the soldier worthy of his hire, sir, or is he not?'

'One good thrashing,' Blewitt said. 'That is what the rebel Maoris most need.'

'Then let us hope, sir, that this latest intelligence answers our difficulty.'

'Exactly, Fairweather,' Blewitt acknowledged. 'It seems that, for once, you might have taken my point.'

News had come of Maori tribesmen entrenching impertinently nearby. The numbers were unclear. What was understood, however, was that Maori ranks had been replenished. A mountain tribe, the Tuhoe, not belligerent until now, had marched into the region to insist on an engagement worth their talent for war. Seasoned rebels, made sadder and wiser by British artillery, felt obliged to provide; their mana as hosts would be diminished if they did not.

Between midnight and dawn next morning Blewitt's company of the 65th moved south into Maori territory. His men had seen no fight for six weeks; since then the war had demanded only the ravaging of rebel harvests and firing of dwellings. Too few Maoris had stood to be slain for Blewitt's satisfaction.

Their moonlit route took them past charred huts, abandoned wheatfields; they forded a river, toiled through swamp, crashed through thick scrub. As the sun rose, and autumn mist thinned, they lurched into an unusually fair and fruitful oasis which had still to feel war. Tidy Maori hamlets, orchards and grapevines long tended. A white wooden church with doors left wide open. Ripened melons and pumpkins rolled away underfoot; spiders webbed the wilting maize. Gorging birds scattered skyward along their line of march; little other life was evident. Human beings must just have judged it timely to decamp.

'Most seductive, sir,' Fairweather observed to Blewitt. 'Has this a name?'

'Orakau, I believe,' Blewitt said.

'Orakau.' Fairweather rather thought he might remember it. 'The need for the Queen's peace is far from apparent.'

'It will be,' Blewitt promised.

Columns of other troops could soon be seen converging dustily upon the terrain; there was the mounting tramp of most of three regiments, the whinny of horses, and the bang and creak of gun carriages along a cart road. Morning lost its spell faster with the first shots. Skirmishers had met Maori pickets.

Then Maori defences were detected. Low parapets rose from a sunny eminence screened by peach trees and post and rail fences.

'We throw a cordon around them,' Blewitt presently announced, 'and then give them hellfire. This time there will be no escape. No palaver. General Cameron has made his impatience plain. We have triumph in our hands today; it is not to slip us.'

'The 65th, sir?' Fairweather asked.

'Alas. General Cameron feels it only fair to allow the Royal Irish first bite at the cherry. You, Fairweather, would surely agree that the 65th has had its heroic hour.'

'In the matter of deportment, sir, a persuasive minute or two. It is my recollection that militant colonists were not heard from for some weeks.'

'More vengeful spirit might not go amiss, Fairweather.'

'Odd you mention it, sir. I was thinking the same.'

'It seems we might have caught this band of rogues on the hop. They haven't finished entrenching; they should fast be flushed out to face British steel on open ground. I give them three hours.'

'Altogether encircled?'

'And nowhere to go,' Blewitt confirmed.

'Would you fancy a wager, sir?' Fairweather asked.

By evening Fairweather was richer by one sovereign.

On the third day the Maori line was shelled, shaken and still there. Artillery and bayonets alike failed to intimidate. Assaults left lonely mounds of imperial dead reddening before Maori loopholes. General Cameron's message offering safe conduct for women and children within the fort won unpromising response; it seemed women and children were to fight too. 'Forever and ever,' was the reply translated. Soon after, by way of emphasis, the Maoris again sallied out from their line to leave British blood on the ground. They had no water. By night depleted warriors fired peach stones and wood chips; they prudently reserved metal for visible menace.

'Madmen,' Blewitt said. 'They must know themselves finished.' He was red-eyed, tense and unshaven; he had just ordered a fresh rum ration for his men.

'That,' suggested Fairweather, 'is a matter upon which we still fail to give satisfaction, sir.'

The men were growing noisy. The rum ration had been liberal.

'Quite,' Blewitt said. 'We yet again make for mockery. Two hundred natives holding Britain at bay? A nonsense. Sir Henry Havelock, who has just joined General Cameron, says he has never seen the like of it before. Not in India; not anywhere. It seems this will be remembered.'

'On that, sir, the enemy appears agreed too.'

'I trust it may never be said that the 65th was lacking.'

'You are making a proposition, sir?'

'Expressing apprehension, Fairweather. If this is much prolonged, the frustration and fervour of our company may run away with us.'

'That is not unfamiliar, sir.' Fairweather understood the rum ration at last.

'Indeed,' Blewitt went on, 'my fear is that men may grow impatient with humiliation. Even hurl themselves prematurely against weakened Maori defences. Would you say that a risk with your platoon, Fairweather?'

'Anything is possible, sir.'

'It would, of course, imperil other platoons who would feel obliged to give support. As indeed I should. We are to contain. Not attack. The 18th is sapping up to the parapets to make the breach. Are we understood?'

'Entirely, sir.'

An order yet not. Fairweather would never be able to protest that he had heard it; he moved to his men.

In shallow trenches his platoon muddled away time much as men in any war; farting, belching, scratching, complaining; some were slipping into alcoholic doze. Frustration might have been apparent; fervour was not. Maori fire was not a large issue.

'They think we are *tutae*,' Fairweather abruptly announced.

'Sir?' That was Corporal Kearon. A fair and earnest Protestant boy, with a dash of Viking, from County Wicklow.

'Tutae,' Fairweather said. 'Turd. The Maoris say we are turd. The 18th. The 40th. And the 65th. They are saying that we *Ickety Pips* are the worst excrement of all; the worst cowards.'

'No, sir.'

'Indeed Corporal Kearon. We give great offence to native nostrils.'

Others were interested now, and indignant.

'There is, of course, a tempting answer to that,' Fairweather allowed.

'Yes, sir,' Kearon said.

'It cannot be countenanced,' Fairweather said sternly. 'Captain Blewitt's hands are tied in this matter. His talent for spiriting up a heady engagement has been quite curtailed. The 18th is busy with saps. When the fort falls, as it must, they won't be slow to claim credit.'

'The 18th,' Kearon said with disgust.

'While our melancholy festers. And Maoris call us turd.'

'It isn't fair, sir,' Kearon said fervently. 'We never have a fair crack.'

'Let us be clear about it, Kearon. It is not to be thought upon. There must be no mad scamper for the honour of the 65th.'

Fairweather had not gone far back to Blewitt when he heard the first shout. Kearon's, of course. Then a salad of other cries. Caps were flung in the air. Two or three dozen men of Fairweather's platoon, and soon considerably more of the 65th, were rising from trenches with rifle and bayonet.

Blewitt was quick to Fairweather's side, and breathless. 'Go with them, Fairweather. Shape them. They are not to be stopped.'

'Then I trust the Maoris have been so informed, sir.'

Fairweather, with pistol drawn, bolted after the men. They had fifty yards of ground to cover, a fence to negotiate; there were just a few scarred fruit trees as shelter. Men erratic with rum drifted, and bunched.

'To the right,' Fairweather called.

To the right, at least, the Maori line had lately been chipped by artillery; to the left the defenders were diverted by the saps of the 18th and grenades flung from within.

But Kearon and his band were deaf to anything not their own yelling. A Maori volley caught them before Fairweather did. Some dropped. Some took shelter. Others went on. Fairweather followed, leaping a felled man, looking for Kearon's fair head in the van. There was a second sturdy volley; Fairweather felt its sting in his arm. Then he was down in a ditch, ducking under the profile of a Maori parapet, with a score or so men. Kearon was not of their number. He was tumbled two yards short, a hole filling with blood where his right eye had been.

Fairweather and his party were trapped. To retire would mean taking more shot; to force further issue with Maoris behind the parapet could call up worse. A ferocious shotgun, first one barrel, then a second, discharged from a loophole not far above his head. There was much shouting and shuffling audible within the Maori defences, along with inflamed oratory cut short by the grenades of the 18th; there was a feebler tide of sound from the wounded and dying. Common to most moans was the word *wai*. Water. There was no *wai*. Prayers were less detectable; it was some time since faltering Maori hymns had been heard. There were chants suggestive of older deities being invoked. Fairweather was an eavesdropping burglar with his hands caught in a slammed door.

'What now, sir?' asked a sobered man.

'Nothing,' Fairweather ordered. He had decided not to hear Blewitt, behind a flax bush thirty yards off, trying to assert command. About Blewitt were men similarly stranded, some embracing the earth, others crawling to his rear. 'We keep our heads down until dark. And trust the Almighty is not of a mind to delay it.'

'You're hit, sir.'

'Now you mention it,' Fairweather agreed.

The fellow tore away sticky tunic from Fairweather's upper arm. 'No one could say we let the regiment down. Not us, sir.'

'I am sure much can be forgiven,' Fairweather said. He winced as his wound was probed; something came free surprisingly fast.

'Just a scrap of rusty old nail, sir. Hardly got going. All the buggers have got left. Wiggle your fingers, sir.'

Fairweather wiggled.

'See? Good as new in no time, sir.' The soldier improvized a bandage from Fairweather's intact sleeve. 'Tight enough for you?'

'Tighter. That may be one scar worth saving.'

The shotgun had ceased reverberating above them. Elsewhere too Maori fire seemed to diminish. Soon the defence had suspiciously less character; the blast of the 18th's grenades called up thinner response. 'Do you hear what I hear?' he asked.

'I don't hear much in there, sir.'

Fairweather checked his pistol, located his sword.

'What is it, sir?'

'Forewarned is forearmed. Look sharp. Maoris don't shut up shop with a memorable battle proceeding apace.'

The mystery persisted; Maori fire grew even more muted. Then, some way to their right, a shadowy river of Maoris rippled free of smoke drifts; they cascaded from their defences to jog quickly and quietly with arms at their side. Lacklustre pickets of the 40th, positioned in that part of the British cordon, were surprised and slow with their weapons. The Maori phalanx began to function. The foremost warriors dropped to their knees and placed an effective volley. The phalanx sped on. More warriors knelt. Another sharp volley. Others pushed staggered fire to the flanks. The 40th melted. The Maoris had the rising terrain ahead to themselves. Open country. Then forest.

Men risen from the ditch alongside Fairweather were equally awed. 'They can't do that,' one protested. 'They can't get away clean.'

'They are,' Fairweather suggested.

'What about us, sir?'

'Until further informed, we are here to take their fort,' he decided.

He led men over the now undefended parapet and into the fort. It was all but emptied of intact Maoris. Drifts of dead. Wounded. A few women and dazed children. Bayonets of more than one regiment were lifting and falling; there were British whoops and Maori screams.

'Stop,' Fairweather cried.

A limping Maori woman, too weak to evade the onrush, took a thrust in the neck. Fairweather grabbed for her killer and found a man of his own platoon. It didn't delay him in felling the man. 'You said they called us turd, sir,' the creature whined.

'And now we are,' Fairweather said bitterly.

By the time Blewitt reached him, he was engaged in pistol-whipping an especially murderous ensign of the 18th.

'We are here to give fight to the Maori, Lieutenant Fairweather,' Blewitt said; and stationed himself before the cringing ensign. 'My hope is that you don't have to answer for this.'

'My hope, sir, is that I might,' Fairweather said.

'Group your platoon; there is no work here. The order is hot pursuit of the Maori column. They are not to escape.'

'They made a pretty picture,' Fairweather said. 'Why not kiss it goodbye?'

'Are you refusing the order?' Blewitt demanded.

Fairweather hesitated. 'I think,' he said finally, 'we should both find that inconvenient, sir.'

'Agreed, Lieutenant Fairweather,' Blewitt said with relief.

Fairweather's platoon joined the pursuit. Close to two thousand British troops were tumbling across fields and up ferny slopes after the fugitive Maoris. Some were lowered; survivors stood again and again to give fight while their fellows hurried clear. There could not be more than a hundred of the original column left.

'So fire above their heads,' Fairweather ordered at length. 'Just keep them moving.'

'Above, sir?'

'You heard me.' He made a point of not being particular who heard; and who shamed. Anyway tiring Blewitt was soon far behind.

There was less than an hour of daylight left when Fairweather's platoon pushed down a quiet gully toward the bank of a modest river; there were still a few shots on their flanks. 'To the water,' he said. 'No further.'

There was an obstacle. An elderly Maori, with impressive facial tattoo, levelled a shotgun. Behind him, three other Maoris, two men with a wounded woman, worked slowly down to the river. The old man covered their escape. He did not shoot. He rose, romped back a few paces, and trained his shotgun again. Meanwhile the trio to his rear gained the water.

'Don't fire,' Fairweather told his nearest men. To the old Maori he called, '*Kaati. Heoi.* Stop. Enough.'

That merely persuaded the fellow to shift his shotgun toward Fairweather. His eyes shone; his finger seemed to tighten on the trigger. Two shots from Fairweather's right left the old man sprawled; a third finished him. The three runaways were well clear, wading up on to the far bank of the river. Fairweather pointed his pistol skyward and fired. They made even more ground. He moved to the corpse and inspected the shotgun. It was much as he imagined.

'He went bravely, sir,' a soldier said.

'Quite creditably,' Fairweather agreed, 'for a man with no cartridge.'

A loquacious civil official of sorts appeared as guest in their garrison mess. The fellow lectured those present on the agricultural virtue of the land over which the 65th had lately battled, the likely crop and livestock yields. Fairweather had drunk more than he ought, and less than required; at first he paid small attention.

'Who is this boor?' he asked Blewitt. 'What is his business?'

'Surveying,' Blewitt explained. 'He is making a flying appraisal of this vicinity. Determining sites for settlement. Townships and farms.'

Fairweather finally had to be held; his second blow went wide.

The interior of General Cameron's tent held little to daunt. A chair or two, a table or two, and papers; an aide in tactful retreat. And a gaunt and whiskered commander who would much prefer not to have Fairweather on mind. 'Colonel Wyatt,' he said, 'has referred your case to me. God knows why. It is a regimental affair.'

Fairweather waited.

Cameron went on, 'I have to presume the colonel's difficulty is with your record.'

'I cannot say, sir.'

'In respect of your recent gallantry, it becomes positive embarrassment.

There could be a decoration for you aboard the next home boat. Won on my recommendation.'

'I am sorry, sir.'

'The New Zealand war has not lately been to your liking. Would that be a fair statement of the position, Fairweather?'

'An approximate one, sir.'

'It is a poor secret that it is not much to mine either. Colonists call me an old woman in uniform. A sentimental old fool. Heard that, have you?'

'I have not been of that opinion, sir.'

'I presume Colonel Wyatt has dispatched you to me with the notion that my notorious skirmishes with our colonist cousins might give me sympathy with your problem.'

'I am not in the colonel's confidence, sir.'

'He is mistaken, Fairweather. I have none with a man who resorts to physically belabouring an employee of the colonial government. I gather there was no special provocation offered.'

'Not of personal nature, sir,' Fairweather allowed.

'And you were drunk.'

'I should not especially plead that, sir.'

'In short, altogether unbecoming?'

'Unacceptably, sir.'

'I hear no regret tendered.'

'Only that satisfaction was short-lived, sir.'

'You don't make things easy for yourself. Or me.'

'Then I regret that too, sir.'

'On further inquiry I find this far from the only cause for grievance. Information reluctantly volunteered suggests that there is a junior commissioned man of another regiment suffering bruises. And there is the larger matter of wilfully misinterpreting a clear order. You go out of your way to make yourself a consistent candidate for court martial. So far you are fortunate your superiors have had no wish to see so recent a regimental hero crucified.'

'With respect, sir, at a court martial I should not have denied that I ordered men to shoot above rebel heads.'

'You would not have argued that you misheard the general order in the commotion of the day?'

'No, sir. I heard it. Hot pursuit. It seemed to me that history was whipped into shape. We had obliged colonists with exterminated Maoris in sufficient quantity. And I should have so pleaded.'

'If you think prolonging rebel lives a kindness, you are mistaken. We are surgeons, not apothecaries. Quick and substantial killing is our cure. With enough hell-raisers dead, other Maoris will lead healthier lives. Leave it to colonists and God knows what might ensue. You have heard of the Tasmanian aborigines? Their fate? Poison bait was laid for them. Like vermin. A stench up to heaven, Fairweather.'

'Your point is accepted, sir.'

'We now appear to have the crushing victory long sought. Think on that. A mercy for all. The inland Maoris have had enough. Likewise their mad mountain allies, whatever they style themselves.'

'The Tuhoe, as I understand it, sir.'

'Their war is over. But I am thinking of yours. Love the army, do you?'

'I have no other home, sir.'

'I seem not to have an answer.'

'Then my reply is yes, sir. For better and worse. Mostly for better, if lately for worse.'

'Then I have an unhappy test for your affection. Colonial politicians and journalists could make much of this affair; they never lose an opportunity to libel us as in sympathy with our Maori foe.'

'If that is the position, sir, I shall have a letter written within the hour. It will confirm that I love the army enough to leave it; my commission will be resigned. I shall, of course, miss my men. And you, sir.'

'Miss me, man?' Cameron found that less than tenable.

'For better or worse, sir. As an orphan learning new tricks of new trades.'

'My gratitude for not making this more difficult,' Cameron sighed at last. 'One other matter. I understand it to be the case that officers of the 65th are raising money for a memorial. To be erected to the fallen Maoris in our most recent affray.'

'Both officers and men, sir.'

'A memorial to the enemy? I have never heard the like of it before, Fairweather.'

'There is always a first time, sir. Even Captain Blewitt, now offensive passion has waned, is making contribution.'

'You have, I take it, a tactful inscription in mind?'

'The words are Biblically provided, sir. *I say unto you, love your enemies.*'

'And may God forgive us all,' Cameron said.

'To take the hopeful view, sir,' Fairweather agreed.

'Finally, what are we to do with this damned decoration if Her Majesty has seen fit to award it?'

'I trust you can rectify the misunderstanding, sir. It was surely meant for Captain Duke. He never flinched from an unfortunate order.'

Nor, though their eyes met for some time, did Cameron flinch now. Fairweather stepped back and saluted. Cameron preferred a handshake.

'I trust your luck improves, Fairweather,' he said. 'If it goes on at this rate, you may very well hang.'

Outside the tent there was a wind with the first sting of New Zealand winter. There was also a senior officer, Whitmore by name, waiting on General Cameron. Colonel George Whitmore. Distressed with soft campaigning and political muddle, Whitmore had sold off his commission in the imperial force and raised his own colonial militia. Currently he was pressing politicians and Cameron to pursue Maori rebels into their forested sanctuaries, rather than leave well alone. Short of temper and stature and often of breath, a veteran of two Kaffir wars and the Crimea, Whitmore had no use for martial modesty; he claimed to enjoy battles best when horses were shot from under him.

'Fairweather, isn't it?' Whitmore said. 'Fairweather of the 65th?'

'Late of, sir.'

'Not before time, I gather.'

'Unless appearances grossly deceive, sir.'

'It need not be the end, man. Will you stay here or go?'

'I have a recently won sovereign to toss, sir. Fate is best tempted.'

'And colonies test character. The damage can be undone; make more of yourself here. In my case, Fairweather, it means shorthorn cattle.'

'I have never quite seen tending cattle as a test of character, sir. But I daresay I have much yet to learn.'

'Not tending. Breeding. On the best land in Hawke's Bay. With the colony pacified, I mean to have a shorthorn stud unrivalled in these parts.'

'My good wishes, sir. I wish my imagination ran so far. And my means.'

'Then think gold, man. Gold. There are still discoveries daily in the South Island. More to the point perhaps, for your peace of mind, no Maoris dwell in the vicinity of the gold strikes. All open country and wild. Ours for the asking.'

'I shall henceforth keep it in mind, sir.'

'Do,' Whitmore urged. He paused before ducking into General Cameron's tent; and looked back with dry smile. 'A new land is a lottery. Even a wayward man of arms has his chance.'

Fairweather paused to think, found his mind empty, and walked off to relieve his pained bladder with the wind to his rear. He that pisseth against it had room for improvement.

3

It took four years for Fairweather to beach in Poverty Bay, and then because it was plausibly drawn on a mariner's chart. He had drifted, with something short of inspired plan, though goldfield and sheepland in the chilly south of the colony. Even the north, such as he heard of it, was less warmed by war. Few Maoris appeared to persist in defiance. Tepid to the last about the royal errand in New Zealand, General Cameron had been shipped back to Britain in gladiatorial disgrace. New Zealand was likewise at pains not to make more of Fairweather. Gold fortunes were few, Fairweather too late, and in the end paints and brushes produced more payable ore than pan and shovel. He cultivated a stylish eye for the remunerative Colonial walls were bare, and fresh wealth best seen. In the sheeplands, founding fathers required portraits painted; their homesteads could also be pictured according to desirable formula, under tall mountains and tassels of forest, with river or lake immaculate in the middle distance. A surveyor or two also found Fairweather useful, if now and then frivolous in his treatment of topography; but his skies were convincingly vast.

Given that matrimony might ease material problems, Fairweather made a playful feint toward a southern sheepman's daughter with whimsical mouth, and was soon outflanked by her father. The man failed to see Fairweather as a credible colonist, which was a legitimate reading; Fairweather wasn't even dependable as a libertine when perverse mood was upon him. So much for a future of fifteen thousand sheep and an increasingly less whimsical wife.

Fairweather went north again. Fate was not to be left to its own devices.

At Wellington, the fresh-minted capital of the colony, there was nothing to detain. A sour and joyless place, the taverns filled with ambitious drunks. Fairweather transferred from steamer to coastal schooner. The skipper disclosed that he was travelling to Auckland by way of Hawke's Bay and Poverty Bay.

'Poverty Bay?' Fairweather said with dawning interest.

'For a day or two,' the skipper said. 'You got business there?'

'Perhaps. I have a sudden vision.'

'You bloody need a vision in Poverty Bay.'

'It displeases?'

'I hate a job half finished,' the morose skipper said. 'Maoris still think they run the show. Another hiding wouldn't do them any harm.'

'Another? Last time I heard of it, the place was pure peace.'

'There was a big fright two years back. Some of these Maori fanatics got going there. The Hau Hau.'

'Forgive me. I find the colonial press mostly unreadable. The Hau Hau?'

'Leftover rebels. If they wasn't pagan again, it wasn't so as you'd notice. Cannibal too. They thought missionary eyeballs was tasty. The colonial militia gave them what for. Those they didn't shoot, they grabbed by the scruff of their necks. And bundled the buggers off to the Chatham Islands. Not that the Hau Hau was so bad in Poverty Bay, not like on the other coast, where some still run riot. But bad enough. They got hurt hard and quick.'

'A change from gold and sheep,' Fairweather observed. 'You must excuse my indifferent geography. You said something of the Chatham Islands.'

'Five hundred miles east. Bare. Winds to freeze your arse off. I took some of the sods over. Kill or cure.'

'And tranquillity again prevails in Poverty Bay?'

'If that's what you like to call it.'

'What do you?'

'Neither fish nor fowl. Neither them nor us.'

'Then it cannot lack interest.'

'You mean you might stay?'

'Promise is debt. I find one outstanding.'

'It's your life,' the skipper said.

There were six days of sailing in combative sea and strident wind. Napier, the port of Hawke's Bay, brought brief peace. It was a tidy enough settlement, with civilized shops, ladies with parasols, beefy Britons on dusty horses, and Maoris not making themselves more conspicuous than need be. Dark ranges rose inland, and here and there tall storms of smoke. Summer burning, for the sowing of fresh pastoral country, had begun.

'Here's one place making sense,' the skipper said. 'The right colonists. And reasonable Maoris.'

'Sail on,' Fairweather said.

That night, after they departed, fire was seen rimming the coastal horizon. Fairweather took to his bunk, as the schooner pitched, and dreamed most pruriently.

At first Poverty Bay was spectral behind thin marine mist. The schooner hovered offshore until risen sun warmed it away; the region surrendered its parts. There was a vast and pleasingly symmetrical curve of shore with pale sand and thumping surf. Beyond was formidable plain flecked with dark native trees and unkempt New Zealand palms. Far wooded peaks, echoing the curve of the coast, made the place seem something of an amphitheatre. A wide river mouth, with silvered mudbanks, filled slowly with tide. The skipper navigated under a bulky headland and cautiously upriver. On the left bank, beyond a cluster of thatched Maori huts, were scattered European buildings of makeshift appearance, some so tentative that they still sat on sledges. A few, among them a motley construction which might serve as hotel, aspired to more than one level. There were no roads worth the name. And no gardens; nothing suggestive of permanence. Whaleboats and canoes hauled free of the water were thick on the shore. Here and there Maoris gazed at the arriving schooner; some ambled toward the jetty and caught mooring ropes.

'Turanga,' the skipper announced. 'Here beats the heart of Poverty Bay.'

'Is there no more to it?' Fairweather asked.

'Not for want of trying. Still want to stay?'

'Give me time,' Fairweather said with waning conviction.

'You have till tomorrow. Anything you need to know, try Trader Read.' The skipper pointed out a sagging seafront building stilted out over the water, and to which small craft were tied. 'Nothing Read doesn't know. Nor no one. He makes more sense than most round here, when he's sober. He did the right thing. Married Maori land right off. Now he sits pretty.'

'Happy the man who has no quarrel with matrimony.'

The skipper laughed. 'See his wife. Marry the devil's daughter and you're bound to finish up living with the old folks. On their quiet days they only take to each other with tomahawks.'

Poverty Bay, this far in, promised little to replenish the spirit. Yet the sun warmed. And there was no impediment to his continuing north tomorrow. He left his baggage aboard the schooner, to spare himself needless exertion in that likelihood, and trod a gritty riverside path to Trader Read's. He found an obese barn of an emporium. Saddles sat on sale among sacks of sugar, salt and flour; harpoons, harness and moleskin trousers hung from rafters. There were Maori customers toying with European attire and passionately protesting the cost. The proprietor was conspicuously in keeping with his establishment, corpulent, baggily suited, replete with years and wrinkles, and resonant of voice. Mounted on a wall to his rear was a shotgun presumably to lend authority in the event of pecuniary quibbles. 'Buy better in the colony and your money back,' he promised his current dissidents. Then he saw Fairweather.

'So,' he called, 'a new face. Off the schooner?'

'In short,' Fairweather said.

'Passing or staying?'

'It remains to be seen.'

'Read,' the fellow said. 'Most call me Trader.' He teetered toward Fairweather on spectacularly short legs; his belt was barely equal to the spillage of belly. 'And what remains to be seen?'

'Seeing, or trying to, is my current vocation. George Fairweather, late of the imperial army. Presently employed, where revenue so provides, as painter of all colonial seasons. I have exquisite credentials.'

'Painter?' Read puzzled.

'Of pictures,' Fairweather explained.

'Just shows you,' Read said. 'Sooner or later we get everything in Poverty Bay.' He considered Fairweather afresh. 'Selling, are you? Selling these pictures you paint?'

'Not currently. Those unpurchased, after modest endeavours in the south, made a melancholy bonfire.'

'There's a man of the market. Never let a surplus play hell with prices; I tip it in the sea. You after land?'

'Are we talking of surplus?'

'Not around here. Unless God gets off his arse and makes a lot more.'

'Do I look a man interested?'

'Most others are. Off the schooners. I'm the only man to see.'

'I seek friends. A woman. By name of Smith, as last known.'

'Meriana Smith,' Read said. 'The belle of the bay.'

'We understand each other.'

'Only one woman by the name of Smith worth asking for here. You feeling lucky?'

'I am a very lucky sort of fellow,' Fairweather argued.

'Just the kind to lead some poor innocent native girl on.'

'Meriana Smith, when last in my vicinity, hardly fitted that bill. Is she still a cheerful widow? Or married again?'

'Married?' Read laughed. 'Once bitten, twice shy. No man here good enough for that one now.'

'Better still,' Fairweather said.

'You know what I see?' Read became roguishly intimate. 'Birds of a feather. Twenty years ago I got off a schooner too, looking out for a woman. And here I am still.'

'I have a weakness for civilization, Trader.'

'Say what you like. I see a right bugger.'

'What real man is not? So where do I find Meri Smith?'

'Upriver. Up the Waimata. Lives with her brothers. I'll rent you a canoe. Take it up on the tide. Only a mile or two. Ask and you shall find.'

'While I think of it, I have another acquaintance hereabouts. Perhaps you could help me there too.'

'Not another woman?'

'A most manly man. When last seen, something of a seaman and merchant. A laugher. A drinker. And great talker. With the cheek of old Nick. A Maori by name of Coates, as I recall.'

Read's face had less jollity.

'Something wrong?' Fairweather asked.

Read was slow to say.

'He seemed,' Fairweather persisted, 'much dedicated to the needs of Poverty Bay.'

'Forget him,' Read said.

'That poses a problem. An unforgettable face. More so his laugh.'

'He's taking a long holiday.'

'Hard earned, if I remember the man right.'

'He earned it. In the Chathams.'

'Forgive my confusion, Trader. I know only two things about the Chathams. One that they are bleak. Second that deported rebels are dumped there.'

'That's right, general.'

'Coates a rebel? Never. I recall loyal passion.'

'Your problem,' Read said.

'I never met a Maori more addicted to the notion of a British Queen.'

'Please yourself,' Read said. 'We knew him better.'

'I daresay,' Fairweather allowed.

'A gutsful of grunts,' Read explained. 'Always pissing more than he drank.'

'And a rebel?'

'On the sly.'

'Live and learn,' Fairweather said. 'And alas for Coates.'

'I don't weep no tears.'

'So I note, Trader.'

There was a short silence. 'What,' Read finally asked, 'is it you really want here?'

'At the least, to pass a few hours free of the intestinal punishments of the Pacific. At the most, what would any right bugger say?'

That put Read in better humour.

'Then you'd best take that canoe,' he said, 'and see how your luck lasts.'

'It never fails,' Fairweather said.

The journey up the buoyant river pleased more; Fairweather paddled without haste. Tree fern shadowed the shiny water. Tiny mullet leapt; crabs scrambled away into seagrass and driftwood. He passed barnacled jetties where

Maori fish traps were hung and nets spread to dry. There were others abroad on the river, all Maori. Some called a genial *kia ora* to the stranger; others distinctly did not. The river narrowed and freshened. Heron and duck flapped from fringing reeds. Riverside dwellings became fewer, and fields of tall corn began to proliferate, orchards with fat fruit, spruce riverland pastures grazed by cattle and sheep. On this February morning Poverty Bay appeared impressively solvent.

Fairweather's estimate of distance covered was soon past a mile. He steered for a dwelling more imposing than most on the river. Wide verandah, curtained windows, a second storey; it looked less rough hewn than others, and had lately been painted. A masculine figure, bare to the waist, worked on a whaleboat beached in front of the building. A Maori or dark approximation.

'Smith?' Fairweather called.

'Here,' the figure agreed, not with enthusiasm.

Fairweather paddled nearer. 'I seek Meriana Smith,' he said.

The Maori was still not impressed. A big man of moderate years, strong shouldered, bulky with muscle rather than fat; a face which currently found no smile and perhaps seldom did. 'Your business?' he asked.

Fairweather bumped his canoe into the riverside and scrambled awkwardly ashore. 'Convivial,' he said. 'I am merely passing this way.'

'You've never passed this way before.'

'That,' Fairweather said, 'is rather the point.'

The Maori, if tolerably well spoken, remained surly. 'You from Matawhero?' he asked.

'Matawhero?'

'The new settlement out on the plain. Biggs' settlement.'

'Matawhero, I confess, is mystery to me. Also anyone by name of Biggs. I am off a schooner this morning.'

'On government business?'

'I am my own man.'

'So you say.'

'Frequently,' Fairweather said.

'What do you want of Meriana?'

'I hope to renew past acquaintance.'

'Past? When? Where?'

'In the port of Auckland, one summer of mixed fortune.'

'What does that mean?' demanded the inquisitorial Maori.

'Largely that I was disporting a pathetic limp, and in British uniform. Which may explain much. Meriana made it her business to feel more kindly toward this country; I have not been quick to forget.'

'Perhaps she has,' the Maori suggested.

'Then that is my loss,' Fairweather said.

He heard horses. To the rear of the house two riders became visible among trees, noon shadow and sunlight. One of the riders was Meriana. She rode astride the horse in sturdy masculine fashion; long hair bounced on her shoulders. If anything memory was on the modest side; Poverty Bay had unmistakeable promise. Her riding companion, so far as Fairweather noticed, was young, slight and male. Her face was puzzled as she closed with the riverside. Recognition came as she reined in.

'No,' she said.

'Yes,' he argued.

She smiled and slid from her horse. 'You.'

'On my honour.'

'And not weary of New Zealand?'

'Only when warring.'

'What happened?'

'Peace that passes understanding.'

Her smile did not diminish; she acknowledged their circumstances. 'You have met my brother Matiu,' she said. 'In English, Matthew.'

She meant Fairweather's riverside interrogator.

'Not formally,' he said. He extended his hand to Matiu; it was held without warmth. 'George Fairweather.'

Matiu chose not to speak.

'And my younger brother,' she went on. 'Pita. Peter.'

Pita, dismounting, was more agreeable. He was handsome, for one thing; perhaps a shade feminine. And with a shy smile.

'*Kia ora,*' he said. 'Welcome.'

He looked toward Meri for reassurance that he had said the right thing; she smiled approval. Devotion was apparent between the pair.

'So you meet the Smiths,' Meri said.

'All?'

'All,' she said firmly. 'It is not too prolonged.'

Matiu was not disposed to make the occasion more extensive either; with no word said he walked back to his whaleboat. Tactful Pita, on the other hand, took the reins of Meri's horse and drew it away, leaving her alone with Fairweather.

She inspected him further. 'No,' she pronounced. 'Not so bad. You do not need your uniform.'

'It is time someone told me.'

'And what are you doing here?'

'Passing, on one view of the matter.'

'The other?'

'Perhaps pausing.' He watched her eyes with care. 'I am now, you must know, an artist of some mean repute. It occurs to me, especially in the past minutes, that I might do better than honour an old promise. I might, with incentive, see Poverty Bay as a fresh base for my business.'

'Are you serious?'

'Sometimes endearingly,' he said.

'Good God.'

'God is always good when I put my mind to a painting. See what I do with Poverty Bay.'

They walked the riverside, away from the house and her brothers.

'So what are you saying?' she asked.

'That I could entertain a weak moment. Such as removing my bags from the schooner on which I arrived.'

'What would you wish me to say?'

'It is difficult to make it more evident.'

'Welcome to Poverty Bay,' she said with decision. 'Does that make for less difficulty?'

'Distinctly,' he said.

There was a short silence; her smile was auspicious. 'Would you,' she asked, 'care to stay here?'

They turned back toward the house. Fairweather considered the offer. Also taciturn Matiu.

'I think not,' he judged.

'You could be made comfortable. You see us as we are. I look after my brothers, or they look after me. I am not sure which. Nor are they.'

'I prefer not to fail domestic expectations. Nor unsettle hosts.'

'Matiu is not all as he seems.'

'I take your word. No. Perhaps closer to the sea.'

'And to departing schooners?'

'That is not my thought.'

'I am thinking it for you,' she said.

'Somewhere near the port might suit best. I shall have to explore such of the coast as can be tamed prettily in a colonial frame.'

'You are serious,' she said.

'You had best believe it.'

'I must believe in you first.'

'Then,' he said, 'you may have the advantage of me.'

There was a call from the house. Pita. Cane chairs had appeared on the verandah. A linen-covered table was likewise set in the shade. Chinaware too, and a teapot of silver.

'Most elegant,' Fairweather observed.

'Did you expect a Maori mat thrown on a mud floor? We manage civilization quite well in these parts.'

They neared the house again.

'Talking of civilization,' he said, 'I am surprised to learn Poverty Bay now lacks one Maori stalwart. I mean Coates.'

She was quiet.

'But for whom we might not have met,' he prompted.

'I heard you,' she said with reluctance.

'What happened? What possessed him?'

She shrugged.

'Well?' he demanded.

'You already seem to know all.'

'Only that he seems to have disgraced himself as a rebel; and that his current circumstances are rightly conducive to melancholy. Little more was detectable in Trader Read's tirade this morning.'

'Then you know all worth knowing,' she said. She had her eye on Matiu, within earshot again.

'All the same,' he protested, 'it makes no sense.'

'Take my word,' she said.

'That it does?'

'Why would he be sent to the Chathams if not?' She seemed even more aware of Matiu; and tense.

'Your answer still begs my question.'

'Then do not ask it,' she proposed. She had not moved her eyes from Matiu. 'Is it necessary to talk further of Coates?'

'It would seem not,' he concluded.

Her relief was plain. 'Good,' she said. 'So it is time for you to take polite tea with the Smiths.'

Luck and elation made that no problem. Even uncommunicative Matiu did not matter; Coates still less.

4

Within a week Fairweather was coherently arranged in Poverty Bay. Meri located a modest native whare a hundred yards upriver from the port of Turanga. One spartan room, slab walls, thatched roof, sod fireplace, and distinctly minus most colonial comforts; even linen was a recent luxury on this largely unreformed coast. With fleas smoked out, Fairweather slept on a mattress of flax mats flung upon crushed fern; a coarse rug or two was sufficient for warmth. Meri came and went irregularly, though at pains never to leave Fairweather alone for long; she was there as often as might be respectably managed. Erotically Poverty Bay left nothing to be desired. Trader Read's store, and a fish net, satisfied lesser needs.

On a calm summer morning Fairweather began making peace with the port; he teased a promising composition from a schooner slumped tideless in mud, rusty whalers' trypots, and finally the ephemeral rooftops of Turanga. An exercise, no more; an unflexing of fingers. He heard a horse somewhere close. Then a dismounting rider interfered with his sun.

'Biggs,' the visitor said. 'Captain Reginald Biggs.' An awkward and angular fellow, narrow-gutted, with wiry beard and bony face. 'You have yet to introduce yourself to me.'

'Is that obligatory?'

'Desirable. You may need me. As administrator or, perhaps, magistrate.'

'Civilization's vanguard.'

'In modesty,' Biggs acknowledged.

'Then let it be said, Captain Biggs, that I have no complaint with Poverty Bay. The summer is warm. The tides are predictable.'

'Or I may need you.'

'Me?'

'Your name is known.'

'Gratifying to learn that my reputation as artist precedes me to so remote an outpost.'

'As soldier,' Biggs said.

Fairweather saw no reason to discontinue drawing; he now found the scale of the schooner excessive.

'You made yourself somewhat notorious,' Biggs went on.

'Your point is made, Captain Biggs,' Fairweather finally said. 'Have you another?'

'While you reside in this vicinity,' Biggs explained, 'I should like you in my militia. Voluntarily, of course.'

Fairweather considered the emphasis. 'Do I hear suggestion that my services could be commanded in other form?'

'Though this is a lately disturbed district, the government stations no armed constabulary. I am empowered to conscript. And fine every defector a guinea a day.'

'Food for thought,' Fairweather agreed.

'Unless circumstances dictate, naturally I conscript with discretion. I don't wish to burden myself with every drunken misfit meandering into Poverty Bay.'

'That sounds a succinct description of present company. Consider me unwholesome, Captain Biggs, and there let this end.'

'Impossible,' Biggs said. 'Whatever your past problem, you are still a trained man.'

'Of the imperial forces. Not the colonial. My 65th has packed and departed. We subdued sufficient Maoris. It is your country now.'

'You put up a memorial to Maoris and marched away,' Biggs complained.

'On the assumption that colonials should have enough character to look after themselves. We came to win a war. It was won.'

'Not cleanly. Witness our recent troubles here.'

'I witness what is, Captain Biggs. This far yours is the only shadow to fall.'

Biggs moved and took less of the light. Fairweather drew.

'We are isolated from the rest of the colony,' Biggs said. 'It may be another year before the electric telegraph reaches us. We have to fend as best we can.'

'Against whom? I understand colonial enterprise has placed surviving rebels across an uncomfortable body of water.'

'Maori insolence cannot be exiled. Land confiscation is still far from settled. Even loyal Maoris turn sullen when the subject is raised. Or laugh. Send soldiers, they tell me, and we'll sit on our land and feed them pumpkins.'

'I never much cared for their flavour myself. Now I know. The taste of treason, sir.'

'Justice has to be seen as even-handed. Maoris elsewhere have been obliged to surrender lands where they or their relatives have defied the Queen's writ. If Poverty Bay Maoris retained theirs, others might again become disgruntled. Loss of land is the only form of retribution they understand.'

'I have heard that song before.'

'Anything less could be construed as weakness on our part.'
'That too. The second verse.'
'It is no joke,' Biggs said.
'I agree, sir, that land confiscation is best conducted in humourless fashion.'
'Theft is frequent here. Burglaries. Sheep stealing. Drunken fights, sometimes with firearms. And from time to time one hears of rebels still loose in the hills.'
'I see your lot as unlovely, Captain Biggs. Try as I might, however, I fail to see it as my largest concern. You are paid for distress. I am not.'
'I am making the point, Mr Fairweather, that Poverty Bay is not all it may seem.'
'Thank you,' Fairweather said.
'I am further making the point that a reliable militia is necessary here to meet all emergencies. So long as you remain, I could yet oblige you to serve.'
'Under your command?'
'Just so,' Biggs said.
They considered each other. Fairweather was less and less taken by what he saw. On an English estate Biggs might have made a useful bully of a manager. Here he was lord, if still far from master.
Biggs persisted, 'Most of my men are untried farmers and tradesmen with rifles. A man with your past capacities would be much valued. Colonial militia is, of course, quite casual. We parade fortnightly. Musketry practice once a month. We also meet for cricket. I make no large demands.'
'You discourage, Captain Biggs. I never was much of a cricketer. Nor have I ever seen soldiering as a weekend hobby. It is a profession for initiates, with daily devotions. Not to speak of the largest of demands.'
'There is remuneration, of course,' Biggs began again. 'And longer term prospects. Men of the militia will have early call on confiscated lands, when the job is finally done.'
Fairweather found the whalers' trypots no longer working to advantage. Nor most of his morning's work.
'You remain quiet,' Biggs said. 'Perhaps you failed to hear.'
'I remain quiet,' Fairweather answered, 'because I did.'
'Well?' Biggs demanded.
'The polite reply, sir, is that I am no colonist. My stay here is unlikely to be long.'
'Despite appearance?'
'You mystify, Captain Biggs.'
'I refer to another matter. My information is that you have an association with a local woman of mixed blood. One of some standing.'
Fairweather considered woody hills rising beyond the river mouth. Hills, then tips of distant mountains, and shadings between. He steadied his hand

and battled for background. 'Am I to take it, Captain Biggs, that you also administer amorous matters in this vicinity?'

'A decade or two ago things were different here,' Biggs said. 'Whalers and runaway sailors came and went. Rough men. Wild. No law, no standards, to constrain them. They bequeathed the mixed blood, and more than a few problems. Some of course stayed to prosper.'

'I have made Trader Read's acquaintance,' Fairweather said. 'Otherwise your drift is far from plain.'

'There have also,' Biggs went on, 'been reliable Christian colonizers who have married into Maori families of distinction, and in that manner become landholders.'

'I hope I do not hear what I seem to, sir.'

'You may be misconstruing me,' Biggs protested.

'I think not,' Fairweather said. 'As a prospectus that seems as inelegant as masquerading in a militia to have call on confiscated land.'

'I may have been a shade blunt,' Biggs allowed.

'At this moment I might be persuaded to see more virtue in the times of Trader Read.'

'It is an unfortunate fact that Read, due to shrewd marriage, and wise dealings, has had most of the useful European land here. Until the Maoris are persuaded to part with more, the rest of us are relative paupers.'

'Then let me ease your vexation, Captain Biggs. My pecuniary interest is of different nature. Natives of these islands can still be deemed useful for pictorial purpose. In a year or two, when they stand even less in our way, I might find a market for decorative Maoris. It is as well to anticipate colonial sentiment. The lady who currently appears to give you pause could prove an especially lucrative subject.'

'I see,' Biggs said uncertainly. 'I am sorry if there has been misunderstanding. I meant merely to pass friendly words.'

'And all most illuminating, sir.'

Biggs, now in light sweat, nevertheless made no move to depart. 'There is more,' he confessed. 'You mix with a family which prefers to pass as Maori. I think especially of her brother. Matiu Smith. You may hear things said.'

'Matiu Smith is at immense pains, in my presence, to say nothing audible.'

'By her, then. Maoris have mischievous tongues. I should be obliged if you gave no credence to gossip.'

'About you?'

'In my official functions.'

'You leave me to presume that Matiu Smith is one of your loyal Maoris lately turned sullen.'

'He took our side against the rebels,' Biggs agreed. 'His stance now cannot be considered friendly.'

'You need not labour to convince me, Captain Biggs.'

'As for the rest,' Biggs said, 'perhaps we could reach an understanding.'

'I thought we had reached one, sir. Largely to the effect that I am a bird of passage.'

'What I have in mind,' Biggs explained, 'is that you might make yourself available to the colonial militia should need arise. No parades, no musketry practice in the meantime.'

Fairweather was tiring; Biggs made poor sport. 'That is more accommodating,' he conceded. 'Especially no cricket.'

'How long, Mr Fairweather, have you been in the colony now?'

'Four or five years,' Fairweather said. 'Perhaps six or seven.'

'Consider,' Biggs smiled charmlessly, 'that you might be past the point of no return. And really one of us now.'

He had a point there, of sorts. Fairweather declined to take it. Not from Biggs. But Biggs, returning to his horse, had more to press home. He unstrapped a slender package from beneath his saddle.

'A rifle?' Fairweather said.

'To save me laboriously issuing you one in the event of urgency. Take it as a loan, if you like.'

Biggs unfastened the package. Within was a well greased carbine, not much scarred. 'I trust it meets with approval. A Calisher and Terry, .565 calibre, breech loading. In bush fighting it cannot be bettered. No more standing to ram a cartridge down the bore. You reload without raising your head.'

Fairweather lifted the weapon to his shoulder and took sight on a distant rock. He felt faint reverberation. Other times, other places.

'With a Terry,' Biggs said, 'I brought down a rebel at four hundred paces. Percussion caps and fifty cartridges come with it.'

'And no more?'

'You have my word. I make no call on you for anything less than large peril. So long as tensions persist I like to see every useful male armed in Poverty Bay. Not all would approve. But colonial politicians stubbornly refuse to comprehend our precarious situation here. In freely issuing arms, I take a liberty. But I know where to turn.'

Fairweather saw the carbine as his licence to remain footloose in the region. He trained it again, on a far tree; it felt most efficient. 'I see ducks dropping already,' he disclosed.

'Capital,' Biggs said. 'By all means keep your eye in. And do visit us at Matawhero, if you can spare a day. Only an eight mile ride south across the plain. We have a tidy little community there. You will see progress. And keen colonists.'

'Perhaps when Turanga palls,' Fairweather said.

'For a man of your stamp, that must be soon,' Biggs said with confidence.

He mounted his horse. 'We may make you feel more at home. Goodbye for the meantime, Mr Fairweather.'

'Goodbye to you, Captain Biggs.'

With Biggs riding south, Fairweather considered the carbine and then his deflated composition. He scored the drawing heavily; the carbine could not be crossed out. He finally carried it home to his waterside whare and rolled it in a woollen rug. Biggs' residue was best out of sight.

He even managed to banish most of Biggs himself from mind. What remained was the vague and sweaty unease of the fellow. An odour of farm animals and fertile earth. Of the keen colonist.

Toward evening he took Meri out in a canoe to empty his net. From the river's mouth the long sweep of the Poverty Bay shore was visible. Streamers of surf coloured with sunset.

'You make a bad woman of me,' she said.

'Of a willing widow? Never.'

'Twenty years ago, even ten, Maori women never went out to fish with men. It was forbidden. *Tapu.* A very bad business. The old ones still frown.'

'Thus does Christianity liberate. It never leaves well alone.'

'You mock.'

'I have always believed there is no work unworthy of woman. I wait upon the day when the masculine function is solely procreative.'

'Your day is almost here,' she said.

There were fat mullet in the net, also two small shark. The mullet were dead, the sharks fiercely alive and tangled; Fairweather battered them on the head until they ceased to twitch.

'We have a saying,' Meri informed him. '*Kia mate ururoa, kei mate wheke.* Better to die as the shark than live as the octopus. The shark fights to the last. The octopus cringes in hope of surviving.'

'My sympathies go to the octopus.'

'And you a soldier.'

'The difference between a warrior and a soldier is that the soldier fights to get drunk tomorrow. My hide is in one piece. I have yet to hear you complain.'

Meri gutted the fish as he paddled upriver. They lit a fire outside his whare. She skewered the mullet on sticks and mounted them above the flame. Fairweather leaned back against the whare wall with no further part to play; Meri remained especially rewarding to watch. Light and shadow moved over her face as she turned the sticks deftly; oil dripped from the mullet and hissed in the fire. There were still cinders of sunset in the western sky. Sound reached them from the port: horses, dogs, voices, splashes, drunken singing. With two schooners moored, Read's rum shop and hotel had business. So had Turanga's half caste whores.

'You are a lunatic man,' she announced from nowhere.
'Thank you. Now I know.'
'You do not care much.'
'If I can help it.'
'I mean about anything.'
'Almost anything,' he said.
'So tell me about almost.'
'I almost care about not caring.'
'Ah,' she said. 'Why?'
'God may know. I do not.'
'But you do not believe in God.'
'Since he seems not especially to believe in me.'
'You English come and give us your God,' she complained, 'and then we find some of you heathen. It is hard to understand.'
'Not with the world, the flesh and the devil. Especially the devil. He cares for the comfort of his troops.'
'And you sooner serve him?'
'Christ says that he who is a friend of this world cannot be a friend of His. My loyalty is here. This world is. This night. And you. Before long those fish and Trader Read's best claret in my belly too. Who could not feel affection?'
'You are pagan,' she judged.
'On my best days,' he said.
'Tell me,' she asked. 'Do you almost care about me?'
'I especially almost care about you.'
She took up a skewered mullet. 'Would you almost care for a hot fish in your face?'
'I especially would not.'
'Then be grateful that I believe in a merciful God.'
'You win a quick convert. Put that creature down and I shall confess all.'
'Confess,' she menaced.
'I had Captain Biggs on my back this morning.'
For a time she said nothing, but with emphasis. 'What did that man want?'
'He wished to apprise me of the fact that Maoris here are above themselves. I should have replied that such was certainly my experience. I can name one Maori consistently above herself, with no respect at all.'
This time the fish was thrown. Fairweather ducked late, and fielded the missile inelegantly. 'There,' he said, wiping sticky hands. 'Which proves the point further.'
'He must have wanted something.'
'To be sure. Principally he wished to recruit me for his colonial militia; I think he might fancy the notion of a sometime imperial officer taking his orders.'

Her silence was interesting. 'And did he?' she asked at last. 'Did he recruit you?'

'We arrived at an understanding. In the event of impending doom I may be called upon to instruct his men to perish with martial propriety.'

'Martial what?'

'Propriety. Decorum. Restraint. Englishmen, especially officers, are notorious for it.'

'Not one I know.'

'No man has dignity with his trousers down. Have charity.'

'You ask the wrong woman,' she said.

She eased the mullet off the skewers into small flax baskets. They ate with their fingers, peeling away skin and scales, picking flesh free of bone. Fairweather was fast satisfied. He poured two tumblers of claret, and lit his pipe. The night was warm. He listened to distant surf, looked up at stars.

'Well?' she asked.

'Splendid. I shall remember this.'

'You always say that.'

'I treasure all which is not witless habit.'

'Might this become so? And me?'

He spoke with more care. 'What is it you want?'

She was reluctant to say.

'Permanence?' he suggested.

She shook her head and looked into the fire.

'I am a most impermanent person,' he said.

'You must not explain. It is all right.'

'It currently seems not.'

'It will be,' she promised obscurely.

'Don't turn morbid Maori on me. Come on.'

A woman's high laugh found its way upriver from the port; and lingered.

'Is it,' he asked, 'not enough that we take pleasure in each other? And from?'

She said nothing.

'Or is it,' he persisted, 'your family?'

She did not contradict.

'If so,' he said, 'they might at least be reassured that I am not seeking some antipodean dowry. My new acquaintance Captain Biggs needed disabusing of that notion.'

She was cautious. 'Most English want land. I tell Matiu not you. He shakes his head. He has never seen such English. Nor any Maori.'

'So life is made difficult for you?'

'*He iti*. A little.'

'I suspect not so *iti*. Would it be best if I left?'

'No.' She was firm.

'Another worm in the apple,' he said. 'Two in one day.'

'This morning you were seen talking to Biggs.'

'So the spies were out. You knew all along and never said.'

'Some say you might really be a man from the government. One meant to work with Biggs. And with some new way to get Maoris off their land.'

'Dear God,' he said. 'I was better off back in the south, grubbing for gold with a frosty arse. I know nothing of the quaint feuds of Poverty Bay. Nor am I anxious to care.'

'If Biggs is to decide who is to have land, and who not, what of those who were not rebel, but now argue with Biggs? They will suffer too.'

'If I must make myself clear,' he said, 'I understand only those Maoris who die in battle with splendid sentiments on their lips.'

'Only?'

'And one other, when less querulous.'

She smiled and let down her long hair.

'As for the rest,' he went on, 'you can inform anyone interested that I am a passing bird on the bough. You must have a harmonious Maori saying.'

'Yes,' she said. 'When a bird has feathers, it flies.'

'Exactly. I am never negligent with my plumage.'

She was quiet.

'Perhaps,' he suggested, 'there is an English avian proverb more to the point for present purposes. A bird in the hand is worth two in the bush.'

At length she rested her hand affectionately on the inside of his leg. 'I pity that pair in the bush,' she said.

'The feeling is mutual.'

Soon more was mutual, garments an impediment. Within the whare she picked open the buttons of his shirt, unfastened his belt. When he was sufficiently undone, she placed his hand on her uncovered breast and eventually and pertinently elsewhere. 'Do you almost care now?'

'Almost fervently,' he confessed.

'Good,' she said, and gave. It was always more than he remembered. The resonance built and then filled his throat. She remained tender and mocking.

'They must have heard you in the port,' she said. 'They will send a search party to see who has drowned.'

The sound of water became distinct again: estuarine lapping, the crash of open sea. Inland there were the nameless birds of the antipodean dark. 'Is it enough?' he finally asked.

'Enough?' She was puzzled.

'To live for.'

'Today has been good,' she said with caution.

'Excellent,' he announced. 'I shall make a noble savage of you yet.'

They dressed. The night had cooled. She placed fresh wood on their fire. Fairweather located his pipe and moistened his mouth with a remnant of claret. He also rediscovered the flaw in his day.

'My uninvited visitor this morning was most concerned that I might, from you, hear things not to his credit.'

'Must we talk of Biggs?'

'Desirably not.'

'Then we shall not,' she said.

'Come,' he urged. 'I may need to interest the man in keeping his distance.'

There was stubborn silence. The night had cooled in more ways than one.

'Please,' he persisted.

'Ask other Maoris if you wish to hear bad of Biggs. He does not make himself liked.'

'I am asking you. Land?'

'Always more.'

'Than is fair?'

'Trader Read was better. When he wanted more land he gave chiefs credit, to buy rum, and when they were enough in debt, he took their land. Until Maoris saw what was happening and put a stop to the selling of land. So Biggs does it differently. No rum. Just law.'

'But Biggs appears to have land. I hear of a settlement at some barely pronounceable place.'

'Matawhero. Land once Read's.'

'That at least cannot be quarrelled with. Having married into more Maori land than he can manage, Read presumably has right to sell off that which he can't. He hinted that he could sell some to me. No doubt at ludicrous price.'

'Ask Biggs,' she suggested presently. 'Ask him what he paid.'

'You appear to know the answer.'

'Biggs and his men paid next to nothing,' she said. 'Perhaps nothing at all.'

'To keep Poverty Bay safe for Trader Read?'

'See for yourself. The port of Turanga has only one trader. Once there was another.'

'Of whom you find it inconvenient to talk.'

There was a short silence. 'Mostly,' she agreed.

'Because Coates hoisted rebel colours?'

'He fought for the Queen,' she said.

'Please,' he said. 'No confusion. Is Coates a deported rebel, or is he not?'

'He is deported,' she said.

'As a rebel.'

'After he fought for the Queen.'

'It cannot be,' Fairweather decided.

'Biggs called Coates a spy in the Queen's camp.'

'Perhaps he was,' Fairweather said.

'Perhaps. Talk to Biggs. Hear what he says.'

'I prefer to avoid upstarts of empire in Poverty Bay.'

'You do not care for your own people much.'

'Not when they call themselves colonists. Give them an acre of weeds and they think themselves monarchs of the realm. They get above themselves in short, even more so than Maoris. I want to hear what you say.'

'There is no more to be said,' she argued.

'I detest mystery,' he said. 'Especially lines left crooked, tales half told.'

She was indifferent to the plea; she judged the moment propitious to take a stick and meddle with the coals of their fire. It seemed their amatory mood might also need much rekindling.

'Biggs was right about one thing,' Fairweather concluded. 'Maoris, by God, do have mischievous tongues.'

He won no response. Finally she stood, looked at him briefly, and then went into the whare. Fairweather smoked his pipe until satisfied that the world was best left awry. Damn Biggs; Coates too. Inside the whare he found welcoming arms after all. Dissonance became distant, crooked lines straight. Their lovemaking this time was more prolonged in duration, more considered in dimension; but Fairweather, at the close, was in no less vocal extremity.

Meri, later, woke him with her own cry. And a crash. Feeling chill, she had risen in the dark to search out further covering. Unrolling a weighty rug she found herself suddenly possessed of a Calisher and Terry breech-loading carbine of .565 calibre. In nocturnal terror she let it fall.

5

Meri left soon after sunrise to help with family harvest upriver. Fairweather slept late, and before noon determined himself to be short of tobacco, bacon and brandy; he paddled his canoe down to the port. The place did not improve on longer acquaintance, nor reek less of dung, dead fish, and urine. Trader Read was abundant behind the counter of his store. He still delighted in identifying Fairweather as a shameless fellow scoundrel, and Fairweather found it advantageous not to disappoint; in better mood Read did not mind the worst of a bargain. Most whites around the river mouth, as distinct from those farming inland, were uncouth strays in casual employment with Read. If Fairweather intrigued, it was perhaps because he remained unbeholden and not altogether graceless. Besides, there was his aberrant occupation.

'Tell you what,' Read said. 'Paint me one of your paintings.'

'You joke,' Fairweather said. Read smelled powerfully of whisky.

'I mean it,' Read argued. 'Something to smarten a tired wall.'

'There is the matter of money.'

'That won't stand in our way.'

'What would you want of a painting?'

'Anything to tickle the fancy.'

'Then you may have the right man. A splendid river vista, perhaps, with this noble edifice rising from the heart of Turanga. The town Trader Read made.'

'We have a deal,' Read said. 'Name your price.'

'I shall think on it,' Fairweather promised.

'The painting or the price?'

'Both.' The painting was not the point: or the price. It seemed that Read disliked the notion of any merchandise in Poverty Bay, even Fairweather's wares, being beyond reach. 'My muse is still a shade weary, and my purse not yet empty. The two need to be on talking terms.'

'I'll pay you out in provisions,' Read decided. 'Starting today.'

'Your risk,' Fairweather said.

'How long do you think you'll last here?'

'Until discomfort begins. Or winter.'

'We never see much frost to speak of. The temperature is over seventy degrees Fahrenheit for nine months of a year.' Read fetched a bottle from under the counter and filled two glasses. 'No cosier corner in this colony. Your health, general.'

'I suspect, Trader, you are still trying to sell me a landowner's life in Poverty Bay.'

'Habit,' Read said.

'And perhaps even land.'

'You could do a lot worse.'

'As seems my custom.' Fairweather took up his unsolicited glass of whisky, considered it for a moment, and drank. It was rough, potent, and too early in the day. 'I believe,' he said, 'that Captain Biggs, whose acquaintance I have lately made, obtained his present land on pleasing terms.'

'Captain Biggs is an asset to the region. Money in the bank, so to speak. No one kept real order before.'

'To money in the bank, then,' Fairweather proposed, raising his glass.

'So let me know,' Read said, 'if you change your mind about land. I might even be generous again. Biggs needs backing.'

'I rather think my vision runs to some more balmy Pacific island. Tahiti, perhaps.'

'Ah,' Read said, with memories evident.

'I shall learn to paint palm trees and girls with golden skins,' Fairweather predicted. 'And plunder the pockets of a few French colonists. They may need an artist to reassure them of paradise as they befoul it.'

'One thing about Tahiti,' Read said. 'The natives fit in with things. They don't fight.'

He filled his glass again and drank most in a gulp.

Fairweather judged that whisky had deployed itself sufficiently. 'The day of my arrival,' he said, 'I asked after a certain native whom, it would seem, most certainly didn't know his place. A sometime acquaintance.'

'Coates.' Read had not forgotten.

'I confess myself still mystified, Trader.'

'How?' Read said.

'About what turned him. Made him a menace.'

'You're asking me?' Read blinked with surprise.

'That appears to be the case. I still have the memory of Coates being a fairly enlightened fellow. Convince me I'm wrong.'

Read grunted opaquely.

Fairweather went on, 'I saw a man who turned the Queen's peace to profit. Not one who would have patience with the pagan and cannibal nonsense of your recent insurgents here. All else aside, the man was uncommonly committed to Christ, never at a loss for words when he had scriptures to quote.'

Read grunted again; and drank.

'Forgive me if the subject distresses,' Fairweather said.

'The bastard can't distress pussy now,' Read said. 'Not where he is.'

'You seem, if I may say so, to take Coates most personally.'

'I ought to,' Read said.

'Enlighten me, Trader.'

'The sod started out working for me. Here. He could add. Price. Write good English. Deal with skippers. And sell a lion's skin before he'd shot the lion.'

Read lapsed into sour reflection, and refilled his glass.

'You make him sound a boon to capitalist enterprise in this colony,' Fairweather proposed.

'He was smart,' Read allowed.

'I take it the labourer proved unworthy of his hire. Perhaps embezzled.'

'Worse. He started his own store across the river.'

'Ah. He lacked loyalty.'

'All the way. He took native trade. Even if they didn't like him, they liked his prices.'

'Human nature is a complex affair,' Fairweather agreed.

'I should of let some daylight into the bugger then and there.'

'You must have been spared much grief when Biggs exposed him as just another native malcontent.'

Read didn't disagree. This time he topped up Fairweather's glass before replenishing his own. 'I'll tell you something else for nothing. The Maoris never liked the two-face bastard neither. Not their chiefs. Coates was a nobody.'

'I recall *tutua* as the word.'

'Right, general. He got too big for his boots. The richer he got, the randier. There wasn't a busier gut-stick around here. Casanova Coates. No chief could say his wife was safe. They were glad to see the last of him; some helped Biggs bundle him on to the boat. Ask your woman.'

'Oh?'

'The Smiths know more than most,' Read said obscurely, and then seemed stricken with intestinal grief. He fast gathered up bottle and glasses and pushed them under the counter. Fairweather saw why. Read's immense Maori wife had surged into the store; peril was apparent.

'Tobacco, was it?' Read asked loudly.

'And brandy and bacon,' Fairweather said.

Mrs Read heaved herself breathily between them. 'You still in Poverty Bay?' she said to Fairweather.

'On the face of it,' Fairweather said.

'You must be looking for something.'

'Interest in life,' Fairweather explained.

'We don't sell much of that here.'

'On the contrary,' he protested, 'and at modest price.'

She made a grab under the counter and held Read's bottle high. Intent to injure was evident. 'Buggers like you make him get his money in a muddle,' she accused Fairweather. 'Buggers like you ruin us.' The bottle hovered above Read's head, then in the vicinity of Fairweather's. 'What do you say?'

'Nothing,' Fairweather decided.

'You?' she said to Read.

'No more today,' he promised.

'Or I have your fat balls,' she vowed.

She waddled from the store with bottle held tight.

'Women,' a chastened Read said, arranging Fairweather's requirements. 'They never come cheap. You better watch it, general, while the going is good.'

'We were talking of Coates,' Fairweather suggested.

Read seemed to think not. 'Am I going to see that painting, then?'

'I never argue with a spirited patron,' Fairweather said.

That afternoon, for reasons other than Read, Fairweather climbed to the shade of a hillside tree, looked upon Poverty Bay, and began work with purpose. His first painterly reconnaissance was without virtue; the second also best burned. The third, though, began to disclose useful intelligence of earth and sky. Fairweather, despite his inclination, was often fastidious. The winnowing of symmetry from the world could make him sweat, for he sometimes believed in its existence. Mystics might fashion God from these glimpses; Fairweather merely felt himself to be a most artful devil of a fellow. He wanted melodies, not symphonies.

There was a short thunderstorm toward evening. Inside the whare, Fairweather kindled driftwood in his fireplace. Meri came. She exchanged drenched garments for a rug, and huddled beside him; he warmed her further with brandy. 'A good day?' she asked.

'Illuminating. I painted. Even Mr Ruskin might be pleased.'

'Who is Mr Ruskin?'

'A *tohunga*, wise man, a priest of my tribe. A man of much mana. We have thus never met.'

'How would he be pleased?'

'To know that his distant pupil took his words to heart. And had this day seen clouds moving in the harmonies he prescribes.'

'So you painted clouds,' she said. 'That is all.'

'All? Mr Ruskin has it that I am gazing at the visible face of God. He writes much of what he calls fleecy citizens of the sky. He sees them as free of earthly passions. Mr Ruskin is a most reverent man.'

'Which you are not.'

'Unlike his most favoured pupil, I can claim not to have run off with his undeflowered bride. On the other hand even clouds never free me from thoughts of terrestrial harmonies. Mr Ruskin would not approve.'

'I am here to sleep with you. Not Mr Ruskin.'

'Tomorrow, perhaps, I shall paint water according to his direction. Shallow, muddied water. He argues that I should see furtive shadows making free with the purely visible. And further insists that I should not be hasty, or flee the tangled skein of true vision. Might Mr Ruskin ingeniously be saying that while we aspire to the condition of clouds, muddied waters are what we are?'

'I think I am fed up with your Mr Ruskin.'

'Via a whisky glass, I seem already to have sipped murky waters today.'

'What are you talking of?'

'Coates.'

'You spoke with Biggs?'

'With Trader Read.'

She was silent for a time. 'Perhaps,' she said finally, 'I would sooner hear more of Mr Ruskin after all.'

'He often talks of the habits of the inferior painter. The kind who, when painting foliage, finds that leaf number one immediately necessitates leaf number two. That is mostly my case.'

'Which means you are a poor painter?'

'Impatient. My quick picture differs distinctly from the one you seemed to paint. Trader Read has it that no one much cared for Coates. Not least certain Maoris. They found him embarrassment also. A twig impertinently posing as a tree. A pretender not only guilty of keen trading practices, but also of transactions with too many women.'

'I can see you have talked to Read.'

'At intemperate length. The general view appears to be that Poverty Bay is better off without Coates. Read visibly is. Likewise miffed chieftains, cuckolded husbands and women of flawed virtue. All is for the best in an untidy world. Just one thing irritates; one muddy ripple. Captain Biggs is better off also. I confirmed services of sorts rendered to Read. A shot in my locker should Biggs not leave me alone. More to the point, perhaps, are you better off without Coates?'

'Me?' She was amused.

'Read hinted that, if pressed, you might have something pertinent to say.'

She laughed. 'Coates pestered most women.'

‘I am not talking of numbers. I am talking of you.’
‘Coates made me laugh. Until he became boring.’
‘And there is no more to be said?’
‘Only that others found him less boring. Wild sometimes, but kind.’
‘Then Read baffles. He said the Smiths knew more.’
‘He means Matiu was one who agreed with Coates being sent away.’
‘Pestering a sister is no great sin.’
‘Coates did not have to pester Matiu’s wife. Not for long. She soon pestered him.’
‘Wife? I saw no spouse of Matiu’s at your home. Is she hidden from all men now?’
‘She has gone too.’
‘You tell me every nondescript adulterer and adulteress is packed off from Poverty Bay?’
‘Not to the Chathams. Back to her family in disgrace. Once Matiu would have been entitled to kill her. Coates too. Some thought he might.’
‘But Coates made a candidate for exile?’
‘Matiu had no quarrel with that. The Chathams are cold and rainy all year. Little grows there. As good as death for a Poverty Bay Maori.’
‘At least one thing seems clarified. You seem not to miss him unduly.’
She laughed again. ‘Do I have to tell you I didn’t love Coates?’
‘I never mentioned the word. I never do.’
‘I have noticed,’ she said.
‘I hear grievance.’
‘You hear a woman. Why do you not?’
‘I see worse than war. I know war. Otherwise what I don’t know won’t hurt me.’
‘And that is that?’
‘With luck,’ he said. ‘As for Coates, it seemed that you spoke with some feeling in the matter; I must have been wrong.’
‘I spoke only of what Biggs is. He told you I might say things. I have and I have not. Coates was your friend. It has been unfair not to tell you.’
‘Where so much is, or seems to be, your sin seems small.’
‘Maoris care less for what has happened. With Coates gone as trader, they pay high prices to Read. Even Matiu now grumbles. And Biggs rules, from the land Read gave him, and tries to get Maoris off theirs.’
‘Is there more to say?’ he asked.
‘Not to make difference.’
‘Good,’ he said. ‘Enough.’
They sat by the fire for a time. Then she prepared food; he uncorked claret. After a time, with the fire low, and talk also ebbing, he reached out for her; she responded in kind. ‘A schooner sails for Auckland tomorrow,’ she said.

'And what,' he asked, 'is the significance in that?'

'You will not be aboard it. Nor the next one, nor the one after. Not after tonight.'

'Is that promise or threat?'

'Wait,' she said. 'See.'

He did not have to wait long; he certainly saw. Hours later another thunderstorm passed in the dark, waking them briefly; her arms tightened about his chest. When the flickering and booming diminished, he was beset by difficult dreams. He was half crippled again, hobbling with a stick, in a summer of war. Healed, he crouched under a Maori parapet and felt guns reverberate above his head. But he woke after all to Meri's easy breath on his face and an immaculate morning. She was right. The schooner sailed without him. Many schooners would, even a steamer or two.

6

On a warm March morning Fairweather rode inland alone. He packed provisions for a day or two and also, more for pigeon than protection, the Biggs carbine. His intention was to see where the bright plain of Poverty Bay ended and shadowy uplands began. He had pillaged the environs of the port of Turanga to some vivid point; and made as much of surrounding seascape as imagination allowed. Now he hoped to tinker with the mechanics of river and mountain, and desirably of waterfalls. Anarchic water was a challenge, not least to Ruskin's first law, that of organic unity. Where water warred with earth and air, nature's design was under siege and less than apparent. It was Fairweather's aspiration to raise the siege and bring relief.

His route took him across patchily pastoral land studded with small and smoky native villages. There were also primitive European buildings, slab houses, barns, storehouses and stables, imbedded among patches of aboriginal forest. After six or seven miles he had a tidier riverland prospect ahead. Meri had drawn a rough map for his excursion; it suggested he was now gazing at the community of Matawhero. Read's sometime land. Biggs' settlement. A small white church sat at its centre. Within walking distance there were several shingle-roof and weatherboard dwellings which argued durability, and others still rising; Fairweather heard a sawyer at work. Older buildings, with a history of all of two years, had fenced-off flowerbeds, rose bushes and shrubs. If short on visual refreshment, Matawhero was at least a trim oasis; and further from the unkempt port than could be counted in miles.

Fairweather veered inland, following a Maori trail, rather than make too close an approach. He was, however, soon viewing another lone rider; one shaping leanly as Biggs. Fairweather, between half harvested fields of corn, had no line of escape. He had to rein in, as Biggs neared, and put a studied face on the encounter. Today Biggs was robustly agricultural rather than magisterial. Shirt minus collar, threadbare waistcoat, soiled corduroy trousers; the muscular pioneer.

'So you are making the acquaintance of Poverty Bay more thoroughly,' he observed.

'Cautiously,' Fairweather said.

'You can now see what decent colonists make of the place.'

'It certainly deserves more than a passing glance,' Fairweather agreed. 'Which is all I can spare.'

'You disappoint,' Biggs said.

'I am moving upland. Hoping, perhaps, for some excess of creation to tease.'

'I trust you will take care.'

'Of what? Or whom?'

'I still hear rumour of stray rebels at the forest's edge. Some Maori villagers are supposed to take them food. They dare not show their faces freely on the plain. I still have a score or two to settle.'

'It is difficult to imagine a few tottering skeletons with rusty muskets doing harm. Or making useful prospects for colonization of the Chathams.'

Biggs was slow to reply. He said finally, 'I understand that you have been asking about Coates.'

'By way of helping Trader Read dispose of a whisky surplus. As Read has also doubtless advised, Coates was a past acquaintance; it was from him I first heard of Poverty Bay. His absence perplexes.'

'For your information, Coates received no more than his due. The man was a nightmare.'

'For Trader Read, perhaps. But hardly for such of civilization as functions here. The man appears to have had virtues. Not least literacy, ambition, and some commercial judgement.'

'Also a weakness for drink and women.'

'A frailty commonly accommodated without the imperial fabric flying apart.'

'No one would contest Coates' sly intelligence,' Biggs said. 'That made him the worse. At the slightest excuse he would go running to law. He had a reputation for driving magistrates insane.'

'You seem to have survived, sir. I presume he remained in character at his trial.'

'Trial?' Biggs said.

'The formalities which preceded his departure.'

'I was not then functioning as magistrate. I was acting in my military capacity.'

'In my military capacity, Captain Biggs, I have always presumed the man in my sights a menace until disabled or dead. You appear to be telling me something. It surely cannot be that Coates had no trial at all. He carried arms for the Queen; he at least earned a court martial.'

'In respect of most rebels deported, we knew faces. And had an instinct for others.'

'Plainly much use could be made of such clairvoyance in speeding the procedures of justice.'

'Deportation itself was problem enough. Finding vessels, for example. We could only pack off two or three hundred of the more troublesome. And finance had to be considered. Guards must be posted over them in the Chathams. Ships must carry over regular supplies. Prisoners have to be fed.'

'Hanging would have been less a drain on the colony's exchequer, surely.'

'There could have been resentment,' Biggs said.

'Men about to be hung commonly exhibit symptoms of resentment. Their cure is quick.'

'I mean among tribesmen friendly to the Queen; their relatives. Trials would then have been essential, of course. All costly and confusing and prolonging the agony. I can assure you that deportations passed off without undue pain.'

'With no trials at all?'

'No,' Biggs said.

'Not even for a man ostensibly serving the Queen?'

'If it makes for peace of mind, Mr Fairweather, powerful evidence could have been called against Coates. He was once caught firing blanks at the rebels. At another time passing furtive messages. He argued that he had a brother in the enemy camp whom he wished to win over to the Queen. His real motive was clear. He wished a foot in both camps, lest the rebels succeed. He was never a true Queen's Maori.'

'Merely a Maori,' Fairweather suggested.

'If you like,' Biggs said warily.

'And one trimmed to size.'

Biggs' eyes grew remote. 'Is it,' he asked, 'your intention to entertain sympathy for Coates? For a less than scrupulous native?'

'It is my intention, Captain Biggs, to entertain no more than wry wonder. To sympathize might mean less low humour in my life.'

Biggs was not eased. 'Accept my assurance that Coates had to go for the general good.'

'Accepted, Captain Biggs.' Fairweather was anxious to end the encounter.

'Besides, deportation was meant for only a few months. Until hot heads cooled down.'

'Two years of cold Chatham wind should have done that handsomely.'

'They remain there on my recommendation. Until confiscation of lands is settled. It is not my fault negotiations have been prolonged. I ask only for twenty thousand acres in compensation for the tribesmen who took up arms against us. This far Poverty Bay chiefs stubbornly offer only ten, mostly hilly and unsuitable for cropping and grazing.'

'What has happened, Captain Biggs, to colonial initiative? The custom elsewhere has been to confiscate first and talk later.'

'I lack the teeth. No armed constabulary, and just a handful of militia. There are fewer than a hundred European males here among a thousand or two Maoris. I have to bargain, not impose. The colonial government wishes costs kept low. They give me free hand, but no men, no money. Typical.'

'I can see,' Fairweather said, 'that the woe is not all on one side.'

'Quite,' Biggs said. 'And I trust you are satisfied in respect of Coates.'

'I have all but forgotten the fellow's name,' Fairweather insisted. 'Today I have more on my mind.'

'Such as, Mr Fairweather?'

'The cadences to be discovered in nature and man. Some plead that divine discontent spurs them; I interpret the condition as meaning no rest for the wicked. I must hasten on. Good day to you, Captain Biggs.'

'And to you, Mr Fairweather.'

As Fairweather pushed his horse toward forested hills he felt Biggs' bemused gaze on his back. When he at last looked over his shoulder, half a mile on, Biggs was still gazing.

The day grew hot. Fairweather travelled up an airless valley, soon beginning to sweat. The last Maori dwelling dropped behind; scrappy grazing land too. He rode among trees growing taller. Their shade was welcome, though lower limbs menaced. Fairweather was soon dismounted and leading his horse along tight forest trail. Birds sang feebly in the heat; cicadas celebrated. He came to a ford, a stream running shallow over pale pebbles. There he lit his pipe and allowed his horse to drink and forage. Meditation did not last more than a minute or two; he had a familiar tremor of gut. If instinct still served, he was not, after all, alone; he was followed. Yet there was nothing to confirm it, no sound save that of cicadas and water. He recalled Biggs' warning. Old rebels? Old scores? With no haste he knocked ash from his pipe, tethered the horse, and unhitched the carbine from under his saddle bags. Then he positioned himself a dozen yards from the bank of the stream, screened by foliage but with a clear field of fire. He had more than enough cartridges to make impression on someone tracking him with injurious intent; the Terry's breech-loading mechanism functioned efficiently. He should get a second shot in fast before his hide was apparent.

The horse browsed. Perhaps five minutes passed. Then Fairweather saw shadows shift. One human shape, or more? One. A scout? Fairweather sighted the carbine, finger on the trigger guard. On balance he felt relieved that intuition was still in working order.

Another minute went. The shape, after a pause, moved out of shadow, into flutters of sunlight, foliage less dense, and disclosed itself as a skinny young Maori male unarmed but for a knife sheathed on his belt. In torn shirt and filthy trousers rolled to the knee he was not especially engaging in appearance. Ragged scars under one eye; a wild mop of black hair. Perhaps not a stupid face, but currently quite puzzled. The youth arrived barefoot beside Fairweather's horse, considered it at length, and then looked upstream and downstream. Fairweather kept the slovenly figure in his sights until convinced that peril was lacking. The youth had made no signal, given no call to companions. He was alone.

Fairweather stood suddenly. 'And who,' he called, 'are you?'

The youth failed to locate his tongue; he stood paralysed as Fairweather burst from vegetation with carbine still ready.

'Who?' Fairweather said. 'Your name? You? *Ingoa? Koe?*'

Fairweather had to rest the carbine before the bush scarecrow made useful sound. 'Hamiora,' it seemed to say.

'Family? *Whanau?*'

'Pere.'

'Village? *Kainga?*'

'Patutahi.'

'Well, Hamiora Pere of Patutahi, account for yourself. You speak English? *Ingarihi*?'

'*Iti.*' Little.

'Try to understand what I say. You do not – never – stalk honourable men about lawful affairs on forest trails. Understand?'

Perhaps Hamiora Pere did. He shook.

'Now smile,' Fairweather said, and demonstrated. 'Smile.'

Hamiora Pere rolled his eyes and swallowed hard; finally he mounted an expression less fearful.

'No use asking what you were up to, I imagine,' Fairweather said. 'Nor scratching among my Maori to try.'

Hamiora Pere did not dispute this. He said nothing.

'My name is George. In Maori, Hori. Hori Fairweather. Now you speak it. You.'

'Hori,' the boy whispered. 'Hori Fair Weather.'

'And I am very little to be curious about. Also little to fear. Fear, no. Good? Understand?'

'Good,' the boy uttered. '*Ka pai.*'

'Very *ka pai.* There. We are getting along famously together, Hamiora Pere.' The boy, by way of confirmation, was ceasing to shiver. 'Come. Let me hear you say all is good again. Good.'

'Bloody *ka pai,*' Hamiora said, bolder.

'God help us,' Fairweather said. 'A master of the Queen's *Ingaringi.*'

Hamiora Pere seemed to see approval. An impudent smile brightened his face. 'Where you go?' he asked, mostly by way of gestures to that effect. 'What you do here?'

'My business,' Fairweather said, with no Maori to that effect. 'If I take pleasure in pathless woods, seek sermons in stones, it does not concern you. Understand? Never mind. I am delighted you are not what you seemed to be. And pleased to pass the time of day. But very soon I shall not be pleased. Clear off. Go. *Haere, whano,* whatever your damn word is. Decamp. And leave me alone.'

Hamiora chose not to comprehend. Or to let Fairweather be.

'Come,' Fairweather said. 'We have had our fun, given each other a fright. Enough is now enough. Bugger off, in brief.'

'Bugger?' Hamiora asked. Familiar syllables.

'Off,' Fairweather said firmly.

'I a bloody bugger,' Hamiora disclosed. 'I a big bloody bugger.'

Perhaps Fairweather was landed with a village rascal; or village idiot. Hamiora Pere of Patutahi. The clown who traps unwary travellers in the woods.

'So listen to me, Hamiora Pere. Hear well. I pursue mountains today, not man. *Maunga.* I wish no friend. No human babble. No you. No.'

'*He maunga*?' Hamiora said.

'Quite. Mountains. And maybe water. Waterfalls.'

'*He wai*?'

'*Wai,*' Fairweather agreed. '*Wai* falling.' He mimed lifting the stream at their feet and letting it drop.

'Ah,' Hamiora said. '*Rere.*'

'Waterfall? *He rere*?'

'*Rere,*' Hamiora confirmed.

'Good. So this enlightening lesson in linguistics is hereby concluded. Good day to you.'

Hamiora protested in Maori and muddy English that he knew the mountains ahead. More, he knew a big bloody *rere.*

'You do?' Fairweather sighed.

'A very big bugger,' Hamiora elaborated.

'True? A waterfall? Big?'

'*E tika,* Hori. I speak always true. I show you. I show my bloody friend.'

Fairweather considered the offer. 'Very well,' he said. 'So find me this marvel. It had best be good. You hear?'

'I carry?' Hamiora asked, meaning the carbine.

'Lead the horse,' Fairweather said. Patutahi's prize clown might be light-fingered in the forest. He might even feed ageing rebel relatives in hiding there; and be shepherding Fairweather into uncongenial company. Hamiora plodded off with the horse, and Fairweather lingered several cautious paces behind, the weapon still loaded; he looked right and left.

Hours later, after floundering through gullies of fern and creeper, teetering across stony streams, Hamiora halted; and beamed.

'*Whakarongo,*' he said. '*Ana.*' Listen. There.

Fairweather listened. There was a bass grumbling ahead; water in unmistakeable volume. It was another hour before they closed with the source of the sound. The forest was cooler, moist with fine mists of spray, and the tumult quite deafening. Hamiora parted last leaves, and Fairweather looked out on an engagingly wide waterfall. The water billowed out of the belly of the land, fine and transparent, frilled thinly with foam, to crash and crackle on rocks thirty or forty feet below. There was much to commend it. The giant ferns and many-trunked palms framing it, for example; the tangles of white debris dumped by flood at its foot.

'Thank you,' Fairweather shouted above the din.

'Good?' Hamiora asked.

'A feast. You, Hamiora Pere, have done well today.' He ruffled the boy's shaggy hair.

The more Fairweather considered the waterfall, the more he saw a week's work. It was late afternoon. Camp had to be made. They steered the horse up a ridge and arrived on a scrubby plateau some fifty yards upriver. The boom of the waterfall was muffled; birds could be heard.

'You go now?' Fairweather asked, with a small gift of money in mind. '*Whano? Koe?*'

'I no go,' Hamiora said.

'You stay?'

'I say?'

'Not say. Stay. You stay here with me?'

'I say here with Fair Weather man.'

'All right, damn it. Say. But you not say too much to Fairweather. This man must think. Work. Much think. Much work.'

'Work?' Hamiora puzzled.

'You shall see,' Fairweather promised. 'So, desirably, shall I.' He had a further thought. 'Your parents?' he conveyed. 'Maybe they miss you?'

It seemed not. Hamiora's parents were *mate*. Dead.

Who then did he live with?

An uncle of sorts. His uncle was not *mate*, though Hamiora's face seemed to wish him so. He worked for his uncle. His uncle was not good.

The scars under his eye, were they his uncle's work?

Hamiora nodded and looked at his feet. Finally and silently he lifted his shirt to disclose scars even larger.

'*Waipiro,*' Hamiora explained. Stinking water; rum. His uncle drank *waipiro* sometimes all day and most of the night. Night was worst. His uncle was wild.

'Consider yourself my guest,' Fairweather said.

Before evening they built a bivouac of treefern logs and canvas. As the sun westered, birds grew noisy in the trees around. Hamiora sat examining Fairweather's carbine with interest. Fairweather explained the function of the parts, then offered the boy cartridges. 'There,' he said. 'Go and make a horror of yourself. I have business with your *rere* before dark.'

Hamiora had no problem with the essential message; he grabbed up the gun and whooped into the trees. Fairweather took sketchbook and pencils and walked downhill to reconnoitre the left flank of the unravelling river; an overhead view of the falls might make for most challenge. He picked his way along dry bank, among boulder and bush, until at last looking down on the water as it leapt. The sinews of its surge were apparent. From a precarious roost, with legs and arms braced against rock, he raced quick visual notes before daylight left. First impressions travelled furthest; the first blow was the best of the battle. It seemed he had a commanding height with the campaign barely begun. Then bravado undid him. Craning forward to consider a diverting stutter in the cataract, he had a difference of opinion with his left leg and lost equilibrium. He slid, clutching air, and toppled. He bounced once, twice, and lay stunned. His tools of trade had gone. So almost had he. His arms were urgently embracing an uncooperative outcrop of rock at the edge of the falls; his legs dangled. Aware of the barrage of water to his rear, he groped upward until he had footing of sorts. There was no safe way higher, and demonstrably none down. He was cast. All evil comedy; the artist in thrall to his theme. He cursed the loss of his notes and contemplated the everlasting loss of his skin. At length, above the beat of water, he heard a faint shout.

'Hori? Hori Fair Weather?'

Hamiora; hope. Fairweather saw the boy's head bobbing about at the side of the falls.

'Here,' Fairweather called, breathless.

Hamiora peered down, blinking, his face pure awe. The carbine was slung on his shoulder. Four blasted pigeon swung from one hand.

There were at least fifteen feet between the pair, and all perpendicular.

'Help,' Fairweather suggested. 'And fairly damn soon.'

'*Taihoa,*' Hamiora said. Wait.

His head disappeared. Fairweather's wait might have been longer, but not much. Light had begun leaving the sky before Hamiora came into view again.

The boy had strips of native flax knotted into a substantial length. He lowered this length gently toward Fairweather. Currents of air, formed by the falls, flicked it out of reach at first. Then Fairweather grabbed it and held. He hoped it strong; and Hamiora sturdy. It seemed the boy was able to find only a flimsy overhanging branch as anchor, not one to detain Fairweather long if he fell; Hamiora would have to take most of Fairweather's weight. Fairweather took a large breath and firm grip. 'Now,' he called.

Hamiora tugged. Fairweather, struggling, angled his boots against steep rock, trying to relieve Hamiora's load. He gained a foot or two upwards. There were still more than twelve.

Hamiora was gasping. Fairweather searched for fissures in which his boots might fit; the flax bit into his hands. Hamiora tried to walk backwards; the flax chafed unpromisingly on rock edge.

Ten feet. Nine. Perhaps less than eight. The flax still held; Fairweather's palms bled. Five feet short, and Hamiora's anguished face began to fill Fairweather's vision. The flax was fraying faster where it chafed and Fairweather's boots no longer finding grip. He skidded. The lethal rumble of water, to his rear, seemed to grow louder.

Improvization arrived. Still gripping the flax with one hand, Hamiora took up the firearm at his feet and pushed it barrel first toward Fairweather. Fairweather clutched at the metal, then at the strap. The flax finally went slack, and with the carbine Hamiora hauled Fairweather the last inches on to reliable terrain. There they collapsed together, the carbine between. Fairweather was first to raise his head.

'Thank you,' he panted. 'Thank you, friend.'

'I always be Hori Fair Weather's good bloody friend,' Hamiora saw fit to declare.

'So prove it,' Fairweather said. 'Cook me the meal of my life.'

They camped within earshot of Hamiora's *rere* for five further and far less remarkable days. Fairweather's abrasions and bruises argued that the waterfall was best wooed from prudent postures. He settled for undemanding sites downriver, where glistening foliage gave perspective, and light did the labour; he harvested rock forms ghostly beyond the green torrent, and made much of the bluish pool misty at its foot. Meanwhile Hamiora hunted, cooked, mused, grinned and found more useful words of *Ingariti* taking his fancy. Fairweather's paintings and drawings perplexed. Why, when the waterfall was there, did he have to make others, and the same? Explanation faltered and finally lost its way in a linguistic maze; Hamiora refused to be tempted by brush and paint. He moodily carved at wood, perhaps as he had seen tribal craftsmen, and presumably to offer images more potent. These were not forthcoming. The most he could dig from the wood were crude and lopsided faces with tongues protruding fiercely in the conventional Maori manner; with sadness he sent them all sailing downriver.

'Never mind,' Fairweather said.

'What,' Hamiora asked, 'means never mind?'

'For me,' Fairweather explained, 'the only way to make this world work.'

'World? All?'

'All earth, all sky, all things. And people. To all I say never mind.'

'I try never mind too,' Hamiora vowed. 'I never mind nothing. I always say very bloody hello to Hori Fair Weather.'

Later Hamiora found the world working to more advantage; he arrived back in camp burdened with the hindquarters of a wild pig fallen to an enlightened shot.

'I tell it never mind,' he explained. 'First with gun. Then with knife.'

'It may have the message,' Fairweather said.

Next morning they broke camp and travelled down country. The waterfall's roar became faint behind. Tracks were seldom apparent, but Hamiora efficiently found his way through gullies crowded with tree and creeper. Scuffling through leaves, they heard something new. Shots, shouts. Then more. Hamiora stiffened, teetered, plainly contemplating flight.

'Wait,' Fairweather said. 'Quiet.'

He unstrapped the carbine from the horse, took cartridges and percussion caps, and loaded. It might merely be an enthusiastic Maori hunting party ahead. It might be more. Either way it was desirable to be certain.

There were more shots. Some near, some far. With further indistinct shouts. If a hunting party, it was apparently intent on putting all life to flight in the forest; too ineffective to be true. The pattern seemed less innocent to an educated ear. Perhaps not a battle of substance, but certainly a mêlée of sorts. Hamiora might have some Maori reason for fright.

'Don't lose my damn horse,' he told the boy. 'I go. I look.'

Hamiora had no quibble, nothing to say at all; he had begun to stream sweat. So much for warrior tradition. Given his current anguish, Hamiora wouldn't pass muster in the most indifferent regiment, though he might serve as a feeble company cook.

Fairweather moved forward. At first there was nothing substantial to see. Light and leaf. Scattering birds. Shots began echoing to right and left, again suggestive of some haphazard affray. He advanced from tree to tree, pausing at each, hastening to the next, then turning fast to consider his rear. He might be in dead ground; he might also be locating himself between belligerents.

Indistinct shouts, repeated, took perplexing colour. Fairweather then heard his own name called again and again.

It was all of ten minutes before he made himself heard, before shots ceased, and the cries; and another ten before Fairweather found himself irritable again in the company of Captain Biggs. Also of what seemed a search party. A couple of Maoris; a clutch of dishevelled colonists presumably of Biggs' militia.

'We feared for your safety,' Biggs explained. 'You appeared to be long overdue.'

'That hardly justifies turning a crazed shooting party loose on the landscape.'

'Anything could have happened,' Biggs protested. 'We also had grounds for suspicion. A loyal Maori told me that a certain youth, of the village of Patutahi, vanished at about the time you were seen riding into the forest. Something of a young ruffian, and certainly with past rebels among his kinsmen. We feared the worst.'

'Then I have the honour, sir, of reporting that this disorder has been successfully contained. The aforementioned young ruffian is in my custody.'

'He made attempt on your person?'

'Not perceptibly.'

'But he took advantage.'

'Of no more than my notorious good nature. Your search party presented more peril. An occasional shot is useful when out on search. Not one damned fusillade after another.'

'My men were nervous. We are close to the mountain Maoris here; the Tuhoe. A surly crew. Most have taken no loyal oath. They remember everything.'

'I also find some things unforgettable, sir. The Tuhoe tantalized us for three lively days at Orakau before waving goodbye. Surly? Perhaps. Their dead didn't look genial. Ours even less so.'

'Had something happened to you, uproar could have ensued here again. You put us all at risk.'

'In which case you have my apologies, Captain Biggs.'

'Major Biggs as from yesterday. The government has belatedly recognized the potential importance of Poverty Bay to the colony.'

'My congratulations, Major Biggs. And my assurance that I have seen no Maori worth a shot this past week.'

'So you wish to bring no charge?'

'You bewilder, Major Biggs. First a battlefield; now a court. Hamiora Pere of Patutahi was last witnessed holding my horse and pissing with fright. The defence rests its case.'

'At least locating you has been a useful exercise,' Biggs said. 'It helps keep men sharp.'

'The pleasure is mine, Major Biggs. Now, if you will excuse me, I have a horse to find, and a friend.'

Easily said. It took Fairweather an hour to find his tethered horse. Hamiora, however, had gone. Fairweather called the boy's name, but he declined to be found. Finally he checked his saddle bags. Nothing had flown.

'Never mind,' he decided at length.

Towards day's end he rode out of the forest, back on to the plain of Poverty Bay, more or less as he had left it, alone.

Next morning he paddled a canoe upriver to tell Meri of his return to the port.

'Was it good?' she asked, pouring tea.

'To the point,' he said. 'I made a waterfall pay for its sins.'

'All that time, and you were never lonely?'

'I found a friend.'

'Up there?' Suspicion was plain.

'Male,' he said quickly.

'Just as well,' she said.

'Or I may have imagined him. Some imp of the woods, perhaps. Anyway he haunted. Later he vanished, as spirits decently should.'

'Perhaps you were drinking again,' she said.

'One Hamiora Pere, if he exists, will swear that I lived a sober life in the wilds. Also a shade chaste, if I may say so.'

'You may not,' she said. 'Quiet.'

Her brothers, after work on their farm, were approaching the verandah. Decencies had to be observed; decorous greetings made. Matiu, however, was short of convincing; his face wished Fairweather elsewhere. He rinsed head and hands in a bucket of water, then sat, sipped tea, and was silent. It was left to gentle Pita to push conversation.

'Does England seem far to you now?' he asked.

'At times,' Fairweather confessed. 'At other times, not.'

'There is one thing that puzzles,' Pita went on. 'Why must the English come so far?'

'Some would say destiny.'

'What do you?'

'That chance is a fine thing. New Zealand parades too many charms to be left alone long. A foolish virgin, perhaps. If not to be wooed and won by us, then by some other. Englishmen may not be dextrous in the wooing; they are in the winning.'

'I should like to see England,' Pita announced. 'I should like to see what makes men English.'

Matiu decided social rite at an end; he stood abruptly and emptied the dregs of his tea over the edge of the verandah. 'See Biggs,' he told his young brother. 'He is all of England, and the English, you need to understand.'

'Perhaps,' Fairweather said. 'On the other hand, all Englishmen are not colonists, nor all colonists Englishmen.'

'You have had business with Biggs,' Matiu accused.

'Of a melancholy sort,' Fairweather agreed.

'You are like all English. You play with words.'

'I am tempted to reply that Maoris play with suspicions.'

'Why then do you remain here?'

'Poverty Bay is compatible. And your sister's company is not to be undervalued.'

'I know her value,' Matiu said. 'You also, I think. There is much good Smith land.'

'I have told you,' Meri said to her brother. 'George remains only so long as he is happy to paint. And I am happy to have him remain.'

That provoked Matiu further. 'These pictures of Poverty Bay, what will you do with them? Will you take them elsewhere?'

'Of necessity. To a settlement of greater substance. A crumb or two may then fall my way from prosperous tables.'

'Colonists' tables.'

'It is in the nature of the enterprise to lighten their purses.'

'Then fill them again.'

'I am sorry. You have now lost me.'

Matiu was all triumph. 'You paint pretty pictures to bring more colonists to Poverty Bay. To bring merchants, speculators. And more men for Biggs' militia.'

'What are you telling me?' Fairweather pleaded.

'You paint for the colonial government. What do you say?'

'That you have a capricious sense of humour.'

'You do not deny it,' Matiu said stubb[illegible]ly.

'Because I do not wish to make this more comic. My vices are commonplace. A talent for conspiracy is not among them.'

'Would you swear before God?'

'In my case that oath might have an empty sound.'

'You see?' Matiu looked to Meri and Pita for vindication. 'He is like an eel. Slippery and wriggling this way and that.'

Matiu stalked off the verandah. There was a silence of some duration after his departure.

Pita spoke first. 'I apologize for Matiu,' he said. 'He has much to anger him. Biggs is beginning to threaten. Biggs says he will bring in a great army, and no one of Maori blood will have land unless he is allowed to confiscate as he pleases.'

'Then his nerve would seem to be going,' Fairweather said. 'Perhaps also his reason. There is no great army left in this land. Nor would England be inclined to lend one again, with bills still unpaid. The army has a phrase for idle boasts. Piss and wind.'

'Some Maoris believe Biggs. Matiu does not. He says what he thinks. Others listen when Matiu speaks. So Biggs hates Matiu the most.'

'Then Matiu must take care. As I understand it, the last Maori here to know too much has indefinite residence far from Poverty Bay.'

'We do not speak of Coates here,' Pita said. 'I think it still best.'

'Forgive me,' Fairweather said. 'But the point must be made.'

'Matiu is safe. He has too much mana and is too high in the church. He reads lessons on Sundays. He is upset because every time Biggs speaks of confiscating more land, there are fewer in church to hear Christ's message. Maoris stay away more and more. Some say Christ is the prow of the colonists' canoe.'

'Which may be fair reading.'

Pita frowned. 'Better not to say that to Matiu. He says that Christ's love is for all. Even Biggs will be forgiven.'

'Then there is hope for me too,' Fairweather said.

Pita rose stiffly, still impeccably mannered. 'Please do not let Matiu's mood stop you visiting again,' he said. 'Or telling of England.'

He left to join his brother in the day's labour.

At length Meri lifted her eyes. 'Does Poverty Bay begin to displease?'

'God spare me from colonists and Maoris both. There is too much righeousness abroad.'

'You are thinking of the next schooner.'

'Also of you.'

'This waterfall,' she asked, 'was it large?'

'And industrious.'

'I could give you better.'

'Are you in the business of creation? I should have known sooner.'

'I am offering you the Urewera mountains. Further than you have been.'

'I understand that my bones might fill a forest grave.'

'Not with me. I have relatives among the Tuhoe.'

'A joint expedition?'

'Of course. I cannot leave you at the mercy of imps of the forest. The next might be a her.'

'Do Tuhoe maidens leap upon the unwary from the trees?'

'You would like that.'

'In moderation. Excess can tire.'

'So what is your answer?'

'You know it,' he said.

Meri arranged four horses, two to ride where equestrian progress was possible, two to carry provisions. They started out on a cool morning in early April. By the end of the first day Poverty Bay was well lost. The steep trail through forest was indistinct, dank, and cluttered with fallen trees; it crossed and recrossed hiccuping streams and sputtering rivers and took insane twists among shaggy stands of rain forest, even seeming to circle. 'Is this the best we can do?' Fairweather asked on the second day.

'It is the best route,' she said.

'It seems designed to taunt and tax.'

'The Tuhoe like their trails rough. It kept other Maori tribes out. Now your tribe.'

'Then they design well,' he said.

Undergrowth and drapes of creeper confounded; trees of wide girth leapt skyward, leaving murky cascades of leaf and lichen behind; even at noon light flickered weakly on the floor of the forest. Strangely coloured and abundant mosses shone in the gloom. It was land impatient with the puny. The mountains of the Urewera, glimpsed beyond giant greenery, teemed in dusky tide under mists. On the third day storm promised to buffet them back to Poverty Bay; they slithered, and horses toiled and baulked. They sheltered and eventually slept under a slender ledge of rock, with a sickly fire for warmth, while their horses rummaged hungrily among fern. Tree and terrain could be felt in their flesh; their lovemaking never lacked vehemence.

As they laboured higher the sound of water became more significant. Torrents stormed through gullies and slammed down terraces of rock and rotting logs. There were few elegant rhythms for Fairweather to consider; it was all uncouth compilation. Poverty Bay's tame pastures and rivers seemed petty irrelevance; this was the land's brutish torso.

Finally their track became more distinct, mountains moved apart, and they had sight of a long lake in the light of setting sun. Below them was a waterside village, a primitive place even by antipodean measure. Thatched dwellings, crooked pallisades, a roughly carved gate. There were canoes pulled up on to a pale beach, and patchy cultivations. There were also fires and voices.

The sunset scene shook figures free; men of the village approached. Most were tall, dark and densely tattooed, with muscular legs and large feet, Polynesians bred to steep mountain trails; they were garbed for the greater part in mats of coarse fibre. Conspicuous among them was an elderly man, his face almost pure purple with tangles of tattoo; he had white hair drifting down to his shoulders and few teeth to speak of.

He recognized Meri and pressed noses with her in traditional greeting. Then, looking sidelong at Fairweather, he spoke quickly and dourly in Maori.

'What does he ask?' Fairweather said.

'That you are not from the government.'

'Which is easily answered.'

'And no colonist.'

'No colonist in his right mind would want an inch of this territory.'

'He is not to see that. The Tuhoe love their high land. They see other tribes lose theirs.'

'So tell him that the Tuhoe are too inconveniently situated. And bound to be forgotten.'

'They wish to be,' Meri explained, 'but they went to help other tribes fight. Their thought was that the colonists must be stopped before these mountains were reached. They fought hard, and now have fear they may be punished.'

'Life here would seem punitive enough. Ask the old fellow if he fought. And where.'

Meri spoke in Maori; the old man, with some brightening of eye, much shaking of head, with chopping hands and stamping feet for emphasis, made lengthy reply.

'He says,' Meri translated, 'that he thinks you must know. He fought at the place called Orakau, against all the soldiers of the imperial army.'

'Then tell him I fought there also. And have come to pay my respects to the bold Tuhoe. No tradesmen of war ever toiled harder; none deserve to be longer remembered.'

Meri worked at conveying the message. A smile dawned slowly on the old man's face. At length he moved to Fairweather and pressed noses with him too; their breath briefly mingled.

'You are now welcome with the Tuhoe,' Meri said. 'You are the guest of Nama. He is chief on this lake, and cousin of my cousins. The Tuhoe sometimes took Poverty Bay people as slaves. We called them destroyers, consigners of men to the spirit world, and thieves of women. It was in that way our blood mixed.'

'Tell Nama we offer flour and sugar as gifts.'

'He wishes to offer dried eel and fresh pigeon.'

'I must learn not to compete. Tell him I have never understood the winning and losing of wars. It seldom seems just.'

'He wishes it known that defeat was never of Tuhoe making.'

'I am sure.'

'It was a Tuhoe who told you that they would fight forever and ever, women and children too.'

'It is recalled.'

'He hopes that forever will not be so.'

'And we are agreed.'

'He most of all wishes you to know that there is no imperial soldier he would sooner have killed.'

'And assure him that there is no Maori, in the length of these islands, I should rather have slain.'

Nama took Fairweather's shoulders with affection for a moment, then led his guests into the village. First impressions persisted. It was a poor, spartan place; not even its situation between mountain and lake did much to beguile. So much for the sublime life of the savage; the thought of existence here left frost in the soul. Fighting had left few men; children were skinny and women mostly lacklustre. Dress was a miscellany of old, new and makeshift. Flax mats, ragged blankets, with a few faded tatters of souvenired imperial uniforms here and there visible. Children plucked at Fairweather's skin, passing verdict on its pallor; plainly most had never seen white skin before.

Nama delivered them to a dwelling set low in the earth, indifferently built, with thatch peeling. It seemed it was theirs as long as they wished. So was Nama's personal guarantee of safety for Fairweather in the mountains of the Tuhoe. With a further measure of Maori oratory, Nama left them in residence. Meri lit a fire; Fairweather used canvas to weatherproof the thatch. Within an hour they had respectable warmth and comfort. Women arrived with flax containers of food still steaming from earth ovens. Fairweather's appetite was not equal to the fibrous fern root in the first container he sampled.

'So try this,' Meri said, pushing another toward him. 'A great Tuhoe delicacy.'

'Such as?'

'Try,' she said.

He tried; tasted. It did not displease. Flesh of some nature, neither fish nor fowl. He filled his mouth again. 'Yes,' he decided. 'So what is it?'

'Mountain rat,' she said. 'Fattened with the very best berries.'

Fairweather ran outside, retched, and returned to sulk until rum and hunger made him reckless.

Later Nama joined them. He wished to acquaint Fairweather with Tuhoe tradition and prowess. The tribe's strength mostly came from shrewd mating. Mountain had copulated with mist, and the far ancestors of the Tuhoe came sighing to life; other ancestors had pushed canoes through vast seas to take the terrain by conquest and the daughters of mountain and mist likewise. So the Tuhoe began, soon men of fierce muscle. It was from such Tuhoe muscle that these Urewera mountains were named. A mighty fighting chief named Mura-Kareke forsook his wife the night before battle, as was Maori warrior custom, but dismally failed to inform his flesh of the discipline needed. While Mura-Kareke slept, his sturdily lengthening penis coupled with his campfire and suffered disagreeable damage. Mura-Kareke in his turn expired of shock and shame. By way of memorial, the mountains were thereafter named Hot Penis. Urewera.

'And beware the fate of Mura-Kareke,' Nama advised, via Meri, with toothless laugh.

'Promise Nama that it shall haunt my mind from this day forward,' Fairweather said. 'I felt there was some nameless sorrow in these highlands. Now I know. He that burns most shines most. Let Mura-Kareke's glowing member be a lesson forever and ever and the day after too. Never forsake a fuck on account of a fight.'

Meri interpreted only with prompting. Nama took his laughter off into the Urewera night.

Morning revised Fairweather's first view. Sky was bright, water blue, and birds loud. In a canoe presented by Nama they paddled about the lake for most of the day. Thin cloud circled mountain summits. New Zealand pines and palms leaned over the waterside, their underside stippled with reflected light. There were theatrical bluffs and silent coves; water flashed luminously from forest gloom. Fairweather had the bitter and sweet of a beleaguered Arcadia if he chose. By the time he beached the canoe back at Nama's village he had so chosen; he had even begun to see statuesque Tuhoe in most melodic setting.

'I may need a month or two,' he told Meri.

'That will take us into winter.'

'Out of season, out of price.'

'Let me hear that when the cold comes,' she said.

7

Winter skirmished and struck. The second half of June was a mix of thunder and downpour, frost and fleeting sunlight. Peaks, when not clouded, were seen patched with snow. Waves flew off the lake with a roar. Fairweather's hands froze in the wind as he worked, and soon his eyes numbed too. Finally they emptied their mountain dwelling; their horses were saddled and burdened. Farewells were made to crusty Nama. The old man said he hoped that Fairweather might again visit the Urewera. But there was a condition.

'Condition?' Fairweather asked.

It seemed Nama had consulted his *tohunga,* his tribal oracle, in connection with Fairweather's welfare. Fairweather, if he wished ever to return to the Urewera, must first watch where the lightning flashed.

Fairweather confessed himself baffled.

'He means,' Meri explained, 'that each person has in life what we call a *rua koha,* a high place where the lightning plays especially for him. If the lightning flashes away from that place, then peril is not for that person. But if the lightning should flash from the *rua koha,* and seem to come closer, then peril is indeed destined for him.'

'I shall keep my head under a blanket,' Fairweather promised.

'That is not the meaning,' Meri said. 'Peril must be met.'

'Not in my book. I let it do all the walking.'

Fairweather leant from his saddle and took Nama's hand for the last time; the old man's energetic grip all but toppled him from the horse. Then, impulsively, Nama threw his personal cloak about Fairweather's neck; a chief's cloak trimmed with the feathers of mountain birds. Nama stepped back and spoke with fervour.

Meri said, 'He still regrets not having the privilege of killing you in fair battle; your mana would have mingled with his. With this cloak, he now mingles his with yours.'

'Tell him I shall wear it as if worthy,' Fairweather said.

'I think Nama already knows that,' Meri said.

Their journey out of the Urewera began in silence; a silence which persisted as days passed on slippery forest trail. It was of their making, not of the mountains. Fairweather was familiar with it: the first and most durable symptom of a spent affair. Perhaps the mountains had postponed its arrival. They knew all they could know of each other, given their circumstances, and Fairweather was not one to meddle with circumstances. Regrets? He was familiar with those too. The Urewera might have persuaded him of the pleasures of the primitive; it had also left him with the conviction that they were best recalled from a civilized armchair with a large whisky in hand. Not a Smith armchair, nor Trader Read's whisky.

She waited with her question until forest fell away and they reined in above Poverty Bay. Plain and coast were sunny; the region was still warm with Indian summer.

'You will leave now?' she asked.

'Soon,' he agreed.

'I shall not be on the shore to watch your ship sail.'

'Perhaps better. For me also. There has been more than I bargained for.'

'What does that mean?'

'Five months.'

'Is time all you count?'

'And riches.'

'How long do you customarily allow an English lady?'

'Sometimes a night. Sometimes an afternoon hour. There is no more to learn, if there ever was.'

'So I must take this as tribute.'

'If you wish conventional endearments, I have those too.'

'I know.' There was a silence of length. She said, 'You are really quite a sad man.'

Fairweather had never been told so before.

It was July's first week when they arrived back on the Turanga riverside. Meri, with few words, rode on to the Smith farm; they were agreed that conversation was unhelpful. Fairweather was left with smaller matters to settle before taking a seaworthy vessel north to Auckland. An overdue painting for Trader Read; a carbine to restore to Major Biggs' armoury. He also needed to wrap and waterproof his work securely, to spare it the ravages of voyaging. Meri was no impediment. For the first four nights he slept alone, close to the fire, waking to ash and a melancholy of flesh, perhaps still at risk. When she did come again, it was on a slow horse out of winter dusk; she found it difficult to meet his eye. But she sat by his fire.

'Where will you finish?' she asked.

'The problem is where to begin,' he argued. 'I must see whether the citizens of that sour town to the north make free with their money. My muddy ventures in Poverty Bay may not sweeten them; the green of the Urewera just might.'

'And otherwise?'

'It seems I am to see which way the lightning flashes.'

Though her intention seemed to waver, she remained with him that night after all. If lightning played from some far *rua koha*, it played unseen.

Through most of the second week of July there was no useful sail in sight; winds were sharp and seas large. On a distinctly midwinter morning he woke to hoofbeats and a male voice calling his name. He reached out sleepily for Meri and failed to locate her; he had passed the night alone.

'Mr Fairweather?' he heard again.

Biggs. And curt.

Fairweather blinked out into cold sunlight, buckling his belt and buttoning his shirt. Biggs sat on his horse; no sociable inclination to dismount was apparent.

'My apologies,' Fairweather said. 'I daresay you have heard of my intended departure. I had it in mind to ride out to Matawhero and return your firearm.'

'I now want you with it,' Biggs said. 'And every capable man. The prisoners are back.'

'Prisoners?' Fairweather asked vaguely.

'Those deported to the Chathams.'

'Released? I have seen no vessel.'

'Escaped. They overpowered the Chathams garrison and commandeered a large visiting schooner. They landed and camped a dozen miles to the south three days ago. Then let the schooner sail on. The idiot skipper didn't think to advise me first; it seems he is on his way south to tell Wellington's politicians the tale. It has only just reached me.'

'Has there been killing?'

'They seem to have let the crew of the schooner live; possibly also the garrison.'

'Then there appears no cause to take great offence. Presumably your natives have become impatient with lengthening exile. I imagine them bedraggled and sea weary, waiting to state their case.'

'They give offence to law and order.'

'To order, perhaps. Of law I have less competence to speak.'

'They have taken it into their own hands.'

'Which seems not unfamiliar in Poverty Bay.'

That dart didn't find Biggs. 'Maori informants tell me the prisoners are armed. They seized every weapon in the Chathams. Not to speak of tobacco, alcohol, and money.'

'If a job is worth doing, it is worth doing well.'

'It appears to have been effectively planned and remarkably executed. But we are talking, Mr Fairweather, of theft, assault and battery, escape from lawful custody, and piracy. A formidable charge sheet; and more. There is some heretical new religion among them.'

'It is new to me that heresy is a punishable offence in this colony.'

'If it proves pernicious, perhaps. It is not our first experience of fanatics. Of Maoris rejecting Christian scripture.'

'I make no secret, Major Biggs, of my own difficulties in that respect. I have as many embracing pagan gods.'

'I said Christian scripture, Mr Fairweather; not the Bible. This new Maori mumbo jumbo seems mostly from the Old Testament. It made for great merriment, I gather, among officers and men of the Chathams garrison. Who now laugh on the other side of their faces, no doubt.'

'And deserve court martial,' Fairweather said.

'For slackness?'

'For being impermissibly witless. The document should never have been allowed circulation. The Old Testament is no fit reading for men exiled. There is too much grief; not to speak of example.'

'The prisoners now think themselves brown Israelites.'

'That was my point, Major Biggs.'

'With their own Moses.'

'Who has found a path through the sea?'

'You would seem to know more than appears, Mr Fairweather.'

'I know the book of Exodus. Who has wooed the waters this time?'

'You hardly need ask. Coates is now better known by the native pronunciation of his name. Kooti.'

'Coates?' Fairweather mused.

'Kooti,' Biggs insisted. 'If you had doubts about my having done the right thing, in shipping him off, I trust they are now allayed. He always made mischief.'

'I see doubt less comfortably in your domain, sir.'

'This could be more than Poverty Bay's problem. It could be the colony's.'

'But especially Poverty Bay's. And yours.'

'At the moment. The prisoners will have to be contained. Persuaded to give up their arms and loot.'

'And surrender themselves to colonial justice?'

'Entirely.'

'Then you have a distinct problem, Major Biggs. Coates, in his past incarnation, has some cause to believe there is none.'

Biggs refused to flinch. 'The short of it is that I desire your services urgently, Mr Fairweather.'

'Are you conscripting?'

'Merely asking you to ride with us today. It may be no more than an afternoon's work. A show of force.'

'Since I have no schooner to capture, a lively canter and little drama will do me no harm. I should still prefer not to be pressed.'

'Excellent. Among other things, you may have some view on which way Kooti will jump.'

'I knew only a chatterbox called Coates,' Fairweather said. 'A man most likely to jump, with great fluency of utterance, in the direction of the nearest hogshead of rum.'

'He must be taken seriously,' Biggs argued.

'Not Coates,' Fairweather said.

8

An hour later, after a hasty breakfast of bread and cheese, Fairweather was riding south, along Poverty Bay's pale shore, with gulls flapping noisily overhead. About and around was Biggs' makeshift troop of militia. There were also twenty or more of the bay's reliable Maoris whom Biggs hoped might serve as intermediaries, also armed by way of precaution. Perhaps a party of seventy all tallied. Most of the colonists had been roused from bed, barn or workshop and told to collect rifles fast. As a show of force they left everything to be desired. Some rode with weapons slung over their shoulders; the more nervous already had them across saddles. Nor was their horsemanship more disciplined. There was much bumping and liverish mumbling among those hanging discreetly to the rear. For a time Fairweather rode beside a twitchy and weedy young Irishman named Mulhooly.

'I didn't know nothing about this,' Mulhooly complained. 'Someone should of said there was wild savages about. I didn't come to Poverty Bay to get into no trouble.'

'So what did you come to get into?' Fairweather asked.

'Boots.'

'Then I must observe that you now wear them handsomely.'

'I mean making boots. Boots for Maoris. They all want them. And wear them out quick. No bloody sense. I got three acres and two cows. And a missus and two kids. No one said nothing about this.'

On Fairweather's other flank was an even less winsome companion, a lean and bleak middle-aged man with badly pitted face named Newman. Fairweather had been long enough in the colony to recognize a last-chancer. Newman spoke little and looked vacantly ahead. Not a man who expected much of life; and Poverty Bay would have nothing to confound expectation. He coughed now and then, with eruptions of phlegm, spitting carelessly as he rode.

'And you?' Fairweather asked.

'Carpenter,' Newman said with reluctance. 'And tidying up for Read.'

'Land too?'

'Not enough to speak of.' Newman confirmed this by releasing another impressive jet of phlegm and falling silent.

The wind was cool in their faces as they struck inland to avoid steep cliffs. Hills slowed them, then patches of fern and scrub, and they veered seaward again. Stops grew frequent. A horse or two had lamed, men were already saddlesore; and Biggs had to muster laggards and candidate cowards back into his band. They moved at slackening pace among rocky hills and yellow ridges whittled by wind. Soon they were looking down into a small cove through which a slender creek found the sea. The sands of the cove were darkened by scores of Maoris. They were camped there in shelters made of driftwood, canvas sail, and blankets. Children shouted. Fires burned.

'Harmless,' Fairweather judged with relief.

'Buggers,' Newman said. He did not elaborate.

Biggs called a halt a hundred yards short of the cove. Then he conversed with Maoris of his party. The upshot was that the Maoris, no militia, continued on to the prisoners' encampment. Fairweather pushed out of the column to join Biggs.

Biggs explained, 'I require intelligence of the enemy.'

'They are scarcely such at this juncture,' Fairweather suggested. 'I see infants and women.'

'Allied with outlaws. I have sent a message that they are to lay down their arms and await instructions from the government. Or suffer the consequences.'

'And we are the consequences?'

'Who else?'

'You see this as a frontal assault, perhaps.'

'As the terrain dictates.'

'Men who have just triumphed over both gaolers and ocean are unlikely to submit soon. It could be costly.'

'We have the high ground.'

'Give Coates – Kooti – a chance to air his grievances. Promise him that, at least.'

'Here?'

'Desirably in court. Before a magistrate with no Poverty Bay connection.'

'A promise to Kooti could go to his head.'

'Then let me make one thing clear, Major Biggs. I am no willing party to a massacre. I should make sure London heard about it. Especially the Colonial Office.'

'I could construe that as threat.'

'I merely give you something to contemplate in a tactical sense. A colony is still a colony. London has the high ground.' Fairweather paused. 'Listen,' he urged. 'There is more to contemplate.'

Singing had begun to rise from the prisoners' camp. Hymns; and presently loudly chanted prayers. The Maoris with Biggs' message were being welcomed with fervour.

'It does not convince,' Biggs said. 'Among those men are the most bloodthirsty we fought.'

'They currently sound most pacific.'

'Let them demonstrate it by surrendering their arms.'

An hour passed; and another, still longer. Silences in the prisoners' camp were punctuated with more hymns and chants. Pickets aside, men of the militia lolled hungry, tired and bored among rocks; complaints grew audible.

Fairweather reclined in the company of a weathered and muscular Yorkshireman named Dodds.

'A right bloody circus,' Dodds grumbled. 'You think Biggs knows what he's up to?'

'It is not for me to pass opinion on your commander.'

'Why not?'

'Because he is your commander.'

'You're army,' Dodds accused. 'Or were.'

'My secret is out,' Fairweather agreed.

Biggs' loyal Maoris straggled up from the cove. The intelligence they carried was of murky nature. The prisoners were celebrating something they insisted on calling Passover.

'The Hebrew festival?' Biggs said.

'Designed to rejoice in Israelite deliverance from Egypt's bonds,' Fairweather offered. 'As I recall, it can last a week.'

'They must be madmen.'

'Or most sincere Jews.'

'Come, Mr Fairweather. You cannot hold with this nonsense.'

'I see men glad of end to exile. The difference seems slight.'

So far as the prisoners had a reply to Biggs' message, it was to the effect that Jehovah had released his chosen ones from an alien clime and placed arms in their hands. To surrender those arms would be to tempt Jehovah's reprisal. They wanted no quarrel with colonists. They wished only their land back, their homes.

'Only?' Biggs sighed.

Told that the wish was unlikely to be granted by Major Biggs here and now, the prisoners had pushed another proposition. That they be allowed open path to the mountains of the Urewera, and permitted sanctuary there, until their wish was considered. Meanwhile they would work peacefully for the salvation of the Maori in accord with Jehovah's command.

'Who said all this?' Biggs demanded.
'Kooti,' a Maori said. 'He speaks for the prisoners.'
'I thought as much,' Biggs said. 'The man speaks gibberish.'
The loyal Maori had more to say. Some in the party bearing Biggs' message had all but succumbed to the evangelical passion of the prisoners' camp; one or two had to be dragged away. Kooti had near to two hundred male followers and most of them armed. There were also perhaps a hundred women and children in his retinue. For most there had been standing space only on the schooner they seized.
'Three hundred,' Fairweather said. 'There is your intelligence, Major Biggs.'
'We may be outnumbered,' Biggs said, 'but that need not be the last word.'
'Three to one, excluding those of their women who might also take up arms; or even some children. I am not sure we can even tally the natives in our party as enthusiastic allies.'
'You are telling me something, Mr Fairweather.'
'That the odds are unacceptable, sir. There is no prospect of early reinforcement. If things go against us all Poverty Bay could be imperilled. Why not give Kooti the chance to prove he means no harm?'
'I did not ride here today to parade impotence.'
'Martial modesty makes no widows. We have no surprise; we are too few to encircle. They need only breach our line once to surround us. At all events we should have an enlivening day.'
Biggs began to have thoughts. Dodds made a querulous appearance beside them.
'What's up?' he demanded. 'Are we still buggering about?'
'Mr Fairweather is acquainting us with his view of the matter,' Biggs explained.
'Time someone had one,' Dodds said. 'Well?'
'I suggest we have the courage to be cowards,' Fairweather said. 'Give Coates, Kooti, a chance to show moderate intention. I should also like to talk to the man. I am better suited than some.'
'I cannot permit that,' Biggs said. 'He might be of a mind to hold you hostage. I should have to bear the brunt of recrimination.'
'A written message, then.'
'Of what nature?'
'Cautionary, sir.'
'So long as you offer the man no encouragement,' Biggs agreed.
Given pencil and notepaper, Fairweather wrote quickly, *He that pisseth against the wind reapeth much moisture. Greetings from George Fairweather.*
A Maori made the descent to the cove with the message and was back soon

with a reply. Fairweather read it aloud and laughed. *Chapter one, verse two. Verily I say unto you that it dependeth how hard the wind bloweth. I hear your word, George Fairweather, and this is mine to you. It was my matakite, my old premonition, that we might meet once more. As a good man of the Queen do the work of peace. Tell Biggs and all colonists that we have nothing left to lose but our lives. They have much. Our work is Jehovah's will. We are not to be prisoner again. Your friend, Kooti.*

'Impudence,' Biggs said.

'Or spirit, sir. What is your intention?'

'To reconsider,' Biggs announced. 'And reinforce. At all events we leave ourselves exposed here.'

'So we are to have no war this afternoon?'

'We have made ample reconnaissance. And confirmed the situation.'

'That always reads instructively in a report,' Fairweather agreed.

'I shall get a messenger down to Hawke's Bay; my information can be put through the electric telegraph to the government. Hawke's Bay can ride to reinforce us in the meantime.'

'To what end?'

'That should be apparent. Emergency now exists in Poverty Bay. We have two hundred mutinous warriors to contain.'

'Or two hundred commendably spiritual servants of Jehovah.'

'It is still a bitter pill to be powerless.'

'Swallow it,' Fairweather said.

Biggs rode at the head of the column back to the plain of Poverty Bay. At Matawhero most of the militiamen dispersed to homes nearby; and Maoris to villages further out on the plain. Daylight was leaving; oil lamps and log fires illuminated windows. Biggs pressed Fairweather to pause. 'Rest your horse,' he pleaded, 'and meet Mrs Biggs.'

Fairweather was reluctant.

'I should be most grateful,' Biggs persisted. 'There are things to be said.'

'For a few minutes only,' Fairweather agreed.

Biggs' house had risen larger than any in Matawhero. The verandah was wide, windows were high, and there was a substantial second storey. Emily Biggs was a soft girl surely half her husband's age, certainly no more than twenty, with black hair, shy eyes, and sunless complexion. Rural Dorset coloured her voice: Fairweather heard larks and saw white villages among hedgerows and cropped fields. He judged her not to have been in the colony long. Nor wed long. She was swollen with child.

'Mr Fairweather has been of help to me today,' Biggs explained. 'We must offer hospitality before he rides on to Turanga.'

He spoke as if to an infant. Emily Biggs stood stiff, confused, touchingly uncertain how to begin.

'The kettle,' Biggs said patiently. 'Put the kettle to the fire. We can at least offer tea. Meanwhile I shall warm Mr Fairweather with something stronger.'

He led Fairweather into a parlour with fire burning. The place served also as office. There were accumulations of printed paper and correspondence on a desk. And maps spread elsewhere.

'My apologies for the muddle,' Biggs said. 'I was immersed in a comprehensive report to the government when news came of the prisoners. One of satisfying nature for once. I am able to say that progress has been made in the matter of land confiscation. Better disposed chiefs see that stalemate is undesirable. We should have our twenty thousand acres before the year's end.'

'You discount today's events?'

'It is more a police problem. We are dealing with rabble, Mr Fairweather. The sweepings of Poverty Bay.'

'But it must give thought.'

First Biggs was silent. Then, surprisingly haggard, he looked into his drink and lowered his head. 'For a moment,' he whispered, 'it seemed the last straw.' He set his drink aside and cradled his head in his arms as if to wrestle an internal ache. There was nothing Fairweather could usefully contribute. At length Biggs lifted his head.

'Forgive me,' he said. 'Pure exhaustion. The frustration of holding the fort alone. Your calm counsel eased matters today. There has been much to harass here. My irritation might have meant death for some. You have my gratitude.'

He was distinctly more human; a beleaguered government clerk. He had quite recovered by the time his wife entered the parlour with a diffident offering of cake and biscuits. She departed with haste.

Biggs further confided, 'I should prefer Emily not to know too much of today. The loneliness of Poverty Bay still makes her fearful. She has no relatives in the colony and next to no friends among colonists' wives. To be blunt, many are no better than they should be. And drunk as often as their husbands. Tolerable standards are few.'

Fairweather examined his empty glass; Biggs did not speed to refill it.

'You cannot walk out on us yet,' Biggs pleaded suddenly. 'Not with things as they are.'

Fairweather was spared a reply by Emily's arrival with tea.

'I was just telling Mr Fairweather,' Biggs said in larger voice, 'that one cannot go to pieces here.'

'No,' Emily said, barely audible.

'Especially not with our responsibilities.'

'No,' she said again, still as quiet.

'With sly Maoris on the one side, fretful colonists on the other, it would be all too easy to do so.'

'Yes,' she said. 'Sugar, Mr Fairweather?'

'George,' he said. 'And thank you; one spoon. When, may I ask, is the happy event due?'

'In a month or two,' she said. 'September, perhaps.' It was a forced confession.

'Then may September blow soft,' Fairweather said, 'until fruit be in loft.'

That won a weak smile from the girl.

'In this clime,' Biggs said, 'I fear it is more a month of uncertain winds. Of falling blossom rather than ripening fruit. Emily has had small chance to observe this colony's peculiarities. She arrived out here only last year. A brave girl; alone.'

'Alone?' Fairweather looked at Emily.

'With other girls similarly situated,' she said. 'Girls of good character.'

'A move of much wisdom on the colonial government's part,' Biggs explained. 'The colony's white female population is being augmented by boatloads of strapping girls. It was undesirable to let the situation drift. The colony is possessed of more than enough half castes already.'

Fairweather was silent.

'Forgive me,' Biggs went on hastily. 'I mean nothing personal. I was not referring to the Smith family. Rather to those with the vices of both races and the virtues of neither.'

'So you,' Fairweather said to Emily, 'have come to save New Zealand?'

'I don't know about that,' she said. 'We were just promised good jobs.' She lowered her eyes. 'I was lucky. I met Mr Biggs right off.'

Fairweather visualized Biggs waiting on a wharfside with other awkward males in search of serviceable brides.

'Emily's past life has not been easy,' Biggs said. 'She now has hopes of something better.'

Intimacy made Fairweather restless. When he judged the moment suitable, he finished his tea and stood. 'I have several slow miles still to ride in the moonlight,' he apologized. 'Thank you, Mrs Biggs.'

'Emily,' she said.

'Emily, then. I am marvellously refreshed. It is some time since I took tea from a sweet English hand.'

Fairweather won yet another timid smile.

Biggs walked his guest outside. 'I hope you manage to overlook my distress,' he said.

'It is overlooked,' Fairweather said.

'And I may well see you tomorrow with further news.'

'I shall hope it good,' Fairweather said.

'The best would be that Kooti's Israelite bubble has burst. But we may have to wait on that.'

'I daresay, Major Biggs. Meanwhile my hope is that the Lord of the Israelites does not, as was his custom, behave irritably toward those who impede his people. I mean by smiting flocks, causing first born to perish, fruit to wither, and rivers to run red.'

'You are joking, of course.'

'Desirably,' Fairweather said.

He left Biggs and rode on to Turanga.

A fire had been lit in his whare. Meri waited. She already knew of the escaped prisoners.

'Did it go well?' she said.

'It seems I may have saved some from prematurely meeting their Maker. At first Biggs was all for a scrap.'

'So Poverty Bay needs you.'

'I could wish the need mutual.'

'You saw Coates?'

'We exchanged written words. He retains a lively sense of his own significance.'

'Maoris don't know what to think. Some who never liked him are laughing now. They laugh because he has outwitted colonists.'

'Matiu?'

'He doesn't laugh. He sees that if there is more trouble there will be even more land confiscated. He says a plague on both Biggs and Coates.'

'That may yet be arranged,' Fairweather said. 'Though I prefer matters frivolous.'

'You are interested,' she said. 'Intrigued.'

'Far be it from me to split hairs.'

'And not a bad man.'

'That is more open to argument.'

'Anyway you are not a colonist.'

'Nor a Maori, as you would be first to agree.'

'You could be trusted,' she said. 'You must not leave now.'

'So Biggs argues too. But he may have martial attributes more in mind than moral character. Attributes mostly designed to produce carrion.'

'Well?' she said.

'I think you see me as soldier again. One who never much thought himself more.'

'I am willing to believe whatever you believe.'

'I'm damned if I don't begin to see this as all your ruse. Something you connived at to keep me in Poverty Bay.'
'Of course.'
'Are we together tonight?'
'Perhaps.'
'Very well, then. I shall not be taking the next vessel out. Is that sufficient?'
'For tonight,' she decided.
'So feed me some warm food,' he commanded. 'Campaigning always leaves me with large appetite.'
Later Fairweather knew relief. To abandon Poverty Bay might be to do fate a disservice. He was far from inattentive to his companion that night.

Biggs was back in the morning. He was making a more extensive muster of colonists, and also recruiting reliable Maoris for two shillings a day with food found. A message had arrived to say there were signs of Kooti's party breaking camp and preparing to move inland.
'Which is no more than he proposed,' Fairweather said.
'He could become impossible of access,' Biggs said. 'We could have the devil's own job fetching him out of the mountains.'
Biggs was all energy again; there was no sight of the woebegone administrator of the night before.
'Surely,' Fairweather argued, 'it is much of a muchness. The prisoners were notionally out of harm's way in the Chathams. They might be equally so in the mountains.'
'The government could not countenance their remaining loose up there.'
'Given a fact, a government can rearrange its countenance fast.'
'I could be held responsible if no formal endeavour is made to deter him. We must stop Kooti short.'
'Kooti? We are talking, surely, of two or three hundred. Not one man alone. You take Kooti too personally.'
'One must. He is the instigator. And of this Israelite nonsense.'
'Sooner or later someone in authority is going to ask a discommoding question or two. Such as why Coates was exiled to the Chathams; why he now resurrects as Kooti. It might spare grief to bargain with him now. You offer only fresh shackles. Promise fair adjudication. Possible compensation. Even land.'
'Land?' Biggs said.
'He surely had some he called his own.'
'Yes,' Biggs agreed with reluctance. 'One way and another, largely through rum trading, he had some quite handsome acres.'

'Who farms them now?'

'Read,' Biggs said with even more reluctance. 'Or men in his employ.'

'The more you stir turd, the worse it stinks, sir. Since arrival in Poverty Bay I have been soiling my boots on something especially smelly.'

Biggs protested, 'You appear not to understand the position.'

'I understand that Read made land available for the settlement at Matawhero on condition that he was rid of Coates. Yes or no?'

'Coates was the author of his own misfortune.'

'With an enthusiastic publisher.'

'An official presence was necessary here. Land was required to bring in colonists who might provide backbone. Read had it. As you know, Maoris are now reluctant to part with theirs. The horns of a dilemma. To be frank, I was not altogether happy.'

'But Coates went. Read had no rival in trade.'

'In the event. It is easy for an outsider to talk. I have to hold things together. Kooti was usurping and undermining all authority, of both races. Promising, in short, to become the most powerful man in Poverty Bay.'

'My impression is that currently he is just that. A chicken home to roost with two hundred warriors. You hope to check him with half that number of green men.'

'We should soon have reinforcement from the south. Hawke's Bay volunteers under Colonel Whitmore.'

Fairweather discovered a large sigh.

'You are evidently intimate with the man,' Biggs said.

'We shared an imperial campaign,' Fairweather allowed. 'After Colonel Whitmore concluded that there was more profit in calling himself colonial, he once failed to enlighten me, with visionary gleam, on the subject of shorthorn cattle.'

'As a colonist he retains his military interests. The Hawke's Bay militia is counted the best drilled in the colony. Men of a better social class, of course.'

'Do you really, Major Biggs, wish war on your hands?'

'I propose no more than a sharp lesson. Turning Kooti back to the coast. We would have surprise on our side. They have no mobility. No horses. With women and children, they must move sluggishly. With luck, they would fall back into Whitmore's hands as he arrives from the south.'

'Then you do talk of war. The greater the carnage, the more Colonel Whitmore will be seen to have risen above insuperable odds. If I remember the man right, he would sooner herd men to battle than cattle to pasture; he never had a tolerable campaign to his name.'

Biggs was thoughtful.

'Detain Kooti with a bargain,' Fairweather urged. 'I am prepared to ride after him and talk. I shall put the case for surrender most forcefully.'

'With one carbine?'

'Under a white flag.'

'Which would mean nothing to most of those murderers. And I do not propose to haggle with Kooti under duress.'

'Then I shall make clear that I act on my own initiative. I shall guarantee Kooti that his grievance will be heard in the highest quarters.'

'You would pursue it?'

'He would have my word.'

'My name would be mentioned.'

'Unavoidably. Your part in Kooti's deportation might be seen as a most human misunderstanding.'

'It might not.'

'Men in government seldom arrive there unsullied. They can be generous to a fault in interpreting misdemeanours in others.'

'Sometimes they need a scapegoat.'

'Only when virtue presses hard on their heels. Virtue currently seems at a loss for numbers in this colony.'

Biggs seemed about to speak, then did not.

'If you require my word also,' Fairweather went on, 'I should see that your case too was put fairly. That the exiling of Kooti is best seen as part and parcel of the confused situation which prevailed in Poverty Bay after the last troubles.'

'What is the bargain with me?'

'That I pursue Kooti with your knowledge. And especially with no impediment placed in my path.'

'The alternative?'

'A parting of the ways, sir.'

Biggs had to consider that. Likewise his need.

'Come,' Fairweather said. 'The risk is mine.'

'What moves you, Mr Fairweather?'

'Any diversion. It would be unseemly to list them.'

'Or honour, perhaps.'

'If seen as a species of vanity. I am not sure I always believe in honour, Major Biggs. But I most certainly believe in dishonour.'

There was silence for some time.

'Very well,' Biggs said. 'I shall allow you to attempt some bargain with Kooti. But only after I have my men placed. We shall, in short, combine the two proposals. Do you find that fair?'

'If I must,' Fairweather said.

9

Kooti appeared in no haste to progress upland; perhaps he felt stately movement desirable. For three days Biggs' clumsy militia had kept watch from a low and uncomfortably moist hill which overlooked a river crossing Kooti's band would have to make. Horses and tents were to the rear, in a scrubby hollow. Biggs' plan had not provided for so long a wait; rations were low, and ammunition spent noisily in pursuit of wild pig. One cumbersome old boar was surprised by a fusillade and soon devoured; its skin and bone finally made a soup of unpretentious flavour.

'Not long now,' Biggs argued. 'He must be near.'

'Intelligence to that effect would be desirable,' Fairweather said.

'Scouts could give our game away,' Biggs said.

'Then we must hope he does not have them.'

'The man is a dreamer,' Biggs said, 'and mostly a drunken one. Nor did he ever make much of a warrior when he claimed to be serving the Queen. Scouts? I think not. And he is all prayers and prophecies now.'

Fairweather did not press the point further. Given Biggs' large quota of aspirant and practising imbeciles, indiscreet scouts could panic Kooti into putting his armed men to test; bullets would end hope of a bargain.

That night there was chilling rain; morning brought weak sun and sodden biscuit.

'We must sight him today,' Biggs said.

Hungry, surly and saturated, his men jostled to warm their limbs by the campfire; and to suck moodily at mugs of tepid tea. By Fairweather's reckoning desertions were due, downright mutiny a day away.

Near noon a picket raced into camp with news. Noises had been heard.

'Noises?' Biggs said.

'Queer,' the picket reported.

'Perhaps your empty gut,' Fairweather suggested.

'No, sir. True. Strange noises. Not ours.'

Biggs was prompted to his feet. 'Every man to his position,' he ordered. 'And fire out fast.'

Biggs and Fairweather climbed up to their vantage point on the hill. Nothing yet to see; the river crossing was clear. The noise could be identified as many voices chanting as one. Rhythmic, devotional, growing louder.

'Thank God,' Biggs said. 'They're here.' He loaded his carbine.

'We have an arrangement,' Fairweather was obliged to say. 'Fire is to be held. I go forward alone.'

'You are still sure about this?'

'I have had four miserable days to consider it. Sure? Only of one thing. Your militia is unfit to deflect a troop of fleas.'

'I shall of course feel obliged to cover you personally as you go forward.'

'I want no armed man within twenty yards. Instruct your men not to shoot even if I draw fire at first; it may be a mistake.'

Fairweather tied a muddy white handkerchief to the muzzle of his carbine; it seemed frugal protection. Maoris were now visible as they moved among flax bushes at the edge of the forest and near the river crossing. Perhaps fifty yards off. They were chanting still; they carried arms. Fairweather took breath, briefly wondering what had brought him to this lunatic pass, and then slid toward low ground. Behind him there was a clatter; Biggs had followed.

'I said to keep a distance,' Fairweather told him. 'By which I mean out of my sight and theirs.'

'You need not concern yourself with my safety.'

'It is mine I have in mind, Major Biggs.'

Biggs dropped back with grudge. Fairweather pushed through a grove of damp treefern, scrambled over a log, and gingerly walked open ground. The Maoris, still not disclosing themselves in large number, were now thirty yards off. Fairweather began shouting and flourishing his truce signal.

With the dense chanting, he went unheard. Then he was sighted. Maoris dropped to their knees; rifles were trained. Sound expired.

'Peace,' Fairweather called. '*Rongo.*' Then, 'I wish to talk to Coates. Kooti. Please.'

He braced for the first shot. Then an elderly warrior placed his hand on a younger man's gun, turning the muzzle downward. Others, after a pause, lifted their heads and lowered their weapons. Fairweather breathed again.

'Kooti?' he asked. 'Kooti?'

He seemed understood. A message was shouted back into the forest along the prisoners' line of march.

'*Taihoa,*' he was told. Wait.

He remained with his carbine and murky signal emphatically aloft. Minutes dragged; his arms ached. Never in his life, however, had a wait been more lavishly rewarded. An improbable figure materialized among the Maoris at the forest edge. Coates? Kooti? Or Moses on Sinai; Joshua commanding the sun to stand still. The apparition stood luminous in a long white robe trimmed with red, hands clasped high as if in prayer, grave, tidily bearded, his hair a cascade of ringlets. After an excessive and effective pause he set sail theatrically toward Fairweather, floating through fern, robe rippling in breeze, and finally stopped ten yards short. He lowered his hands; Fairweather rested his carbine.

'George Fairweather.'

'As you knew him.'

'No other *pakeha* of Poverty Bay would wish to meet me alone. You are not of them. This I have heard.'

'I am not of them yet. This day do not make me so. From whom have you heard?'

'Villagers. People of Poverty Bay who know of the new Israel.'

'It is not incumbent upon you to talk that nonsense to me.'

'Much is incumbent, George. There is Maori lamentation through this land.'

'It is not to be stilled by conspiring with Jehovah; nor by trying to awaken old Israel's woes. As a joke it has been splendid. Let it go now. You have made your point, scared colonists witless. Already your name is possibly making panic in government. Soon it will be famous. "Who is this Kooti?" many will be asking up and down the land, soon in England too. "Who is this daring escaper, this laughing outlaw? Why. How did it happen?"'

'George, you wish not to take me seriously.'

'I take your two hundred sincerely.'

'Three hundred now. Men are swift to join us. Jehovah gave his word it would be so.'

'What word, and how?'

'To me, George. In vision.'

'If I didn't know better, I might fancy you did believe it all. Give it away. Get out of that fancy dress. Talk sense.'

'What sense, George?' There was still some promising humour in Kooti's eyes. 'Colonists' sense? Biggs' sense? Such sense placed me in the Chathams for two years. Such sense could keep me there ten more. Is it such sense you wish to talk to me? Then it is too late, George. I make my own sense now.'

'I understand that some people need to lead. Rebels and rulers always promise the world as they flourish the sword. But the promised world is forgotten when the sword begins work. Means not only become ends; men become that which they battle. And worse. Hell has no half price; it has to be paid.'

'You threaten, George.'

'Plead.'

'Then I still hear you.'

'Push at a boulder, and it must begin rolling. Then another and another. An avalanche under which virtue and evil alike are lost.'

'Where is Biggs?'
'Is that important?'
'Biggs is what has happened to me. Biggs is what has happened to others. He is not one man, but many. All go by the name colonist.'
'I know you have grievances. So I promise this. Trust me, and I shall make those grievances heard loudly, to ensure you are soon your own master again. It is not too late. There is no need for that clown's costume. Everything is still possible.'
'Everything?'
'Your men have only to place their arms at their feet.'
'That was Biggs' message.'
'Mine also. There is no other way.'
'Would Biggs' men likewise place their arms at their feet?'
'I cannot answer for Biggs and his men. Trust begets trust. You are best placed to father it.'
'With your word you would tell of what Biggs and Read did to remove me from Poverty Bay?'
'Until all is known,' Fairweather promised.
Kooti was quiet. 'Then, George Fairweather,' he began, 'let this be my word to you.' He raised an arm presumably in blessing.
The shot came from Fairweather's rear; he felt the breath of the passing bullet. So did Kooti. They went to ground as the bullet rattled into foliage. Warriors were racing from cover. Kooti rose, his robe stained, and looked down on kneeling Fairweather; his eyes were humourless.
'It was not my doing,' Fairweather protested.
Kooti said nothing.
'You must believe that,' Fairweather said.
'I will believe it when you depart this place, George, and leave Biggs to me. Go. Go now.'
Fairweather needed no long urging; he leapt clumsily for cover. There were shots behind. He found Biggs crouched behind the log he had earlier passed. Biggs was sighting his carbine for a second shot.
'Now you have your damn war,' Fairweather said bitterly.
'He raised his hand. Surely calling up fire. Perhaps I panicked.'
'And perhaps you did not.'
'One true shot could have put an end to this thing,' Biggs allowed. 'It could have been all over.'
'Now,' Fairweather predicted, 'it has all begun.' He knelt beside Biggs and tore the truce token from his carbine. Shot chattered through the trees above. Biggs fired blind. 'We need height on the matter,' Fairweather argued. 'Regain the hill while I cover.'
Biggs scurried uphill. Fairweather shot into suggestive shadow and re-

loaded; he fired again and followed Biggs. Hauling on root and branch, they made high ground. There they found disarray. Men on the hill were taking shot not from one side, but from three. The party of chanting warriors at the river crossing had been a pious feint. Two other parties had quietly worked their way into positions of advantage; the militia was near surrounded.

'Whose ambush now?' Fairweather said.

'They deceived us,' Biggs lamented sweatily, 'while Kooti parleyed.'

'You have made it justified precaution. I should say Kooti had his force split in three from the first. They knew we were waiting. Whatever Kooti is or is not, he is not yet anyone's fool.'

Ricocheting bullets whined around.

Biggs bit his lip. 'What now?' he asked.

'What we make it. Fall back, give fight, and fall back again.'

'To what end?'

'Escape. Failing which we must ensure the day is not altogether one of shame for British arms. If life is lost, let it be to effect. For the sake of all concerned, and especially Kooti, we cannot permit too heady a triumph.'

There was noise downhill to their rear. Cries, shots. A shocked militiaman came running. Mulhooly, trembling, trying to speak. 'They have taken our camp,' he finally got out. 'Our horses. Ammunition. Everything. Gone.'

'That simplifies matters,' Fairweather said.

'The natives have gone too,' Mulhooly said. 'Our natives. They ran.'

'Better now than later,' Fairweather suggested.

Biggs protested, 'Better?'

'Disaster, sir, does us service by playing all its cards. It abets enterprise, perhaps even sanity.'

'You mean surrender?'

'You are our liability there, Major Biggs.'

Biggs was silent.

'So make a point of keeping your head especially low. With Kooti felled, there would have been no colonial breast beating, no lamentations about the unedifying affairs of Poverty Bay. I believe I had the man interested in a bargain. But that did not suit your book. It could not. My mistake. I should have seen.'

'All spilt milk,' Biggs muttered.

'Fat in the fire, sir. You may just have confirmed Kooti as a worker of martial miracles. First a garrison overpowered. Then a schooner seized and sailed. Now a militia troop in tatters. That should be worth another hundred dazzled volunteers.'

'You persist in thinking well of the man.'

'He impresses more by the minute. Meanwhile I suggest you instruct your men not to be heroes.'

'That is rather unnecessary,' Biggs said.

'Also to use ammunition sparingly, now we have none in reserve. To keep Maori heads down. No more.'

'What then?' Biggs appealed.

'I am thinking on it,' Fairweather said. 'So, I respectfully suggest, should you, Major Biggs.'

If Biggs had any useful thought, as the day lengthened, he was not disposed to confide it to Fairweather or to his marooned men. His orders became fewer and weaker, until barely audible. He was not even especially visible. Guns echoed and re-echoed off surrounding ridges. Sometimes smoke showed itself; seldom a warrior. The militia appeared in no large hazard, unless from hellbent assault, so long as fire was maintained. Fairweather tried to give it authority. He moved back and forward among the men, sometimes crawling, sometimes leaping between leafy patches of cover, to cosset, encourage, and instruct each in his short-term function of keeping Kooti at bay. Long term? There was only one prospect. A breaching of the Maori line, desirably in poor light, which would leave a path for escape. That implied a respectable rearguard; men who might have the wit not to argue with his orders to deter Maori pursuit. Newman, he of the listless gaze and careless spittle, was one likely candidate. Dodds, the cursing Yorkshireman, might have enough bile to make himself murderous. But Fairweather's belated discovery was Larkin, a stocky and silent Irishman with ferocious black eyebrows, a sometime colour sergeant of the imperial 18th who had taken discharge in New Zealand; the sort of soldier who had absorbed so much shot in his lifetime that it was marvellous he did not rattle when he moved. He took an intelligent interest in Fairweather's plan.

'You mean like them Maoris at Orakau?' he said.

'You were there too?' Fairweather said.

'My last fight, sir.'

'Mine too, Larkin. We have much in common.'

'It's not going to be easy, sir. Not with this lot.'

'Given bad light, enough smoke and racket, a nervous enemy firing this way and that may do most of our work for us. While they riddle themselves we make graceless exit.'

'Sounds good, sir,' Larkin said, though plainly with doubts.

'We shall make it good, Larkin. You and I.'

'What about Major Biggs, then? Where does he fit in?'

'Major Biggs may be spurred into taking more interest in matters. When word is given I want you to muster men into a reasonable column. Those at the head of the column will have bayonets fixed. Those to the flanks will present staggered fire. Men of the rear will have to make their chances. All must be kept moving.'

'What if the sods don't?'

'Offer a bullet up the backside.'

'Pleasure,' Larkin said. Then, 'You and me, sir, we could get out of this together. Why don't we?'

'A wonder to me too,' Fairweather confessed.

In the late afternoon the Maori guns quietened. Fairweather crawled back to Biggs. Biggs still hugged earth. 'An attack?' he whispered.

'That depends on how many casualties Kooti finds comfortable. Also on how sharp a lesson he means to teach us.'

'If you were he?'

'I should be laughing. We have our lesson; he has our horses.'

'He may want more.'

'Coates would not. Kooti may well.'

A bugle sounded somewhere near. One woeful and experimental note.

'Part of their Chathams loot, no doubt,' Biggs said. 'What are they telling us?'

'That we may need to use our next rounds point blank.'

An attack did not come. A voice did. Kooti's; and confident. He did indeed want more. He wanted Biggs. 'Give him up,' Kooti called, 'and all may go freely back to their homes in Poverty Bay. The *taniwha* will be toothless. It will no longer bite.'

'Dragon,' Biggs interpreted. 'He sees us as a dragon in his path. And me as the teeth.'

Though Kooti was hardly paying credit where due, Biggs had stiffened obligingly.

They listened further. Kooti had begun Biblical embroidery. It was Israel's wish that Biggs be given up. It was Jehovah's will. Kooti was not one to make a point once if thrice enthralled him more. Biggs must move forward alone. The men of the militia must rest their arms.

'He wants more than capitulation,' Biggs said. 'He wants humiliation.'

'Which should not surprise.'

'What would you have me do, Mr Fairweather?'

'Prepare to repel attack, Major Biggs.'

'It has not been a creditable day,' Biggs said. 'On my own initiative, without instruction from government, I have led good men into what might yet prove a massacre. And made matters worse by miserably failing to lead.'

'It is a remarkably fair summary,' Fairweather agreed.

'It might even be said that I alone have brought the situation to its current pass. Not only by exiling Kooti; also by recommending extensions of exile for them all. Your own feelings are plain.'

'We are not here to search souls at this juncture, Major Biggs. We are here to save them.'

'You misunderstand, Mr Fairweather. I suggest that the day could yet be redeemed.'

Fairweather comprehended. Courage, even in probationary form, was not to be undervalued; it won out against martial contempt. 'No,' he decided. 'You will not surrender yourself to Kooti.'

'It is my decision.'

'And will guarantee no lives.'

'Kooti professes godliness.'

'Not of the insipid cheek-turning kind. They scan a different text now. An eye for an eye.'

'I might be of value as hostage.'

'As the man who exiled most of them, you might last a minute. Kooti takes keen personal interest in you. That much is apparent. The Achilles heel of the prophet; vengeance. A flaw we might yet find use for. Besides, there is Mrs Biggs. You may not be the best husband in the world, but she has no other.'

'Thank you for the thought.' Biggs set down his rifle and made to rise. 'If things do not go well, I trust you will make fair report. To Emily also.'

'With respect, sir, I can promise a shot from behind before you have gone five yards. I should try for the leg. But I cannot guarantee my elevation; a soldier is only as good as his gun.'

'You cannot mean that.'

'Anatomically there is much to be said for it. Better that than a tomahawk in the skull. Nor would you be the first weak commander to suffer the indignity.'

'You, Mr Fairweather, were the one who urged moderation.'

'All things being equal. They must be made so again. I have the hopeful notion that Kooti may be trying to bargain your surrender less from strength than uncertainty. He is still not confident of pushing men up at us; nor of their resolve. He has us conveniently pinned, no more. So far their shooting is as slipshod as our own. He may also worry that we are due for reinforcement.'

'The fact is that reinforcement must still be many miles off.'

'You know that. He does not.'

'All you offer is mind-reading, Mr Fairweather.'

'More to the point, then, men are braced to breach Kooti's line at a time of our choice.'

'You are revelling in all this,' Biggs accused.

'In survival,' Fairweather said.

'Biggs?' Kooti called from somewhere near. 'Biggs?'

'You are not going to him,' Fairweather said.

'It would seem not,' Biggs agreed.

'Tell him so. Also that we are waiting on overdue reinforcement. It may incline him to consider withdrawal.'

Biggs recovered his rifle and shouted accordingly. There was a silence. Whatever Kooti was considering, it was not withdrawal. 'Then fight, Biggs,' he announced. To those of his followers near he called, *'Ruia taitea, kia tu ko taikaka anake.'*

'He expresses himself proverbially,' Biggs explained. 'Scatter the sap-wood, let only the heartwood remain. Which means women and children are best out of the way while warriors begin work. We have an attack.'

Fairweather moved among the men, instructing them to shoot only when ordered, and with targets plain. A maximum of five rounds per man was to be expended. Some were inclined to quibble. 'What then?' they asked.

'One prayer per man is permitted,' Fairweather said. 'Then bayonet, butt and boot.'

Scattered Maori shots mounted into continuous detonation. Smoke from spent gunpowder gathered over the forest. Many bullets hummed overhead; others trimmed leaves, and took residence in trees. Sometimes a man cried out, and was tended; there were no serious wounds. An arm here. A leg there. Creases and grazes. The embattled militia made no reply.

'Can we let it go on?' Biggs appealed.

'Let them make mince of the landscape,' Fairweather said. 'We can afford to hurt once and once only.'

Emboldened Maoris began showing themselves above fern and scrub, or rising from behind rocks, to stand and shoot. One or two, soon more, leapt uphill. Fluttering lines thickened; a convincing circle took form. Among the weaving heads and bare torsos there was no familiar face, no robed figure; no Kooti. Perhaps it was his privilege as Jehovah's general to judge victory secure. It meant piquancy was lacking, perhaps also spine.

'Fire,' Fairweather proposed.

'Fire,' Biggs shouted hoarsely.

There was no need for a third order. Some warriors toppled; others were nipped. Most soon found an exposed stance undesirable. The second fusillade located a few dazed targets still standing; the third was superfluous. Maoris could be heard scuttling away through undergrowth, shouting recriminations, and dragging wounded. The day became less agitated, with only wild shots overhead.

'They won't forget that,' an enlivened Biggs said.

'Unfortunately,' Fairweather said.

'Does nothing satisfy you?' Biggs said.

'Not if I can help it. If Kooti is half the man I think he may be, he will have taken note. Disciplined firepower can always beat rifles in bulk. We may yet rue the demonstration.'

'You talk as if there will be no end to this thing.'

'And you talk as if a skirmish is triumph. We live to see sunset; sunrise is far from assured.'

Fairweather was now free to make it more probable. With the turned attack too recent, the militia undesirably cocky, he judged dusk inopportune for escape; men had best sober to their situation again, with Maori fervour likewise allowed to wane through the winter night. The column would form in the last hour of dark, launch itself through the Maori line in the first dim minutes of day. Kooti's men, if denied sleep, should be at their most inattentive. To ensure their low ebb, and keep the militia alert, he mounted randomly placed volleys at intervals through the night; there were satisfying cries of alarm. Later, with Larkin, he cajoled men into formation. Biggs would take the head of the column and use surprise and the bayonet to cut Kooti's line. Weaker men were placed in the middle to provide staggered fire. The making of a formidable rear still vexed; Fairweather could be certain only of Larkin beside him, and hope on Dodds and Newman taking example. As signal and feint, he had them place shot in a direction other than the militia was to take.

Biggs and the head of the column careered downhill. There was a confused flash and crash of firearms, then silhouettes rising and falling; men battling trees and terror; cries and improvized orders. Men dropped, and two distinctly dead were abandoned; wounded were dragged and carried. Full daylight found the din less numbing, hostile fire fading, and most Poverty Bay men disentangling from the terrain. With Larkin, Dodds and Newman grunting and cursing beside him, Fairweather withdrew slowly while Biggs tried to control the remainder of the men. Once the column broke they were not, for the most part, to be rallied. Sometimes solitary, sometimes in parties of two and three, they were pointing themselves roughly in the direction of the Poverty Bay plain. Some even discarded weapons to speed their departure. A rout. Many might have been hunted down had Kooti's more persistent warriors not been given second thoughts by the rearguard. Not until late afternoon was Fairweather satisfied that pursuit had been deterred. By then the four left fighting had barely a round remaining apiece. Fairweather gazed at Larkin, Dodds and Newman, as filthy and ragged a trio as had ever been led, and found himself unable to manage more than an affectionate grip on the shoulder of each man in turn; words would not come.

'It's all right, sir,' Larkin said charitably.

They followed a fast river toward the coast. They caught up with shivering survivors complaining of sprained ankles and hunger. The four of the rearguard pushed on; the survivors hobbled behind.

After a time they came to a temporary camp, a fire. Biggs was there, most of the wounded, and a number of red-eyed pickets indifferently placed. Fairweather irritably ordered them spread further and higher; he saw no cause to persist with the pretence that Biggs had command. Then he looked to the wounded. None seemed in current peril of expiring.

To Biggs he said, 'My advice is to sign Poverty Bay over to Kooti, with interest, and no undue delay.'

'You saved us,' Biggs protested.

'More fool I,' Fairweather said. He collapsed under the nearest tree and felt sleep fill his limbs. He had never done a better day's soldiering, nor a worse. Rain did not wake him. Not even Kooti could have.

10

Morning brought no reprieve. In the wan light there were groaning wounded, and unwounded blaspheming with black fervour. Fairweather could not tell where his aches ended and despair began. Raw fronds of young fern made a barely digestible breakfast. Litters were fashioned for the disabled; the journey to the coast resumed among dripping trees; most of the landscape was under fine mist.

They had not marched a mile when they heard shouts and horses. Kooti, perhaps. Kooti cutting off path to the sea.

Fairweather found purpose again. He nudged wounded to the rear and ordered others to take cover, kicking and cuffing men slow to move. Then, carbine loaded, he moved forward with Biggs.

Through trees they glimpsed the first horsemen. Shouts took an English tint; faces too. For footsore Poverty Bay colonists it was a sight to fatigue still more. The contingent from Hawke's Bay was at hand, and distinctly looking for sport. All they lacked were dogs baying after a fox. Riding ahead, stout, red-faced, and resonant, was a figure as inauspicious as Kooti. Colonel George Whitmore, in faded imperial regalia, sword at his side, was cutting a martial dash through the colony again. Around him rode lusty pastoralists and their sons.

Biggs, Fairweather and others of Poverty Bay rose bedraggled from cover; Biggs called out. Whitmore steered toward them and reined in.

'What in hell is going on here?' he asked Biggs.

'A disaster,' Biggs pleaded.

'I can see that, man. Speak up.'

'Two dead. A dozen wounded. We tried to stop the prisoners.'

'Damned if you did. On whose authority?'

'Mine,' Biggs admitted in puny voice.

'My writ runs here now,' Whitmore announced. 'Plainly not before time. You're a bloody madman. Half trained soldiers. An untested enemy. And this wretched country. What possessed you?'

'We thought to nobble Kooti,' Biggs confessed.

'Kooti?'

'Their leader. A difficult fellow.'

'Plainly,' Whitmore said with humour. He took note of Fairweather nearby. 'I have seen you before.'

'When General Cameron prevailed upon me not to complicate my departure from the 65th,' Fairweather said.

'The infamous Lieutenant Fairweather? I remember telling you to make more of yourself in this colony.'

'You remember right, sir.'

'You make less of yourself with these Poverty Bay louts.'

'That might currently appear the case,' Fairweather agreed.

'Looking for trouble again, were you?'

'To put it perversely.'

'You seem to have been one with their lunacy.'

'Mr Fairweather became as my right arm,' Biggs explained. 'I regret I did not listen to his advice earlier. He urged that I leave the prisoners alone.'

'And wait for me?'

'Just to let them alone. Let them be.'

'There was a case to be made for the prisoners,' Fairweather argued. 'Not least for their leader.'

'Was?' Whitmore said.

'There is now an even better case for letting this fizzle out in the mountains. It is winter. Kooti and his companions will have warmth to think about. Food. Survival. The pursuits of peace. They will finish by eating the horses they stole. Devotion to the God of Israel should soon dim.'

'You deny me enlightenment, Fairweather. Israel?'

'Kooti seems persuaded that he and his fellows are fleeing bondage to Egypt and battling home into the land of Canaan.'

'Jews?'

'In brief.'

'What excuse will they find for themselves next?'

'Meanwhile there is more the smell of vendetta than war. Kooti does not much care for Major Biggs, nor Major Biggs for Kooti. It might be desirable to let matters cool.'

'They have set themselves against lawful authority.'

'As the Pharaoh might once have been so seen.'

'Come, man. We don't have to indulge native extravagance.'

'Nor to mock it, sir. It may help to think as men from captivity might.'

'There are now colonial dead.'

'My point entirely.'

'Let a mad Maori leader run riot and we could have half the colony in uproar again. The issue has been joined with the gun. It hardly matters what Kooti thinks he is; it is what he might mean. He is best trampled now in tried and true way.'

'There is another tried and true way, sir. Leave him alone for a year or two to ripen for a Queen's pardon. Perhaps even for a native seat in Parliament, where he can orate in his dotage. His past could be seen as picturesque.'

'Are you telling me, Fairweather, you wish to wash your hands of the whole thing?'

'Consider them scrubbed, sir.'

'You suffer misapprehension,' Whitmore said icily. 'You are now under my command. You. Biggs. Everyone. Martial law is proclaimed and I administer it. You hear me, Biggs?'

'Indeed, sir,' Biggs said wearily.

'Fairweather? I daresay you are concerned about your standing with this force.'

'Not noticeably,' Fairweather said.

'How does Captain Fairweather sound? The posting can be made official later.'

'To what end, sir?'

'To press this Kooti. Run him to ground and put an end to his humbug.'

A muddy group of Poverty Bay men, some carrying wounded in litters, had crept from cover to form an abject half circle before Whitmore. Behind Whitmore the gallants of the Hawke's Bay militia lounged, still dapper, with clipped moustaches and tidy beards; they lit cheroots, laughed, and looked upon the shaken and saturated colonists of Poverty Bay with indifference. The Hawke's Bay men groomed their horses and passed silver whisky flasks around among themselves. There was a picnic atmosphere, though parasols were lacking. To their rear, a large group of hireling Hawke's Bay Maoris observed the proceedings with vacant faces. A light drizzle fell as Whitmore began to boom.

'Every fit man is to turn back with me,' he announced.

'And who the hell would you be?' drawled Yorkshireman Dodds.

'Colonel Whitmore. Further questions?'

'Well, Mr Colonel Whitmore,' said Dodds, 'maybe you're who you say you are, and maybe you're not. It's no odds to me. I'm on my way home.'

'You're defending your home, man.'

'What would you bloody know?' Dodds challenged. 'I never seen you before.'

'In which case,' Whitmore said, 'brace yourself to see much more of me.'

'That's what you think.'

Newman spat eloquently towards Whitmore's feet.

Young Mulhooly found courage to whine, 'I got nothing against this Kooti. I never heard of him. I only been here a year. I'm going home too.'

Whitmore turned to Biggs. 'I suggest, Major, that you call your rabble to order. I have urged upon the government the need to settle outlying districts only with colonists of some mettle and breeding. The point is now proved.'

'We have not had the land to attract desirable colonists,' Biggs protested.

'And at this rate you'll never have it. Where are your friendly Maoris?'

'Fled,' Biggs said miserably.

'And these oafs are the best Poverty Bay can provide?'

'They have had several difficult days,' Biggs pleaded.

'They are embarked upon an even more difficult one. There is a word for this. Mutiny.'

'Use any word you like, Mr Colonel Whitmore,' Dodds said. 'We got wives. We got families. We're still going home.'

'I didn't put no prisoners on the Chathams,' Newman said. 'Nor let none loose.'

Other Poverty Bay men mumbled more colourful sentiments.

'I could arrange a firing squad,' Whitmore mused.

'Try it,' Dodds said, and lifted his rifle.

Men of the Hawke's Bay militia were ensuring that their own firearms were near to hand; hilarity was in check.

'Major Biggs,' Whitmore ruled, 'your men are now one minute from a court martial. I suggest you inform them accordingly.'

Biggs was confusion.

'With respect, sir,' Fairweather intervened, 'I am under the impression that you are here to give fight to Kooti. Not the colonists of Poverty Bay.'

Whitmore was incredulous. 'You take their side? You?'

'Some have just acquitted themselves well. Others have had an unholy nightmare, and are not of a mind for another. They have neither eaten nor slept much for two days. There are no horses, and wounded to be borne out.'

'Perhaps I can shoot just one of them,' Whitmore proposed. His stare suggested he had Dodds most in mind.

'Again with respect, sir, a clash between two contingents of colonial militia is no way to begin a campaign. Not the most ingenious report on the affray could make it explicable.'

There was silence while Whitmore performed mental calculations. The sum of these calculations, it seemed, was that he needed Fairweather, or might.

'I put it to you, Fairweather,' he said, 'that Major Biggs no longer appears to enjoy the confidence of his men. You do your worst. Give them an order.'

'Then I order them home. To eat, see wives, and sleep. With full bellies and emptied loins they may have more enthusiasm.'

'Is this war,' Whitmore asked, 'or is it not?'

'Desirably not. But I shall not belabour the point.'

'Do these men have land and lives at risk or do they not?'

'That is best asked of Kooti. I was of the belief that his intention was mostly pacific; that he was striking a decorative stance with scriptural trimmings. I am less sure now that shot has been fired. Certainly Major Biggs cannot be called safe.'

Biggs looked even more uncomfortable in his soiled skin.

'We have ridden scores of miles,' Whitmore said. 'All of us damnably inconvenienced. Now we find these wretches unwilling to help themselves.'

'They are only human.'

'You protest too much, Fairweather. They go far to convince that this fellow Darwin might have it right. Some breeds of human might best be classified with apes. Poverty Bay seems a stud.'

There was laughter among Hawke's Bay men.

'You are not endearing yourself,' Fairweather observed.

'When is a British commander obliged to endear himself?'

'With colonial militia, perhaps.'

'They make a poor fight, flee for their worthless lives, and expect others to patch Humpty Dumpty together again.'

'I shall remain at your disposal here,' Fairweather offered. 'Consider me hostage for the return of the Poverty Bay men. Major Biggs can shepherd them home for rejuvenation, and ensure swift renewal of duty. I suggest Major Biggs might then best busy himself with organizing a commissariat and a route of supply.'

'I failed,' Whitmore said, 'to hear Major Biggs requesting your protection. I trust he is touched by your concern.'

'A martial consideration only,' Fairweather argued. 'Major Biggs has an incendiary effect on Kooti, and vice versa. It is not the time or place for a private war. And let this expedition at least be supplied adequately.'

'We have provisions for a week. More than sufficient.'

'I respect optimism in a superior, sir,' Fairweather said. 'My belief, however, based upon recent observation, is that it makes thin breakfast and worse supper in New Zealand forest.'

'Provision us for an additional fortnight,' Whitmore instructed Biggs. 'And see your men get back here. No shirkers. Otherwise the colonial government may well see fit, on my recommendation, to appoint an adequate guardian of Poverty Bay. Is that understood?'

'Entirely,' Biggs said.

He could not have been seen more humiliated. After marshalling Poverty Bay men for departure, he whispered to Fairweather, 'Thank you.'

'My own interests are uppermost. You draw too much fire.'

'Whitmore is a brute and bully, nonetheless.'

'Whom we may now have need of.'

'You would defend him?' Biggs said, astonished.

'And any commander who makes himself credible.'

'God help us.'

'Quite so, sir,' Fairweather agreed.

Biggs shambled off feebly; Fairweather, after all, found pity for the fellow.

Reliable Larkin approached. His whiskers had been singed by the blast of a Maori gun; he had a reddened bandage about his head. 'You're set on staying, Mr Fairweather?' he asked.

'Captain. Captain Fairweather. I am now due splendid courtesies. And yes, Larkin. I do seem set on it now.'

'Then I'll stay too, sir,' Larkin announced. 'I got nothing much to go home to Poverty Bay for. Besides, I can't leave you alone with that Whitmore bastard. You need a mate. Me too, the way things look. You'll do me.'

'In which case, Larkin, you shall do me also. More so if you watch your language.'

'Sorry, sir.'

'That's more like it. Now, Larkin, here's your first order. Get us a bivouac built and a fire lit. Then steal, if you must, some Hawke's Bay bacon. Desirably also liquor of some potency.'

'Understood, sir.' Larkin went.

Fairweather sat on a riverside rock, tugged off his boots, and tipped out water surplus to his requirements. He suspected he might have begun to enjoy himself.

11

'Sometimes,' Larkin said, 'it's hard to see more to life.' He slurped tea and wiped his mouth with the back of his hand; he had been listing the joys and woes of a colour sergeant in the 18th. A chilly sunlight played among the cooking fires of the forest camp. Three days had gone in waiting on the return of the Poverty Bay men.

'More?' Fairweather asked.

'Than soldiering, sir. When you're at it. It's honest. Ask no questions and you get told no lies. All I need to know is I'm over here, Jacko's over there. It's Jacko or me. It doesn't leave nothing else worth thinking about.'

'Then why did you ever give it away, Larkin?'

'Others was quitting here. Going for land. I thought I'd be in the swim too. Now or never, I thought.'

'And now you wish it was never?'

'My woman went. The land was worse. Cows got bloat. I owe money to Read. There's things going on I never knew about. Maoris. Biggs. I don't want to know. All lies. Simpler when it's Jacko or me.'

'It is Kooti we are presently considering.'

'Just another Jacko to me, sir,' Larkin said.

'Then we must trust he obliges you. My suspicion, Larkin, is that he may not.'

'Sir?'

'He may not be quite where you require him. He may be up your backside.'

'What are you telling me, sir?'

'What I am trying to tell myself, Larkin, if not yet to useful effect.'

With breakfasting finished, Colonel Whitmore could be heard airing robust views on the delay in the return of Poverty Bay's incompetent colonists. With the drag of time and winter's damp, Hawke's Bay spirits were in diminuendo, not to be lifted by Whitmore's ferocious drilling. Packs of playing cards were hourly muddier. The Maoris were likewise fretting.

At length Whitmore made his morning round of the camp. He halted in that quarter where Fairweather and Larkin had set themselves apart.

He found only Fairweather; Larkin had made a well timed exit.

The colonel, hands behind his back, looked skyward for a time. 'Define war, Captain Fairweather,' he suggested.

'I was always weak on the academic side, sir. It is something which enables men to feel important. There is that to be said.'

'I put it to you, Fairweather, that war is God's formula for choosing between peoples when one gets in another's way. An experiment to set His mind at rest on human matters; to ensure our advancement. We serve large ends, Fairweather. Large ends.'

'An enlightening thought, sir. When placing my next shot I shall remember divine requirements.'

'Trivial as this campaign may appear, it is nonetheless no subject for jest. In short, Fairweather, I should welcome less levity. It can be interpreted as dissidence.'

'You make yourself understood, sir.'

'More to the point, I detect some sympathy for Kooti.'

'Originality always appeals, sir.'

'You feel he was done ill by colonists?'

'And by his own. He had no standing in the Maori order of things; and now none in ours. Kooti seems to see God choosing too; he wagers on the chosen people. Their God is garrulous on the subject of justice.'

'I must further put it to you, Fairweather, that any merit in Kooti's case must be seen as irrelevance, in the overall scheme.'

'Or will be with a little Queen's lead. Chances have been missed. Things are as they are. I accept that, sir.'

'I can rely on you, then?'

'So far as I may be found useful.'

'Do I hear quibble?'

'I should prefer to see Kooti contained rather than again pushed to making desperate statement with the gun. If we are to write a postscript to the New Zealand wars, let it be edifying.'

'I shall take note of those feelings,' Whitmore said. 'Finally, however, that which has to be done, must be. We have three hundred armed warriors making for the mountains ahead, already with some days' start. They cannot be permitted to provoke fresh Maori commotion. Otherwise, Fairweather, I find you a most interesting fellow.'

'That is decent of you, sir.'

'I cannot, however, let the occasion pass without noting that this far you have failed to exert yourself socially. You must not let my lack of commiseration for the dregs of Poverty Bay deter you. Carr, Canning and Herrick, my three Hawke's Bay captains, are fine fellows in all. I see no reason to slight them by hovering over here in the woods with your man.'

'We are conscious, Larkin and I, that we hold the line for Poverty Bay here. We cling, sir.'

'So where is confounded Biggs?'

'Perhaps rallying those faint of spirit.'

'I may yet have the man mocked the length of the colony.'

'Major Biggs, whatever his failings, has his conscientious side, sir. It has already almost been the death of him. Mockery cannot add much to the humble pie Kooti has made him eat.'

'Slackness is the colonial vice, Fairweather; I will not allow it rein here. We must use time. Use it. Keep up morale. Where is our bugler? Let us put today's drill behind us.'

'Yes, sir,' Fairweather sighed.

Four hours later, having trampled sufficient of the forest floor to mud, Whitmore's militia was permitted rest. Exhausted men tumbled; some crawled painfully into bivouacs and slept. The Maoris still gaped at the rituals of the British parade ground which demanded victims before the enemy was met.

With rations even more restricted, and Larkin's dedicated pilfering producing no more than mildewed flour, Fairweather thought to make himself less remote to his fellow captains and win some salt pork. Captains Carr and Canning did not prove enlightening company. Carr was of middle years, vague, reedy and rather deaf, due to sometime service with the Royal Artillery and gunnery disaster; his mellow smile suggested a man currently more in touch with sheep than fellow men.

'It is all quite an adventure for me,' he disclosed to Fairweather. 'D'you think we'll get some shooting in?'

'My experience suggests a surfeit,' Fairweather said, meanwhile making a mental note to place himself at a remove from genial Carr in the event of martial exertions.

'You mean that? A jolly good fight?'

'A fight, at all events,' Fairweather agreed.

'Splendid,' Carr said.

Canning was sharp, bony, less disconnected, a weathered grazier who had made one colonial fortune in Australia and had sailed to New Zealand to make a second in the sunny uplands of Hawke's Bay. He chafed in the greasy forest.

'I hear you know this Kooti we're hunting,' he said.

'Knew,' Fairweather said.

'Mix with Maoris, do you?' Suspicion was apparent.

'I have been known to break bread,' Fairweather allowed.

'With any old native malcontent?'

'If we last long enough in these mountains, I might introduce you to a very fine line in cooked rebel rat.'

Canning's humourless mouth twitched. It seemed he had Fairweather summed up: a man gone half native. 'Nothing surprises me,' he said.

'Then I shall forgo any further attempt to astonish,' Fairweather promised.

'What about Kooti, then? You think we'll find him in this country?'

Fairweather shrugged.

'One clear shot could settle things,' Canning insisted. 'Flush him out. Then one clear shot.'

'So Major Biggs thought.'

'Always go for the gut shot first,' Canning said with conviction. 'Always leave the head till later.'

'Are we talking of Australian kangaroos?'

'And blackfellows. Bloody thieves.'

So much for social pleasantries. Canning failed to offer whisky. Fairweather set off for his bivouac, no more than two meagre handfuls of meat to the good. He was obliged to step over the outstretched legs of Captain Herrick beside a fire. Herrick was of a different order. For one thing, he was youthful; his soft face suggested unfamiliarity with the outdoors. For another, he was mostly seen separate from Canning and Carr; currently he was reading a book of some dimension. Possibly he was punishing himself with a martial tome to compensate for lack of experience in the field; Fairweather understood Herrick to be a colonial official whose commission had come in accord with his civil status.

'Last minute illumination?' he asked.

'Shakespeare,' Herrick said. 'The works of.'

'Sweet are the uses of adversity. If nothing else, someone is improving mind and character on this expedition. My congratulations, Herrick. I should have known. You have a poet's name.'

'My family does claim descent,' Herrick said. 'My name is Robert too.'

Fairweather quoted, 'I write of hell; I sing and ever shall of heaven, and hope to have it after all.' He added, 'Thank you, Captain Herrick. You have quite made my day. Surprise me more. Tell me you flirt with the family muse.'

'On occasion,' Herrick confessed.

'Here? Now?'

'Alas,' Herrick said. 'All too untidy; the darks too drear. I can't persuade myself that innocence dwells in these trees, or that the sour can be made sweet.'

'Give yourself another hundred years,' Fairweather urged. 'You may then get it right. Or your grandchildren.'

'I am not much of a pioneer, even with rhymes,' Herrick lamented. 'Still less a soldier. Yet here I am.'

'Here we all are,' Fairweather said. 'But for Kooti, the rain and cold of this forest, not to speak of bloodthirsty insects and two dead upriver, we might spend many an hour considering the wildflowers and festive virgins of your ancestor's Devon.'

'We might,' Herrick said, with altogether winning smile.

Just short of dusk Herrick crossed the camp to find Fairweather alone at his fire. The evening pickets had been posted, Larkin among them; the sounds of the camp were subdued. Fairweather had sketchbook on knee, pencil in hand, trying to find harmonies in men, horses and trees in the fading light. When Herrick arrived, he was acknowledging an imaginative reverse.

'So you have a secret talent too,' Herrick said.

'As far as lack of accomplishment makes it so,' Fairweather agreed.

Herrick sat. Observed. Finally produced a flask. 'What did you have in mind?' he asked.

'The market,' Fairweather said. 'If Colonel Whitmore makes more of this miserable campaign than need be, there may be demand for its depiction by an artist of elevated character.'

'I wish I could see more than inconvenience.'

'That is no way for an apprentice hero to talk.'

'The colonel is again in rage about the overdue Poverty Bay men.'

'Who may be doing us service with the delay. Many go out for wool and come home shorn. Direct further inquiries on the subject to Major Biggs. Is it your intention, Herrick, that we empty this flask?'

'By all means.'

'Excellent. A friend is never known until a man hath need.'

'You are an odd sort of companion to find in these woods. Not that I am complaining, you understand.'

'Nor I, Herrick, of being found.'

Before they parted that night, Fairweather took the younger man's arm. 'One thing,' he said. 'If and when events become vexing, Robert Herrick, do not place your carcass at too great a distance from mine. Killing without tears is a matter of experience and correct deportment.'

'I shall remember that,' Herrick promised.

'Please,' Fairweather said.

In the night Fairweather was woken by an uncomfortable bladder and Larkin crawling clumsily into their bivouac. 'It's getting colder out there,' Larkin reported. 'Why don't the sods sit up on a hill and wait for a fight like they used to? It isn't the same, not knowing where Kooti is or he isn't. The world seems full of whispers and things stirring.'

'The world, Larkin,' Fairweather said sleepily, 'is always full of whispers and things stirring. Otherwise it wouldn't be the world or you would be quite dead. Now do be a good fellow, shut up, and go back outside and perform a large proxy piss for your distinguished officer.'

12

On the fifth day the Poverty Bay contingent returned. Among them were faces now familiar. Mulhooly was there, Newman too, and Dodds. They were diminished in number. Some had taken to bed with nameless fevers or gone mysteriously lame after their forest fight with Kooti. Those who returned had largely done so out of respect for Fairweather. Or at least according to Larkin. 'Staying here with Colonel Whitmore, you shamed them, sir,' he reported.

'You and I both, surely, Larkin.'

Larkin was adamant; and loyal. 'You, sir, you being a stranger to Poverty Bay. They had to come back. And they think you'll look after them.'

'Then they are quaint dreamers,' Fairweather said.

The conspicuous absentee was Major Biggs. Biggs was still toiling somewhere behind with packhorses, in difficulty with ridges and rivers. It might be another day before he brought up provisions and further ammunition. Meanwhile he had sent a message to Colonel Whitmore. When Whitmore had loudly reaffirmed his contempt for the colonists of Poverty Bay, he considered the message; he took a large breath, then a second, until fury became less inhibiting. 'It seems,' he announced, 'that our Major Biggs has heard of a dispatch on the way recalling this expedition. He says he is unable to confirm the story. He has a man riding to fetch the dispatch. He suggests we wait here until the position is clarified. What is the man talking about? Wait?'

No captain found it expedient to speak. Whitmore crumpled the message and trod it into mud.

'I don't know about you gentlemen,' he went on, 'but I haven't come up here to sit saturated as sin in this forest while the spineless politicians of this colony make up their minds.'

Captain Herrick, rather heroically, discovered his voice. 'Perhaps, sir, it is thought that a band of escaped prisoners is not worth the time and trouble. Or the money, sir.'

'Politicians counting pennies again.'

'Money is always a consideration, sir,' Herrick said cautiously. 'Since the imperial regiments departed, expenditure on defence is begrudged. It is felt it might be better spent bringing in fresh colonists from Britain. There is greater security in numbers.'

'When I wish you to put the view of the colonial government, Captain Herrick, I shall indicate accordingly. Meanwhile you answer as my officer.'

'Sir,' Herrick said, eyes lowered.

'I find no justification for turning aside. Or for permitting Kooti to manufacture dissension.'

'No, sir.'

'Certainly not on the strength of some tale Biggs may or may not have heard. I shouldn't be surprised if he had invented it. His own excursion having proved a fiasco, he would like to frustrate ours. What do you think, Fairweather?'

'You appear to have thought of everything, sir,' Fairweather judged.

'Good. Then we move.'

'Now, sir?' Herrick asked.

'I didn't say tomorrow. I didn't say next week. Within the hour.'

'What of Biggs, sir?' Fairweather asked. 'And the supplies?'

'I see no reason to burden ourselves unnecessarily.'

Nor, Fairweather saw, did Colonel Whitmore mean to be burdened by a last-minute recall. Not with a campaign he could comfortably call his own.

'With respect, sir, that must limit our range.'

'Would you think Kooti well supplied, Fairweather?'

'Tolerably, sir.'

'Excellent. We shall make pursuit hot enough for him to begin ditching his fodder. Meanwhile I note that your Poverty Bay men have had the foresight to bring private rations. They are hereby commandeered. We shall leave markers on our trail for Biggs. Damn the fellow. Does he think we've got the rest of the century?'

The mêlée of horses and men on the campsite needed most of an hour to shape into a column. There were more than a hundred men, inclusive of Maoris, and as many horses. Poverty Bay and Hawke's Bay militias were kept apart to risk no tetchy exchanges; Whitmore made the Maoris a rearguard where, if caught, they would have to fight. The column shook out and began to move. Fairweather, familiar with the immediate terrain, scouted the line of march; he took Larkin and Dodds, and left the other Poverty Bay men in Herrick's hands. Impatient Canning had charge of Hawke's Bay; and Carr, who claimed a way with natives, had the Maoris to nurse.

The first day's journey brought no surprise; they followed the route along which Poverty Bay men had made spirited withdrawal the best of a week before. There were items of torn clothing which had proved impediment, discarded boots, and firearms and ammunition belts unrecovered by Kooti's scavengers, now presumably with a surfeit of loot; in places the vegetation was still levelled by the stampede.

Morning gave them unmolested view of the trampled ground where Kooti had made himself felt. His dead, if any, were buried. Noisy flies announced the location of the two lost to Poverty Bay, a half caste adult and a gingery youth, both in displeasing condition after taking shots to head and gut at close range and bloating for days since. Never having known either, other than as terrified faces, Fairweather found no cause to pursue intimacy now. They were still as they fell; there had been no mutilation. He ordered Larkin and Dodds to scoop out temporary graves. Then he walked over the ground, wishing it less memorable, and arrived at the riverside; the stench of the dead still clung. Before he could sink his face in the water, he saw a message scratched into the bark of a conspicuous tree. At that moment Whitmore and Herrick rode up.

'What impertinence now?' Whitmore asked.

The first part of the message was in Maori, which Herrick translated; it disclosed that Kooti was on his way inland, following the traditional trail into the Urewera mountains; that he would be making camp on the height called Puketapu.

'Puketapu means holy hill,' Herrick explained. 'I must say the fellow is unusually daring. He tells us where he is heading.'

'Or prospective recruits to his cause,' Fairweather said.

Whitmore asked, 'You don't think, Fairweather, that this is some bluff?'

'The second part of the message would seem to cover your query, sir.'

It was in the best King James English: *Thus the Lord saved Israel that day out of the Land of the Egyptians; and Israel saw the Egyptians dead on the seashore.*

'No mistaking for whom that is meant,' Fairweather argued. 'He knew that sooner or later we must return for our dead. Possibly he hopes us too stung and awed to follow. My reading is that he intends us to remain awed. Likewise his retinue. I imagine him preaching with much conviction. To the effect that his people should fear the Lord, and believe in the Lord, and especially His confidant Kooti.'

'Bloody brown Jew,' Whitmore said. 'I daresay he'd crucify Christ too, given hammer and nails.'

'Or Major Biggs, most certainly.'

'We are not to be mocked, Fairweather. Are we understood?'

'Entirely, sir.'

Herrick was considering a map. 'We appear to be approaching terra incognita, sir. The region has been most speculatively drawn. I can find no indication of a place called Puketapu. Or holy hill. Nothing, sir.'

'We may take it that it rests close to the traditional trail obligingly mentioned,' Fairweather said.

'No suggestion of a trail either,' Herrick objected. 'We appear to be on the bank of the Hangaroa river. Inland to the west there is another river called Ruakituri. It is difficult to get bearings.'

'Then we take Kooti as guide,' Fairweather proposed. 'Not only does he make no secret of his route; his three or four hundred should leave the trail decently flattened.'

Canning and Carr rode in. 'What is the problem?' Canning demanded. 'Who makes the delay?'

'Our dead,' Fairweather said curtly. 'We can inter them no faster.'

Canning continued to gaze with grievance at Fairweather as he examined and amplified Herrick's map. 'We cross the Hangaroa here, where we stand,' he told Whitmore and Herrick. 'Then we meet and master a wide dividing range of mountains. Finally we descend to the Ruakituri and follow that river up to its headwaters. That brings us to the gate of the Ureweras. Also to the home of the Tuhoe people, a pained memory for most who fought them. Kooti's holy hill should be somewhere there. Kooti would need to ingratiate himself with the Tuhoe, perhaps even try winning them to his flag, before proceeding further into the interior.'

Whitmore at least was impressed. 'You are a sudden fund of information on this region, Captain Fairweather,' he noted.

'I have quarrelled with a good deal of it, sir.'

'Surveying?'

'Acquiring local knowledge, sir.'

'In the course of what?'

'Carnal knowledge, sir.'

Whitmore was less impressed.

After the river crossing, days were tallied with difficulty. All had cold and damp in common. Horses had to be dragged, cursed and kicked across streams; and nursed down spellbinding slopes. Sometimes men and beasts slid away in muddy tangle. Whitmore soon despaired of imposing form on his column; the mountains had more authority. There were more meandering ravines, more murky valleys. Rain fell, and water brimmed underfoot; streams aspired to become brawling torrents. Kooti's trail was always apparent, though he was moving with no consideration for those in pursuit; everything suggested he kept his people moving fast.

'With women and children too,' Whitmore mused.

'Perhaps the more reason, sir,' Fairweather said. 'He may wish to establish them in safety before risking another engagement.'

'What drives them, Fairweather? What keeps them together in this foul country?'

'The book of books, sir, to the best of our knowledge.'

Whitmore proved better at asking questions than considering answers.

Some days had more surprise than others. The first day of snow, for example. The second was no more tolerable. The snow drifted so deep as to make the trail indetectable. Fairweather and fellow scouts circled for hours; they shivered back to tall campfires.

'We could,' Whitmore hazarded, 'turn back with no dishonour, Fairweather.'

'Conceivably, sir.'

'Most of our party would now be of that opinion, don't you think?'

'Many or most, sir.'

'Then inform all of that opinion, Fairweather, that we shall not. On no account. We shall not be turning back.'

Every heart had its own ache. Whitmore's was having to play second fiddle to lukewarm commanders and lacklustre politicians most of his military life. In these forests he called his own heady tune; hardship intoxicated. The more punishing the march, the more impeccable the melody.

Sometimes they camped where Kooti had. There was the ash of campfires, charred potatoes and pigeon bones picked clean; and horses dismembered and meatless. There were also hogsheads quite emptied of rum. It was clear that Kooti retained his numbers. His band ate and drank amply, rested sufficiently, and pushed on again.

'They lack compassion,' Herrick mourned. 'Never a scrap of creature comfort discarded in blind panic.'

Whitmore's men were down to flour, which made a sorry damper bread for the evening meal, and a soggy breakfast. The commander's itinerary did not provide for hunting; Biggs would now never catch them with supplies.

Meanwhile there were more messages carved on trees, again to the effect that Kooti was proceeding to holy hill, and with Biblical notations. *Hide me from the secret counsel of the wicked,* said one, *from the insurrection of the workers of iniquity.*

As the current prime worker of iniquity Whitmore demonstrated that he could still, on his day, swear the devil out of hell.

They came to the loud river called the Ruakituri. Clumps of flax fringed it; spouts of foam flecked it. There were glistening cliffs crowned with tall mountain palms.

More to the point, a corpse of a Maori male of middle years lay near the river's edge, on ground left soft by many feet. A tomahawk had divided the skull. Formal execution was plain; the body had been stripped and abandoned to rodent and bird. The flesh had the scar of old gunshot.

Arriving militiamen led their horses past slowly; some stared with fascination. Whitmore took seconds to see a desirable omen. 'Dissension in their camp,' he deduced. 'Their nerve is going.'

'It could be construed as less comforting, sir,' Fairweather objected. 'Kooti could be seen as enforcing stiffer discipline. Learning as he goes. This man may have been an indifferent disciple. He may also shape as a message to us. That no one is to inconvenience Kooti. A change from Biblical texts, sir.'

Whitmore thoughtfully turned the corpse with the toe of his boot. Finally he grunted, 'One less to hunt. Damned ugly brute anyway.'

'Certainly a sighting of sorts, sir.'

'I think I can do without it,' Whitmore decided.

'Larkin,' Fairweather ordered.

Larkin dragged the body from the colonel's view. Whitmore considered the busy water and the heights above. 'So,' he said meditatively, 'the Ruakituri. You ever have the notion, Fairweather, that the rivers in this country feel obliged to prove something?'

'Since you mention it, sir.'

'What about this one?'

'It doesn't mean to accommodate, sir. Neither men nor horses.'

'If it slows us, it must slow Kooti. We may start picking off stragglers soon.'

That day went in crossing and recrossing the Ruakituri to find level ground; it took four hours to gain a hundred yards. By nightfall Whitmore decided to abandon horses and leave a half dozen Hawke's Bay Maoris as guard. Then some decided it timely to abandon Whitmore. He found a deputation of Poverty Bay men hovering before him in the firelight. Dodds was again the spokesman.

'We're a long way from home,' he announced.

'Agreed. Make your point, man.'

'As militia,' Dodds said, 'we are only obliged to serve in our own region. This river isn't in Poverty Bay.'

'By God,' Whitmore said, 'we may have that court martial yet.'

'There's regulations,' Dodds said with easy insolence. 'You can't make us go no further.'

'Can't I? Wait and see.'

Herrick intervened. 'I'm afraid the man is right, sir. Technically.'

'The way we see it,' Dodds said, 'there's no point in getting Kooti's goat. We done that once. Much good it did anyone. Two graves is enough to dig.'

'And you want fellow colonists to do your dirty work now?'

'We don't want anyone to do nothing,' Dodds said. 'If we leave Kooti alone, maybe he'll leave us alone. He's clearing out. Let him. We got homes and families. We just want to live peaceful.'

'Dear God,' Whitmore said.

'And there's more,' Dodds said. 'You'd march us till we rot. The likes of you can't do that to the likes of us no more. Not in this country. We got rights. And the vote.'

'From Hell, Hull and Halifax, may the good Lord deliver us,' Whitmore sighed. Then, 'You remain extremely quiet, Fairweather.'

'The situation seems sufficiently agitated, sir.'

'In short, you prefer not to be helpful.'

'Dodds argues that Poverty Bay men have homes and families. That, sir, appears beyond dispute.'

'And you would let an advocate of cowardice go unchallenged?'

'I have had no complaint with Dodds' capacity as scout, sir. Nor with his talent in a rearguard.'

'So what are you telling me, Fairweather?'

'That I hear reason of a hard earned sort, sir.'

Canning lumbered into the wrangle. 'You,' he told Fairweather, 'put them up to this.'

Fairweather was silent.

'It's what you've said,' Canning pointed out. 'You said to leave Kooti alone.'

'Captain Canning has an argument of substance,' Whitmore ruled. 'The view of these wretches accords remarkably with your own. Would you deny it, Captain Fairweather?'

'I deny discussion with Dodds. This deputation is their own notion.'

'You expect us to believe that?' Canning asked.

'I am indifferent to what you believe, Canning,' Fairweather said.

Whitmore said, 'For fomenting discontent on this expedition I could have your guts, Fairweather.'

'I don't doubt it, sir.'

'In the matter of making headway up this river, are you with me, at this moment, or are you not?'

Fairweather considered his reply, and found nowhere to go. 'It would seem I must be, sir.'

'I think I should like bolder tone, Captain Fairweather. Yes or no?'

'Yes, sir. I am.'

'And with no further quibbles?'

'Not of conspicuous nature, sir.'

'Good,' Whitmore said.

Herrick finally asked, 'Is the position of these Poverty Bay men to be left unresolved, sir?'

Whitmore walked three paces to his left, three paces to his right, and then repeated this contemplative procedure. At length he addressed himself to Herrick.

'Do you, captain, often consider why God arranged for this world to turn upon its axis once daily?'

'Not often, sir,' Herrick allowed.
'Or caused the sun to shine equally upon us all?'
'Not especially, sir. No.'
'Think on it, Herrick. You will come to only the one conclusion. Divine folly. He should have left the bloody place dark.'
There was a long silence. 'These men, sir?' Herrick asked again.
'I see no men,' Whitmore pronounced. 'He who has no stomach for the fight, let him depart.'
'*Henry V*, sir?' Herrick said helpfully.
'Not a quotation, Herrick. An order. Remove them from my field of fire.'
Dodds and his fellow Poverty Bay colonists found no cause to persist as targets.
Fairweather soon made his own more tactful retreat from Whitmore's fire. He shed his clammy boots, unbuckled his belt, and climbed into the ungainly bivouac Larkin had designed. Larkin was already in residence.
'In case you're wondering, sir,' he said, 'I won't be off with Dodds and the others in the morning. I'm staying with you.'
Fairweather was moved. 'That is unnecessary, Larkin.'
'I'm the best judge of that, sir.'
'Then thank you, Larkin. It is much appreciated.'
'Dodds didn't know he was feeding you to Whitmore. Nor did I, sir. I could have a word with Newman and others. They'd see it through too.'
'No need,' Fairweather said.
'I mean, sir, what's in this for you?'
'And for you?'
Larkin was quiet.
'You see,' Fairweather said. 'Birds of a feather. Two fools who still think they make most sense soldiering.'
'Not easy with Whitmore, sir.'
'Do shut up, Larkin. Officers do not, as is well known, discuss their commanders with non-commissioned men. You tempt the devil in me.'
'You don't make it no secret, sir. Not the devil in you. No.'
'Goodnight, Larkin. Sleep without supping and wake without owing.'
The prince of sinners, nonetheless, had business with Fairweather that night. He dreamt excruciatingly of the woman called Meriana Smith, and woke with ardour uncomfortably spent and Larkin snoring in manly rhythm beside him. In the morning he composed a brief letter, mainly to assure her that he remained in fair health, no thanks to his commander or Kooti. Before the Poverty Bay men began their return to the coast he gave the letter to Newman and asked safe delivery.
'I shouldn't be saying this,' Newman observed, 'but have you thought of a last will and testament?'

13

That day the scramble upriver became robust. Banks tightened and misty water sped between boulders; men formed chains to fight the current. Yet Kooti had pushed his people through with no further dissenters tomahawked. Nor did he oblige Whitmore with limping stragglers to be lowered; not even with lame horses. Whitmore's problems were not diminished by the departure of the Poverty Bay men; already three or four men of the Hawke's Bay militia had taken example and crept off too.

The winter day lengthened and brightened. Cruel cold dispersed; the antipodean sun substituted cruel heat. Steam rose from giant fronds of fern; sweat flowed from faces and swilled under tunics.

At noon Fairweather was scouting ahead with Larkin. He paused to consider the river and ease his thirst; and listen. Water. Wind. Birds. No forest could seem more unfurnished with human presence. Yet Fairweather had the sure conviction he was watched. No shot came. Perhaps foliage somewhere stirred as feet withdrew. The landscape left everything to the imagination. Fairweather filled his pipe with damp tobacco, and managed to get it smouldering before Larkin crossed from the opposite bank of the river.

'I like this less,' he told Larkin.

Larkin cupped water to his mouth with grimy hands. 'A fair bugger of a day, sir.'

'I mean the terrain, Larkin.'

'Mad,' Larkin agreed. 'We can't do ourselves much good in this kind of country.'

'I suspect Kooti may be of that view too.'

'You'd know, sir. You know Kooti.'

'I rather think that even Kooti does not know Kooti. Or not yet.'

'What are you thinking, sir?'

'That we might again be contributing toward his self-knowledge. More especially if an ambush is set. Some height on the subject is desirable. Hold the colonel here. Explain that I feel some form of contact with the prisoners imminent.'

'Prisoners, sir? Or the enemy?'

'Prisoners, Larkin. Until further advised.'

Larkin looked up at the tall bluffs rising from the river's edge. 'You're tackling that climb, sir?'

'I could be some little time. You may need all your sergeant's tact to curb the colonel. If and when rage subsides, tell him that I appear to know something you don't; that should keep him pleasantly baffled.'

'Do you, sir? Do you know something?'

'Only that we may now be marching as prisoners; I need to peer over the wall and see if Kooti is rattling the keys.'

He left Larkin and began to climb. The weathered rock resisted his grip; he grappled with tufts of scrub and followed eccentric ledges. At length he was gasping a hundred feet above the river. The next hundred were even less charitable. His heart thumped and sweat stung his eyes. As he teetered from foothold to foothold he recalled another and recent climb; this time he had no Hamiora Pere helpful with a length of flax. Nevertheless trees suddenly rose around, and there was soil of rancid sort firm underfoot. No more than scraps of sky could be seen through interlaced trees. For the next hour he heaved still higher. Then, from a cliff left clean by landslide, he looked out on mountain after mountain with deep valleys between. He was surely seeing into the Urewera. Nama's territory; the home of the tall Tuhoe and the toasted penis. Never forsake a fuck for a fight? Too late now. He recalled Nama's half-toothed laugh with mixed feelings; also a cloak of fine feathers.

More to current matters, he picked out the erratic route of the Ruakituri river in the green maze; he determined the probable location of its head-waters. He let his eyes wander. Then he found cause to look with concentration, blink, and look again. No; no mistake.

Smoke. Smoke lifting and drifting. And from more than one fire. Possibly four miles off, or two days as Whitmore travelled. The source of the smoke was on some elevation shut from sight by nearer ridge and mountain; distinctly not from a riverside trail.

Besides, noon fires were not lit by men on the move. Evening fires of necessity; morning fires maybe. Noon fires never. Kooti had called a halt. He had arrived on holy hill.

One way and another, then every way and a few others, Fairweather slithered and crashed back to the riverside again. Fatigued men of the Hawke's Bay militia were collapsed and sleeping among rocks and fern; their Maori allies looked even more languorous.

'You have held us for more than two hours,' Whitmore said. 'Hours which we must now endeavour to make good.'

'With caution, sir,' Fairweather suggested. 'We are closing with them fast.'

'You call that news?'

'Fires are,' Fairweather said.
'Fires?' Whitmore pondered.
'Cooking fires, sir. Of substantial nature.'
'Surprise me still further, Fairweather.'
'It suggests two possibilities, sir. One, that the prisoners are now moving at leisurely pace and either unaware of pursuit or indifferent. Second, that they may be consolidating and preparing to repel pursuit. I favour the latter, sir.'
'You could not be mistaken about these fires?'
'I think not, sir.'
Whitmore wanted no fires complicating the command picture. 'They could be mere hunters,' he argued. 'You have said, Fairweather, that we are on the edge of the Urewera country here. The land of the Tuhoe. And the Tuhoe, as I understand, are tenacious hunters. They, knowing nothing of recent events, nor of Kooti, would still be lighting fires whenever and wherever so inclined.'
'They could be,' Fairweather had to agree.
'There are your fires, then, Captain Fairweather.'
'If you say so, sir.'
'The fact of the matter is that Kooti must have run his crew ragged. They must all be at sixes and sevens.'
'Desirably, sir,' Fairweather said.
Whitmore turned to Herrick. 'Get men on their feet again, captain.'
Herrick hesitated and said, 'I am impelled to observe, sir, that the men are feeling the strain.'
'Thanks to Captain Fairweather's forest browsing,' Whitmore judged. 'Loss of impetus always plays havoc with men's spirits.'
So might the environs of holy hill, Fairweather thought, but said nothing.
Herrick protested, 'The morale of even the best Hawke's Bay men isn't the same, sir. Not since the Poverty Bay men left. They see less point. They also see we are fewer than a hundred rifles against perhaps three times our number.'
'We make our rifles matter more, Herrick. Trained rifles against ruffians win every time.'
'And there is the food, sir. The prisoners have been disinclined to favour us by abandoning provisions. We have flour only for another day. No more.'
'Is that all, Herrick?'
'It would seem so, sir,' Herrick said feebly.
'Captain Herrick,' Fairweather suggested, 'is putting forward the familiar martial dilemma, sir. Men are made of flesh; gut upholds heart.'
'There is another proposition,' Whitmore said. 'Give guts no time to think. Keep men moving. Make monotony a virtue.'

'Sir,' Herrick acknowledged.

'You may yet learn, Herrick, that tired men are the most receptive to firm orders. Also the bravest. The more a creature is burdened, the less it is inclined to buck. Disobedience hardly seems worth it. Even in the mouth of enemy guns.' Whitmore turned to Fairweather. 'You, captain, seem agitated by something unsaid.'

'Regardless of the fires, sir, Kooti is somewhere between us and the Urewera mountains. He cannot push into those mountains without presenting his credentials to the Tuhoe people and trying to win sympathy and sanctuary. Given their past addiction to suicidal enterprise, some might be disposed to turn armed Shylock too.'

'All the better,' Whitmore argued, 'when we thrash Kooti within their gaze. Thank you, Fairweather. You confirm my feeling considerably. Kooti must be nipped in the bud. We push on.'

'That was not my point, sir. Kooti must win time to ingratiate himself with the Tuhoe. That means deflecting us forcibly.'

'Your theme eludes me, Fairweather.'

'I would urge playing observer, sir, rather than tempting Kooti to excess. He could get a cold shoulder from the Tuhoe. They have been baffled by passing Catholics and Protestants trying to convert and reconvert them; to learn of Jews too might be the last straw.'

'All this could take weeks,' Whitmore objected.

'The dead are dead longer,' Fairweather said. 'Give Kooti time for second thoughts. He may conclude he has called sufficient attention to himself.'

Captain Canning made a querulous appearance. 'May I ask what is happening, sir?' he said to Whitmore.

'You may well,' Whitmore said. 'Fairweather currently appears of the view that nothing should.'

'I didn't come up here for nothing,' Canning announced.

'You heard that, Fairweather?' Whitmore asked.

'Distinctly, sir.'

'Would you have me waste Canning's time?'

'As a man of substance, Captain Canning would appear to be an asset to this colony. I trust he is permitted to remain so.'

'You trying to scare?' Canning asked.

'Fairweather,' Whitmore explained, 'fancies that the currency of the gun may buy us difficulties.'

'So let him sod off back to Poverty Bay with the rest of them,' Canning said. He felt he had licence for dislike of Fairweather now.

'I cannot have this,' Whitmore decided. 'Not between officers. Captain Fairweather has given well of his services as scout. Apologize, Canning.'

'For what?' Canning said. 'I am just stating the fact of the matter. He could reckon the same regulations were on his side.'

'You class a fellow captain with cowards.'

'My ewes are lambing back in Hawke's Bay. I am classing him as a fellow who holds us up with gab.'

'Apologize, Canning,' Whitmore insisted. 'Make it clear the imputation of cowardice withdrawn.'

'In return,' Fairweather offered, 'I shall apologize to Captain Canning's neglected ewes. I had not understood there were matters of gravity at issue.'

'That will be enough from you too, Fairweather,' Whitmore ruled. 'Canning?'

'I apologize,' Canning said with grievance.

'So where is Carr?' Whitmore asked. 'Where is the fellow?'

Delicate Captain Carr was roused from a riverside doze; he made his way unsteadily to his fellow captains and Whitmore.

'We have differences of opinion here, Carr,' Whitmore informed him. 'You are entitled to make your views known.'

'My what, sir?' Carr had the apologetic smile of the deaf.

'Views, man. Views.'

'I have no news,' Carr disclosed.

Whitmore persisted, 'It is Herrick's view that we are at the limit of our resources. Fairweather's that we should begin a waiting game. Canning, on the other hand, would appear to want this over and done. My present inclination also. How do you feel about it? You right for a scrap?'

'I've had my nap,' Carr agreed pleasantly.

Whitmore despaired. 'I think we can take it,' he said, 'that Captain Carr is still with us. At all events the decision is mine.'

With groans and more explicitly subversive sounds, the column began moving again; Fairweather and Larkin pushed forward to scout the river.

Toward nightfall they came upon a modest campsite with ashes still warm. Fairweather left Larkin to await Whitmore, and warily travelled on another hundred yards upriver. The sun's heat had gone; the air was fast cooling to frost. It seemed he had suffered a surfeit of forest and river; as he went forward, from cover to cover, a twitching took over one eye. He had almost persuaded himself that the area was free of menace when something flicked to his right. His carbine flew in that direction, then a shot, though he retained no memory of engaging the trigger. He had never fired a less considered shot, nor one more in dread.

There was a thump. Then a chilling sound of distress beyond fern. Gurgling. A windpipe wound.

'Dear Christ,' he said loudly, and reloaded quick.

There was no fire returned. He closed slowly with the sound, all the forest watching.

His victim lay among the debris of large trees; and needed a shaky second shot. Kooti's party was poorer by one deceased colt.

Whitmore found vindication in the fresh campsite. 'We are less than a day's march behind them,' he said. 'Almost on top of them. They have to be flagging.'

'On one reading, sir,' Fairweather said wearily.

'Is there another?'

'I should not care to make too much of it, sir. This campsite is queerly small. It suggests a less substantial band. Perhaps an outlying picket. A passive rearguard instructed to withdraw.'

'Your imagination runs away with you,' Whitmore said.

'I should be last to deny that I have one, sir. And I prefer to resist the thought that some game is afoot; that we are being tactically tempted.'

'You are unduly fascinated by this fellow Kooti,' Whitmore decided. 'Tactics? Pickets? A passive rearguard?'

'He is an uncomfortably quick learner, sir. Certainly in peace, perhaps too in war. Otherwise he would never have been in exile; nor should we be hunting him here.'

'And you would have me believe that the man places a passive rearguard, perhaps to lead us on?'

'I should sooner not have myself believe any of it, sir.'

'Maoris stand and fight,' Whitmore said. 'All for the first shot. Show me a passive Maori and I'll show you a painted Dutchman.'

Nevertheless Whitmore seemed of the view that reinforced pickets were desirable.

Fairweather's colt was stripped and stewed, no sinew left to waste, and drained of every nourishing juice; there was consolation for three or four score slack bellies. After they had eaten, Herrick reclined alongside Fairweather and sighed, 'If tired men are bravest, then I am the most fearless here.'

Fairweather was quiet. The twitch in his eye had gone; it had taken residence in the old Maori wound in his left knee, perhaps searching out further flaws.

'It could be tomorrow,' Herrick said suddenly.

'Or the day after,' Fairweather agreed.

'How is one supposed to feel? How do you?'

'If it helps, Herrick, there are two circumstances in which I know I am alive. The second is when guns begin to sound.'

'What,' Herrick asked, 'of art?'

'A feeble third.'

'I suspect you might be as much a monster as Whitmore.'

'On my day,' Fairweather said.

Fairweather sagged, slept the night through, and woke to drama. Six so far obscure Hawke's Bay men had been intercepted while trying to steal off downriver. Whitmore was not of a mind for a lecture. He ordered a court martial and a gravedigging detail.

'With respect, sir,' Herrick protested, 'this is an improper procedure. You are virtually confirming the sentences before evidence has been heard – that is, if you were empowered to pass the death sentence, which you are not.'

'Canning and Fairweather will preside,' Whitmore announced. 'You, Herrick, if you choose, may defend these cowards. I warn that lengthy speeches will not be tolerated. We have business on hand.'

The prisoners, already blindfolded on Whitmore's order, were dragged on buckling knees before Canning and Fairweather. Also on Whitmore's order repetitive confessions were cut short. Herrick was allowed a minute to argue a breathless cause for compassion. The men, he said, had suffered the cruellest march made by Britons in melancholy New Zealand forest, and their flinching at this point might be forgiven; they should have a second chance.

Fairweather had whispered conversation with Canning. There was only one verdict possible. All had allowed themselves guilty.

'But what of?' Fairweather pondered.

'Of being bad buggers,' Canning hissed. 'Say what you like.'

'Have you arrived at a verdict?' Whitmore demanded.

'We have, sir,' Fairweather said. 'We hereby find all six as human as sin.'

Whitmore was not to be taken aback. 'Nothing further?'

'Only,' Fairweather said, 'that Captain Canning seems to wish a rider concerning unnatural practices. I feel bound to observe, however, that no evidence has been tendered in this respect.'

Whitmore still did not blink. Sentencing was in his province. 'I have,' he disclosed, 'already briefed Captain Carr to instruct a firing squad in the correct procedure.'

The tearful men were led away from the campsite toward the dug graves. One was heard pleading with Carr's detail for a five yard start before shots were delivered.

'I must challenge this, sir,' pale Herrick told Whitmore.

'By all means,' Whitmore said pleasantly.

'It is, sir, not even within your rights to order a flogging of men in this militia.'

'Then this affair,' Whitmore suggested, 'should go far toward illustrating my need for such rights. That is, when sufficiently publicized. You will oblige me, Herrick, if you make it your business to do so.'

He walked off in meditation, hands behind back.

Extended protest was made impossible by the volley nearby. Herrick swayed, perhaps about to faint. Then cries of anguish rose. Fairweather took Herrick's arm.

'It is all right,' he said. 'Sweet Carr has just made his marksmen give heaven a fright. Had the colonel been at all serious he should have assigned Canning or myself as executioner.'

Herrick still shuddered. 'And what should you have done?'

'Ordered the firing party to place shots as mercifully as possible.'

'In the air also?'

'In the heart,' Fairweather said.

'Dear God,' Herrick cried, 'what are we?'

'Soldiers,' Fairweather proposed. 'We have to be now.'

'Yet you urged against this.'

'That was yesterday's lost fight. The next cannot be. And rest assured that the six currently recovering their wits are privileged among us; they are now going to find Kooti sweet company.'

'I still don't like it,' Herrick said.

'It's an acquired taste,' Fairweather agreed.

Those were not the only shots heard that day. A mist lingered over frosty trees as Fairweather and Larkin felt out the rest of the Ruakituri. They now signalled silently from each side of the river before moving on; one never lost sight of the other. When the last mist lifted, and the sun warmed, they heard the guns and lingering echoes.

The shots were from upriver, some nearer than others, coming and going with no apparent consistency. One, then several, and singly again. Echoes sped away; fluttering birds settled.

Fairweather signalled. Larkin waded across the river.

'At least it gives interest,' Fairweather said.

There were more shots. Larkin's black eyebrows lifted.

'What are you thinking?' Fairweather asked.

'I'm still at it, sir,' Larkin confessed.

Echoes receded. Herrick joined them, breathing fast and crouching with revolver shaky in hand.

'They seem very close,' he said hoarsely.

'What do you say, Larkin?' Fairweather asked.

'As close as God's curse to a whore's arse, sir,' Larkin said.

'And on the face of it otherwise engaged,' Fairweather suggested. 'So do be a dear fellow and put that revolver away, Herrick. You might do hurt.'

Whitmore toiled up to them on short legs; his sweaty arrival coincided with fresh shots upriver. 'Hunting?' he asked Fairweather.

'If they are herding along a half hundred wild pig, sir. I rather think an intoxicating surplus of ammunition and rum. Perhaps some new Semitic festival.'

'I read feud,' Whitmore eventually decided. 'They are now viciously at odds with themselves. If so, we let them fight to the finish and then move to apprehend the survivors.'

Canning and Carr appeared. Canning had his twopence worth too.

'Signals,' he said. 'They herald our approach.'

'I think not,' Fairweather said. 'There is no system. And most seem to issue from the one locality.'

At least a score of shots sounded. They penetrated Carr's deafness and moved him to contribute. 'They seem,' he suggested, 'to be having a jolly old time.'

Whitmore winced. It seemed he was not; and for the first time uncertain.

'There is,' Fairweather said, 'one opinion still not offered here.'

'Whose?' Whitmore barked.

'Larkin's, sir,' Fairweather said quietly.

Larkin had never stopped listening, and thinking; he looked up with surprise. 'Mine, sir?'

'Yours, Larkin,' Fairweather said. 'Your opinion. What does it sound like to you?'

'Musketry practice,' Larkin said.

14

Whitmore judged a halt wise; they could be caught in winter dark on terrain vulnerable to surprise. They camped without fire or food. There was a muster before dawn, and blankets and haversacks were abandoned. In the thin dark the roused men were pissing, shitting and sighing shadows, less than a picture of enterprise; some found it an effort to stumble into line with weapons.

Whitmore undertook to make armed opposition seem insignificant. 'This far,' he told those assembled, 'we have trailed our coat through some of the world's wildest country, and no one has dared jump upon it. May it be so today too. Let each man recall that in this forbidding solitude he serves in the front rank of empire. Am I understood?'

Silent men shifted from one foot to another, resigned to further inspiration.

'I see men,' he declared. 'British chips of the devil who would march another hundred miles with no complaint. And still have strength to plant the flag at day's end. As, by God, we shall.'

The cheer which followed could have done with more volume, and some orchestration.

To Herrick, Fairweather said, 'Take a deep breath if matters begin to displease. Then two or three more. Your first fight will be with yourself. Win that; the second is easier.'

'I take your word,' Herrick said.

Fairweather moved off with Larkin; the column was to follow fifteen minutes behind.

'So what are we up to, sir?' Larkin asked.

'You heard the colonel,' Fairweather said. 'We are planting the flag.'

The sun found a path between hills, travelling down valley from tree to tree; the birdsong which heralded it did not diminish. Melting frost dripped from overhead fern. The river began to fatten, the valley to widen. Mountains no longer leaned brutally above; there were spaces. Moving towards an intrusive bluff, Fairweather heard voices, a laugh. Larkin, covering Fairweather from the opposite bank, stiffened at the sound too. Fairweather signalled Larkin to remain in place. Then he rounded the bluff, uncovered and alone, flecks of shingle crackling underfoot; the sun on the river dazzled.

Voices again; another laugh. It played with memory. Then it did not. A Maori laugh certainly. But not quite Kooti's nervous neigh.

Gaining height on a large rock, Fairweather saw movement beyond flashing water. Three figures solidified perhaps sixty yards away; three men surfacing from riverside trees with wooden buckets in hand. While Fairweather watched, they gathered water; and conversed. No arms were apparent. Laughter was frequent and loud. Finally they carried their buckets back into the trees.

Too innocent to be true. Yet might be if Whitmore's advancing column had never been watched.

Still making sense of the scene, Fairweather had it again. Three figures from trees. Buckets. Conversation. Moreover, the same three males. This time their laughter seemed higher in pitch. Their campsite had to be within very few paces; they had emptied their buckets remarkably soon.

Either all was awry, or Fairweather was. Useful inference had to be won; Whitmore was fewer minutes behind. On each side of the river were low slopes, the ground gently rising; the greenery was thick and then tall. The river featured a slender and rocky island, scrappily vegetated, its banks buried under the limbs and trunks of dead trees dumped by flood. The Maoris were on the riverside beyond, retreating into trees again.

While Fairweather chewed on an empty pipe, Larkin crawled wheezily alongside him.

'What do you have, sir?' he asked.

'A scene of some character,' Fairweather said.

The same water carriers returned to the river.

'The third time,' Fairweather explained.

Larkin said presently, 'They don't fill them buckets too full, sir.'

'Thank you, Larkin. That had escaped me.'

'What's up, sir?'

'I'm damned if I know. And we might all be damned if I don't. We have to be looking at an outpost of sorts. Not the major camp. There is no height.'

Holy hill? He lifted his head to scrutinize surrounding summits; the most considerable candidate had steep rock faces, deeply fissured flanks and a blunt top, all desirable features for a Maori citadel, perhaps one used in the past by coastal tribesmen trying to tame the Tuhoe. From that elevation Whitmore's column could have been watched for the past two days. And it would command an ample view of the riverbed before them, the banks, the island. Fairweather could detect no movement, hear no voices, see no fires. It was only as sinister as the mind made it.

'Sprats,' Larkin said.

'Sprats, Larkin?'

'To catch a mackerel, sir. Bait. What else can the buggers be?'

'Stay here,' Fairweather ordered. 'Neither nibble nor bite. I shall intercept Colonel Whitmore.'

'What'll you tell him, sir?'

'Nothing to make much difference, Larkin.'

Fairweather skidded and splashed downstream. He met Whitmore, with Herrick, moving at the head of the column.

'We have sighted prisoners, sir,' Fairweather reported.

'In force?' Whitmore asked.

'I cannot say, sir. So far there are three unarmed men only in sight. They may be of an outpost.'

'Then we take it,' Whitmore said.

'We shall be further exposed sir,' Fairweather said. 'I should be foolish to understate my suspicions. All may be as peaceful as appears to be. All may not. If we are to proceed, might I request that we do not fire the first shot? There is still the chance that no fire at all need be exchanged.'

'Blood has been shed, Fairweather. There are dead to be avenged. Maoris understand that. Their word is *utu. Utu,* Fairweather. Vengeance. I am all for respecting the customs of the country. Within reason, of course. Souveniring and smoking of heads can no longer be countenanced. Nor cannibalism, needless to say. Otherwise *utu* is a word well suited to our business here.'

Canning joined them. 'What's going on?' he asked. 'More talk?'

'Captain Fairweather,' Whitmore explained, 'is favouring us with his view of the situation ahead.'

'Fairweather,' Canning said, 'would favour us with his views for the next fortnight.'

'It is not my intention to leave your ewes bleating,' Fairweather said.

'You can,' Whitmore said, 'hardly deny that you yet again appear to argue procrastination.'

'Negotiation, sir. Especially if Kooti can be kept guessing at our number.'

'Negotiation, Fairweather, is best conducted with a few bodies on view. Sharp punishment administered, then surrender accepted. Aside from which we must have something to show for our pains.'

'I take your point, sir. A few bodies.'

'Let's get on with it,' Canning said.

With Whitmore, Fairweather climbed on to the vantage point where Larkin waited. 'Still no more than we've seen, sir,' Larkin said, and moved aside to make room for rotund Whitmore.

Whitmore took in the sunlit prospect, the river, rocky banks, and trees. He also watched the three Maoris make their appearance and vanish into growth. 'Interesting,' he presently observed. 'That island especially attracts. If Kooti cannot see its merit as a strongpoint, we can. It is really rather pretty. Like an arrowhead planted at the heart of things. Or perhaps a sturdy vessel. I think a vessel. One from which boarders might be repelled.'

Whitmore had never disclosed much sentiment for the New Zealand interior before, nor a capricious naval inclination.

'With the difference, sir,' Fairweather said, 'that an island cannot be eased into a different tack. Or persuaded to gather speed by clapping on sail.'

'It commands both banks of the river, nonetheless,' Whitmore said.

'And can be commanded by both, sir.'

'There is only one way to see, is there not? We may encourage Kooti's men to reveal themselves. Furthermore, the island cannot be left. It could be used to drive a wedge into any salient we establish.'

'Possibly,' Fairweather had to agree.

'Distinctly,' Whitmore decided. He scanned the quiet terrain once more. 'It always bemuses me, Fairweather, to look upon some such tranquil haunt of nature, under the bright orb of day, before all becomes smoke, dust, and the delirium of battle. How does it affect you?'

'Rather liverishly,' Fairweather said.

Canning was ordered forward with thirty men to feel out the left side of the river and secure the island; they had first to contest chilling and chest-high water while lifting arms and ammunition belts above their heads. They moved in silence, with a few gasping loudly in the struggle for footing. Captain Carr, misunderstanding Whitmore's requirements, hastened after Canning too; the Hawke's Bay Maoris, of whom Carr was still notionally in command, made no point of following. Whitmore preferred not to chance premature exposure by shouting a recall; he let Carr labour on through the river after Canning's men.

Fairweather and Herrick remained with Whitmore until further disposition was made. They watched the jogging heads of Canning's men, and Carr doggedly trailing.

Fairweather waited for the water carriers to reappear upriver. They did not.

Herrick shivered violently. 'Where are they?' he asked. 'And Kooti?'

Canning gained shallow water on the river's left. His men were soon abreast of the island with eroded cliff to their rear.

Now, Fairweather thought. Now, if ever.

There was a short blast of bugle somewhere above. Vegetation twitched on the island. Wherever it moved a warrior with firearm made magical appearance. Certainly a dozen, perhaps even a score. Their guns banged. Canning and his men were caught with no cover, still dragging their heels through the river. As shot fell among them they scattered, splashing, tumbling, half hidden by spray; most reached dry ground and dropped flat while the Maoris reloaded.

'To think,' Whitmore said, 'that someone in my vicinity was concerned about who fired the first shot. Casualties?'

'Perhaps not at this point, sir,' Fairweather said.

'Good,' Whitmore said with satisfaction. 'I told you that island was the key. We have to outflank it, then take it. Stand by to broach the right of the river. You, Herrick, and the militia remaining.'

They were momentarily deafened. Canning's force had won sufficient equilibrium to return Maori fire from the island. The Maoris made scrappy targets. They leapt up unpredictably, discharged their weapons, and ducked again. Their shooting encouraged Canning's men to heap up rocks for shelter. Captain Carr, having belatedly joined them, was earnestly emptying his revolver.

'No reserves, sir?' Fairweather asked.

'I shall retain our native allies. And deploy them if need arises. You will oblige me by ensuring that the need does not.'

'One other thing, sir,' Fairweather began.

His voice was lost under fresh musketry. Canning's party now appeared to be holding its own in terms of commotion, though Canning was plainly bewildered about what best to do.

'Kooti, sir, has not chosen to populate that island as densely as he might have.'

'Are you trying to tell me something, Fairweather?'

'That we observed three men further upriver, sir. There may be more placed about.'

'Unless they notify us otherwise, let them be seen as withdrawing before bold advance.'

'I cannot, sir, believe that Kooti is merely using that island for nuisance.'

'Well, I damn well can, Fairweather. I believe what I see. It is a nuisance we isolate and eliminate. What would you have me do? Recall Canning, certainly at cost, and abandon the field to those wretches on the island?'

'I agree that we now appear to be committed to this ground, sir. I make only the point that it is not ground of our choice.'

'Have you made it, man? Your point?'

'It would seem so,' Fairweather decided.

'Move,' Whitmore ordered. 'Draw fire from the island, give back what you can, and Canning can contemplate assault.'

Herrick was bringing up men. Larkin was braced. Fairweather edged around the rock which had protected observers. He had slim footing above the river; dark pools turned beneath. Larkin, then Herrick and the rest of the militia followed awkwardly in single file. Though now exposed to the marksmen on the island, they made twenty yards up the right of the river before detection. Finally there was a twang of metal on rock above Fairweather's head; a similar sound behind. A third shot kicked up water. Seeing Fairweather under fire, those following lost pace. One or two fell on their bellies to examine the riverside at close quarters. Herrick could be heard manfully urging along laggards.

'Go back and help him, Larkin,' Fairweather ordered. 'Prod them with your rifle. Bash them with the butt. Regardless of rank; we apologize to lieutenants later. We need the numbers.'

'My pleasure, sir,' Larkin said.

Fairweather ran on alone, sometimes through water, sometimes across rock, until he had the length of the island in view, and was roughly on a par with beleaguered Canning on the opposite bank. Shot sputtered into water near his feet or swished into overhead fern. Maoris on the island were now more consistently dividing their fire, to contain Canning's party on one bank, and curb Fairweather on the other; Fairweather they took personally. Their diving to load and leaping to shoot did not allow great accuracy; Fairweather could further test the hypothesis that the ratio of air to flesh was much in his favour. While waiting on the others he made himself small and selected a first target, a Maori a shade less transient than most, at forty yards. If his bullet did damage, it was not apparent. There was perceptible increase in the shot snapping around. Larkin, with evil vocabulary, was still bullying along militia. Meanwhile Herrick arrived.

'What do we do now?' he asked.

'Our best,' Fairweather suggested, looking to send a second shot.

'Easy for you to say,' Herrick replied. Fitting his own carbine to shoulder, he flinched as Maori shot brought wet clay down on their heads.

Fairweather fired, again without satisfaction. 'It is never easy,' he said.

Herrick loosed shot at another fleeting Maori; and trembled as he pushed a fresh cartridge into his carbine's breech. 'But you make it look so. How is it done?'

'When you see a man leap ahead of his fellows, you may take it as desperation. He is merely more terrified of terror than not.'

'I must try to believe you,' Herrick said. His next shot chipped a sapling above a Maori head.

'And your elevation will improve,' Fairweather promised.

Larkin arrived with a collection of discountenanced militiamen.

'Keep them moving,' Fairweather said. 'And spread. Stay behind them.'

'Sir,' Larkin said.

'Come, Herrick,' Fairweather said. 'We must make this bank of the river fit for the colonel's promenade.'

Taking more fire from the island, they led the men on. Among slimy boulders footing was poor; some slipped away into the river and floundered back again. Soon they had gained most of the bank parallel to the island. From the other side they could hear Canning's party still giving noisy fight.

Then they had more to consider. They met an abrupt and ample volley from their front; not from the island. Smoke showed the Maori position to be approximately where the water carriers had been. Most shot seethed into water. Men dropped flat, Herrick included. A man to the rear called out, evidently struck.

Fairweather noted a small creek feeding the river about fifteen paces ahead; the mouth promised shelter. 'Move,' he said.

'Into that fire?' Herrick asked.

'Or remain a miserable target. And before their next volley.'

They ducked under the second volley as they arrived at the creek. Others, driven along by Larkin, tumbled and sprawled as chips of rock and metal flew. At least one other man was hit, though his howl suggested not mortally. Soon all were gasping in the mouth of the creek; a third volley bit into vegetation overhead.

'Most disciplined,' Fairweather said. 'How many guns ahead, Larkin?'

'Between two and three dozen, sir.'

'Their shots never fall far of the mark. Nor those from the island.'

'No, sir. There is no wild shooting.'

'So what would your impression be?'

'My impression is that they are bloody good, sir.'

'Thank you, Larkin. See to the wounded.'

Herrick found breath. 'What next, then?'

'I fight an uncongenial thought, Herrick. This far fifty men at most have been deployed against us. Kooti, if on hand, could have five times that number in reserve. We may soon not be able to see the woods for the warriors.'

'We are taking fire from two directions,' Herrick said. 'We could soon be cut off.'

'Perhaps if we take fire from four. Larkin? Arrange men to keep up fire to the front. Inactivity might encourage a demented native charge to flush us out. And send some up the creek to our rear.'

They could now see only as much of the island as the mouth of the creek framed. Sometimes a cautionary bullet came in from that direction, but the defenders were now concentrated on Canning. Smoke misted the riverbed.

Between blasts of militia rifles, Herrick said, 'So what does Kooti think he's doing?'

'Counting gifts. Confining us to the bed of the river up which we have helpfully advanced.'

'That is not consistent with his defence of the island.'

'True,' Fairweather conceded. 'We have yet to see what the island is consistent with.'

There was an increase in powder and shot expended on the unseen side of the island; and in British shouts and curses. Canning's voice lifted desperately above others. He was storming the island.

Above the riverside, the Maori bugle sounded again. Two blasts this time. The warriors on the island began to withdraw; they could be seen weaving through scrub, sliding around rocks, with one or two turning to discharge last shots toward Canning. It was a disciplined withdrawal, all moving fast toward the upriver end of the island.

'Shoot at will,' Fairweather told men with clear view.

He took up his own carbine and placed a shot among the Maoris departing the island. They may not have been hindered; they were surely hastened. Then he grabbed Herrick's undischarged weapon. With his second shot, a Maori found his legs failing. He wobbled on after his fellows, wading into the river, now a slow target. Fairweather's third shot, from a weapon loaded by Larkin, brought the man down; his body bobbed in the water.

'You mystify,' Herrick said. 'You argued against firing the first shot. Now you do these natives more hurt than any other.'

'I see nothing incompatible. Not in saving my skin.'

'Come,' Herrick said. 'There is more.'

'Pride in the killer's craft,' Fairweather allowed.

'That seems apparent,' Herrick said. The body of the Maori had begun bumping downstream.

The heads of Canning's men rose on the island; they were scouting it to ensure the last Maori had left. At the upriver end they were checked by a volley from the same Maori rifles which subdued Fairweather. Canning's men, after returning fire, began retiring to cover.

The Maori bugle brayed again. Three blasts, the third lingering suggestively.

Seconds later there were shots and Maori cries to their rear. Men Larkin had placed further up the creek now staggered back in fright. 'They're down on us,' one shouted. 'Dozens and dozens.'

'Allowing for colonial arithmetic,' Fairweather said to Herrick, 'Kooti would seem to be deploying the first of his reserves. Hold men here. Come, Larkin.'

They moved carefully up the creek. Shot scattered among trees overhead; leaves drifted down. A few militia still huddled under banks. Their shooting was blind. Maoris had height and a screen of foliage. Larkin and Fairweather fired off deterrent rounds, and then crouched to load.

'How many?' Fairweather wondered.

'Too many,' Larkin said.

In confirmation, a shot passed between them, discharged from around a bend in the creek. Maoris were moving on lower ground too. The next to snipe around the bend met two shots. Fairweather's took him high, Larkin's low. The shots spun the Maori altogether from concealment. His weapon clattered among rocks; he lay awry across a rotting log.

'There is luck in odd numbers,' Fairweather observed. 'I think we have had ours.'

'I wouldn't argue, sir.'

'Muster these men and retire.'

'Where to, sir?'

'An intelligent question,' Fairweather said.

He hurried to the mouth of the creek. 'Our lease on this sanctuary appears to have expired,' he told Herrick. 'We can proceed upriver into fire. Or downriver away from it. I have no pride in the matter.'

'Nor I,' Herrick admitted.

'In both instances we expose ourselves to firepower which may not have made itself apparent.'

'There is the island,' Herrick suggested. 'A shorter distance to move. Canning seems established.'

On the island Canning's men were still directing fire at the Maori outpost upriver; their shooting might give cover while the river was crossed and the island gained.

Then Fairweather saw it. The island and the dour walls of Urewera wilderness rising to its rear. He had been blinkered.

'No,' he said suddenly.

'No?' Herrick was puzzled.

'We wondered what that island was consistent with. A killing ground, Herrick. We have been bewitched. A light defence, then rehearsed withdrawal to tempt us aboard. Canning is already placed for the inferno. It is now just a matter of nudging us there too.'

'Then Canning should be told.'

'That is my notion. Canning could need some persuasion on my part. His men may not.'

'You would intervene in his command?'

'To deprive Kooti of too lurid a triumph. I would wager that whatever has happened, and whatever has yet to, will have been watched. I suspect the Tuhoe are arranged in box seats across the river. And waiting to see which way the cat jumps.'

'You could suspect too much.'

'I saw only that this situation had character. I did not ask myself what kind.

Theatrical, Herrick. In the third act we are butchered to make a Maori holiday.'

Herrick's composure was ebbing. Embattled Larkin arrived to report that all but the mouth of the creek was now Maori. 'What now, sir?' he asked.

'You will help Captain Herrick get men downriver, moving singly at five second intervals, and with all possible haste. Wounded of course will need help. Jolly Maoris with as much fire as you can manage along the way. I shall depart first, but the island will be my port of call. No one is to follow. You will all report to Colonel Whitmore.'

'Who won't be happy,' Herrick said.

'And may be denied more joy if Canning holds men in an abattoir. And while I think of it, Herrick, I shall hold you to account if Larkin is mislaid. Don't let him manage alone.'

'You have my word,' Herrick said.

'It's not your word I need. It's Larkin. Or I may be lost too.'

'Thank you, sir,' Larkin said.

Filling his lungs, Fairweather leapt from the mouth of the creek, scuffing through gravel and teetering across boulders. Behind him Larkin ordered the next man away; and the next. For a minute Fairweather met no impediment. He looked back and saw men strung out, some supporting wounded, finding a slow path through boulders and driftwood. Canning's force was still drawing Maori fire from the upriver outpost. When shot fell near, it was more an irritated spitting than a robust fusillade. Fairweather judged the moment auspicious to make for the island; he held weapons and ammunition belt high and veered into the river. It soon numbed to the neck. Underwater rock and sunken limbs battered his shins and scraped his belly. He was most of the way across the river before shot flicked the surface. Over his shoulder he saw Herrick herding along the last men to escape from the mouth of the creek; they were now scattered for fifty yards on the right bank of the river. From behind a boulder Larkin was deterring Maori pursuit, with four men loading weapons as fast as Larkin could fire them. Fairweather was freed to toil on to the island, fight through driftwood, and find Canning.

'I see men fleeing the fight,' Canning said sourly.

'Considered withdrawal, after harassment from their rear. My orders.'

'Imperial orders?' Canning mocked.

'Makeshift,' Fairweather said, 'and in that respect decently colonial. We did not read the terrain. Kooti controls it all above head height. We are here on his terms; he gave us this island.'

'We won it,' Canning insisted.

'A mirage, Canning. I fancy he has been training guns upon it for two days. Before sport begins in earnest I suggest you consider a fast route for evacuation.'

'For retreat,' Canning said.

'For a tactical movement to the rear,' Fairweather argued. 'So styled by a Greek general. Few commanders in two thousand years have found fault with his elegant wording.'

'Because you back off, you now need us to justify it.'

'This has the makings of a wearisome conversation, Canning.'

'You are terrified by Kooti.'

'Impressed. In a month he has turned himself from melancholy exile into a tolerable student of martial enterprise; we promise to inspire still further.'

'When all's said and done he's no more than another Maori.'

'When all's said and done a fool knows more in his own house than a wise man in another's. For God's sake, man, get everyone off here.'

'My men are readied for further advance,' Canning announced. 'We are launching across the river to quieten that outpost. If the truth be known, the Maoris there are covering Kooti's retreat.'

'Dreamland,' Fairweather sighed.

'We shall,' Canning said, 'undertake the task you shirked.'

'Captain Carr?'

'Forward. Waiting on my word. You are welcome to participate.'

'At least give me time to see the colonel. If his judgement is yours, then he may provide you with my militia and Maori reserves.'

'I have already requested the reserves. They are slow arriving. I cannot wait.'

'Why?'

'Because, Fairweather, if we are fit to rule, it has to be here.'

'With all respect, Canning, I hardly think the Queen's peace of mind imperilled if one puny island is abandoned to psalm-singing rebels.'

'If we cannot exploit hard advantage, then we have no business hanging on to this colony.'

Canning rose from cover, indifferent to the shot skipping among the rocks and wispy vegetation of the island. Fairweather considered felling the man, and found he could not. A coward yes. A Canning no. In martial impotence Fairweather knew the day overdue for disaster; and much else besides.

Canning was shouting, rallying men, urging them off the island toward the upriver guns. There were four blasts of bugle this time, the last almost lost under Maori cheering. Canning reached the river as gunfire grew. Fairweather, following, felt the wind of malicious fusillades to left and then to right. Ahead, the first man toppled. Then Canning himself. No inch of air seemed free of lacerating metal. Men who had reached the riverside flung themselves down and were taking what cover they could among rocks and logs when Fairweather crawled among them. One or two were trying to return fire, but confused about where best to send bullets.

'Disengage,' he ordered. 'Get back into the centre of the island. Take wounded. And quick.'

Carr was further forward, groping toward Canning; rocks were splintering as more Maori shot sped in. He looked back to Fairweather with dazed eyes.

'I have ordered men to disengage,' Fairweather shouted.

'Engage?'

'Disengage,' Fairweather roared in despair.

No use. Carr's deafness did its worst; resonant fire did the rest. Carr was quick on his feet and raising his revolver. 'Forward,' he called, with some dignity.

Then he thought to look back and reconsider his solo offensive; Fairweather had no time to tug the man down. Perplexity waned in Carr's face as shot struck; half his tunic and much of his torso shredded as he was gusted to one side. Fairweather didn't need to determine Carr lifeless; he scrambled on to Canning. Canning lay half submerged in reddening water, head on a boulder. When Fairweather reached out, Canning fell away. So did some of his jaw. His open eyes still held the shock of the firepower.

Fairweather, swerving and jumping among waspish ricochet, followed the survivors of the attack back on to the body of the island. Fire had not perceptibly diminished; smoke seeped from trees on both sides of the river. Even in the centre of the island there was no safety. Shot from three sides was trimming the vegetation, with leaves raining down, twigs and branches snapping. There were twenty or more men bunched there, a few wounded, the rest mostly whimpering with apprehension or burrowing among stones.

'Build up,' Fairweather raged.

Walls grew as Maori shooting became measured. There was soon a hollow in which wounded could reside. Fairweather arranged men still useful in a circle, so all likely fording places could be watched. He urged them to train guns under the greatest concentrations of Maori smoke. 'We might knock a few off their legs,' he explained. Intent on showing how, he pushed shots into foliage across the river while disabled men loaded carbines and passed them up to him.

Arranging a damaged elbow, bracing to shoot again, he heard a familiar voice. Larkin had arrived from God knew where. Also Herrick. Larkin was no surprise. Herrick was. Both were breathless.

'You told me to stay close in the event of trouble,' Herrick explained. 'Here I am.'

'You interpret me perversely,' Fairweather said. To Larkin he said, 'And you?'

'A message from the colonel, sir.'

'I have one for him. Canning and Carr are gone, and all those on the island as good as. Why, Larkin, did you not boot Captain Herrick's arse when he followed?'

'He was firm, sir. And a captain.'

'You told me on no account to lose Larkin,' Herrick said. 'And I have not.'

'The colonel's message, Larkin?'

'To make your own judgements, sir.'

'And accept blame? Where are these native reserves Canning requested?'

Larkin was silent. Herrick said, 'It seems half fled when Kooti disclosed his firepower.'

'I could make do with the other half to help men off here.'

'That's a horse of another colour, sir,' Larkin said. 'They went off to join Kooti.'

15

The shot beating about their position diminished. They heard a long, shaky note of bugle; after which there were no further Maori guns.

'Hold fire,' Fairweather told his men.

The quiet grew.

'Uncanny,' Herrick said. 'What now?'

'No offer of safe conduct from this river,' Fairweather suggested. Men breathed raggedly around; he could still hear the ring of Maori shot.

A voice rose from somewhere above the right bank. 'Biggs?'

Kooti? Kooti.

'I have been here before,' Fairweather whispered.

Herrick was awed.

'Biggs?'

Fairweather found breath and shouted, 'Major Biggs is not of this company.'

'Not?'

'Not,' Fairweather called. To Herrick and Larkin he said, 'Watch for movement. Try to locate the position of that voice. It cannot be far.'

'Who speaks?' the voice across the river asked. 'George Fairweather?'

'As before,' Fairweather agreed.

'You still do Biggs' work, George.'

'The Queen's work. For the Queen's peace.'

'Did Her Majesty request you, George, to move after me with many armed men?'

'Others, not I, endeavoured to construe her likely wish in the matter.'

'Biggs?'

'Not Biggs either. It has become larger than Biggs; larger than you.'

Laughter. The old nervous neighing.

Larkin said, 'That split rock, sir, half way along the bank. There's some low fern above it. Then a big tree. To the left of the tree. Movement there. Maybe one in something white like last time.'

'Good fellow,' Fairweather said. 'Load two rifles for me. A third for luck.'

Kooti's voice travelled across the water again. 'Who has made it larger, George? Do many armed men march for peace?'

Split rock. Low fern. Big tree. To the left was shadow and sunlight, a fog of foliage. He watched for more to make itself seen. At least he now knew where to direct his voice. At most?

'You and I, Kooti,' he announced, 'could have many a long *korero* on the subject. Much is not of any man's making. Much is in the careless disposition of peoples on this planet; much may be divine misjudgement. Much is what is and always has been.'

Fairweather would have to estimate likely human height on the sloping terrain to the left of the tree; and place a shot to the centre. The gut shot was to have been Canning's pièce de résistance; there would be no room or time for a coup de grâce.

'I must protest,' Herrick whispered. 'You are still talking to the man. It is what Biggs did by your account. And not honourable.'

'I think our present situation can accommodate a little dishonour,' Fairweather said. 'And there is no flag of truce.'

'All the same,' Herrick said.

'My reading is that Kooti is enjoying the sound of his own voice before he urges eloquence upon his guns. He may even be using this to move men into advantageous position.'

'Two wrongs don't make a right.'

'Then we try three, Herrick. Honour is best seen as bonus, not as tactical virtue. And triumph the sum of enlightened treachery.'

'George?' Kooti called. 'George Fairweather?'

'I hear you,' Fairweather said.

There was another pause on Kooti's part. Perhaps hesitation.

Herrick said, 'I see you as of more than one mind. Kooti may be too.'

'No longer. We pushed him to fight. Now we push him to win. As he must, and be seen to, over our bodies.'

'You still lack conviction.'

'I wish an enemy to believe in,' Fairweather agreed. 'I may make myself plausible.'

'Now I have heard everything,' Herrick said.

'Persuade men to fall back toward the lower reach of the island. Slowly, and as much under cover as possible, while absence of fire persists.'

Kooti again. 'The children of Israel, George, have shown they can fight. Is that not so?'

'You have done a day's work of which the best British regiments might be proud,' Fairweather answered.

'Have we killed many?'

'Some,' Fairweather allowed.

'You mean I must kill more?'

'Jehovah,' Fairweather suggested, 'could well feel his servants have kept faith sufficiently.'

He estimated the range at just under forty yards. Already he seemed to know every twig to the left of the big tree. Larkin nudged a second and third rifle into place beside him.

'Do you think, George, that I shall be troubled again?'

'It is not for me to say, Kooti. I am a modest figure in this enterprise.'

Behind, he heard Herrick urging men to move. Then men moving.

'Must I ensure, George, that I am never troubled further? Must I behead the fish?'

'You see only the tip of a snapping tail. Beware making it more ill-tempered. It swims all the world's seas.'

'You threaten.'

'Caution,' Fairweather argued.

To Larkin he said hastily, 'That bugler must be with him.'

'He'd have to be, sir.'

'That would seem his one form of control.'

'The only one we know, sir.'

'If we fail to incapacitate, we at least cause confusion.'

'If we haven't cut our lucky, sir,' Larkin said. He was now loading rifles for himself. Most men were vacating the position; Herrick was pleading with wounded to stifle their groans.

'Caution, George?' Kooti called. 'It still sounds like threaten to me. My Maori ears are deaf to the difference.'

'Forget the past,' Fairweather proposed. 'It can never be cured.'

'Forget?' Kooti cried.

'Even Biggs,' Fairweather said provocatively. 'Especially Biggs. A prophet surely knows the noblest vengeance is to forgive. Some call it divine revenge.'

'You joke,' Kooti said. 'Biggs?'

Herrick crawled back to Fairweather with query on his face.

'At first shot,' Fairweather said, 'tell men to run for the water with wounded. Then make their own route to safety. You too. You may have a minute. You may have much less. Weapons may be abandoned.'

'You? Larkin?'

'We may muster more interest in events.'

To Kooti, he said, 'I cannot joke. Not here and not now. Nor am I placed to bargain. I say only that the stain of most piss can pass. But a man pissing blood to excess begs for foul medicine.'

Laughter again.

'I always,' Kooti announced, 'enjoy *korero* with you, George.'

'On my side I suspect pleasure less mutual,' Fairweather replied. 'We were better over a convivial quart of rum.'

More laughter. Humour made Kooti careless where rage with Biggs had not. Something pale showed briefly from shadow beyond vegetation; perhaps a robe over quivering belly. Fairweather smuggled a carbine under his body and levelled it at the vanished flutter of white. Then he paused. The past could not be cured; the future might be even more terminal. Honour, on the other hand, bought no beef in the market, nor mercy for that matter; Canning and Carr made indifferent company.

Yet he still did not fire. The detonation in his right ear came from Larkin's gun. Fairweather hurried his shot. Across the river there were Maori cries. He and Larkin emptied the rifles beside them into the same few square yards of forest. Success could not be measured, nor was Fairweather in mood to.

'Move,' he told Larkin.

They tumbled toward the water, sheltered from fire on the right bank by the profile of the island, but more vulnerable to Maoris on the left. Stupefaction persisted among the attackers; there were scattered shots, no fusillades. Fairweather and Larkin were well into the river, and speeding Herrick's flock on, when Kooti's bugle bleated weakly. By the time shot proliferated, they had the island behind them, most of the river, and a shielding clay cliff above. It was possible to tease small groups along the bank toward Whitmore's position, and take more advantage of the unadventurous covering fire from that quarter.

Not many minutes later Fairweather was downriver reporting to numb Whitmore that offensive operations were at an end; that among others Canning and Carr were dead. Unless the Ruakituri river was swiftly abandoned, he argued, Kooti might entrap yet again.

'Again?' Whitmore stuttered.

'With a vengeance,' Fairweather promised.

Men unfit to command others were seldom distinguished in commanding themselves. The sweaty panic in Whitmore's face was not an elevating sight; Fairweather had to look elsewhere.

'We have been fortunate so far, sir,' he insisted.

Whitmore did not seem altogether to hear.

Fairweather persisted, 'Our dead could have been ten times as many. And might yet be. I should not care to put any other assessment of our situation to the test, sir.'

Clearly no command evaluation was offering. The last of the sun was leaving the valley; the forest was shadowing, and soon some of the river.

'Canning? Carr?' Whitmore could be detected as asking. 'Their bodies are impossible of recovery?'

'Distinctly, sir.'

'So be it,' Whitmore muttered. 'I detest having to leave them.'

'Very naturally, sir.'

Whitmore knew, or soon surely would, what Fairweather was witness to. Nor was Whitmore likely to forgive very fast.

'As my most recent officer in the field, Fairweather,' he said in stiffening voice, 'what would you say on the prospects of resuming our initiative at daybreak?'

'I find I have nothing to say on that subject, sir.'

'Then I shall, this once, entertain your advice, Fairweather. We may have to account for this soon.'

'You may, sir. I have no accounting to do, unless to tally funds to buy my way out of this colony.'

'What is wrong with you, man?'

'One colonial battle too many,' Fairweather said.

Dusk was not prolonged; darkness was. Staggering downriver in unravelled column, men bumped wearily into boulders, waded through tributary creeks, limped over high ground to low. There were barely enough undamaged men to bear the badly wounded, with six hands to each litter. The wounded often cried out. Two died on the journey; they were deposited with quick prayers, and the column heaved on. Frost stung. Tunics and trousers were heavy with icy moisture. Nor did hunger diminish. The moonlit terrain filled with false alarms.

Herrick, Larkin and Fairweather remained in a rearguard, often prodding men on. One mercy was that Kooti did not fall upon them. Again retreat could have become rout.

Toward dawn, with survival apparent, Herrick asked Fairweather, 'How do you feel about it now?'

'As a bruised Egyptian, perhaps, or bleeding Canaanite.'

'What does that mean?'

'That I am less than I was,' Fairweather said.

Herrick needed no further explanation. They moved in silence again.

As the sun rose a third man expired. They had just reached the campsite where blankets and haversacks had been abandoned the day before. A break was taken for the digging of a grave and less comprehensive attention to the living. Daylight, and continued absence of peril, did much to animate Whitmore. After upbraiding men for conspicuous lethargy, and ordering several to their feet, he sought Fairweather's company.

'It is time,' he suggested, 'to take a more considered view of the matter. I am interested in how many of Kooti's band we may have brought low.'

'Perhaps a dozen, sir,' Fairweather sighed.
'We could not possibly have witnessed all his casualties. He could have sustained double that number. More.'
'Anything is possible,' Fairweather agreed.
'Let us say between thirty and forty. Would you call that a fair estimate?'
'It is certainly an estimate, sir.'
'That would suggest we left them licking their wounds.'
'On a single-minded view of the matter, sir.'
'There is one other thing I neglected to ascertain. Did they reoccupy the island as you left?'
'I didn't dawdle to see, sir. There would be no point; it had most usefully served its purpose, as Canning and Carr might testify.'
'It would seem they died well.'
'Extremely well, sir. They are extremely dead.'
'So,' Whitmore summed up, 'the enemy neither attempted to reoccupy the ground from which we retired, nor to follow us by a single yard. It is reasonable to conclude that we left him dazed, counting casualties, in full retreat. In short, we appear to have gone off with the honours of war.'
'We are all grateful for that news, sir,' Fairweather said. 'I trust the colony's politicians are as appreciative.'
'I shall most certainly report that all credit is due my officers and men, but for whose entreaties I should never have thought to pursue Kooti so far.'
'That could be construed as a shade generous, sir.'
Herrick, to Whitmore's rear, could be seen trying to kill a tired smile.
'Even so,' Whitmore went on, 'I must be blunt about the squalid aspect of this affair. I mean the departure of the Poverty Bay people. It is my duty to make clear that their defection rendered it impossible to press home such advantage as we won. Canning and Carr might still be with us this morning.'
'I have to observe, sir, that Poverty Bay has colonists devilish enough to argue that point. Such devil's advocates could press the view that this expedition would have suffered no casualties at all had Poverty Bay's experience of Kooti been heeded.'
'Are you,' Whitmore asked sharply, 'one who would urge such a view?'
'I remain weary spectator, sir.'
'You deceive yourself,' Whitmore judged. And walked off abruptly.
Herrick drew breath and said, 'I do not believe it. Two captains dead. Graves marking our retreat. Too many wounded to manage. Holy hill never seen and half our natives to be numbered with Kooti. Another victory like that and we can all pack our bags for Mother England. And should there be query about pushing so far and perilously into the interior, then the misguided zeal of officers and men can be blamed. And not least the mutinous colonists of Poverty Bay.'

'That, Herrick, is called protecting the flanks.'

'You want my opinion? Whitmore will speak well of you in his report.'

'Probably,' Fairweather said. 'An officer liable to spread the word that he has seen his commander with his trousers down must be either blackened or wooed. Whitmore seems currently for wooing. I must expect some colonial medal. If Kooti is now converting the Tuhoe, then a great many medals are due for quick minting.'

'Would you?' Herrick asked. 'Would you spread the word that you had seen him with his trousers down?'

'I should not make a point of it. Not when I have had mine rather vexingly soiled, and more than once, in the past two days.'

'That's a relief,' Herrick said. 'I thought the problem was my own.'

The march to the coast resumed through forest and gorge. Men lurched and fell and had to be helped; the pace was pained and halts frequent. Impatience with human frailty was apparent on the part of their commander, also the desire to put more miles between his force and Kooti's. Whitmore might draw energy from phrasing his report; others found the well of vigour dusty. They came to the riverside site where horses had been left. There they met a belated Major Biggs, with provisions and an embarrassing supply of ammunition.

'What happened?' he asked with awe.

'We administered a sound thrashing,' Whitmore disclosed. 'One Kooti won't forget in a hurry.'

Biggs made bold effort to reconcile the intelligence with Whitmore's bandaged and hobbling band, and the litters of wounded.

'That makes matters awkward,' he said. 'The word from the government is that the prisoners are to be placated, and not pursued into inaccessible territory.'

'Placated?' Whitmore glowered. 'Not pursued?'

'They are to be given to understand that nothing will be held against them, except for those who might have committed some atrocity. Others are to have unconditional pardon and opportunity to vent grievances. It is all, I must confess, akin to the course originally urged upon me by Fairweather.'

'Too late now,' Whitmore pronounced.

'I can see that,' Biggs said bleakly.

Meanwhile, Whitmore's column had advanced with spirit on Biggs' packhorses. Men were breaking open bags and hungrily plundering; bottles of rum were lifted high and borne from the scramble.

'The escape from the Chathams has been avenged,' Whitmore said, 'and your own shameful escapade. Had we the numbers we could have had Kooti pleading for return to captivity. Your Poverty Bay deserters have much to answer for.'

'Unfortunately,' Biggs said, 'Poverty Bay colonists were, as you know, within their rights.' Still perplexed, he added, 'I fail, sir, to see Captains Canning and Carr.'

'Dead,' Whitmore said. 'I shall make it plain to the government where responsibility falls.'

Biggs was shaken.

'Further,' Whitmore said, 'I shall make equally plain that it would be a kindness to relieve you of your job in Poverty Bay. To cut our losses in that cantankerous region.'

'You shall argue that?' Biggs said feebly.

'As distasteful duty,' Whitmore insisted.

'I was hoping for something more, sir.'

'Doubtless you were, Biggs. Alas.'

'I mean, sir, in the event that your expedition fell short of its mark.'

'Fell short, man?' Whitmore asked with vehemence.

'It would appear to be the case, sir, that Kooti has not been apprehended. Naturally I must now hope that additional militia, or desirably armed constabulary, will be stationed in Poverty Bay so long as Kooti remains at large. Perhaps, sir, under your personal command.'

'You have a sunny sense of humour, Biggs.'

'Colonists could be extremely vulnerable,' Biggs protested. 'Kooti might ride out of the mountains.'

'In which case call upon me by all means, Biggs. I should delight in a final reckoning with the fellow on open ground.'

'You are talking of our farms, sir. Of families at risk.'

'The problem is one you made. To be frank, I think your fears pathetic. Kooti is not to be reckoned with for some months, if at all. My report to the government will read accordingly.'

Whitmore considered the cloudy sky, as if to determine whether there was more rain in the offing, and at length walked away.

Biggs said, 'You might prevail upon him, Fairweather. We cannot be left.'

'I have been failing to prevail on all concerned for some weeks,' Fairweather said. 'It might be more painless to believe what Colonel Whitmore believes.'

'Do you believe it?'

'No. But I am not Colonel Whitmore.'

'He cannot either.'

'Yesterday perhaps not. Today I would swear to it.'

'There are facts,' Biggs argued. 'You have all suffered severely. There are dead. It could not, it seems, be worse.'

'On the contrary,' Fairweather said. 'Worse is the Tuhoe announcing themselves the last lost tribe of Israel and flocking to shed foreskins for Kooti.'

'Is that how you see it?'

'It is how I would sooner not.'

'Then he'll be the death of us,' Biggs sighed.

'Kooti?'

'Whitmore,' Biggs said.

Fires had been lit. Rum revived men as meat cooked. There were soon intestinal cramps and showers of vomit as they overburdened their bellies. Yet there was occasion; and relief. These were men who had survived forest and Maori fire. Whitmore's decorative version of events became more acceptable with a warmed gut. Fairweather and Herrick sat beyond the commotion.

'Where now for you?' Herrick asked.

'Where hell is not,' Fairweather said.

'A woman?'

'I do have some fancy of that kind,' Fairweather admitted. 'I am an extremely weak man.'

'I understand your condition to be endemic among soldiery, and more especially after combat.'

'You are finding excuses, Herrick. I have never relied on the inconvenience of combat for arousal.'

'One woman in particular?'

'Gentlemen never tell, Herrick. Each to his own garden.'

'I hesitate to say so, but your company has almost made this misery worthwhile.'

'Take that as mutual. And you?'

'I shall return to polishing this jewel in the imperial crown.'

'You may feel loss pushing a pen. Never quite the honourable son of empire again.'

'It sounds like cynicism talking. Or rum.'

'There is a German philosopher of war I read when I had a morbid passion for his subject. He argues that the play of probability and chance makes war a free activity of the soul.'

'Free?' Herrick said.

'Within the limits of flesh.'

'Surely,' Herrick protested, 'art frees the soul more.'

'Not in my imperfect view of the matter. My life is not on the line. Merely my purse.'

'You are a complicated fellow,' Herrick observed.

'What does that mean?'

'That I am glad I am not you,' Herrick said.

Biggs could be seen in fresh and intemperate conversation with Whitmore. Biggs was still protesting Poverty Bay's need for protection. Whitmore was unmoved.

'So this,' Herrick said, 'is our parting of the ways.'

'For true friends there is never parting,' Fairweather said. 'By way of a commemorative dinner, minus champagne, what would you say to more bacon and biscuit?'

Whitmore decided on overnight camp. Men were too boisterous and bloated to be pushed through the dark; there was risk of injury and drowning, or of losing further men to the forest and Kooti. Kooti appeared to be much on the colonel's mind when he ordered a doubling of pickets and, on third thought, a tripling. He roamed the camp fretfully and asked if Fairweather thought the location safe.

'Tolerably,' Fairweather said. 'If Kooti has the will left to repay his hiding, it would seem he has passed up his chance.'

Whitmore grunted, then ordered silence and fast extinguishing of fires. There was equally swift extinction of spirits. In the dark the river took on daunting rumble; air became colder and trees blacker. Silence prevailed so far as animal function permitted: men pissed, retched, belched and farted. They were also felled in brutal contest with overhanging branches.

Fairweather pulled a dank blanket over himself. Larkin, just back from picket, was attempting rest too. 'I detest playing prophet,' Fairweather said, 'but I predict this night's sleep doomed from the outset.'

'Not for me, sir,' Larkin said, and soon after confirmed it with an aweing snore.

In the middle of the night, surely its darkest hour, a couple of pickets halted a wild boar's nocturnal ramble. Taking exception, the boar snorted and bellowed into the camp before intelligently careering clear. There was snorting and bellowing of far more ferocity as Whitmore called men to arms. Militia thudded to right and left in the mounting racket. Horses whinnied, broke loose and stampeded. Panicky shots produced more; a picket was carried into camp with a leg wound, and the corpse of a perforated horse found. That was the least of several alarms. At dawn the campsite was all bristling rifles and red-eyed men.

'I felt more comfortable on the island,' Herrrick said.

'You must stifle surprise,' Fairweather warned. 'In the official version we may just have repelled more of Kooti's killers. And without grievous loss.'

'Speak for yourself,' Herrick said. 'I shall never find that night's slumber again.'

Separation came later that morning. Whitmore, Herrick and the men of Hawke's Bay had to take an easterly course homeward; Fairweather, Larkin, Biggs and men of the packhorse team were to ride a northerly route to Poverty Bay.

With matters of significance on mind, Whitmore was not inclined to ceremony. 'I trust you have safe passage,' he told Biggs.

Biggs waited for more. There was no more. Finally he said, 'If I may, sir, it is the subject of safety I should like to raise with you one last time. Poverty Bay's safety, sir.'

'We have reviewed that subject sufficiently,' Whitmore ruled. 'You are becoming tedious, man. If your colonists are so deficient in character, set about raising morale.'

'How?' Biggs asked.

'By example,' Whitmore said. 'Start by forgetting your fears.'

Biggs was silenced. Fairweather and Larkin shook hands with Herrick. Fairweather then found his hand in Whitmore's grip.

'We have shared much, Fairweather,' the colonel said.

'It has all been most stirring, sir,' Fairweather agreed.

'If I have one regret about our excursion, Fairweather, it is that no scribe is likely to do justice to our difficult experience.'

'I conceive that as a likelihood too, sir.'

'I trust that should any such scribe approach you, in the near or far future, you will endeavour to give fair account of all parties concerned. And of the difficulties.'

'I should make much of the difficulties, sir,' Fairweather promised. 'Otherwise the fact is that my memory is going fast. I now find it a problem to distinguish one action from another.'

'There was only the one,' Whitmore objected.

'I mean, sir, that in fatigue it becomes difficult to distinguish Major Biggs' engagement from your own. They shape already as one; I make a most unreliable witness.'

Whitmore had to consider whether he found this acceptable, and appeared to conclude that on balance he must. 'Despite your apparent inclination, Fairweather, there is still a future for you in this colony. But you would do well to put Poverty Bay behind you.'

'That is something I don't need to be told twice, sir.'

'Agricultural qualities to the contrary, the place is well named. An impoverishment of spirit, Fairweather. Let the likes of Biggs sink in that cesspit. Should you make your way to Hawke's Bay, by any chance, I may do more than make you welcome. I could be of a mind to put material advancement in your path.'

'I shall remember that, sir,' Fairweather said, with less and less comfort. A bribe? Anyway Whitmore was distinct in not wanting hair nor hide of Fairweather near Poverty Bay.

'Do remember it, Fairweather. Do.'

Biggs and Larkin were a little way off, horsed, and waiting with Fairweather's pony. Fairweather set off toward them and saw Biggs' tragic face; he abruptly reversed course and faced Whitmore again.

'There is one other thing, sir,' he began. 'I should be obliged if on second thought you lent a compassionate ear to Major Biggs' concerns. I should part company with Poverty Bay more peaceful of mind. If Kooti's warrior spirits survive the winter, there may be further vexations in store. There are accounts still unsettled.'

'Your point is muddy, man.' Whitmore's irritability rose to the occasion.

'If the people of Poverty Bay, sir, were left defenceless, it could be seen as an invitation to Kooti to romp back into that region. In which case it could also be said, by those of a mind to say so, that people were being used as tethered goats to tempt Kooti on to clear ground.'

'It could be said?'

'Perhaps would be, sir.'

Whitmore might have been outmanoeuvred; he was not yet outgunned. 'I should hope, Fairweather, that you were not one of those of a mind to say so.'

'I should hope not also, sir. Some thoughts are unthinkable.'

There was a pause which grew longer.

Whitmore sighed, 'I take it you have said all you mean to say, Fairweather.'

'It would seem so, sir,' Fairweather decided.

'Good. Then I trust we never meet again in other than amicable circumstance.'

Whitmore urged his horse forward. Fairweather watched the colonel's back recede along the cheerless trail to Hawke's Bay, until sure it was gone, and then joined Larkin and Biggs.

16

The shadow and slime of the forest had an end. There were clumps of palm, slopes of low fern, and then growing vistas of bright sea and green plain, pastured animals and distant dwellings. The sun had warmth.

'Poverty Bay seems fair substitute for civilization after all,' Fairweather observed.

'Tell Whitmore,' Biggs said.

He was still smarting.

'And you, Larkin?' Fairweather asked. 'How do you feel?'

'Alive,' Larkin said.

They steered their horses downhill, crossed several small creeks, and then passed a nondescript native village. Habitations were not of generous dimension, and mostly ramshackle; a medley of European and Maori construction.

'Patutahi,' Biggs said. 'I never know how things stand here. Some are for us, some against.'

A few villagers rode out to inspect the muddy party of colonists passing; they held their horses at a tactful distance.

'We are not winning friends,' Fairweather said. 'They seem to know what has happened.'

'Kooti may well have sent messengers,' Biggs said. 'They would move faster and more sure-footed than we.'

Fairweather heard his name called. 'Hori? Hori Fair Weather?'

One of the Maoris parted from his companions and galloped toward Fairweather. A skinny youth with vast smile and scarred face.

'All I need,' Fairweather sighed. 'Hamiora Pere the comedian, no less.'

'*Rere,*' Hamiora reminded him. 'Big bloody *rere*. I find you the waterfall.'

'Of course I remember,' Fairweather said.

'You my big bloody friend,' Hamiora said. 'Very damn hello, Hori Fair Weather.'

'To you likewise, Hamiora.'

Larkin was too tired to take interest. But Biggs looked askance as Hamiora rode alongside them.

'You keep well, Hori?'

'I have kept better, Hamiora. My compliments on your *Ingaringi*. You have begun to turn a fine phrase.'

'Where you been?' Hamiora asked. Perhaps innocently, perhaps not so.

'In difficulty,' Fairweather said. 'Perhaps you have heard.'

Biggs whispered, 'See what you can learn. The boy is a lout, but he may know something.'

'Difficulty?' Hamiora repeated.

'A thing of many guns. I think you know.'

'Kooti?' Hamiora said obligingly.

'Quite. Kooti.'

'Ah.' Hamiora's smile was less certain.

Fairweather asked, 'What do your people think of Kooti now? Your village. Your *kainga*. Do they think Kooti good or bad?'

'Good? Bad?' Hamiora weighed one word, then the other.

'They must think one thing or the other,' Fairweather persisted.

Hamiora looked from Fairweather to Biggs, and back to Fairweather again; he did not speak.

'He is a fool,' Biggs pronounced. 'We are wasting our time.'

'Wait', Fairweather said. Then, to Hamiora, 'Speak not to please Hori Fairweather. Speak true. *Tika*.'

'E tika?'

'Very damn *pono*.'

'They think,' Hamiora said with difficulty, 'no thing or the other. Not good, not bad. They think Kooti is big.'

'And clever?'

'Big,' Hamiora said.

'And what do you think? You, Hamiora Pere?'

Hamiora was silent.

'Come,' Fairweather said.

'I think Kooti is no more a *tutua*.'

'Then we are agreed, Hamiora Pere. Kooti is most certainly not a nothing. Nor does he mean to be again.'

Hamiora was pleased to have given satisfaction, though Biggs was far from happy.

'You must excuse us, Hamiora,' Fairweather went on. 'We have travelled far and need peace. We meet again soon, perhaps.'

'You are my friend more?' Hamiora asked, rather anxious.

'A man who speaks *tika* always shall be,' Fairweather promised. 'A man who speaks *tika* is no *tutua* either.'

Hamiora wheeled his horse away. 'Then I think we meet more, Hori Fair Weather. Today very bloody goodbye.'

They rode on. Fairweather said brisk farewells to Biggs and Larkin at the settlement of Matawhero and continued alone toward Turanga; he was free to acknowledge himself depleted. A giddy fit grew with first sight of the port; herald of perhaps postponed fever. When he set foot in his dwelling the ground shifted underfoot and delirium began.

Soon, or so he remembered it later, there were cool female hands. He might have wished a reunion less emasculated. The Ruakituri river became leaden dream; even Poverty Bay passed him by.

It was days before coherence came. More days passed before Meri said from his bedside, 'You still choose not to talk of it.'

'I should sooner talk to you. You make a competent nurse.'

'You are different,' she said.

'The ill are always different. They are, the saying goes, not themselves.'

'The illness is leaving, yet you are not the man I know.'

'Who, then?'

She shrugged. 'Someone harder. I wish to know why.'

'Men tend to become so without the softness of woman. All the native ugliness of the male has rein.'

'You have more to say,' she insisted.

'You may have. I have not.'

'I shall win in the end, you know.'

'I am not sure I care for a woman who wins. As the weaker sex men must be granted illusion. Otherwise they wilt on the human vine; their gaudy flower fertilizes nothing. Then where would women be? Pass me that brandy.'

'When you tell me what is wrong.'

'Nothing that cannot be cured with a little fertilizing.'

'One thing at a time.'

'The brandy, then. You make a sinister habit of hiding the bottle.'

'You might be still better if you talked freely. The illness may now be less in your body. It is still in your mind.'

'You are quite a physician. What next? Some vile Maori potion?'

'I have used all those. Stewed flax. Berries. Leaves. You did not notice.'

'Thank God,' he said.

'For the body,' she explained.

'I see where your preference resides.'

'You shouted, you raved. I think something still burns.'

There was a long silence.

'Very well,' he said. 'The brandy.'

'One sip,' she said.

'And of you?'

'Later. One thing leads to another. You would escape with nothing said.'

'It was a fair ploy,' he lamented. 'And it seems my last.'

He managed a respectable gulp before she grabbed back the bottle. 'Now,' she said. 'Talk.'

'Four walls to keep out winter wind,' he said. 'A roof to hold off hellish rain. No wading through mud to see to the posting of pickets. Food and drink for the asking. And you. It seems somewhat excessive.'

'What did you do?'

'It is what I didn't. I thought to tamper with the inevitable, bring it to heel. Instead I helped fashion it. Fate enslaves all.'

'What was inevitable?'

'Kooti.'

'Kooti is only Coates,' she said.

'On one view of the matter. It did not serve reliably for long.'

She was quiet.

'Now,' he suggested. 'Tell me what you know.'

'What I see. It went well for Kooti, badly for you.'

'I am more interested in what you have heard.'

'The same, only Maori. The morning tide was his.'

'That suggests he may make an unwholesome day of it.'

'It is the word from the mountains.'

'What else trickles down?'

'He preaches that the star of Israel is in the ascendant. He reads from the Book of Joshua. Where Joshua says the Lord hath driven out great nations and strong.'

'You seem wonderfully informed.'

'Maoris make a feast of informing each other. The more gossip a Maori knows, the more mana. Some say that if Kooti had not been hurt, no colonist would have escaped.'

'Hurt?'

'A leg wound. It slowed him.'

Fairweather considered that. There were two possibilities. The second was a carbine discharged by Larkin.

'I require further brandy,' he pronounced.

'It upsets you?'

'I prefer to think of Kooti in a mood of tranquil rejoicing. Hurt creatures of the wild are not notorious for social graces.'

'You hunted him.'

'It is moot who was huntsman. I retain the memory of residing in a snare. Our departure lacked much in dignity. At least it is over.'

'It does not seem so for you.'

'The considered colonial view is that he is best left alone. And my late commander seems persuaded that we made a quick Maori breakfast of Kooti's men.'

'What do you think?' she asked.

'As much as a soldier ever knows. The price of everything, and the value of nothing.'

'I still see one,' she said.

'From that distance? Never. Come closer.'

'Better not. I should fear for you.'

'This soldier has lately earned a glorious death.'

'Must you win with words?'

'The way the best battles are won.'

'Move over,' she said.

She was gentle beside him. His tide, when it came, rose opulently high. 'All is not lost,' he disclosed. 'There is a God.'

'Quiet,' she said. 'You have already told most of Poverty Bay.'

'Two needs,' he said, when she departed for further provisions from Trader Read's. 'A more considerable supply of brandy. Also a Bible, by fair means or foul.'

'Repentance?' she asked.

'When my vision is less impaired, I might meander among the pages of the prophet Joshua. Since he is not sprightly reading, I may require the brandy to counter deep lassitude.'

'What could Joshua tell you?'

'What Kooti may be trying to.'

'There have been others trying to tell you something,' she said. 'I have had to chase away visitors.'

'Biggs?'

'And others. One called Larkin. A rough man.'

'And good one.'

'Also a boy. A Maori boy.'

Fairweather did not have to think long. 'Hamiora.'

'He seemed to think he had some right to you too. They all do.'

'And they are wrong, I take it.'

'I should know,' she said.

With Meri gone, Fairweather sat weakly in sunlight, and watched canoes pass on the river. Poverty Bay was warming with spring; plum and apple trees were blossoming, peach too. Time to take leave.

The feeling was confirmed when Biggs arrived, tethered his horse, and sat companionably by his side. 'For a time,' Biggs said, 'we feared the battle of the

Ruakituri might be claiming another fatality. I have a message from Captain Herrick in Hawke's Bay. He also wishes speedy return to health. I shall reassure him in my next communication. Your recovery will be vast relief to us all.'

Fairweather was interested in where Biggs' emphasis fell. 'Vast, Major Biggs?'

'Naturally. You have been a valued comrade in arms.'

'Of whom further use might be made?'

'We must trust not,' Biggs said.

'You must indeed,' Fairweather said. 'I am filthied to surfeit in a colonial squabble which need never have been.'

'We all know that now,' Biggs agreed.

'Wisdom after the event does not raise dead. Nor heal wounds.'

'It should please you to know that there is definitely to be no further offensive action against Kooti. The government, perhaps, has made the right decision for the wrong reasons. Whitmore's account of putting Kooti to rights has been warmly embraced by politicians. It relieves them of need for more martial expenditure. Not just for offensive measures. For defensive too.'

'Whitmore made no case for defence?'

'Had he done so, of course, his triumph might have seemed less than complete. He cannot say in the one breath that he left the enemy trampled, and in the next urge Poverty Bay's need of men and money. The two do not square.'

'I should have known,' Fairweather said.

'Moreover, he has recommended that Poverty Bay's militia be disbanded in disgrace. He says that in the unlikely event of Kooti ever showing his face again, he, Whitmore, will deal personally and decisively with the fellow.'

'Major Biggs, I prefer not to know.'

'I prevail upon you to persist longer here. We need you.'

'I need myself more.'

'I am empowered to make it worth your while,' Biggs said.

'How many Maori acres this time?'

'I mean monetary remuneration for inconvenience suffered.'

'You have already told me the government is voting no money.'

'This is from well-meaning and appreciative colonists.'

'You overstate your case, Major Biggs. Most of your colonists can ill afford to pool pennies to keep me in my present elegance. I imagine we are talking of Trader Read.'

'Read would be a substantial contributor,' Biggs confessed.

'Thank you,' Fairweather said. 'You have just allowed me to escape with a tatter or two of self-respect; it makes a late bonus.'

'You confuse,' Biggs said.

'I celebrate, Major Biggs. It seems I have discovered the depth to which I cannot sink. A drunkard, yes. A fornicator, often. A coward on occasion. A godless man always. But a hireling never. And especially not of a drunken freebooter in Poverty Bay.'

'I am not one to argue Read's character is of the highest,' Biggs allowed. 'But he has more at risk than most. And more unease.'

'No one could say it unearned.'

'It is not for me to pass stern judgement.'

'Whitmore might be right. Disband the militia. Evacuate all of European blood from Poverty Bay. Let Read, if he will, fend for himself. And things run their course.'

'You cannot be serious.'

'More and more,' Fairweather said.

'Much of the colony could be equally abandoned to the Maori.'

'I fail to feel anguish.'

'Others of us have our future here; families too. And no other life. We cannot voyage back to Britain. We should be impoverished strangers in our own land.'

'As Kooti in his?'

'After all you have been through, you still seem to sympathize.'

'With less heart for the subject. And when there is not better to contemplate. Fortunately, at this very moment, that is not the case.'

Meri could now be seen, paddling strongly upriver in a canoe laden with provisions. Biggs watched her too.

'I see,' he said. He could not forgo adding, 'Life is long but lust is short.'

'The reverse is my impression, Major Biggs. Convey my respects to sweet Mrs Biggs; I hope her condition remains no problem.'

'It cannot be more than a week or two now,' Biggs said. 'Emily remains quite saintly in all our trials, and despite my absences.'

'You are a fortunate man, sir.'

'I know it.' There was a long and painful pause before Biggs added, 'The fact is that without Emily, and our child to be, I might not find the strength to persist here either.'

Talk of a man sapped. Fairweather was dismayed; he preferred Biggs to be Biggs.

Biggs went on, 'There are, as you will doubtless soon hear, Europeans departing Poverty Bay on every passing vessel. Abandoning land and livestock and dwellings. Most are poor of spirit, lacking the courage of their convictions as colonists; people we can well do without. The riddle is that you, who have nothing to abandon, are one we cannot do without.'

'Material appearances to the contrary, Major Biggs, I do have something it vexes to leave here; I may also be lacking the courage of my convictions.'

He watched Meri as she paddled nearer and beached the canoe.

'Then it is better that I distract you no longer,' Biggs judged.

'On the whole,' Fairweather acknowledged.

Biggs retrieved his horse and rode away before Meri arrived.

'What did he want?' she asked.

'Me.'

'Does he have you?'

'Tell me what you think.'

'That is all right, then,' she said.

'It seems he has fewer colonists to muster.'

'No schooner leaves empty now,' she confirmed.

'Then peace may prevail. Kooti can make spirited return to Poverty Bay without firing a shot.'

'Easy for you to say. You are not Maori.'

Her vehemence surprised. 'My apologies,' he said.

'A Poverty Bay Maori cannot pack and leave on a schooner. He has nowhere to go. Some are even less keen on Kooti than the colonists.'

'Your brother Matiu for one?'

'And others with no wish to be children of Israel.'

'I see. A Maori Smith cannot a Cohen make.'

'It is not amusing.'

'Forgive me. It is just that I still cannot give Kooti's pious tantrum all the respect he might wish. His guns yes. His theology no. I imagine it might have begun as an evening's entertainment for prisoners cooped on the Chathams. Then, perhaps with purloined rum, it may have got out of hand.'

'Others know it as serious.'

'Don't talk of others. Rather of you.'

'I find it difficult enough to be Christian,' she said.

'Because of me?'

'Many now see me as no better than the whores of the port. Your half Maori wench.'

'Many? Or merely Matiu?'

'Matiu is not alone in his feeling.'

'You no longer go with your brothers to church?'

'Not so often now.'

'I am sorry.'

She considered that for a time. 'I should be too,' she said.

17

It was a September of hybrid weather, confused harbingers. The sun could toast. Then remnant winds of winter nagged; rain crashed. Fallen blossom frosted the river's tides; the ardour of early corn was cooled. Yet cows calved, lambs fattened, earth broke to the plough; and people, for the most part, found Kooti less a shadow with a day's labour in hand. Rumour said the Tuhoe were converting to Kooti. Rumour also said the Tuhoe were not. It was said that Kooti's anger was undimmed. It was also said he lived devout as the day was long, his rage in retirement.

When Meri judged Fairweather fit to care for himself, she returned upriver to the Smith land to help Matiu and Pita with planting. In her absence Fairweather took a shaky turn or two around the landscape on horse. He found himself shivering in the sunlight; he trusted his fitful aches were the residue of fever. He felt need to make sense of himself, and it seemed he still could not.

It also seemed he was still in Poverty Bay.

On such an excursion Major Biggs rose suddenly alongside. For once his bony face framed a smile.

'I bring news that could hardly be bettered,' he said.

'The government is giving protection,' Fairweather suggested. He felt relief; it proved premature.

'Our blessings still come singly,' Biggs said. 'Maoris here are changing their tune about land confiscation. Most are now disposed to part with the land we want.'

'My congratulations, Major Biggs.'

'I am in Kooti's debt; his reappearance has ended two years of strife and despair.'

'You surprise me.'

'It's an ill wind which blows no good. Sober Maoris fear that should Kooti make further trouble, involving fellow tribesmen, there could be even larger confiscation. Better to part with what they must now, rather than lose more later.'

'Then may they have a gambler's luck.'

'Of course,' Biggs said, 'there is more than meets the eye. Chiefs know that Kooti could erode their traditional power should his confounded religion spread. Some Maori families, not notable for religious practice in the past, have taken to singing psalms with fervour. It cannot be coincidence. You may recall that senior Maoris were as convinced as colonists about the desirability of Kooti's deportation.'

'I am more inclined to recall that Kooti's religion was mostly the rum trade, getting the better of Trader Read, and the merry pleasures of women and money. Innocent days, Major Biggs.'

'Perhaps.' Biggs was grudging.

'An odd pass when the singing of psalms is seen as malign.'

'Those psalms, as you well know, are now associated with a man who can play fast and loose with a great many guns. Responsible Maoris see colonists leaving in fright, and now panic that they may be abandoned to Kooti. Another reason for surrendering land. The prospect of fresh acres should check the flow of colonists from the region; the risk in remaining here may seem more acceptable.'

'Poverty Bay begins to seem a gamester's carnival, sir.'

They had descended to the riverside, where their horses nibbled on rank grass.

'You have not given further thought to remaining?' Biggs asked.

'Not conspicuously, Major Biggs. No.'

'Fertile Poverty Bay land will be worth much more on the market in another year or two, perhaps double or triple present values. The prospects even short-term are promising. Alternatively such land can be profitably leased.'

Fairweather lifted his eyes to consider river and plain.

'You are still not to be tempted,' Biggs concluded.

'Try Kooti,' Fairweather said. 'Test his faith with enough acres and he might see that Jehovah offers an impecunious route to salvation. He could always plead a message on a mountain top, perhaps an eleventh commandment. Thou shalt profit as a colonist, say. His Jews might be overnight gentiles.'

'You are not serious.'

'In a middling way.'

'There could be uproar from colonist and Maori alike.'

'Then you would best woo Colonel Whitmore with a lion's share of land. The result might be magical. He would be winning arms, money and men from bewildered politicians. Poverty Bay could soon be as safe as London's Tower. Your situation demands that either Kooti be nobbled or Whitmore nullified. One or the other.'

'I am doing my best in connection with Whitmore. I communicate with the government almost daily, and not just to counter his stigmatizing of Poverty Bay's people as cowards, down and outs, and drunkards. Also to emphasize that his appraisal of Kooti's condition may err on the side of optimism.'

'Pleasantly put, Major Biggs.' Fairweather began to feel impatience. 'Might I, finally, inquire after Mrs Biggs?'

'She has perhaps only a week now,' Biggs said warmly. 'I shall tell her you were asking. She speaks of you often; it seems you made much impression.'

'So goes my fate,' Fairweather lamented. 'Only women see my worth.'

That night Meri was back sooner than expected. It seemed it was less easing of an absent heart's fondness than a response to matters domestic. 'Matiu,' she explained, 'would like words with you.'

'With me?'

'Very much.'

Fairweather had to consider this. 'Matiu,' he said, 'has always shown more inclination to nausea than speech in my presence.'

'Perhaps he regrets his rudeness now.'

'Meaning what?'

'You will have to let Matiu tell you.'

'You cannot?'

'Not altogether,' she said warily.

'A damned queer turnaround. Does he come to me, or do I go to him? What is Maori etiquette in these matters?'

'His suggestion is that I bring you for a social call tomorrow,' she said. 'Smith etiquette. We show our *pakeha* face. I have even baked a cake.'

'What is going on? Are there to be others present?'

'Only family,' she promised. 'At least try the cake.'

It was mostly as it had been on Fairweather's first visit. Linen, fine china, a tea service of silver; a table on the verandah, and sunlit river riding past. One difference was that Matiu and Pita were groomed and in dark suits, as if formal for church. In muddy boots and tired trousers, Fairweather felt altogether unkempt. Conversation was largely of climate and crops, with recent events avoided; Pita and Meri had less and less to say. At length, perhaps on some furtive signal from Matiu, they withdrew.

Matiu had still made no great effort to present an agreeable face. He looked at Fairweather across emptied cups and crumbs of cake. 'You have,' he said, 'had a difficult time.'

'It was short of an idyll,' Fairweather allowed.

'Word spreads. It seems you did your best to behave well.'

'That may be credited to training.'

'You tried to avert trouble.'

'I am afflicted with common sense on occasion.'

'There are some who appreciate what you did, or tried to. Much might have been worse.'

'Much might also have been postponed.'

Matiu made no answer; his gaze wandered away and was slow to return. Fairweather understood that their conversation had still to find its centre. It circled again.

'It was not, I think, what you came to Poverty Bay for,' Matiu said. 'It is now many months.'

'Seven or eight,' Fairweather agreed.

'It is not Kooti who has detained you this long.'

'I think that apparent.'

'You are fond of Meriana?'

'That needs no stating either.'

'She also, of course, is fond of you.'

'It is,' Fairweather said with caution, 'always gratifying to know that affection is reciprocated.'

'I have not been of a mind to take account of her feelings,' Matiu confessed.

'You have not?' Fairweather managed surprise.

'I did not see you as a suitable friend. I believed you might bring harm.'

'It was never my intention.'

'You had an intention?' Matiu was interested now.

'No more than a masculine disposition to make the most of her company.'

It appeared that Fairweather had refused a flank; Matiu looked frustrated.

'I wish you to know,' he said, 'that I have become more of a mind to take account of Meriana's affections.'

Fairweather might have been safer scouting the Ruakituri. 'That is most generous,' he said. 'I have no wish to be cause of family ill feeling.'

'I alone was the cause,' Matiu insisted.

'In Poverty Bay,' Fairweather suggested, 'there seems to have been reason for suspicion. Especially of passing strangers. They suddenly cease their passing. Worse, they cease to be strangers, yet never friends.'

'You are tactful in a Maori way.'

'Land is easily understood.'

Fairweather seemed to have struck rock. Matiu was silenced.

'Though men may appear to be discussing other things,' Fairweather suggested, 'it always seems to be land that is most in mind.'

Matiu was not moved to quibble. 'It could be so,' he acknowledged. He was more visibly Maori, much less a Smith, and evasive.

'I have the impression,' Fairweather pushed, 'that you are telling me more than is said.'

'Perhaps it is that I wish to say that our door is open to you. This house is.'

Fairweather was slow to understand, then unwilling to. 'I should be glad to visit again, in circumstances less constrained,' he said.

Matiu was involved in some large inner struggle. 'I mean,' he explained, 'that you might make this house your home.'

'It is difficult to know what to say,' Fairweather answered with truth. 'I wish to give no offence.'

'All will be understood,' Matiu promised.

'An answer cannot be given lightly. Not in a minute.'

'I should not expect it,' Matiu said obligingly. 'Not from a man of your standing.'

It seemed Fairweather was not to be found lacking on any score.

'Arrangement would be made for your comfort,' Matiu went on, 'and all wishes satisfied.'

In short, and translated, he was surely saying that Fairweather might bed nightly with Meri; no pretence needed.

'I shall take that into account,' Fairweather said.

'Your dwelling near the port,' Matiu persisted, 'is far from suitable for one like yourself. It has not always been easy or desirable for Meriana to visit you there.'

'The arrangement you suggest is by no means unsullied. It could be interpreted unfortunately; you might appear to be blessing the unseemly. It does not sit well with prevalent Christian thinking.'

'Christians of Maori blood,' Matiu said, 'take a more tolerant and traditional view.'

'When the situation arises?'

'As it has,' Matiu agreed.

'And you tell me that the situation now arisen is that I am seen differently? A better man than before?'

'You must believe it,' Matiu replied.

'I should like to,' Fairweather said.

Travelling downriver with the tide, he said to Meri, 'The cake was splendid.'

'Thank you,' she said. And paddled.

'It did not altogether sweeten the ambush.'

'Matiu said he alone should speak. He did not wish you to think that I had prevailed upon him.'

'Which was not the case?'

'It was not,' she said, and continued to paddle. Fairweather was content with the pace of the tide.

'All the more intriguing,' he said. 'There is more to this.'

'Perhaps,' she said with reluctance. 'I would not know.'

'At the least,' he said, 'Matiu seems set on making a more honourable man of me.'

'I cannot pretend to know Matiu's mind.'

'It requires no clairvoyance.'

Her paddling slowed and then ceased. The river fluttered against the canoe.

'Or would you sooner not talk of this?' he asked.

'I told Matiu he might be making a mistake. He would not listen. I am sorry.'

'No need. It gives this day colour.'

'We will not talk of it,' she decided, and paddled with new vigour.

Fairweather let a minute pass. 'Surprise never ceases,' he said. 'Not just Matiu. I have also seen Major Biggs parading jubilation. It seems some Maoris now plead for speedy confiscation lest Kooti complicate further. Biggs cannot believe his luck. Is it all true?'

'If Biggs says it is.'

'You cannot be unaware. Matiu has been opposed to Biggs in the matter, or so you have said.'

'Have I?' She had grown unpromisingly vague, perhaps set on proving that she could be as Maori as Matiu.

'Matiu would appear to have lost out to Biggs. He must be bitter.'

'Things are uncertain,' she said.

'That was not quite my drift.'

'It is time for you to paddle. Exercise will do you good.'

'It would do me more good to hear you speak without inhibition.'

'Tonight,' she said.

'That is different.'

'It is also better.'

'I should be last to deny it.'

'I should think not,' she said.

There was a mild dusk and a magic sunset. They finished their meal and sat in silence for a time. 'There is,' he said, 'a small local matter you might help me understand.'

'If I must,' she sighed.

'Your land. The Smith land. Is it seen as European or Maori?'

'It was of my mother's *hapu*. Her family's.'

'I am still unclear. Your father was a Yankee.'

'Happy just to live among my mother's people. When he deserted his ship they gave shelter. He wanted only my mother, not land in his name. He thought much, read much, and smoked his pipe. In most things he became Maori. He was never greedy for more.'

'I take your point.'

'Good,' she said, and seemed to think the subject finished.

It was not.

'So,' he said, 'you would appear to be telling me that the Smith land is Maori.'

'Yes,' she allowed.

'And therefore currently at risk?'

'It is not yet clear.'

'You leave me even less so.'

'My mother's *hapu* may surrender some traditional land. Yes.'

'Including, possibly, some Smith acres?'

'Possibly,' she said.

'Many or most of the Smith acres?'

'Possibly many. Perhaps most.'

Fairweather summed up, 'In retrospect it now seems a pity that your father was not a man more demanding. Had he embraced those acres along with your mother his children might be less troubled.'

'You could say it a pity,' she agreed. 'Matiu has.'

'I see,' he said. Or began to.

In bed he was subdued. 'What is wrong?' she asked finally.

'Matiu might have been more honest. You also.'

'I know what you are thinking,' she said.

'Then you must keep me advised. It seems I do not.'

She rolled away from him, and seemed to become smaller. Her voice was. 'You think we wish only to use you,' she said.

'Most in Poverty Bay seem anxious to find a use for me; I should have known there were no exceptions.'

'It is not true of me.' Her voice had diminished still more.

'Of Matiu?'

She was quiet. Also loyal.

'Perhaps,' he said, 'I should tell you what I surmise, for better or worse.'

'It is not necessary,' she protested.

'Mostly for worse, I conclude that my residence in the Smith household might go far toward retention of the surrounding Smith soil. Lawful matrimony even more so. It might be Fairweather land, at least in name. European and safe. Thereby making good your father's dereliction of the white man's duty. If I read the matter wrong, I am open to correction.'

He was not corrected. Minutes passed.

'Is it over?' she asked. 'Are we?'

'Damn Poverty Bay,' he said.

He woke early to a voice outside his walls. Meri sat up in fright.

He heard, 'Hori? Hori Fair Weather?'

To Meri he said, 'Relax. I know who it is.'

He pulled on trousers and tunic and went barefoot to his door. It opened to warm daylight. And Hamiora Pere holding a horse.

'Very bloody hello, Hori,' Hamiora said sunnily.

'What is it you want at this hour?' Fairweather asked.

'To talk,' Hamiora explained. 'I like *korero* with you.'

'I am not, Hamiora, much of a mind for *korero*. And not at this time.'

The boy's smile shrank; he lowered his eyes. 'I am sorry,' he said. 'I am a very big damn bugger.'

Fairweather relented. 'What is it, then? Be quick.'

'I think, Hori, you need many soldiers for Kooti now. Many.'

'You do?' Fairweather said wearily.

'I think you are soldier, Hori.'

'When I must be,' Fairweather said.

Hamiora heard no reservation. 'And I,' he argued, 'must be soldier also. I come to you.'

'I am the wrong man, Hamiora, to help in such a matter.'

'I help,' Hamiora said, still misunderstanding. 'I a very big bloody help. I help you, Hori. I find *rere* for you.'

'And I am grateful,' Fairweather conceded.

'I shoot. Bang. I shoot your gun well.'

'We do not speak of the same thing, Hamiora. Soldiering is more than tramping and camping and hunting. No. It is not happy business. Some would say bad.'

'Bad, Hori?'

'*Kino*. Very damn *kino*.'

Hamiora took the word personally. 'I not *kino*,' he protested. 'I very bloody good.'

'All the more reason, Hamiora, for you to go home to Patutahi and forget this.'

'Forget?'

'And be good. Better still, happy.'

'Patutahi is not happy, Hori. I think you need many soldiers now.'

'Not my business, Hamiora. Others arrange soldiers. Not I.'

Fairweather's negative theme at last found its way through the verbal haze. Hamiora sulked, and looked down at his grubby feet. Fairweather gripped the boy's shoulder.

'I am sorry,' he said. 'You make me feel a big bloody bugger too.'

Meri moved within the whare, making a distinct sound. Hamiora looked toward the open door, eyes fast cheeky again.

'You have woman?' he asked.

'And therefore not all the time in the world,' Fairweather said.

'Ah,' Hamiora said. 'Then I see you more, Hori.'

'And I shall doubtless you see again also, Hamiora.'

They shook hands. Hamiora scrambled bareback on to his horse and, after a last rueful gaze at Fairweather, rode away without looking over his shoulder. Meri emerged from the whare, a problem of more substance.

'You heard?' he asked.

'All,' she said. Her voice was dull.

'A droll little fellow. I might have been more receptive.'

'You said what you had to say.'

'Perhaps. Now I have this confounded feeling he was telling me something.'

'Like what?'

'I should have listened harder. Mostly to his excited story that many soldiers are now needed. If true, that means he may know something I don't.'

She was quiet.

'The Tuhoe have made up their minds,' he suggested. 'Perhaps the message of invincible Israel now rings from mountain to mountain.'

He saw her expression; he knew it true.

'When?' he said.

'A week,' she shrugged. 'A month. Does it matter to you?'

'That is for me to determine.' He felt a drag of gut. 'Nama?'

'Nama also. All the best Tuhoe fighting chiefs have declared for Kooti. They say that they have found another Maori who wars as well as they.'

'His religion?'

'It entertains them at their fires. And Kooti's way with women.'

'The most dedicated prophets put them aside.'

'He is now a man of many wives. He chooses from his followers. He tells their husbands that it is Jehovah's wish.'

'Thou shalt honour the prophet and see his seed is fruitfully sown?'

'It is not so humorous. Not for the women. Nor for their men.'

'I prefer to think of Kooti philandering rather than fighting. He might take a hint from the Tuhoe tale and refuse to risk the tool of the amorist's trade near the womanless fire of a war party. It also suggests Kooti might be the same, only more so.'

'Like you?' she asked.

'I am not best placed to judge that.'

'Very well,' she said. 'Now that you know all, do you wish to see me again?'

'I have generally been helpless in that regard. That seems not to have changed.'

'Good,' she said. Her smile went far to mend the morning. 'And Matiu?'

'In your case deception is easier to forgive. Beauty and honesty seldom agree. Tell Matiu I prefer men who speak their whole mind.'

'It is not easy for Matiu. He cannot confess fear.'

'Unnecessary. I know what I see. Colonists of Poverty Bay fear they will never get land. Maoris fear they will never hold it.'

'I mean fear of Kooti.'

'So. Now I know.'

'Matiu would feel safer with you in our house. We all would.'

'Had that been said, I might have interpreted matters more charitably. It makes Matiu more human.'

'It is being said now. Matiu sees you, after all, as a good man.'

'A good man with a gun?'

'A good man. What shall I tell him, then?'

'In the meantime, while I meditate,' Fairweather said, 'tell Matiu very bloody hello.'

Soon after Meri left, Fairweather found a deputation of three at his door. Sober Larkin, excitable Dodds, and taciturn Newman.

'We was wondering,' Larkin said, 'if you might see your way clear to helping again.'

'If another expedition, Larkin, you know my answer.'

'This is different,' Dodds said.

'Did Major Biggs send you?'

'Major Biggs is busy with a son and heir. Emily Biggs delivered last night. She had a time of it, I hear.'

'My question remains. I imagine fatherhood has not altogether unhinged Major Biggs. Did he send you?'

'We came for ourselves,' Newman insisted.

'The colonists around Matawhero have been talking this over,' Dodds explained. 'Talking you over.'

'And keeping colonists and their families safe,' Larkin said. 'It looks like Whitmore's done for us. We got no protection. Only what we manage ourselves. Whitmore gets Kooti's blood up, and leaves us to it.'

'It was, I recall, a Poverty Bay shot fired first.'

'It could have been forgot,' Dodds said. 'We didn't want to go on with it. We saw.'

'We know as you did your best, Mr Fairweather,' Newman said.

Larkin had no interest in post mortem. 'We been trying to organize ourselves, sir,' he explained. 'Patrols. Keeping watch. Looking for fires in the hills. It's what has to be done.'

'I thought you were fed to the teeth with Poverty Bay, Larkin.'

'Things might get better,' Larkin said obscurely.

'For us all,' Newman said.

'I imagine,' Fairweather said, 'we are talking of land.'

'We been waiting long enough,' Dodds said.

'It makes things worthwhile,' Newman agreed.

'So,' Larkin elaborated, 'we have to do things proper for protection.'

'Doing things proper is in Major Biggs' province,' Fairweather argued.

Newman spat on cue. 'He's got no idea,' he said. 'Biggs never has.'

'Too many things on his mind,' Dodds said. 'Reports to the government. Maps and boundaries. *Korero* with Maoris at all hours. Scab on his sheep. Now his wife and baby too. He doesn't know whether he's coming or going.'

'We need you, sir,' Larkin said. 'Things got to be done right.'

Fairweather looked at Larkin. Larkin looked back unblinking. Fairweather felt an old weakness. Fidelity nailed coffins tight.

'It could be said that I owe you, Larkin.'

'I'm not saying it, sir.'

'Then perhaps I must.'

'Something's got to be done, sir. I can't organize men how I'd like. They worry about their families and wander off. They got to learn to take orders. You and me, sir, we can work together. We can make them useful.'

'With enough cursing and kicking?'

'The better from you, sir. They know what you are.'

'How many men are we talking about, Larkin?'

'Never much more than a dozen, sir.'

'We are also talking about tens of thousands of acres of tree and mountain.'

'That's it, sir. A tall job.'

'Desperate,' Dodds said.

'Not if Kooti finds content in his current kingdom,' Fairweather suggested.

'He's no mountain Maori,' Dodds said.

'If the stories are true, carnal campaigning might hold unhappy passion for Poverty Bay in check. The best protection might be to arrange regular shipments of women and rum.'

'It's no joke for us,' Dodds said. 'We don't know what he's up to. Maybe he doesn't yet.'

'Look,' Fairweather said finally, 'I must think on all this.'

'If you would, sir,' Larkin said.

Late in the afternoon Fairweather took up the leather-bound Bible Meri had located. So far he had laboured through a score of chapters. The Book of Joshua was still not forthcoming; Fairweather had still to find the reference he wanted. The Lord hath driven out great nations and strong?

This time he found the words waiting. Chapter twenty-three. Verse nine.

As an hors-d'oeuvre, however, verse five had the most nutriment. *And the Lord, your God, he shall expel them from before you, and drive them from out of your sight; and ye shall possess their land, as the Lord your God hath promised unto you.*

Land? Alas the Canaanites; goodnight all enemies of Israel.

Fairweather reached for his carbine. It required oiling. So did he.

18

Next morning he rode to the settlement of Matawhero and took his respects to the Biggs' house. A colonist's wife was about kitchen duties; Biggs greeted Fairweather with pen in hand and steered him toward the marital bedroom. Then Biggs withdrew to continue applying pen urgently to paper. Emily Biggs was wan in her bed, child sleepy in arms, and heroically smiling. 'It is good of you to come,' she said. 'I hear you have had a difficult time also.'

'Less productively,' he said. 'I have nothing of joy to show for my confinement.'

'We are calling him George,' she said. 'Reginald wished for Albert, but I thought George more handsome as a name.'

'I have always found it tolerable,' Fairweather said. 'May this one be a fine, strapping and gallant fellow, unlike some mediocre namesakes.'

'Much is owed to you in this house,' she argued. 'Perhaps Reginald does not say it to you, but he does to me; he has several times sung your praises.'

'That is not easy to fathom. Your husband and I cannot often bring ourselves to agree.'

'You saved his life.'

'In not neglecting my own.'

'Reginald would have it otherwise. He talks of your level head. And of your taking the side of Poverty Bay colonists against Colonel Whitmore.'

'For once in my life I could enjoy the risk of enraging a superior. The colonies do afford pleasures.'

'You did what you did,' she said stubbornly; and looked into the tiny face of her child. 'I am glad we called him George. I knew you were important to us from the time you first set foot in this house. Perhaps it comes from my grandmother. She had the second sight.'

'It is something we could do with here.'

Her face shadowed. 'Reginald assures me that all will be safe.'

'Of course,' he said quickly. 'Major Biggs has a more commanding view of the matter. He sees the wood, and I but the trees.'

'There will be no more expeditions?'

'Not if I can help it.'

'That is relief,' she said. 'I sometimes fear Reginald might not tell the whole truth. I do not care to imagine myself a widow alone in this colony.'

'Never alone now. There is your son.'

'There is,' she agreed.

The child was quite asleep now.

'Would you,' she asked, 'care to hold him?'

'He might wake and take fright.'

'Not of you,' she promised.

Fairweather lifted the child awkwardly from her arms. Nursing it proved, after all, no great feat. 'Welcome to the world, young George Biggs,' he said softly.

The baby did not waken.

'He is a New Zealander,' Emily said. 'That is the extraordinary thing. Born of this country.'

'I daresay he will manage the notion. His children still more.'

'I mean,' she said, 'that he may never see England, or know it as home.'

'He has a brawny young land to call his own. He could go far. And further than elsewhere.'

'I cannot imagine it,' she said. 'I cannot imagine the future at all.'

'Young George is a fact to embrace,' he urged. 'All you need to.'

She smiled. 'You make it your business to bring comfort.'

'No effort in the presence of a new mother's pride.'

Confident now, Fairweather began to rock the child in his arms lightly.

'Would you wish one of your own?' she asked.

'He that has no children brings them up well. In short, I am selfish.'

'Never,' she said. 'My second sight again, perhaps. I see a good father and fine son to be. Also, I think, a New Zealander.'

He felt unease in his belly; and returned George Biggs to his mother. 'Love the child for her that bore it,' he said. 'You make a pretty mother, Emily Biggs.'

'And you must come again, George Fairweather,' she said boldly. 'You make my day sweet.'

Fairweather, in retreat, saw a woman; no longer a numb bride. He wished envy away.

Conversation with Biggs had less pleasure. He announced himself available to scout and patrol. 'I will make it no secret,' he said. 'Some of your unhappy colonists did much to win me over. They seem at sixes and sevens. Their need for leadership is evident.'

'True,' Biggs said with relief.

'On the other hand, their need for security is no greater than that of many Maoris here.'

'I could not have hoped for more,' Biggs said.

'In which case you may listen with tolerance to my conditions. An understanding must be arrived at. No unnecessary provocation to be offered Kooti and his kind. Not even to suspected sympathizers here if they burgeon with praise of Jehovah. Live and let live.'

'You would be well placed to see to that,' Biggs pointed out. 'In any case we no longer have the numbers to provoke anyone.'

'So long as it is understood. And approved.'

'It is understood,' Biggs said.

'My second condition may not be much to your liking. I am talking of land. You will take no advantage of current Maori fears.'

'If they press land upon me,' Biggs protested, 'what am I to do?'

'Tell them to think twice. Until now Maoris have seen you only as a zealous taker of land. Let them see a more sympathetic side. A man with displeasing duties, but with a heart.'

Some anguish apparent, Biggs promised, 'I shall do my best.'

'You must,' Fairweather said. 'If Kooti learns that more of Poverty Bay is passing into colonists' hands, he may judge the moment desirable to make muscular return before numbers are against him. All to do with land must be slowed.'

'It will not be easy,' Biggs said. 'Like learning to walk backwards and yet keep my balance.'

'Think on Emily and young George. The balance will come. Are we understood?'

'It seems we must be,' Biggs said.

That afternoon Meri came downriver. His dwelling was stripped, his possessions packed.

'What is this?' she asked.

'Decision,' he said.

'You are leaving?'

'If the door to the Smith house remains open.'

She embraced him. Fairweather looked beyond her shoulder. 'It must mean only what it seemed to,' he said. 'I am not to be relied on as more than a guest.'

'That is agreed,' she said.

'I seem to have business beyond the call of whim,' he explained. 'I need a base with comfort. Matiu's need coincides with my own.'

'And mine?'

'That can be accommodated too.'
'Promises,' she said.

Located in the Smith homestead, Fairweather prepared for his first patrol. He gathered all that might be useful for martial purpose, checked and fired his carbine, also a revolver, and counted out ammunition; he fitted new boots and borrowed a thicker blanket. Matiu remained agreeable; Pita innocently conversational. Meri watched as he packed paper, pencils and paints and filled space still free in his saddlebags with two bottles of brandy.

'It looks more a picnic,' she said.

'And I shall make it one,' he promised.

Last, he squeezed in the Bible.

'So,' she said. 'I should be grateful to Kooti.'

'For our meeting?' he asked. 'Or for keeping me here?'

'For fascinating more than I can.'

Matiu and Pita appeared while Fairweather tightened his saddlebags. Pita had a short, bashful speech to make. 'We of this family will pray for your safe return,' he said. 'Many people of Poverty Bay will.'

'Then my hope is,' Fairweather said, 'that Kooti's mountain roost does not mean that his prayers are heard first.'

Pita smiled uncertainly. Matiu was even less partial to levity.

Fairweather swung up into his saddle. 'As for other things,' he told Matiu, 'I have spoken to Biggs. I hope land matters may shape more fairly. I shall do what I can.'

'Your presence might be half the battle,' Matiu said.

'Then may the other half be as bloodless,' Fairweather replied.

Matiu and Pita made a discreet move toward the house, allowing Fairweather to lean from his saddle for a more intimate farewell.

'You will be back soon?' she whispered.

'I should lose all respect for myself if I were not.'

'You worry too much about respect for yourself.'

'I need to,' he said.

Fairweather steered his pony along the riverside, turning to wave at the three figures on the Smith verandah, and then took a ford and crossed on to the plain. The homestead grew small and was gone.

At Matawhero he gathered up Larkin, Dodds, Newman and other armed colonists offering; and had final words with Biggs.

'What if we detect extensive movement?' he asked.

'You inform me,' Biggs said.

'To what end? Another report to government? More paper on the rustling mountain?'

'It depends on the intelligence afforded.'

'Intelligence afforded will be of peril, Major Biggs. You must evacuate. Remove people from Matawhero and outlying places to the port and fill all boats offering.'

'We have a presence to uphold here. We would lose face with the Maoris if we panicked needlessly.'

'You might lose more by lingering. With colonists of Matawhero hostage, Kooti could bargain for more than the redress of his grievances; he could claim all Poverty Bay. And if I were a colonial politician I might be tempted by the line of least resistance.'

'Perhaps you think too far,' Biggs said.

'His Jews must have a land they can call home,' Fairweather pressed. 'He would fail them with anything less.'

'I shall of course plan for extreme contingency. And list procedures to be followed.'

'A redoubt at Turanga to contain colonists and threatened Maoris would not go amiss. Not all could be shipped out fast.'

'I have pleaded for a redoubt,' Biggs said. 'There has been letter after letter to the authorities. Whitmore's information remains more agreeable to the penny-pinchers.'

'Then, Major Biggs, perhaps you should have gone to Wellington and battered down a few doors. Or if that informal measure failed, gone to some mischievous journalist of the colony's press.'

'I am in my present post, Fairweather, because I am familiar with correct procedures.'

'I daresay, Major Biggs. And I suggest that the most fitting procedure is now not to lament Colonel Whitmore, but to consider the sturdy timber in Poverty Bay's hills. Men unfit for scouting could turn a hand to milling. Trader Read might be cajoled into providing the nails. Use some of your famed colonial enterprise. Get a redoubt built fast. Otherwise a warning will be waste.'

'You seem suddenly to take Kooti more seriously than I.'

'History, Major Biggs. A country which has none borrows badly. If Kooti were only a Maori we might manage. But he may make himself more its slave than we.'

'I am not sure I understand.'

'And you might not wish to. Good luck, Major Biggs.'

Fairweather rode into the hills with men in straggling file behind. If history could not be tamed, it might be tickled.

19

September slid away; October was calm and warm. Fairweather moved fluently into the rhythm of patrolling, of scouting landscape for symptoms of flux. From a leafy summit he watched the Urewera ranges rise from the dawn and fade into dusk. Fire on the campsite was kept brief, especially smoke, with only dry wood burned; horses were always saddled for sudden move. Men slept fully dressed, firearms to hand. Small parties of Maori travellers were observed, never approached. By day Fairweather broke his party and rode, mostly with Larkin, over the irregular and patchily wooded terrain between Poverty Bay and the mountains of the Tuhoe. They looked at all likely outlets from the Urewera, noting footprints on such trails, and their number. Silences stifled. They seldom heard more than birds, muted at noon, and wild pig scuttling clear. Human sound never. Yet he and Larkin talked often in whispers, as if the land might take alarm and unleash itself direly. Petals of wilted spring flora, red, gold, and nondescript, wandered down on to their tunics; elegant spirals of fern uncurled into vast fronds; native pines encumbered with creeper rose into glimmering mists of fresh leaf; muddy creeks became silver and fed transparent pools. Fairweather made use of his sketchbook. Colour and form could divert, but symmetry was best left unconsidered. Serenity was sufficient to his days. None were mindless; calm came with method.

With routine established, men made receptive to discipline, Fairweather could lean more on Larkin; and ride back to Poverty Bay. First to report to Biggs. Second to bed with no ache in the Smith household.

Biggs had news. The government had shifted an inch and agreed, in view of persisting anxieties, to pay Fairweather a militia captain's salary to assist in the keeping of Poverty Bay's peace. No further finance was offered. Nor men.

'At least they begin to acknowledge need,' Biggs said.

'I can see bankruptcy does not stare me in the face,' Fairweather said. 'Otherwise far too many mountains still do.'

'But Whitmore no longer prevails,' Biggs protested. 'We have driven a wedge.'

'Driving deep foundations for a redoubt at Turanga might be more rewarding.'

'Read has been generous with materials, labour and land. When I pointed out that he might later convert the redoubt to a warehouse, he couldn't have been more helpful. He also communicates with the colonial press. He urges that one hundred men of the armed constabulary be shipped in.'

'I foresee Turanga booming. And especially Read.'

'I can imagine worse,' Biggs said.

Emily Biggs was about again, with unblushing smile for Fairweather, and pots of fresh tea. She often carried her baby out into the spring sunlight. Young George Biggs refused to be impressed by the wider world; he blinked and yawned under the bright sky, and called for more than visual nourishment.

'He wishes to be at breast all his waking hours,' Emily complained. 'He is never satisfied.'

'Nor should I be,' Fairweather teased.

Even then Emily was not inclined to colour.

Fairweather left the migrant daffodils and bluebells of the Biggs garden for the untidy native reeds of the Smith riverside. It seemed, after all, there was a place he could call home; he even had something which passed plausibly for family. All was opulence after his lean days outdoors. There was fire without risk, and roast lamb and duckling; also, reliably, a bottle of claret fetched from the port. In table talk Fairweather discovered that he could pay his dues convincingly to the commonplace; mixed feelings became fewer as his belly filled and the bottle emptied. Moreover Matiu could be depended on to play a mean hand of poker, and Pita a thoughtful game of chess. When he had to, Fairweather spoke of the terrain he was scouting, of the follies and fears of his men, though he tended not to make much of fears.

'It will all be for nothing,' he predicted. 'But if it brings comfort it is best seen to be done.'

Matiu was silent. Pita, however, found optimism expedient. 'When you have finished,' he asked, 'will you remain here?'

'Perhaps,' Fairweather said.

'Forever?'

'Forever begs questions. Perhaps for no little time.'

'What does that mean?' Pita asked, always polite.

'Thought, for the most part,' Fairweather explained, more aware of Meri listening from the fireside.

'What thought?' Pita persisted. 'I see you happy.'

'As erratic visitor. Here today and back in the hills tomorrow. My temptation is with things as they are; thinking few thoughts at all.'

'Why?' Pita said.

'Because a man who is neither one thing nor the other is nothing much; and has few friends. A voyage with no harbour is inconvenient to contemplate.'

Pita smiled. Fairweather might know how to shape an answer to serve present matters best; he was also knowledgeable in respect of the hair lately greying his scalp.

Alongside him that night Meri said, 'You are careful?'

'Of course.'

'You go off looking for trouble.'

'In a sense.'

'I see no other.'

'I appear to find more trouble within.'

She knew when to remain quiet.

'You go far to convincing me that it might be extinguished,' he went on. 'The cause and the cure.'

'You leave me confused,' she said.

'No more than I.'

'Confusion? That does not sound like you.'

'I am less like me,' he said.

Riding alone out of Poverty Bay, back to his hilltop camp, Fairweather was mostly alert. Bushes on both sides of the trail bristled with uncertainties; shadows at the forest edge shifted suggestively; ridges required scanning through binoculars. Open ground was not necessarily reassuring either. It was just that; open. He could push his horse at distressing pace.

Expectation did not go wanting. Near the end of October he paused his horse on a steep climb and imagined he heard hoofbeats behind. There were. He stationed his horse among trees and provided himself with the choice of already loaded revolver and quickly loaded carbine. A single rider appeared on the trail, bareback and barefoot, and soon recognizable. Fairweather's bad penny; Hamiora Pere had turned up again. His undistinguished horse was toiling and fretting. Hamiora sighted Fairweather and whooped.

'Is this necessary?' Fairweather asked.

'I follow you, Hori,' Hamiora explained. 'I follow my friend. I find you again.'

'Your friend is about business,' Fairweather said. 'I have too much on mind.'

Hamiora understood imperfectly, though enough to be hurt. He gazed at the ground; his horse shuddered and sweated.

'If soldiering is still what you want,' Fairweather said, 'this is not the way in. There is no back door. Forget it. And now.'

Perhaps Fairweather was sterner than warranted. Hamiora sank low on his horse. His eyes did not lift.

'Then just a little way further with me,' Fairweather said. 'Not far. Then home fast to Patutahi. Good?'

'Good,' Hamiora grinned. Impudence again.

'There must be quiet,' Fairweather ordered. 'Not too much talk. Much *korero*, no. Understand?'

Hamiora nodded. 'Kooti?'

'Or his wild men. There is always the chance.'

Hamiora rolled his eyes appreciatively; it seemed he could not ask more. 'You shoot, Hori? Bang?'

'I think not, Hamiora. I think I ride back to Poverty Bay very damn quick.'

Hamiora enjoyed that too, though shaking his head; he refused to see Fairweather fleeing.

'Now silence,' Fairweather said. 'If Kooti does not have your hide, I will.'

They arrived on a ridge; Fairweather considered wilderness, and especially that south and west toward the hazy Urewera. Hamiora might after all be useful.

'Tracks,' he said. 'Tracks, Hamiora. *Ara.* From the Urewera. From the mountains. Mountain *ara.* I watch all. Understand?'

Hamiora seemed to.

'There may be more,' Fairweather said. 'More than I know.'

'Ara?'

'I wish to know all.'

It had first to be conveyed which *ara* Fairweather had been watching. This meant much pantomime, pointing, naming of known rivers and heights. Hamiora appeared to take intelligent interest.

'Ah,' he said finally.

'You know one I do not?'

'I think, Hori. I very bloody think.'

'So show me,' Fairweather said. 'Be my big bloody friend.'

Hamiora beamed and led Fairweather back toward Poverty Bay and then inland; after an hour they came to an accommodating hole in the hills Fairweather had never much noticed. There was a wide gully thinly vegetated, and a wandering creek. Then deep forest. Hamiora dismounted; Fairweather also. They tethered their horses and continued on foot. Hamiora brushed aside foliage and stopped.

'Ara,' he announced.

'Here?' Fairweather arrived at Hamiora's side. It took him some time to see a strip of vaguely worn ground, eroded with rains, and now muddled with undergrowth. But still vestigially a track. Flecks of sunlight found it here and there. No birds could be heard.

'Old?' he asked.

'Old,' Hamiora said.

'Used now?'

'I think not much, Hori. I think never much.'

'Not much or never?'

Hamiora was unable to say.

'For war?' Fairweather said. 'An *ara* for war? Very old war?'

'I think, Hori. I think bloody maybe.'

Hamiora was interestingly uncomfortable. Fairweather asked, 'Your people in Patutahi, do they think this a *kino* place? Bad?'

'They not come here, Hori.'

'Yet you know it. You.'

'One day I hunt with my uncle. I run after big pig. I kill it here. My uncle, he say never eat that pig. We never. We go quick.'

'Why?' Fairweather asked.

'*Kehua*,' Hamiora said, still as tense.

'Ghosts?'

'I think many, Hori.'

'Maybe very many. Much old blood.'

'How you know, Hori?'

'Because,' Fairweather decided, 'I think I am feeling them too.'

Yet he had to see where the remnant trail took him. Hamiora followed with no enthusiasm, but concluding that it was best to stay close to Fairweather. They worked through high trees, and some fallen. There was less and less light as their feet crackled over rotting debris. Enough of the trail persisted to tempt Fairweather into the gloom. His shivering soon appeared to be more of the mind than the flesh. There was never a footprint as the trail dipped, almost lost in greenery, and rambled up into robust timber. Again it became almost indetectable under debris. Fairweather had seen enough, Hamiora more so; they made their way back. The sun was relief; his shivering left. There were no *kehua* pressing misty sorrows. Just their horses grazing in daylight without dread.

'It is good for you?' Hamiora asked. 'The *ara*?'

'You have a genius for places,' Fairweather said.

'Genius?' Hamiora understood only that it was something meant kindly; and smiled.

'Never mind,' Fairweather said.

He had surely partaken of the past. Anything else was unthinkable, or at least out of character; he was superstitious only when it suited a lacklustre hour.

Yet he felt bound to ride back to Poverty Bay with Hamiora. On a riverbank their paths parted. The left fork took Hamiora home to the Maori *kainga* of

Patutahi. The right, across the river, would take Fairweather to the colonists' *kainga* of Matawhero. There was a handshake.

'Genius?' Hamiora said, still puzzling at the word. 'I?'

'For being Hamiora Pere, perhaps,' Fairweather suggested.

'That is good, Hori?'

'Very. You must keep at it.'

'I bloody try,' Hamiora promised; and galloped away.

Biggs was not to be inconvenienced by Fairweather's intelligence. 'Overgrown, you say?'

'Most,' Fairweather said.

'Then it can be discounted. You make a poor case for return.'

'Intuition always finds indifferent advocates. It leaves me with unease I should share.'

'What unease?'

Emily Biggs appeared on the verandah with tea and cake. Her baby was sleeping. Talk of unease was postponed until she had poured tea and gone, with a smile for Fairweather as she passed.

'The track,' Fairweather explained, 'is miles to the north of the territory we are watching. And that much closer to Poverty Bay; almost a back door. If Kooti were to suspect southerly approaches watched, he might rediscover this northern way in. That is, should he move.'

'I have reports to finish and place on tomorrow's schooner,' Biggs said. 'I should be grateful if you were more to the point.'

'I argue that the track must be kept in mind.'

'I shall henceforth ensure so,' Biggs said. 'I shall note it as soon as I return to my desk. And shall mark it on the official map of the region.'

'Two or three men keeping watch might cover the point more adequately.'

'How many do you have currently?'

'Resting men regularly, sending them home for a night, seldom more than a meagre ten at one time.'

'And you propose reducing their number to watch an obscure and forgotten trail? You heard nothing? Saw nothing?'

'Of material nature,' Fairweather had to agree.

'There you are, man. Besides, fresh Maori intelligence confirms that a watch there would be waste. It seems Kooti is beginning to break camp on holy hill. Parties of his men have been seen moving in southerly direction. More toward Hawke's Bay than here. Perhaps Kooti has further indignity for Whitmore in mind. If so, nothing could suit better. Alarms would be sounded the like of which this colony has never heard. Poverty Bay too would have to be made safe.'

'It makes tactical sense,' Fairweather said. 'If his true target is Poverty Bay, which he must know to be vulnerable, then there would be virtue in striking first in the direction from which assistance would be afforded us. His coup would be complete.'

'You feel he thinks that far?'

'We should pay Kooti less than his due if we did not try to out-think him that far.'

Biggs was quiet for a time. Remorse? God knew. And Biggs.

'I might be wrong,' Fairweather said. 'But Kooti can never be. A prophet has to deliver on promises; his intimacy with Jehovah must be tested. I can clothe myself in tattered mana. He cannot.'

'A wretched word,' Biggs said.

'For which there is no substitute, Major Biggs. His stake in it, also in Poverty Bay, must not be underestimated. It is distinctly far more than yours, and certainly mine.'

'You appear to have larger investment here yourself,' Biggs noted. 'You have been modest about mentioning your move to the Smith household.'

'Because there is much to be modest about, Major Biggs. I need somewhere now and then to retire saddlesore buttocks.'

'I will not quibble with that,' Biggs said, much as he seemed of a mind to.

'In which case the subject is best left alone, sir.' Fairweather found himself rising from the table abruptly; chinaware rattled.

'Forgive me,' Biggs said. 'I did not think to arouse sensitivity. I meant only to suggest that you are now more one of us. In the same boat.'

'Or on Maori land?'

'It could be said that way.'

'Then it had best not be said, Major Biggs.' Fairweather tightened his belt, preparing to ride.

'What can be said, then?' Biggs asked.

'What I say, sir. Never what I do not.'

'I understand,' Biggs said with complicity.

The damnable thing was that Biggs possibly did.

Emily arrived, ending tension as she cleared the table. She looked with reproach at Fairweather. 'You are going so soon?'

'It was a flying detour,' Fairweather said. 'With information which seems happily redundant.'

'And now back to the hills?'

'Alas,' Fairweather agreed.

'I say often to Reginald that I feel safe with you there.'

'Then my days do not pass in vain. Young George thrives?'

'And fattens. A sweet little pig.'

'Embrace him for me when he wakes. I shall see him again soon.'

'Next time you must stay longer.'

'I shall make a point of it,' he promised.

Biggs walked Fairweather to his horse. 'As for that old track,' he said, 'I trust your mind is more at rest.'

'Present circumstances do not permit it repose, Major Biggs.'

'New Zealand's less civilized parts are notoriously teasing. Men can go mad. They see things they should not.'

'I do not care to either,' Fairweather said.

Small and vivid Emily Biggs waved from the verandah as Fairweather rode out of Matawhero. Biggs made a less memorable figure as he trudged back to the procedural burdens of his day.

20

It was now November; temperatures were summer's. Valleys were ovens, and breezes were few. Bright sky was empty of all but brown native hawks circling prey. Little other movement drew tired eyes. There was always the temptation to puncture the day, to test menace, with a quick single shot. On Fairweather's order no firearm was used, not even on incautious wild pig. Fires were no longer lit; men had to make the most of cold mutton and stale bread. Flies swarmed by day and mosquitoes by night. Much was conducive to discontent, with grumbles on the edge of earshot, but rebellion was bred more by the dragging days than Fairweather's discipline.

'It's all for nothing, sir,' young Mulhooly complained.

'With luck,' Fairweather said.

'I think of all the boots I might of been making, sir.'

'Think rather, Mulhooly, of the tale you can cobble from this for your grandchildren. Of the time you sat single-handed on this hilltop waiting to fight off savage hordes.'

There was an unimpressed silence. 'Is this what it's like, sir?' Mulhooly finally dared ask. 'Is this what it's like being a hero?'

'But for the frills. Like seducing a difficult woman. Hours of tedium for a few seconds of sensation.'

That appeared to be outside Mulhooly's experience. He waited on Fairweather to say more.

'I begin to feel, Mulhooly, that you haven't the makings of a hero. Worse, that you don't even want to be one much.'

'No, sir. Since you ask. I'm missing my Millie, her and the children. I'm not one for being with other men. It's just not the same.'

Fairweather said gravely, 'Were you with Kooti, perhaps, you could have the best of both worlds. Women and warriors mix except, as I understand it, the night before battle.'

'I'd sooner you didn't talk about him, sir,' Mulhooly said. 'He still gives me a shiver.'

Fairweather had already once found Mulhooly tearful in the moonlight; and packed him back to Poverty Bay on a brief connubial visit next morning. He couldn't be excused service entirely. Whatever his deficiencies, Mulhooly still had two useful eyes and the lungs to produce a warning shout. With a kick in his rear, Mulhooly might even expose himself to retaliation by pointing a rifle in a direction Fairweather nominated. Of such, for the most part, was Poverty Bay's protection fashioned. Fairweather could be confident only of Larkin, and sometimes of Newman and Dodds. Newman and Dodds could take orders. Larkin could anticipate them and even contrive some himself. There was no hope of more like him. The latest message from Biggs said no further assistance could yet be expected, not with Fairweather's pay as militia captain depleting the colonial treasury.

'They give us our inch,' Biggs scribbled, 'and Kooti a mile.' Biggs had fresh Maori confirmation that Kooti was moving more toward the south from holy hill; Fairweather's conjecture of a tactical strike at Hawke's Bay might yet be proven. 'Do continue keeping sharp watch,' Biggs pleaded, 'while I battle the obtuse misers of officialdom. I am now obliged to argue that swift settlement of the land question will make Poverty Bay more precious to the colony and deserving of larger government expenditure. You may not find this ploy much to your liking, but I must try everything now.'

It was not to Fairweather's liking; he would have to make time for further words with Biggs. Nor did he much care for the apprehension seeping between the lines of the Biggs letter.

There was also a communication forwarded from Herrick in Hawke's Bay.

If official reports are true, Herrick wrote, *you have become an addict of bush picnics. Or is it just that you like walking with your head in the clouds? If your current enterprise proves as jolly as the last, I shall not be jealous. Colonel Whitmore, you may be glad to know, has taken himself off to the western coast of the colony where he is doubtless bringing fresh heart to the Hau Hau rebels who have dared again raise their scarred heads there. Any day now we expect to hear of his next stunning triumph, which will leave us free to imagine the Hau Hau controlling such of the colony as Kooti does not. It may come as no surprise that Whitmore has been called to his present post as the man who scorned treacherous terrain and weight of numbers and put the terrible Kooti to flight. Mysterious are the ways of the world and more so of men. Almost as inexplicable is that, with Whitmore gone, Canning and Carr deceased, I appear to command the Hawke's Bay militia. Fortunately, and unlike you, I also command some experienced men of the armed constabulary made available for regular patrols; Whitmore's political influence does not go for nothing in respect of Hawke's Bay needs. The point of this letter is that should you want me, shout long and hard, with as much despair as you can muster, and I shall come running with all the men I can fetch. Until then I fear my hands are tied by politics and regulations. All I can say is that I am willing, though that may not make this letter large consolation.*

A friend, however fettered, could freshen a dead day. Otherwise Fairweather had only Mulhooly's unhappy confessions or Larkin's melancholy tales of the swamps and fevers of the Burma war, after which his 18th was a regiment mostly of unmarked graves. The soul of martial optimism, Larkin argued that Kooti couldn't do worse.

'Perhaps not to the 18th,' Fairweather said.

'No, sir,' Larkin said. He looked over the trampled hilltop, at Poverty Bay colonists on uninspired picket or felled by heat. 'With this lot, sir, my feeling is we still got a long way to go.'

How long?

They arrived at the fifth of November; it seemed the ghost of Guy Fawkes was not to be given its due. 'Unless Kooti is at this minute burrowing under Parliament,' Fairweather said, 'and with enough gunpowder to dismember the colony's politicians.'

'There are some things devoutly to be wished, sir,' Larkin said.

They were on dawn watch together.

'I imagine you're Catholic, Larkin.'

'If I'm anything, sir.'

'Pray,' Fairweather ordered.

'Pray, sir?'

'To your Holy Virgin, whatever her name is. It might come less intemperately from you. Anything to end this damn nonsense.'

Among Fairweather's other irritations, the night's insects had kept vigil on his exposed flesh. Watching the summits of the Urewera shed mist as they rose to the sun, he considered assigning himself another solo excursion back to Poverty Bay, perhaps tomorrow, and again leaving Larkin in charge. In the Smith homestead Fairweather might imagine himself again his own man. He might also impress more as commander in the remaining twenty-five days of November. There was no need to rationalize further. What was good for his men was good enough for him, and probably better.

Perhaps Larkin did make the Mother of God familiar with Fairweather's need. In late afternoon the day became distinguishable from others.

'Smoke,' Larkin said.

Fairweather had been dozing, prone in deep fern with cap covering his face while flies noised around. He stood and claimed the binoculars from Larkin.

'To the west,' Larkin said, 'and half to the south.'

Fairweather moved the binoculars. Ridges and valleys rippled across his sight, and everywhere dense stands of timber.

'Four miles, sir,' Larkin added. 'Maybe five.'

Fairweather found it. The smoke rose slender in the still air. The source seemed to be just short of a summit footing the Urewera ranges. Though he looked with concentration, he failed to do more than confirm its existence. When he lowered the binoculars, he saw that the smoke had thickened enough to make itself plain to the unaided eye. All his men were watching with fascination; they were not, after all, alone in this landscape.

'Thank you, Larkin,' he said. 'At least we seem more alert. Hunters?'

'Could be, sir,' Larkin said with caution.

'From Hawke's Bay, perhaps,' Fairweather wondered aloud. 'Hawke's Bay Maoris, you think they come so far north in this season?'

Larkin made no reply. Nor was any other man ready to chance one. Fairweather was obliged to answer himself.

'It's possible,' he decided, though wishing conviction. 'At all events we must keep it in view.'

No need to make that an order. Men were disinclined to move their gaze.

'Also,' he added, 'for anything more provocative in nature.'

'Provocative?' Dodds asked.

'Anything that moves,' Fairweather said. 'Anything that might.'

He passed the binoculars to Dodds, then found it necessary to take Larkin aside.

'The heroic thing would be to charge across there and investigate,' he suggested.

'Yes, sir,' Larkin said, with the certainty that heroism was not here the issue.

'We risk disturbing hornets. Or something perfectly peaceful. Either way we betray our presence. Our value would be impaired. Poverty Bay might get no early warning. Kooti could push men through the territory in small parties, or perhaps just hunt present company for sport. Neither prospect appeals.'

'No, sir,' Larkin said. 'A difficult business, in all.' He knew when not to say more; when to leave officers to embroider that which was plain.

'Infernal,' Fairweather said. 'Yet it seems, for the moment, that we must sit it out.'

'And it's getting near dark, sir,' Larkin said, deciding it time to relieve Fairweather of vexation. 'We could never get across that country by night.'

'So we shall have to see what we see in the morning,' Fairweather concluded.

'That seems the short of it, sir. Extra pickets tonight?'

'And extremely discreet scouting tomorrow. Perhaps I shall take Dodds, while you ensure the safety of the others.'

'Whatever you say, sir.'

'And no man gets leave to return to Poverty Bay. Luxuries are past.'

It was not something Fairweather could say without pang. Tomorrow now had a less generous colour, though not necessarily commonplace. Doldrums were gone; they were in livelier waters, perhaps even deep.

They walked back to the other men. Mulhooly approached his captain with eyes rather wide.

'Kooti, sir?' he asked.

'Smoke,' Fairweather said.

Through the first watch of the night it was possible to pick up a faint and far glow. Not flame; just irregular illumination among trees. By dawn it was gone.

Fairweather and Dodds rode in that direction soon after first light. They kept to leafy low ground, following creeks, exposing themselves on ridges seldom and briefly. Dew dripped from overhead foliage; gullies brimmed with loud birds. Finally they tethered their horses and proceeded on foot. It was difficult to locate the minor height upon which they had seen the fire burning; there was no distinctive landmark to give bearings, and all slopes seemed alike. They sometimes paused, when they had pushed to a vantage point, to listen and look. There was nothing to quicken the heartbeat, though much to leave conversation ragged. It was some hours before Fairweather lit his pipe and passed his tobacco to Dodds; as good as a signal to retire.

'At all events,' Fairweather said, 'we would seem to have established that there are no men moving here on any large scale.'

'Thank God,' Dodds said, 'I think of my family.'

'You are not alone in thought of others,' Fairweather said.

Dodds, filling his pipe, looked up with surprise. 'Even you?'

'It would seem,' Fairweather said.

'You want to talk about who?'

'Not especially, Dodds. No.'

'I been thinking you're some bugger at this for the fun of it. Or maybe the money. Not that you don't do a fair job.'

'Thank you, Dodds. And, by the way, even if circumstances are not currently conducive, I still expect to hear you say sir.'

'Yes, sir,' Dodds said with reluctance. 'It's just, sir, that you do things a bit cool and casual, and I haven't got the hang of you yet. Sir.'

'I am not hard of hearing, Dodds. Occasional utterance of the word will remind me of responsibility and stop rot setting in. Cool I can be. Casual never.'

'Kooti, he might just be bluffing. Laughing while we run this way and that.'

'You know your Bible, Dodds?'

'I'm not a great reader, sir.'

'Let me assure you it is seldom uproarious reading.'

'I take your word, sir.'

'Not mine, Dodds. Kooti's.'

'So you don't think he's bluffing?'

'You tell me,' Fairweather said. 'Then we shall be both well informed.'

They arrived back at camp in the afternoon. Men crowded about, some visibly anxious, but it was Larkin to whom Fairweather spoke.

'As bare of Kooti as a new baby's arse,' he said. 'We wait.'

'Understood, sir.'

'Carry on,' Fairweather ordered. 'Keep the men sharp.'

He went to find food, drink and shade; finally he slept. Until he heard Larkin.

'Smoke again,' Larkin was saying.

Fairweather was quick on his feet. 'Where now?'

'Same hill, sir. Same place.'

He took the binoculars from Larkin; his eyes travelled across contours already familiar and lit on the smoke. Larkin could not be contradicted. Same hill; same place. This time the smoke had a curl where it met breeze.

'And about the same time of day, sir,' Larkin observed.

'Perhaps a relief.' Fairweather lowered the binoculars. 'It does suggest hunters. Same time, same site.'

'Except for one thing, sir.'

'And what might that be, Larkin?'

'I talked to Dodds, sir. I questioned him close. He tells me you travelled hard up against those hills. If not right to the place.'

'Well?' Fairweather said, impatient.

'He says you heard nothing, sir. If there were hunters, you should of heard shots.'

Larkin could be right too often; it tended to irritate. Fairweather argued, 'Perhaps the place is barren of game.'

'Then a queer place to camp, sir. And stay on a day more.'

'Or they could be,' Fairweather persisted, 'Maoris trapping pigeon in the traditional way.'

'If you think so, sir. But I seen enough Maoris now. Most have got a great liking for guns. Traps don't seem the same.'

'Damn it, Larkin, all we have is smoke.'

'Yes, sir.'

'The explanation may be simple in the fullness of time.'

'Yes, sir. I can't help being curious.'

'Remain so,' Fairweather ordered, 'and keep a sharp watch. I shall go looking for my lost sleep. And in case I have neglected to say it this far, Larkin, you are quite a fine fellow. Even if you do think thoughts of your own.'

'Thank you, sir. It is much appreciated.'

'And the best of officers sometimes know not what they do. Or what to.'

'No need to tell me, sir. You get your sleep.'

The fullness of time, perhaps all of fifteen minutes, hardly allowed Fairweather to doze.

'More smoke,' Larkin said. 'Not the same place.'

When Fairweather reached Larkin's side no binoculars were needed. The new smoke rose perhaps a mile to the north of the old, at approximately the same elevation, in the same range of foothills. 'Well?' Fairweather said.

'Hard to know what to make of it, sir.'

'I think it weighs down my side of the argument, Larkin. Hunters. Hunters dividing their party.'

'Perhaps, sir,' Larkin said quietly.

The two skeins of smoke grew taller; they had identical twist.

'Wisdom still rules,' Fairweather decided. 'We cannot risk crossing the country between by night. We wait upon morning.'

'Yes, sir,' Larkin said. 'All the same, it's queer you and Dodds heard nothing. Saw nothing neither.'

'You may soon become tiresome, Larkin.'

'Yes, sir.' Larkin stood stiff.

'Rest assured that if men in number were moving over there, Dodds and I would have picked up their trail. There is no way in which they would have escaped our attention.'

This was more to comfort himself than to convince Larkin.

He added, 'Whatever we are watching has to do with small parties. Also static. They cover no ground. It may all be meaningless.'

Yet neither he nor Larkin shifted their gaze. As smoke climbed and met more air currents it became quite rococo. That night, for a time, there were two indistinct points of light for pickets to watch.

In the morning he and Dodds rode out to take in even more territory. The result did not enlighten. There was no sight of anything recently or currently human, nor any reverberation to give pause. Wherever the fires cooled, it was in forest too deep.

'You begin to think they lit themselves,' Dodds said. 'It gives me the willies.'

Fairweather said nothing as they rode back to camp. He let Dodds report to Larkin and the other men, and sank fatigued under a tree. At length he lit his pipe. Larkin judged it timely to make an approach.

'You still think hunters, sir?' he asked.

'If so,' Fairweather said, 'very damn few.'

'I see, sir.'

'Damn it, Larkin,' Fairweather snapped, 'what else can they be? Who else?'

'I know no more than you, sir.'

'Exactly. And until you do I require no further harassment. Whoever is over there, the one thing we know is that they aren't shy about announcing their presence. The imagination has no other front to work on. Which is not to argue that we neglect our rear.'

'Yes, sir. Any orders?'

'The same,' Fairweather said.

Other things were too. Towards the end of the afternoon the smoke of two fires lifted from distant forest, from hills identifiably yesterday's, again a hawk's mile apart. On one theory of the thing, reassuring. On any other, not. So much for November the seventh.

Fairweather woke Larkin before dawn. 'You try your luck today,' he said. 'Go out with Dodds. He knows where we've been.'

'Anything special, sir?'

'Instinct,' Fairweather said. 'Mine may be lacking.'

'And if we see anyone, sir?'

'Observe. Don't reveal yourselves. Then back to tell me. I shall have a difficult wait.'

Through the morning and most of the afternoon Fairweather kept his distance from the other men on the hilltop. Their profane mumbling now maddened. Sleep was impossible. With binoculars he retraced his steps to see if a foot had somewhere been put wrong in search. If so, no other man was to blame. There were no bad soldiers; there were only bad officers. Even with half trained colonists deployed against rumour and riddle, the maxim could still be upheld. Even at his worst Fairweather still had to know best.

Dodds rode back alone.

Fairweather said with anger, 'What have you done with Larkin?'

'It's what he did to me. Sir. Sergeant Larkin told me to report back here smart.'

'Report what?'

'That he'll be longer. We was going on foot, up a hill he thought likely. He had another think and said two made twice as much noise in that steep kind of country. He reckoned he wanted to finish the job alone. He's a persistent bugger is Sergeant Larkin. He said to give you his promise he'd be back sharpish.'

But Larkin was not. An hour passed. Two.

For the first time it was not Larkin who gave the familiar word as the afternoon waned.

'Smoke,' Newman called.

'The other place too,' Mulhooly reported.

There was satisfaction, as if the absence of smoke would now leave them at a loss, the day's end empty. Fairweather used his binoculars. The hills were the same; today wind made for more fluttering as the smoke rose.

'Where is Larkin?' he appealed, but to no one present.

Dodds arrived at his shoulder. 'I hate to tell you this, sir, but you better look off to the south, maybe a mile. And see if you see what I do.'

Moving the binoculars Fairweather framed the wisp of a third fire beginning to burn. He could not believe it. He had to. The wind soon gave the smoke similar configuration to that which lifted twice to the north.

'Damnation,' was all he could tell Dodds.

Three bursts of smoke stuttering above trees. Three in a line, the same elevation, one never more than a mile from another.

'Where does that leave us, sir?' Dodds dared to ask.

'Speaking for myself,' Fairweather said, 'even deeper in turd.'

It was dusk before exhausted Larkin rode into camp. Men had to help him from his horse and lower him gently to earth. Wit was slow returning; also breath.

'You saw something?' Fairweather asked.

'Women,' Larkin gasped.

Fairweather produced a bottle. Larkin tipped it into his mouth and shuddered as the brandy bit.

'What women?' Fairweather said. 'Where?'

'Just women, sir. Maori. None I seen before. Old ones and young. They was just sitting, talking, laughing a fair lot. Up a hill over there. Maybe a dozen. Maybe more. I crawled close, but I couldn't see plain.'

'Armed?'

'Not so as I saw. It was like they was having a picnic.'

'And definitely no men?'

'I waited and watched a long time. No men turned up.'

'Hunting?'

'They had food, sir. They wasn't going hungry. But no feathers nor carcasses around. It didn't seem like they had any real business at all.'

Larkin took brandy again.

'Well,' Fairweather said, impatient, 'what do you think? That they lit the fires and are lighting them still?'

'Who else?' Larkin asked.

Fairweather had to think. 'Get some rest,' he said before turning away. 'I need to mull over this before morning.'

He moved only a few paces, stopped, and walked back to Larkin.

'One more thing,' he said, 'and I shall not trouble you again. Were there any manifestations among the women? Did they sing hymns, chant psalms, or the like?'

'Now you mention it, sir,' Larkin said.

Fairweather managed an hour of sleep, then woke with much certainty. He had been here before. A trio of Maoris taking water from riverside; a trinity of fires lit in these hills. The first an overture to talented carnage; the second also signalled orchestration. If a snare, though, where was the net? If a feint, where the thrust?

His mind coloured with a tale told too often. There was one circumstance in which warring Maoris saw women as tempting poor fortune. Perhaps the fires had first been engineered by men. It was women's work now. The men, without libidinous diversion, were upon business elsewhere.

His gut simmering, he walked among sleeping men and woke Dodds. 'I need you,' he said. 'Get ready to ride as soon as night allows.'

'Me?' Dodds said, sleepy.

'And quick back to Poverty Bay. I need a man who can talk sense to Biggs. Larkin's too tuckered. And you have a loud voice.'

'Right, sir.' Dodds stood, shedding his blanket, understanding urgency at last.

'If Biggs quibbles and queries, outshout him. Let everyone in Matawhero hear what you have to say. That is an order. This too. Tell Biggs that all at Matawhero, every outlying colonist, must be evacuated. Moved to whatever exists of the redoubt being built at the port. Those whom the redoubt cannot contain must be bundled into every vessel available, whaleboats, dinghies, canoes, anything; and sped well clear. If Biggs wants to linger at Matawhero, from fear of losing face, tell him mana is no longer an issue.'

'Mana, sir?' Dodds was not familiar with the word, but anxious to get it right.

'Not mana. Nor land. The issue is life. Tell him as much as you care to of what we have seen. And say I interpret peril, and not just to flavour a report to the government. Argue that every horizon in Poverty Bay is now unsafe. In short, Dodds, I am sending you to spread panic. I want nothing less than a stampede down to Turanga, the redoubt and the boats.'

'You can rely on me, sir,' Dodds said, if troubled.

'Finally,' Fairweather said, 'make it clear that the word must be spread also among Maoris. Especially among those not yet convinced they are Jews. Biggs is not to be selective. All must be warned.'

'I get your drift. Everyone, sir.'

'There is one other thing I ask as special favour.' Fairweather took a large breath, then disclosed himself wholly. 'I should be grateful if you made it your business, before riding back here, to go personally to a family on the Waimata river known as Smith.'

'I know the family, sir. Matiu Smith. A confounded morose bugger with no liking for us.'

'Nor for Kooti. I ask that you impart the same tidings. Instruct the Smiths to make a quick move. Tell them I beg. If Matiu should jib, talk to his sister. Her wit should prevail.'

'You leave it to me, sir. This sister, this woman, she's the one you don't talk about.'

'And it is not my inclination, Dodds, to begin now. Get yourself ready. And ride quick with the light.'

Fairweather walked away to find Newman on picket. 'I'll take over,' he told Newman. 'You need some sleep.'

'You're not getting much, sir.'

'Nevertheless, Newman, tonight you need more. You are familiar with the ground between here and Hawke's Bay?'

'I've ridden it, sir,' Newman allowed.

'And you could find your way across it again?'

'Taking it easy. Watching my way.'

'I want you to go to the port of Napier, where a certain Robert Herrick, captain of militia, resides. Understood?'

'Robert Herrick,' Newman repeated. 'I get the name. Remember him too. One of Whitmore's Hawke's Bay bastards.'

'You are about to find them entirely legitimate,' Fairweather promised.

'If you say so, sir.' Newman was unconvinced. 'So what do you want me to tell him?'

'Just this, from me. Tell him despair is at hand and please travel with speed.'

'At hand?' Newman queried.

'And please travel with speed,' Fairweather confirmed.

'You don't need to write it down,' Newman judged.

The day could not have been longer. It dawned with Dodds riding to the north, Newman to the south. Fairweather journeyed in imagination with both men, more especially with Dodds. He urged Dodds' horse across creeks and up ridges; he whipped it down to the Poverty Bay plain. Dodds, with the best will in the world, might not make Matawhero until middle afternoon. Newman, pushing across terrain stranger, would take more than one day. It might be all of another two before Herrick heard Fairweather's plea.

Meanwhile he made a more tangible excursion with Larkin, yet again into that territory where smoke had been seen. The known tracks from the Urewera were still sparing of clues. There were few recent footprints, and old waterside camps had no one at home. There was no suggestion of numbers or nocturnal movement. Higher, they looked for the women Larkin had watched. Larkin was unable to duplicate his route of the previous day, not having risked blazing a trail through the trees; they were baffled by vicious stands of nettle and towers of eroded rock. The women, if about, were at pains not to disclose themselves. Larkin cursed. Fairweather remained quiet. They finally rode back to camp; their faces reported frustration.

Late that afternoon the first fire began to burn. Then the second, and soon three. Perhaps a fourth was considered redundant; three were sufficiently taunting.

'Damn,' Fairweather said. His pipe had no flavour; liquor was on short ration.

Larkin approached. 'I been wondering, sir,' he began.

'Wonder away, Larkin. Feel at liberty to mention all musings to me.'

'Have you considered withdrawing to Poverty Bay, sir?'

'I have considered that, Larkin. And still do.'

'Well, sir?'

'We must persist a day or two longer. We have a presence across there. If Kooti knows we are scouting this territory, it might be a useful ploy to light those fires until we tire of investigating. If we relaxed vigilance he could speed his men through. He must buy surprise.'

'Yes, sir.' Larkin was thoughtful.

'All we know is that something is up. We remain on our guard.'

'And just watch those fires burn?'

'For once in your miserable life, Larkin, you might have it about right. Napoleon told his marshals never to lose the sound of the guns. Here we never lose the known.'

'I see, sir.'

'You have doubts, Larkin.'

'If you say so, sir.'

'Whatever they are, I have them tenfold; and a few others to boot. Obtuse though I may seem to you, I sometimes make sense.'

'I know that, sir.'

'And it cannot have escaped your notice that I am not a free agent. I answer to Major Biggs. His wish was that we remain here until we have something comprehensible to report. Lacking which, I have sent stern warning with the hope that he listens. We must wait on Dodds' return before leaving this territory all Kooti's.'

'I understand your problem, sir.'

'And I understand yours, Larkin. You mean no offence, but you wish to help me think.'

'Something like that, sir.'

'If it helps you sleep easier, Larkin, you do. But it helps my sleep not at all.'

'I'm sorry, sir.'

'To demonstrate contrition, then, fetch me something not too far gone to be edible. Otherwise I shall make you a pitiful spectacle and boot your hairy Irish arse.'

In the last of daylight Fairweather took up his Bible. He seemed to have drained all red juice from the Book of Joshua; he dabbled as displeasingly elsewhere, and especially in Deuteronomy. Where Jehovah was not smiting, his chosen people were, and to effect. Canaanites upon the land promised had not just to be slain, like the Midianites, the Amalekites, and the deluged Egyptians before them; they had to be persuasively so under the sky of the Jew. A killer of lesser conviction could flinch; Fairweather perceptibly did.

'I didn't know you'd gone holy, sir,' Larkin said.

'The Bible is literature, Larkin. The religion of the Protestant; the reading too. I daresay a bog Catholic wouldn't know.'

'Literature, sir?' Larkin was perplexed. 'You mean like the Queen's regulations? The manuals officers read?'

'Let us hope not, Larkin.'

'Sir?'

But Larkin was left to puzzle at what might have been said to turn his captain so quiet.

Sunset. Dusk. Dodds should be at Matawhero, doing his best to dismay Biggs, and then riding from door to door. Newman? Likely well on the way to Hawke's Bay, munching a crust and winding a blanket about himself for the night.

'What is the day?' Fairweather asked suddenly. 'We must be close to December.'

'Only November the ninth, sir,' Larkin said.

'The ninth?'

'Only, sir. True.'

Across the territory they watched, as daylight left, the reflected glow of three fires grew brighter. There was no illumination in the sky above; no moon or stars. All afternoon cloud had poured around Urewera summits and begun to spill further. Wind was rising too.

'A change for the worse,' Larkin diagnosed.

'There is no need for a formal report,' Fairweather said.

'It could turn things nasty, sir. Come to think, wherever the sod is, for Kooti too.'

'Then think on the wonder of it, Larkin. One touch of nature making all men kin.'

'Kooti? He's no kin of mine.'

'There, Larkin, we differ. We must see him as brother. Try to think as he might; get into his skin.'

'You mean be a right bloody savage?'

'Just an indignant Jew for the present,' Fairweather said. 'Though it might amount to that too.'

Rain began after dark. It was soon vehement, backed with rumbles of thunder and embellished by lightning. This last touch of nature lit a memory. As Fairweather bedded in his leaky bivouac, tugging a waterproof sheet over his blanket, he heard old Nama, of the tribe called Tuhoe, talking again. Finally he crawled outside and called Larkin from picket.

'There is something I wish you to note,' he said. 'I have just, Larkin, nominated this hilltop as my *rua koha*.'

'*Rua* what, sir?'

'Never mind. Let us just say as our special place.'

'Can't argue with that, sir. If we're here any longer they'll have to dig us out by the roots.'

'The point of this, Larkin, is that I want the lightning watched.'

'The lightning, sir?' Larkin might conclude that Fairweather was due for confinement; Larkin might even be right.

'The lightning,' Fairweather insisted. 'I want you to watch where it plays.'

'I see, sir,' Larkin said with grudge. 'And what for, sir, may I ask?'

'You may, but the answer might daunt you. I want you to observe whether the lightning plays toward this place, or away. And if away, where.'

'Where, sir?'

'Where, Larkin. But first whether toward us or away.'

'I'll do what I can, sir,' Larkin said. 'It would help, though, if I knew more.'

'What you don't know won't hurt you,' Fairweather said. 'On that, this once, you have my most melancholy word.'

Fairweather dwelt among green pastures, still waters; he walked a shadowless land with life only in dream. Then a saturated hand brushed his face and shook him awake; he was returned to forest and frustration.

'You told me to wake you after midnight, sir,' Larkin was saying.

'Did I? Then I am a damned fool.'

'So you get your sleep, sir. I'll carry on.'

'No matter, Larkin. The fun has quite gone.' Fairweather rose from his bivouac and buckled his belt. The rain had cleared. There were stars. 'Anything up?'

'Unless you mean the lightning, sir. You told me to watch.'

'Indeed I did,' Fairweather remembered, locating his carbine. 'And?'

'It played this way and that, sir. Hard to get a straight sight. I reckoned it played mostly away. Mostly away from us, sir.'

'So perhaps we are blessed, Larkin.'

'I expect you know what you are saying, sir. It makes no sense to me.'

'Your report omits vital detail, Larkin. Which way did it play? Where did it move?'

'Roughly north, sir.'

'Toward Poverty Bay?'

'Generally, sir,' Larkin agreed.

Fairweather considered that. Portent was at its best when it confirmed common sense.

'What is it you are thinking, sir?' Larkin finally asked.

'That I am glad I sent Dodds,' Fairweather said.

At first light he ordered a fire built, for men to be warmed and clothes dried; also for tea to be brewed and laced with the last of the rum. Larkin was surprised at the abrupt breach of routine.

'There is no sense,' Fairweather said, 'in playing with the pretence that they don't know we're here. Kooti, I mean, his women and warriors. We have not been fooling them. Merely ourselves.'

Their fire rose higher, the smoke likewise.

'All the same, sir, they can now mark our position. Maybe move in on us quiet.'

'I think not, Larkin. And it is for me to decide.'

'Yes, sir,' Larkin answered with grievance.

'Speaking for myself, I have a fine sense of security. I wish I could say as much for others elsewhere.'

Larkin was still unconvinced.

'You and I, Larkin, have both lived, even quite lately, what is called a charmed life.'

'Yes, sir.'

'Carry on living it,' Fairweather ordered. 'Tell men to make preparation for breaking of camp.'

'Today, sir?'

'And perhaps very soon.'

'You mean if we're attacked, sir?'

'Do shut up, Larkin. You're becoming a grumpy old bore. I am talking of Dodds' return; we should then know what we must.'

Dodds did not arrive that morning, which was far from surprising; even with a fresh horse he had another demanding ride. The passing afternoon hours made the wait cruel. All eyes were watchful. Men took their tension from Fairweather; for once he found concealment too great a duty. Thwarted by time, besieged by flies and humidity, his temper went fast. Larkin, observing the symptoms, stayed at a remove.

At last, at a distance, two riders were seen. Men moved to prepared positions; carbines were trained. Fairweather did not shift, nor did Larkin, at least not until danger or otherwise had been determined by binoculars. It was difficult for Fairweather to hold the riders in view; they travelled too fast, heads bobbing, weaving beyond rock and tree. At last the approach to the hilltop slowed them. They urged their horses up rising ground, whipping, digging boots into sweaty flanks; faces became passably clear.

Neither was Dodds.

'Dear God,' Fairweather whispered.

One was a chunky and unidentifiable Maori with fretful face. The other was a colonist and sometime scout by name of Daniels, a lanky and cadaverous fellow whom Fairweather had lately retired with an afflicted gut. His face held no elation either. Whatever his anguish, it was now more than intestinal.

Otherwise nothing was clear. Still a hundred yards off, the pair could be heard shouting; their voices wound incoherently into one and streamed away in wind. Men rose from their positions, curious, carbines still ready.

'I know that Maori,' Larkin disclosed. 'He shears for colonists round Matawhero. Name of Jonah, as I recall.'

'Thank you, Larkin,' Fairweather said. 'That's all I need.'

Having taxed their lungs too early, all but riding their horses into the last yards of ground, the pair arrived gasping and gagging; hoofbeats ceased.

'Murder,' was all the Maori could say, and toppled from his saddle. Helping hands reached out too late; he crashed dumb into fern.

'What?' Fairweather asked. 'Where?'

It was Daniels who answered. Still horsed, he found himself the equal of his distress; and hissed through his teeth. 'Hell,' he said. 'Hell is broke loose.'

It seemed Fairweather already knew what had happened, and how. While he persisted in thrall to the smoke of three fires, disaster had forced entry by the back door. He hardly needed further enlightenment. 'Kooti?'

'Hell,' Daniels said.

21

Fairweather swore his party back to Poverty Bay through surviving daylight and a night feebly moonlit. Given the terrain, the hazards of night riding, the pace was consistently intemperate. Horses broke legs and had to be shot; others became doubly burdened. Nor did men go unmarked. Creeper strangled, and ambushing branches bashed some from saddles. There were cries, bloody abrasions, and crippling sprains. And the shocked colonist named Daniels, the sorry Maori called Jonah, had to be nursed. Neither grew much more informative. They just knew, for God's truth, that they had seen what they saw, and found it mostly unspeakable. When they could talk, it was of terror and fire, tomahawks flailing, guns flaming, death storming abroad in the night and their own lives at risk. Of the lives of others they proved less competent to speak. Neither knew anything of Dodds, though they had heard of his warning; the message had travelled through Matawhero, toward the port, on the eve of the ninth; most colonists and many Maoris were preparing to leave the next morning. Biggs? They knew nothing of him either. They could not even assign a role to Kooti. They made it seem less the work of man and more an act of God. Flood, perhaps; avalanche or earthquake. Their experience seemed to partake of all three. Over Poverty Bay some lethal blight had settled. With words again failing, the two lapsed back into stupor. With Fairweather urging them on, they needed their breath anyway.

Most was confirmed in the morning. Fairweather lay in damp grass on a knoll overlooking the southern half of the Poverty Bay plain. Behind him horses frothed and men fretted. Before him, as he moved his binoculars, the worst slowly marched. Old fires smouldered; fresh fires burned. Impossible to see a home left standing in the south. Such as he could view of Matawhero amounted to stables, sheds and barns; otherwise he noted blackened walls and smoking ground.

A loud moaning rose nearby. Mulhooly. 'My wife,' he wept. 'Where is my Millie?'

'Larkin,' Fairweather said, 'that man may spread panic. Shut him up. Say our only recourse is to shoot.'

'Look, son,' Larkin told Mulhooly, 'we know as some must of got away.'

'Not Millie,' Mulhooly lamented. 'She wouldn't go nowhere without me.'

'Shut him up,' Fairweather ordered. 'Now.'

Larkin launched an accurate fist. Mulhooly was quiet.

As daylight strengthened, Fairweather picked up movement. Parties of men on horseback, firearms slung on their backs, were abroad on the plain; soon some were passing quite near. They appeared to be patrolling their scorched domain. Certainly they were shutting Fairweather's party off from the port.

'Tell men not to show themselves tall,' Fairweather said to Larkin. 'Drag horses down too.'

He used the binoculars to see north. Toward the port of Turanga all seemed much as he had last seen it; there was no smoke rising, and rivers took the first sun.

Larkin crouched alongside. 'What now, sir?' he asked.

'My notion,' Fairweather said, 'is that we must get through to the port. Yet to cross the plain is madness. I see too many down there; and we are too few.'

'Then we go by sea, sir,' Larkin suggested. 'Go down to a coast village, dump our horses, and grab a boat.'

'Does it ever come to you, Larkin, that you might best command this party?'

'Never, sir,' Larkin asserted.

Within the minute Larkin had men horsed again and moving as inconspicuously as broken country allowed; Fairweather travelled in the rear. At length, from a ridge, they looked down on a promising Maori coastal *kainga*. Larkin gave it a name. 'Muriwai village, sir,' he said. 'They catch the biggest fish in the bay. Peaceful sort of place.' No inhabitant was visible. Nor were armed raiders evident. Fishing nets were strung above the shore; whaleboats and canoes rested on the sand. Larkin elected to ride down to the village with the Maori Jonah, who claimed relatives there.

'If there is trouble,' Fairweather promised, 'we shall ride in. In which case you and Jonah fall flat. Our shooting may not discriminate.'

'Sir,' Larkin said, and cantered away.

Fairweather watched through binoculars as Larkin and Jonah arrived in the village. Soon most of its inhabitants were roused. Men appeared, then women and children, all fully dressed. It was clear that none had known a night's sleep; they had been cowering under cover. The *korero* with Larkin and Jonah took a vigorous turn. Waving arms could be discerned, sometimes fists. Shouting came faintly. Fairweather judged the time for negotiation past.

'We ride in,' he ordered. 'Shoot if I say.'

Even tattered and bloodied, Fairweather's party made impression as it entered the village with weapons on show. Maoris backed against walls and gave a clear path. Fairweather placed men to watch approaches to the village and then reined in alongside Larkin. Jonah was in agitated debate with several elderly men.

'The problem, sir,' Larkin explained, 'is that Kooti's got these people in his pockets. Whether they're for him or against is difficult to say. They tell Jonah that if they help us Kooti might come down hard. He's already taken off young men. They don't want worse.'

Fairweather moved to Jonah. 'Which of these old roosters,' he asked, 'is the senior?'

'Him,' Jonah said. A tall greybeard backed away, sheepish about acknowledging his distinction; more so when Fairweather tugged his revolver free.

'Tell him,' Fairweather said, 'that whatever Kooti can do, I do better. Especially in respect of scattering his brains, then those of his fellows. He has ten seconds. We want a whaleboat.'

Jonah hardly needed to interpret. Given Fairweather's fast breathing and bloodshot eyes, the old men were unanimously pleased to oblige with a boat. They led the way to the beach, where fresh *korero* rippled about the craft best suited to Fairweather's need.

With minutes going, menace festering near, Fairweather and Larkin took the nearest. Packs, saddles and weapons were bundled aboard, and it was dragged to the water. Horses were set free.

'Explain that we'll be back to collect them,' Fairweather told Jonah. 'Also to return their boat.'

Jonah nodded. 'I think they understand that. What they worry about is whether they should follow. They now have much fear.'

'Say it is shared.'

Fairweather waded after the launched whaleboat, still with revolver in hand, and with wary eye on the village and villagers behind. He urged Jonah aboard, and then followed. 'Pull,' he called to the oarsmen. They found a stuttering rhythm; the boat lifted over the surf and fell into flat sea.

They were fifty yards off shore when Larkin sighted a horseman. Soon there were a dozen strung out on the sand near the village named Muriwai. None were slow to dismount and train rifles. Their shot splashed short, or skipped wide. 'Point to open sea,' Fairweather ordered. 'Present a thin target.'

A shot struck the boat. There was damage only to woodwork. Another hissed interestingly past Fairweather's ear. There was desirable response. Men on the oars cursed others too clumsy and slow. Fright gained another hundred yards. A last bullet passed overhead, and they were abandoned as quarry.

Ashore the shooting persisted. This did not prove a puzzle for long. People of Muriwai could be observed fleeing. Men were afoot with guns, loading and firing. It was some time before their sound slackened. When it did, single shots sickened more; likewise the intervals between. The dwellings of Muriwai began burning.

'Punishment,' Jonah grieved from the stern. 'It is as their fear.'

'And goodbye our bloody horses,' Larkin muttered.

Fairweather was not disposed to listen to either. As the boat stood further out to sea, at last turning north toward Turanga, he watched the smoke of several fires form one foul cloud. He could take half the credit, or all.

'Do you believe, Larkin,' he asked finally, 'that what must be has to be?'

'Pardon, sir?'

'Never mind,' Fairweather said.

Turanga was undamaged; it was merely deranged. Colonists and Maoris jostled on the banks of the river, bitter men raging, women ugly with weeping, children still wailing alarm. The unfinished redoubt had been occupied by panicky Maoris. Others were sheltering in the courthouse, in Read's store and hotel. Two schooners seen becalmed in light airs off the coast had been brought in by oil-burning bonfire; they had discharged cargoes of live cattle, multiplying the waterside confusion, and were taking aboard refugees. Colonists and villagers from outlying districts were still arriving in, by horse or canoe, or afoot and tottering the last yards. The sweaty shape of Trader Read rose from the ferment, his hat askew, his unbuttoned shirt retired from contest with his belly.

'Thank God you got here,' Read said. 'We need some authority.'

Biggs?

Read shook his head. He also knew nothing of Emily Biggs and her child. Nor of Dodds and others of Matawhero. The best hope was that they were held hostage. The least that their anguish had been brief.

A familiar lament went up. Mulhooly again. 'My Millie,' he cried. 'I can't find her.'

Fairweather had a search of his own. He pushed among Maoris and colonists and addressed the same question to all. He had the one answer from all.

No one had seen anything of the Smith family. Seen or heard.

Someone had to salvage those visible and mountingly audible. Fairweather imposed himself first on the schooners. No able men were to be taken aboard. Those found huddled among women, or under hatches, he booted off again; and Larkin similarly humiliated them when they were ferried ashore. Fairweather placed a sentry to ensure that no further males of an age to bear rifles attempted escape. So much for manpower. He sent pickets running to cover approaches to the port; and dispatched weary Jonah with telescope to find a high point and observe any outlaw advance. He emptied squatters from the redoubt at gunpoint, and established system within. Sand was passed in buckets from the river, along a line of men, and emptied between weatherboards and linings of buildings which could be defended; slots in the walls were sawn for firearms. Women and children cheated of a schooner passage were taken indoors. Men were arranged in ranks and harangued by Larkin on the usage of weapons. Finally, there was food. The abandoned cattle were slain, gutted, and hoisted on spits over fires. Fairweather also commandeered all the foodstuffs, likewise the drink, in Trader Read's store.

'This is nothing short of looting,' Read protested. 'I trust there will be compensation.'

'I am not empowered to speak for this skinflint colony,' Fairweather said while uncorking brandy. 'I can for Kooti. He has compensation of more informal nature in mind. By tomorrow he could be back in business in Turanga. And with no rival.'

That did not leave Read in good heart; it was not meant to. Fairweather carried his confiscated bottle to Read's hotel, already selected as headquarters. Men kept watch on the rickety upper verandah, among them Mulhooly. His eyes were to Matawhero in the south as the last hour of day passed; he surely saw little through his tears. Fairweather pressed the brandy upon him. 'Get your belly around this,' he said. 'Which is an order.'

'I never had a head for strong drink, sir,' Mulhooly argued feebly.

'All to the good. Come on, man. Now.'

Mulhooly shakily lifted the bottle, gulped, and then gagged and spat.

'And the rest,' Fairweather said.

'Sir. Please.'

'Hurry along. I have better to do with my day.'

Less than a third of the bottle was all Mulhooly required. When his knees sagged, Fairweather shouldered him inside the hotel to sleep with the women. Of a mind to make the most of the remainder of the bottle, Fairweather walked out to the verandah again. There Larkin lurked to remind him of duty.

'I think, sir,' Larkin reported, 'that we've got this ship in shape.'

'For quicker sinking, perhaps.' Fairweather viewed southern plain. With the going of day distant fires burned brighter. There was no gunshot in remote hearing. That did not mean much; Kooti was out there. Meanwhile the port was quietening.

'There's still a few arriving in,' Larkin added. 'Mostly Maori now.'

'No one I'd know?'

'I'm sorry to say, sir. I ask all of them just like you said. No one by name of Smith.'

'Thank you, Larkin. You are a considerate fellow.'

'It doesn't bear thinking about, sir, what's been going on. And maybe still is.'

'No, Larkin. I also try not to.'

'Lucky you've got other things to occupy you, sir.'

'Yes, Larkin. Fortunate indeed.'

'I'm sorry, sir, if I'm not helping matters.'

'Then perhaps we must find some more feats for ourselves,' Fairweather said. 'Putting Read out of misery for one.'

'He's still on the rampage about his lost grog, sir. He says Turanga is in the hands of a drunk thief.'

'In which case, Larkin, you must assist in disposing of this evidence of felony. It is by no means desirable that I empty the bottle alone.'

Larkin took the brandy. 'I thought you was never going to ask, sir.'

'At least it is one which Kooti won't get.'

'Yes, sir. I know my duty.'

'And make sure other men tonight get the same. Not to excess. One mug for each. Enough to cheer until dawn, if they see it. If not, I should much prefer happy corpses.'

'You're going to drive Read fair mad, sir.'

'In my book of martial etiquette,' Fairweather said, 'only soldiers should profit from siege. Civilians come second, and prosperous merchants a pitiful third. You play to your strong points, and God knows we have few.'

The brandy kept Larkin quiet. There was a fresh ripple of light out on the plain.

'I'm the lucky one, sir,' Larkin confided.

'You must work hard to convince me, Larkin. Meanwhile you might consider returning that bottle.'

'I don't have no wife or woman still out there,' Larkin explained. 'My house might be gone, but land don't burn easy. Even if I grizzle about it, it's still there.'

'And perhaps more yet and better.'

'I'm not thinking that far, sir.'

'Wisdom speaks,' Fairweather said.

They saw the sun rise, after all, next morning. Kooti seemed set on puzzling. He had more than enough warriors to mince the port and its defenders; he could have pulled off that coup thrice over. Why no attack?

'Perhaps he thinks we're stronger,' Larkin said.

'Or given himself a fright,' Fairweather suggested. 'A commonplace happening. One cannot quite believe one's own success; nerve suddenly goes.'

'If you say so, sir.'

Larkin was dubious. So too was Fairweather. Speculation served to keep him awake; it was sixty hours since he last slept.

'On the other hand,' he went on, 'it may all be simpler. He might just be instructing fresh conscripts in the lively pursuits of Old Testament tribesmen, before Christ came along.'

'Christ, sir?'

'And the humbug of sweetness and light. If my skin were brown I might need no convincing.'

'Yes, sir. Poor sods.'

'The same poor sods may be in sufficiently rabid shape very soon. Aside from which, Kooti could be trying to call his more seasoned followers to heel. One thing he does delight in is discipline, and the enforcing of same.'

'Yes, sir. You got to admire him for that.'

'Still ever the fighting man, Larkin.'

'You got to do things proper, sir, or not do them at all.'

'In that case, go and wake Mulhooly. Give him a turn on watch. You should find him more of a soldier this morning.'

Before Larkin left, he looked again to the south. 'It's still a bloody teaser, sir. Whatever we say.'

'It is,' Fairweather said.

They also saw the setting of the sun. The swampy ground beyond the port remained empty of peril. Outlying pickets were called in and replaced by men with more sleep. Orders had still to be improvised and enforced with promise of personal injury. There were disputes to be settled among those comfortlessly crowded in the port, grievances about food and accommodation to be heard, altercations to be quietened. The most commanding of these was a brawl between Trader Read and his inflamed and weighty Maori wife along a distance of riverside. There was much staggering, falling and heavy breathing in this contest of corpulence. Missiles were made of objects promisingly lethal. When his nearest and dearest got the best of it, Read waded out into mud and tide, fully dressed, and rowed out to midstream in a dinghy where he rocked panting and groaning. With the undivided attention of all in the port, Mrs Read denounced her husband as promoter of Poverty Bay's woes. Her most strident complaint was that Read had taught Kooti how to turn a quick penny, filled his fool's head with ambition, and initiated him into the lucrative magic of the rum trade. Otherwise Kooti might still be a pious idler about the port; and not an aggrieved exile with bloody hands. With asides to her audience, and vividly obscene gestures, Mrs Read won rising applause. Finally she sent a scrap of rusty metal spinning in Read's direction, and walked off to restore her taxed vocal chords from the most convenient bottle.

'Kooti himself couldn't do better,' Larkin judged. He assigned Read a guard.

The wind had changed; it now brought the smell of burning in from the plain. Far conflagrations again punctured the dark. The marvel was that there was anything left flammable over the greater part of Poverty Bay.

The sea mirrored moon and stars; there was the beat of Pacific surf. For a time, on watch, Fairweather was beset by memory of his first frivolous weeks here; he wished himself less cursed with recall. A shadowy Larkin finally moved into place beside him.

'I think you can risk some sleep, sir,' Larkin said. 'You're a right mess and getting no better.'

'It's too calm, Larkin, altogether too quiet. You would think he might make a probe. A thrust here and there.'

'He hasn't, sir, and he isn't. I'd very soon wake you. Is it the Smiths still worrying you?'

'I ask myself questions,' Fairweather conceded.

'Who doesn't, sir? I mean about Biggs, Dodds, all them out there. There's one thing about your Smiths. Being half Maori, they might have a better colour for Kooti.'

'I should like to think so, Larkin.'

'Try thinking it, sir. And get your sleep. Otherwise you'll be no use to us. As things are, you can't even stand straight.'

'Shut up, Larkin.'

'I order you, sir.'

Fairweather was ineffective as Larkin fell upon him like a wall and heaved him into the hotel; he lost communication with his feet, and collapsed to the floor. A pillow of sacking was pushed under his head, a blanket thrown over him. With something between shudder and sigh, he soared into void.

He woke to sunlight, the voices of children. He heard Larkin shouting orders, men banging up and down stairs. An attack? He threw aside his blanket and raced out to Larkin.

'Just placing new pickets, sir,' Larkin said. 'Nothing to report.'

'Nothing?'

'Only that it's gone uncanny quiet, sir, out on the plain.'

Fairweather blinked in the light. Smoke had gone; so had its smell. He took binoculars and looked from left to right, from sea to mountain, and slowly back again. He could pick up no movement on the plain. No horsemen. No life at all.

'You're feeling all right, sir?' Larkin asked.

'Aside from an uncomfortable bladder, which is overdue for relief. As for last night, and your mutinous liberties with my person, I may overlook it for now.'

'Thank you, sir.'

'Which is not to say it can happen again. Decencies and distances must be observed between officers and men. The colonies cannot be permitted to corrupt old imperial men.'

'I know a reprimand when I hear one, sir. If you don't mind me saying so, you'd look more like an officer if you had a piss and a wash and got some food in your belly. That's if you want to make some impression.'

'I'll have your balls one day,' Fairweather promised, and then did mostly as Larkin said.

Noon was the same. Bright sunlight and empty plain. The beginnings of blue summer haze.

'I think I understand,' Fairweather said.

'You do, sir?'

'In moderation. I am a moderate man, as you well know, Larkin. Which leaves me with a sore problem. A moderate man can believe only moderately in moderation.'

'So what is it you reckon, sir?' Larkin asked.

'That Kooti is much more concerned with making himself felt on the land hereabouts. So that no colonist can further feel safe. The port would be a shabby prize. And irrelevant. Land is the thing.'

'Maybe, sir.'

'Also taking the port might entangle him too deeply. Difficult to defend. Artillery could soon warm his arse. He has seen those schooners arrive; he is not to know whether we have been reinforced. He can play ducks and drakes out on the plain. Not necessarily here.'

'I get your drift, sir.'

'Each hour that passes means Captain Herrick another hour closer from Hawke's Bay. Word will also have gone out on the electric telegraph from there.'

'Yes, sir, I keep thinking of that. I tell the men this isn't forever. There's some don't believe it. Mulhooly for one.'

'In Mulhooly's case I shouldn't argue, Larkin. He is by far the best judge of forever in present company.'

'Yes, sir.'

'I also understand that Kooti could be counting on that. Our impatience. Our need to know. In short, the quiet out there could be deceit. A ploy. He may be trying to tempt us out on to the plain. We reveal our strength, or our lack. And he practices every trick in the ambusher's trade, then cuts to size all who give him offence in the port. To oblige him we need only go out there and investigate.'

There was a long silence.

'All the same, sir,' Larkin protested at last, 'it's hard just to sit here. Hour after hour.'

'Then you must practice,' Fairweather said. 'Practice with diligence. Hour after hour.'

'I'll try, sir. And tell others too.'

'And remind me also, Larkin. Often.'

'You, sir?'

'I need telling, Larkin, that it is the right thing to do.'

Nor did nightfall bring change or challenge. For the first time there was no gleam of fire out on the plain. It was a warm night, flecked with the whine of mosquitoes, not conducive to sleep. Nor to the comfort of those intentionally wakeful and fretful in thought. Fairweather took first watch from the hotel verandah; Larkin relieved him at midnight.

'Nothing,' Fairweather reported. 'And no Herrick.'

'He won't let you down, sir.'

'I am grateful to have my own feeling confirmed. But you bring him no closer.'

'No, sir. I can't play at God.'

'Someone may be. And perhaps not an impostor. Things have that hellish feel.'

'You been letting things get under your guard again, sir.'

'You would seem to be telling me, Larkin, that concern for the fate of individuals is unbecoming to a professional; that I must keep larger ends in view.'

'It's not for me to tell you one thing or the other, sir. But there's one thing I will say. As for the Smiths, nothing you do now will make no difference. Whatever has happened, it's done. And you'd be the better for more sleep.'

'When Herrick arrives, come hell or high water, we move out across the plain. Only one thing might make me think twice. If Kooti has people hostage, we could expect a messenger soon. If so, we reconsider. And think on the bargain to be struck.'

'You think that's possible, sir? A bargain?'

'I think mostly everything, Larkin. And I trust your hours on watch are not quite as long.'

Fairweather limped inside, his body a burden, and found a place to fall. He thought he might be slower to find sleep this second time. He was wrong. It arrived as a deluge; he drowned.

22

In the middle of another hot morning Fairweather spied a flicker of motion out on the plain. The sunlit landscape trembled as he trained binoculars. There was a lone human figure rising most of a mile off. This figure was following a worn path to the port.

'We may have our messenger at last,' he told Larkin.

'Armed, sir?'

'Not that I see. Get word to pickets. He is not to be hindered or hurt.'

Larkin sent a man running with the order. 'How's it look now, sir?' he asked.

'Odd,' Fairweather said.

The figure was making indifferent progress; there was a wobbling, a wandering. More, the figure seemed to shrink; it continued to shrink. No illusion. Just one conclusion was possible.

'Dear God,' he said to Larkin, 'we have a child out there.'

'Maori?'

'Too soon to say. We ride out to bring it in.'

'You don't think a trap, sir?'

'A child is a child. It may not make the distance.'

Fairweather and Larkin hurried to horses, and galloped out of the port. To take more men might impede; it had to be a dash by two with an understanding. Larkin rode wide, to draw fire, while Fairweather made fast for the child.

In the last yards it could be seen as male and pale, a feeble and barefoot boy of five or six years in filthy nightshirt. He shivered with fright as Fairweather and his horse bore down. Fairweather was not disposed to friendly overtures. He swooped and gathered the boy kicking on to his saddle; and swung for the port.

'I have you safe,' he promised. 'Whatever it is, or was, it's all over now.'

Larkin closed, rode level and looked at the boy. 'Mother of God,' he shouted over hoofbeats. 'That's young Jimmy Newman. Jack Newman's son.'

They cantered past pickets and into the port. A sighing crowd gathered. Fairweather dispersed it with efficient obscenity. He passed the boy to

Larkin, who carried him up hotel stairs. Inside they arranged the boy on a blanket and pressed water between his lips. He shook less violently, though with eyes still timid.

'What is it, son?' Fairweather asked.

'I been walking,' the boy confided.

'So we see,' Fairweather said.

'Days and days. Round and round. Sometimes in trees. The trees were all big.'

'Sometimes trees are,' Fairweather said.

'And there was Maoris riding everywhere. The night they came, Mum pushed me out a window. I hid in a bush.'

'What else can you tell us, Jimmy?' Fairweather persisted.

'Where is me Dad?' Jimmy demanded. 'I want me Dad.'

'Your father,' Fairweather explained, 'has been performing a mission for me. And should be back soon. What do you want to tell him?'

'It's me Mum. She's hurt. She's hurt bad.'

He held up a skinny fist; Fairweather undid it. There was a stained scrap of paper within. The message scrawled was brief and barely decipherable. *Is there,* it read, *some Christian to save me? I am very Much wounded and Suffering terrible. I am in a shed at the back of our Property. I send my boy Jim. come quick Whoever reads this for the Love of God and Christ our Sweet Saviour. ALICE NEWMAN.'*

'How long?' Fairweather said with difficulty. 'How long since you left her?'

'I don't count good,' Jimmy said, and held up three and then four fingers. 'I just kept walking and hiding. I got things to eat from houses. I didn't think it was stealing if nobody was home.'

'It wasn't, Jimmy,' Fairweather reassured.

'Sometimes when I went back to the houses they was burned. I didn't burn them. I just took things. True.'

'All is forgiven,' Fairweather insisted.

He called women to wash and feed the boy and locate fresh clothes. Then he turned to Larkin. 'Four days,' he said.

'At least, sir,' Larkin said.

'And there might be others barely clinging to life.'

'One's enough, sir. Jack Newman would never forgive us.'

'Could you forgive yourself either?'

'Not easy, sir. No.'

'To hell with Herrick,' Fairweather decided.

Gathering men, finding and saddling horses, distributing ammunition and checking weapons, took most of an hour. The party was ready when a cry came from a man on watch.

'Steamer,' he called.

Herrick; it had to be. Fairweather would be less alone. Someone to share decision; also someone to blame. In that respect Larkin gave too little satisfaction.

He climbed to the verandah. The plume of the steamer smudged the horizon as it came in from the south.

'We wait,' he told Larkin. 'It's only good sense.'

'You won't get much from Newman, sir, when he hears. I already got problems holding Mulhooly back. One madman is enough.'

'We may soon, Larkin, need all the madmen we can muster.'

'If that's what you think, sir.'

'More and more,' Fairweather said. 'Why can't that steamer move faster?'

The prudent skipper chose not to enter the river, with God knew what loose in Poverty Bay. He hovered off the mouth, engine still working, and had passengers ferried ashore.

Newman and Herrick were in the first boat to beach. Fairweather took Newman's hand first. 'I knew you would not fail me,' he said. 'Now go along with Larkin. There is much to explain.'

Confused and still on sea legs, Newman shuffled away alongside Larkin; Fairweather did not care to watch further. To Herrick he said, 'I should like to speak what I feel.'

'Save your breath,' Herrick urged. 'News?'

'Only that we now know Kooti's bite even worse than his bark. We shall very soon know more.'

'I bring seventy, and a number of horses. Twenty of militia, a dozen armed constabulary, one surgeon, and the remainder Maoris. Reliable all.'

'Also the Maoris?'

'It is a matter of pride with Whitmore not to be able to distinguish one native face from another. I know mine. Men greedy to fight for two colonial shillings a day and all food found. Mercenary ambition may prove a match for Kooti's mana.'

'There,' Fairweather said, 'is the damnable word again.'

'Look who is talking,' Herrick argued. 'You appear to have kept control. And a calm head. From where else does it spring?'

'Consider fear,' Fairweather said.

They heard Newman's cry. It said that he had found his son and knew of his wife. It said more. Even Herrick, who knew little yet, had a face losing all colour.

They rode out from the port in three parties. Two were to spread protective wings; the third was to make directly for Matawhero. Fairweather ordered that no engagement was to be countenanced; in the event of ambush all were to extricate themselves with speed, to the point of abandoning wounded. Kooti still had the numbers; the port could not be imperilled. Herrick rode between Fairweather and Larkin, with Newman, Mulhooly and Jonah behind.

They met desolation, fences torn and trampled, dwellings looted and burned; these were farms of Maoris and colonists close enough to the port to escape without personal hurt. Their abandoned livestock had been slaughtered. Sheep here, cattle there, and horses and pigs. After days of hot sun, the stench was tidal; flies rose in shimmering haze.

'Sweet Jesus,' Herrick said. 'It is like plague.'

Others kept silence as they closed with Matawhero. Newman was soon bolting ahead, with Fairweather trying to keep pace. Useless to urge discretion on Newman. But he did shout back to Larkin, 'Hold on to Mulhooly. He must not go alone. Never.'

Matawhero was magically still; a few freed ducks and chickens squawked away as men dismounted near the charred Newman home. Newman had no eyes for it. They heard the low moaning before they reached the shed at the rear.

Within was what persisted of Alice Newman after bayonets had pierced her, and rifle butts bashed again and again. Much of her breast had been laid open, some of her abdomen too. The marvel was not just that she lived, but that she had crawled to the shed, found water, and written the note for young Jimmy. Newman spluttered and wept. Fairweather could not see where to begin. Someone more competent might put Alice Newman together again.

He left the shed to find Herrick dismounting. 'There is work for your surgeon,' he said. 'I trust he has the stomach. God knows I have not.'

To Larkin he said, 'Assign men to Newman and his wife. Keep pickets circling Matawhero. We need time to know all.'

'Sir,' Larkin said.

'Ensured of our safety, you may investigate the Biggs house. Then report to me.'

Larkin mounted and rode away.

Mulhooly stood before Fairweather with twitching face.

'Captain Herrick,' Fairweather said, 'I should be obliged if you kept the pair of us company. We have a brief visit to make. Jonah? I think you too.'

Fairweather dropped an arm about Mulhooly to curb a precipitate dash. His property adjoined Newman's; there was only a short walk. Herrick and Jonah followed behind. Their boots could be heard on the hard earth. Mulhooly's breath came in shudders. The walk was already the longest of his life.

'Bear up,' Fairweather said. 'We know nothing yet. Nothing.'

But Mulhooly knew, and was right. Stench became stronger as they neared the rubble of his home. He broke free and ran on. Fairweather followed breathless. Sense told him to tackle Mulhooly, pinion him, send him away. Sense was one thing, Mulhooly another; he was not to be caught.

Or not until they reached the wreckage of rose bushes in Mulhooly's front garden. His wife rested there. Her head was fragments of skull and pulped brain; her throat had been ripped, her torso superfluously shredded. Three children lay near, similarly used, the youngest quite headless. The drifts of feeding flies were not shifted by Mulhooly's bubbling whimper.

'Get him out of here,' Fairweather told Jonah, the least afflicted, with more notion than most of what to expect. 'Don't stand on ceremony. Render him unconscious if you must. But remove him from this.'

Jonah bundled Mulhooly away; he had to call on others for help as Mulhooly bit and kicked.

Herrick backed away from the site. 'Women,' he said hoarsely. 'Children. This cannot be called war.'

'What else?' Fairweather said.

Larkin rode down on them. To Fairweather he said, 'I shouldn't go over to the Biggs place, sir. I can handle it myself. No sight for a Christian to see.'

'Then I qualify,' Fairweather said. He and Herrick recovered their horses and followed Larkin. The smell did not diminish as they rode through Matawhero. Stray dogs and reprieved pigs were foraging among human remains. Men were shooting, driving the beasts off.

Where the Biggs house had stood the difference was only in particulars. Emily Biggs was a torn doll, naked and hardly identifiable in the dirt. Her breasts had been hacked away; she had been split from the fork of her legs up to the navel. What might have been her womb was exposed to the world. Baby George was beside her, many times run through with bayonets, hardly to be seen as more than meat. Biggs had been decapitated after blades and bullets had done their worst elsewhere; his head had become a nourishing plaything for pigs. The sockets of his eyes had been emptied, yet he still seemed to stare astonished at the sky. Scorched and bloody papers, documents and maps, fluttered about the three corpses. Fire had quite levelled the house behind.

Herrick, somewhere near, began retching. Fairweather said to Larkin, 'Temporary graves must be dug, and all known names marked. There will be some more decent and formal interment later.'

'We could say a prayer, sir,' Larkin said.

'If brief,' Fairweather said.

'A fair few not accounted for, sir. Dodds for one.'

'I shall check Dodds' house.'

'At the far end of the settlement, sir. Likely the first hit. I'll get on with the digging. The sooner done, the sooner we're rid of the stink.'

Herrick was bent, a trickle of bile spilling; Fairweather persuaded him upright. 'You will need to do better than this,' he said. 'You set no example.'

Herrick pleaded, 'It is worse than anything said of the Indian mutiny. Worse than Cawnpore. I shall never see anything more hateful.' He mopped his mouth with a handkerchief. 'I shall remind myself I am a Briton. Is that what I do?'

'And find your horse. We still have work here.'

'Looking for survivors?'

'Numbering the dead.'

They moved inland with men riding defensively on each side. On Fairweather's order some dropped away to check other houses reduced to debris and look for slain. Presently a last composition of blackened timber and fallen roofing iron was sighted. Fairweather paused his horse.

'You need come no nearer,' he told Herrick. 'I had a good man here. A scout. A troublesome fellow at times, but no more so than most colonists, and with never a mean streak among comrades.'

'Perhaps this time you will need help more than I,' Herrick suggested.

'You will see no grief.'

'Would it not be better?'

'Our wits are more wisely employed.'

'You still think we might be attacked?'

'Rather less. I think Kooti has withdrawn from the plain. He may need the satisfaction of someone seeing that he has been about Jehovah's business; someone alive to report.'

'How even to begin?'

'The words are provided already, Herrick. Cursed be the fruit of thy body, and the fruit of thy land, the increase of thy kin, and the flocks of thy sheep. And thy carcass shall be meat unto all the fowls of the air, and unto the beasts of the earth.'

'You would say that?'

'As Deuteronomy does. A recipe for obstinate Canaanites and disobedient Jews. Also a plan of campaign.'

'Perhaps Kooti should be made to understand that the Jews are no longer as in the Bible, and tolerably civilized. Indeed passive, if one is to give them a name.'

'The information would come too many lives late in the day. Shall we proceed?'

'You lead,' Herrick said. 'I follow.'

This time they did not dismount to view death. Fairweather ordered men to begin digging. The corpses of Dodds and his family were more wholly clothed than most seen; they appeared to have been about to depart Matawhero. Unpacked possessions were strewn about, abandoned as poor loot by the raiders. There was one other distinction. A smashed carbine lay beside Dodds; he had perished giving fight. In consequence of which, presumably, his trousers had been tugged to his knees; he had been emasculated.

Fairweather rode a little way off with Herrick. The reek was not lost, nor much else.

'I know it small consolation,' Herrick observed, 'but there is one thing to be said. There has been no reversion to traditional Maori custom. No cannibalism is evident.'

'You are missing the point, Herrick. Jews don't even eat pig.'

They trotted their horses back to Larkin, past burial parties and men patrolling. It appeared that Kooti had taken no hostage, done nothing to prolong matters; the massacre was pure in its plan. With pencil and paper Larkin was keeping tally as men reported in. Already thirty colonists and their women and children had been counted dead; also more than that number of Maoris dwelling nearby.

'More?' Fairweather queried.

'He hasn't been kind to his own colour either,' Larkin said. 'Not if they were in his way, sir.'

To Herrick, Fairweather said, 'I leave you in command here. Do not allow the return to the port to be that of a rabble.'

'Where are you going?' Herrick said.

'Where it is best I ride alone.'

'It sounds most unwise,' Herrick protested.

Larkin looked up from his calculations. 'I'd leave Captain Fairweather to his business, sir,' he suggested to Herrick.

'If I must, then,' Herrick agreed.

'Should chance arrange that I cannot join you this evening,' Fairweather said, 'no men are to be sent abroad on the plain or tempted into traps.'

'I understand,' Herrick said with reluctance. 'But I should still like to know more.'

'At least I soon shall,' Fairweather said.

He rode across the plain on an erratic course designed to frustrate snipers in wait. No shots sounded, but silence did not mean safety. It certainly meant death. There were more stricken dwellings; more slaughtered beasts bloating, and hawks overhead.

The Smith homestead rose beyond the river. No dark shell; it stood undiminished. Relief was short; apprehension returned. Why? Why of all places left?

He pushed his horse across the river; it whinnied and baulked at the mud and depth, but was brutally persuaded to locate footing, to climb drenched with its rider upon the far bank. Riverside trees, scrub and shadow signalled caution; likewise absence of life. He took revolver in hand and rode the last yards with care. No marksman disclosed himself from door or window of the homestead. He dismounted and walked. When he paused, which was often, he could hear faint birds, perhaps even leaves falling. The sound of twigs and grass underfoot became audible as he moved on; his boots were even more resonant on the boards of the Smith verandah.

The front door stood partly ajar. Taking breath, he kicked it wider; the bang echoed briefly within. Silence again. Flies. After the sun's glare his eyes had to labour, for a time, in the gloom of the hall. He thought himself past horror. It seemed not. Human segments were distributed the length of the hall. Darkening blood patched carpet and streaked walls. He tried to lift his eyes, as he forced himself through the hall, but still managed to note that two limbs did not match; that two butchered males were on view. Matiu and Pita had been dismembered with method, and for effect. It was not clear that there had been bullets first; he did not care to make a deduction.

Meri? God knew. Gone. The homestead remained soundless.

He arrived in the kitchen. Devastation could not be more comprehensive. Everything was askew, smashed, overturned and trampled as if an army had marched through. Then he saw that an army of sorts had. Plundered foodstuffs, empty bottles, discarded bones and dirtied bedding said that men had camped here in number; that the building had been a base while Kooti transacted business on the plain. A blemished slaughterman's knife had been driven into the kitchen table; it held down a note. It took some time to read, though it never strayed far from its purpose.

Kia ora Fairweather

I much regret your absence. Informants had told me that this was your dwelling place, which was convenient, for I had long planned this call. I would have been better for the drinking of your liquor with you. We might have had one last and long korero. I should have given you this word, that I am not to be pursued, not to be hunted. No more. Let it be known that those who pursue with murderous heart shall be rats who die in their own dung. I could have killed all the soldiers who guarded us on the Chatham Islands. I did not. I could have killed the crew and captain of the ship we took. I did not. I could have killed Biggs and all of his poor party who asked us to lay down our arms when we landed. I did not. I wished only work of peace and praise of Jehovah. The idea of your people was that killing must be, that the godly of Israel should be hunted as beasts. I have begun to adopt the idea of your people and kill better. So, beware. Do not say Jehovah's wish cannot be. Do not say I cannot be.

For you, Fairweather, this is my word. We may meet again, for it is once more my matakite that this will be so. I even think we might meet again forever, but I know not yet how to interpret this dream. Hear this well. Do the work of dead Biggs no more. The workers of evil here are gone, but for the one, and I may yet drown Read in his own rum. Hear this also. Which way does the wind bloweth now? If you dislike my words, what does it matter? All the worse for you.

One more word of mine to you. I am much recovered from my wound, which delayed my visit to Poverty Bay, but I think yours will be the longer to heal. Too many wives make a burden. May she be my gift. If I make my bed in hell, behold, thou art there (Psalms, Chapter 39, Verse 8).

Na to koutou hoa riri, from your enemy,
Kooti (Coates)

Kooti's way with words left Fairweather with a question; it was answered as he asked it. There was a faint sound; animal. Then he was scrambling from room to room, pounding up stairs and along a passage, the ravished interior of the homestead pouring past. Toppled furniture, axed tables, smashed mirrors; his boots crunched over glass.

Meri sat small in a dim corner, naked but for a stained blanket. Around was a drying pool of faeces and urine. Her face was bruised and festering with cuts. When she lifted her eyes, there was no recognition in them, no light at all.

Later he groped from the house, found a spade and a site for a grave which might take the remnants of Matiu and Pita. He sensed a world made of malevolence; he was its servant.

In hell, then, he promised. I shall be there.

Before dusk he was back in the port with all he had recovered of Meriana Smith. She was passed into the care of Herrick's surgeon, a muscular and middle-aged Scot named Gibbs. Gibbs was bent on making Alice Newman's departure from the world more painless. He examined Meri and announced no serious wound, nothing worth urgent attention; he would do what he could, when he could.

'Please,' Fairweather said.

He remained with Meri while Maori women bedded her between clean linen in a schoolhouse which had been fast converted to hospital. She turned her face from him; she still did not speak. At length Fairweather acknowledged duties elsewhere.

Herrick was on the hotel verandah with a tumbler of liquor soon poured. It seemed Herrick already knew all.

'I hardly know how to begin,' he sympathized.

'Consider it said.'

'Would it not help to talk? Your hands still shake so.'

'I can guarantee my hands,' Fairweather said. 'Now please, Herrick, no more.'

With a sudden abundance of men to deploy, pickets had been strengthened, old defenders rested for the night. The port was prematurely quiet, even children subdued. There were still fitful wails of mourning from Maoris with relatives slain. Colonists, for the most part, wandered in trance. Poverty Bay was a place now disfigured and cursed.

'What of Alice Newman?' Herrick ventured.

'It seems she lingers,' Fairweather said.

'Look at it this way. Life is something, at least.'

'For what?' Fairweather asked.

With a second tumbler of liquor, he looked into the night. The moon was behind cloud, and stars mostly dim.

'I am only saying,' Herrick explained, 'that in your case all is not necessarily lost. Forgive me for saying it. I do not wish to tempt rage. But it would seem she meant much to you.'

'Even the most dedicated lecher, Herrick, can find his battle plan flawed by the terrain.'

'Terrain?' Herrick puzzled.

'And such as grows there. There is always a tree whereof it is commanded that we shouldest not eat.'

'I am sorry,' Herrick said.

'According to the best information available, our miserable ancestor was driven from the garden to till earth where only thistles and bitter herbs grew. And where men could be bred to begin the business of extinguishing each other.'

'I think I take your meaning.'

'You must help me embrace it.'

'Nonetheless I tell you all is not lost. She lives.'

'Quite,' Fairweather said.

Herrick brought himself to ask, 'It is, perhaps, that you wish she did not?'

'I might know what I felt,' Fairweather said.

'Dear God,' Herrick said. Then, 'What power of darkness has laboured to make this?'

Fairweather lifted his tumbler, drank, and on further consideration drank again. There would never be enough to drink; never. He said, 'The craftsmanship is distinctive.'

'To call it of man's making hardly seems adequate.'

'Credit where due,' Fairweather said. 'We are an ingenious species. If you want to know what makes men excel, consider cupidity and vanity. Lately and respectively served by Biggs and Whitmore. As for power, that was our brew too; we can hardly wonder at Kooti being a bad drunk.'

'Given such a day, I am surprised to find you still reasonable.'

'Only because you invite me to skirt the true issue. One does not need to know what turned a dog mad. The fact is that it is so. And must fast be destroyed.'

With uncomfortable effort, Herrick said, 'I see.'

'I think not, Herrick. But you very soon shall. Tomorrow you will see men driven and cursed and training to slay. If Larkin and I have one left with charity in his soul, then we shall have failed.'

'In defending Poverty Bay?'

'Of the past. Herrick. We take the offensive. Our excursion upriver with Whitmore may soon seem salad days. We leave no tree unfelled, no rock unrolled. Nowhere for Kooti to hide.'

'Is vengeance sufficient?'

'If we make a feast of it.'

'I have always seen it as clothing a multitude of sins. Pride, say. And ambition.'

'And a chance to make the world change its tune. My German philosopher argues that war is too dangerous to permit a spirit of benevolence.'

'In what way, then, if you forgive my asking, will you now differ from Kooti?'

'You split hairs,' Fairweather said.

Alice Newman died toward dawn. Candles left shadows fluttering on the walls of the schoolhouse hospital. The sobbing of her husband and son could be heard, and the voice of a clergyman commending her soul into Christ's care. Fairweather removed himself from the bedside when life was no longer apparent. He then found Meri's bed. Surgeon Gibbs had dispensed laudanum; her breathing was shallow, her body still restless. Fairweather took her inert hand for a time, then made himself leave.

He sought comfort in Herrick, and a fresh bottle.

'You wished for an enemy you could believe in,' Herrick noted.

'Tact,' Fairweather said, 'is not your strong suit tonight.'

Soon after, Larkin went bellowing through the port, calling upon every adult male of every hue to make himself visible and available. Larkin further gave it to be understood that those on deathbeds need not think themselves excused. When ranks formed, in an open space before the hotel, Fairweather noted that Larkin used Mulhooly as a marker for the first. Among the last to shuffle into line was Newman, with shoulders soon stiffening; he remained indifferent to Larkin's plea that he might serve grief best by nursing his son for the day.

Satisfied, Fairweather emptied the bottle to brace himself better for the dry day ahead. His legs were suddenly insensitive to his needs; he staggered, and had to hold a verandah rail for equilibrium. Herrick took his arm.

'I do wish you would drink less,' Herrick said. 'I must be frank, Fairweather. You terrify.'

'Rest assured,' Fairweather said, 'that I terrify myself more.'

At noon a second steamer arrived from Hawke's Bay with the remainder of Herrick's contingent. Fairweather had close to another hundred men, mostly Maori. He could also send more women and children to safety, so making the port less a responsibility. On the other hand there was a message from the colony's government untidily transcribed from the electric telegraph. This instructed Fairweather to secure the port of Turanga, protect life and property, and not to engage in enterprises which might promote reprisal. Colonel Whitmore had been instructed to return from the west coast of the colony to punish Kooti again. Fairweather was to wait on Whitmore's orders.

Herrick was unable to hide relief. 'So there are to be no risky ventures,' he said.

'I can make no sense of the thing,' Fairweather said. 'The handwriting is poor. The page is sea-stained; the ink all a blur.'

'I cannot deny that the telegraphist's hand could be improved. But there is no stain of sea.'

'There will be,' Fairweather said, and crumpled the message.

'So that is how it is to be.'

'Conceivably, Herrick.'

'Live and learn,' Herrick said. 'I remember Whitmore ignoring undesirable information. You promise to match him.'

'This is different. We know that Kooti still hovers nearby.'

'Who knows? And how?'

'By way of acid gut. Perhaps prickling of scalp.'

'Your knowledge. Not mine.'

'In which case, Herrick, you must remain in the middle of the column when we move. You must not be at risk.'

'What are you trying to tell me?'

'That we do no one kindness, not even the colonial exchequer, if we again let Kooti drift off into inaccessible parts. We know what that means. And the arrival of Whitmore. Again the will for the deed. Again a counterfeit triumph to placate politicians. And Kooti flourishing as the green bay tree.'

Herrick was quiet.

'Come,' Fairweather said. 'We present Whitmore with Kooti dead or alive. My preference needs no stating.'

'The marvel,' Herrick said, 'is that you can put a persuasive face on something so wilful.'

'Are you with me, and your men?'

'On one understanding. Should you find Kooti before you, you are to recall that there is also a man beside you; and that he is to be given second thrust of the bayonet.'

'You have my word,' Fairweather said.

In the distance Larkin was flintily drilling militia and Maoris; he also had musketry practice in hand. Awe had replaced mourning in the port. The interment of Alice Newman was not, after all, the day's most conspicuous occurrence. The chores of war were.

Fairweather called up Jonah. 'These Maoris from Hawke's Bay,' he said, 'seem too fat to me.'

'Fat?' asked Jonah, himself no mean girth.

'To fight well,' Fairweather said.

'Maybe,' Jonah said. 'Hawke's Bay Maoris, they didn't have much land confiscated. They sold it instead. Some chiefs sleep on mattresses of money. They eat well down there.'

'They must learn to eat less,' Fairweather ordered.

'If that's what you say, boss.'

'Each ounce of blubber will slow us,' Fairweather said. 'Make them sweat. Make them groan.'

Herrick was within earshot. He closed with Fairweather. 'Does your German philosopher,' he asked, 'prevail already?'

'Since you ask, Herrick.'

'Might not more milk of human kindness serve the same end?'

'Tell Kooti,' Fairweather said.

He went again to the hospital. Surgeon Gibbs was at pains to define the limits of his vocation. He could keep Meriana Smith alive. The rest had to be more of God's making than man's. Fairweather could not contest the diagnosis. On her second day she was persuaded to accept a bowl of bread and warm milk. On the third there seemed to be some recognition of Fairweather; she flinched, hid her face, and shuddered. Gibbs led Fairweather away.

'You seem not to help matters,' Gibbs said.

'So there is nothing I can do,' Fairweather said.

'I think not. You seem to bring pain.'

'Talking of pain,' Fairweather said, 'tomorrow we move.'

'I shall be ready,' Gibbs promised.

'What of her?'

'She will be in safe native hands. If there is further failing of health, I have instructed that she be placed aboard a boat for Hawke's Bay to receive decently qualified attention in the hospital there. Don't distress yourself; all that can be done will be.'

'It is what cannot which distresses.'

'A man letting slip the dogs of war will have more on his mind,' Gibbs consoled.

'When they bite,' Fairweather agreed.

23

With Larkin and Jonah alongside, Fairweather halted his horse on a rise and looked over the column as it climbed off the Poverty Bay plain. Three hundred men wound past tree and river for much of a mile. Some straggled on foot; others rode. Packhorses trailed.

'More haste and closer order,' he told Larkin. 'Kooti could waltz through us anywhere with ease.'

'I still got problems,' Larkin complained. 'I could of done with a few more days drilling sense into the sods.'

'Each of those days could also have been gift to Kooti.'

'Yes, sir.'

'Which is not to say, Larkin, that you haven't done all you could.'

Larkin looked more driven than his men; he had shed weight.

'While I think of it,' Fairweather went on, 'make a point of mingling Maoris and militia. They keep too separate.'

'It's natural, sir.'

'No longer, Larkin. Offence has been given to both races. It is now more natural for them to compete for the taking of Kooti's head. He is never again to be seen as a rebel serving native grievance; as anything but an insane killer serving himself.'

'Understood, sir.'

'I wish to see our cause stated clearly. I wish to see the two races fighting as one. Jonah? Is that understood too?'

'All the way, boss.'

'I require you to ride at all times with Larkin. But you answer to me. It would help if you just called me captain.'

'Yes, boss. Captain.'

'It is merely to establish our roles. I am not here just to chase you along.'

'No?' Jonah said with comic surprise.

'You are my left arm, and Larkin my right. It makes for more effective punching if one fist knows what the other is doing. There are two fists, but only one head. Fists cannot be allowed to think for themselves.'

'You talk in a Maori way,' Jonah said.

'Then listen longer,' Fairweather said. 'May I do so much more.'

Larkin and Jonah wheeled off, riding back down the column, delivering Fairweather's message as they moved; Larkin's barking left no room for misunderstanding. Tiring men winced.

Herrick rode up to Fairweather. 'Just where are we going?' he asked. 'Or is it impertinent to ask?'

'The way Kooti came. And surely the way he has gone.'

'And then?'

'We close with him. His force may be too glutted with food and loot to move very fast.'

'Intuition again?'

'Until hell freezes, Herrick.'

'I don't doubt your purpose. But a man is only as strong as his weak moments. Not only Kooti. You too.'

'Your thought eludes me,' Fairweather said.

Coolness between them was evident again.

'Kooti,' Herrick said, 'could have remained a wandering Jew in the wilderness. We could still have let him go. But he would not leave well alone. He had to have vengeance. He did not think the thing through. As things stand, he calls down retribution; sooner or later he has to be squashed as a flea on the British rump.'

'You are still less than clear,' Fairweather said.

'My point,' Herrick sighed, 'is that vengeance does not permit tidy thought. There is more than your life at risk if we rush blind.'

'Yours, for example?'

'I am not a disinterested party. I cannot forget Carr and Canning.'

'In which case, Herrick, consider yourself still free to depart.'

Their eyes did not meet. Men and horses laboured past.

'What detains you?' Fairweather asked.

'You,' Herrick said. 'Fear for you outweighs my own.'

'As friend I should be decently grateful. As a Johnny come lately commander not so. I see a man less committed to the hunt than he might be.'

'Hunt? Is that how you style it?'

'In sane moments, which I do have, Herrick, I know that we may not be able to do more than hound Kooti. But I also know there will be a day when he is torn root and branch from this territory. I hope to be there.'

'It is a relief to hear you talk of what is humanly possible.'

'My intention is not to set limits in that respect. Or have I still to make myself clear?'

'I am neither deaf nor blind,' Herrick said.

Fairweather rode on. Herrick jogged beside him.

'And by the way, Herrick, I should have said thank you.'
'I heard it anyway,' Herrick said.

At the head of the column again, Fairweather arrived at the beginning of the old way into the Urewera. The location differed impressively from that as he last saw it. Axes had been working, and men in large number. Growth had been trimmed, intrusive branches chopped back, and most debris cleared. It was now a modest highway, with hoofprints and footprints pointing seaward and inland again. By way of confirming his route of withdrawal, and as a last message to Poverty Bay, Kooti had left three elderly Maoris mangled by tomahawk. Jonah named them as chiefs who had favoured Kooti's deportation to the Chathams; they would certainly have remained contemptuous of a rogue tribal *tutua* proclaiming divine law. Nor were they the only captives shed. When Fairweather scouted the track further with Larkin and Jonah, he found younger Maoris less formally executed, commonly in places where land rose steeply and roots of trees hindered. These failed candidates for conversion had been shot where they tripped and aired pain and protest.

'Dead wood from his tree,' Jonah said bleakly.

Fairweather found his sense of evil here sanctioned; it had yet to be seen whether one of the corpses had a familiar face. Hamiora Pere had shivered this way beside him. Perhaps he had since been prodded the same way. Kooti had plundered Poverty Bay of most of its young; Hamiora had made no appearance in the port among refugees. Nor did he make an appearance now. While grieving Jonah identified faces, and Fairweather ordered corpses quickly covered with earth, Larkin's concern was entirely professional. He kept watch with carbine to shoulder, moving the muzzle from left to right, no twig or leaf uncovered for long.

Repellent diversions became fewer. Kooti could again be observed imposing form on his band. Compassion might be missing; martial sense was not.

When the column could be hurried no longer that day, Fairweather ordered camp made in a deep gully where smoke might be inconspicuous; pickets were set on high ground around. There was tea, a rum ration, salt beef and biscuit. The Maoris fetched from the south showed dissatisfaction with both food and Fairweather; Jonah reported their grievances. Hawke's Bay Maoris felt they had demonstrated sufficient aggressive intent; their inclination was to go home with unblemished glory, and a tale of Kooti taking to his heels upon their appearance in Poverty Bay.

'Tell them,' Fairweather said to Jonah, 'that soldiering cannot be scrimped in these parts. Explain it as a game of cards. Say Kooti has made a large wager. And that it would be shame and disgrace – a disgusting loss of mana – if we failed to meet it in full. Does that sound Maori enough?'

'Leave it to me,' Jonah said.

'Further, tell them that those seen cultivating fatter arses will have their daily pay cut from two shillings to one.'

'They won't like that,' Jonah said.

'If you wish to sugar it, do. I can make it no sweeter.'

Soon afterwards Jonah harangued a Maori assembly. Each word of Fairweather's marvellously became scores in translation. There were theatrical pauses, with tactical throat clearings and fluttering of fingers. Jonah seemed embarked on the story of creation; his oratory soared for all of an hour. Most listeners were visibly numbed. Speeches in reply to Jonah appeared to lack vigour and invention.

He returned to report, 'They wish it known they are with you to the death.'

'Theirs or mine?'

'Mine if you get me to do that again. They say it is natural for tired men to grumble.'

'Likewise for tired captains. I promise less pedestrian employment.'

'It would help,' Jonah said. 'I'm buggered too.'

With Jonah gone to look for his blanket, Herrick said, 'Today, for a time, I fancied I was riding alongside Whitmore again.'

'Then wait upon tomorrow,' Fairweather said. 'Whitmore is only a bully. As a brute he is not a beginner.'

The subdued camp was soon quieter still. Even Maori chatter did not last. Fairweather slept poorly, his dreams ugly; he might have known images of massacre could not be postponed. He woke with reassuring venom, and gave men no time to dwell on their rations; the column was soon moving on. Larkin rode with him at the head.

The track led them on to a shoulder of land overlooking a broad and bright valley. Fire in the recent past had levelled most vegetation; a few lifeless trees survived ghostly among low scrub and saplings. The track was plainly printed across the valley, descending and rising, pointed west to the mountains.

'Seems safe enough, sir,' Larkin judged, and Fairweather did not disagree.

Herrick joined them; the column banked up behind. 'Problems?' he asked.

'A lack,' Fairweather said. 'More territory like this and we shall make better time.'

The wind, a stiff westerly, blew into their faces.

'A change from Whitmore's mad rivers and gorges,' Herrick said.

'Keep men moving,' Fairweather said. 'That doesn't change. Larkin and I shall dawdle a little and tighten the column. If you have cause for a query, signal with a shot.'

Herrick led down into the valley while the column swayed and shuffled past Fairweather's gaze. It was still tolerably coherent, though Larkin found sufficient flaws for complaint; in Larkin's view nothing men did on this earth could be cause for complacency. After a time they fell in with the column again, moving toward the front; Herrick was in clear sight, five hundred yards ahead, fording a river and then taking steep ground on the far side of the valley. There was a growing whine of wind through the scrub. Otherwise sound was of sweaty horses and men, of harness and heavy breathing. Fairweather's thoughts were shaped more by the motion of his horse than by things human. After forest scouting, open ground deserved celebration, if only by way of being off the qui vive for an hour, and letting his mind sleep. He followed Larkin across the river, the column splashing and groaning alongside them, and Herrick winding up the high ground ahead. Kooti might safely concentrate matters soon.

Safely? One shot. More than a signal. Because suddenly two. Then they heard rifles in number from the spur of the valley above. They saw Herrick veer, the head of the column bend.

Fairweather and Larkin dug heels into their horses; the lifting ground did not favour great speed. On their way upward they met Jonah among halted men. 'Get the rest across the river,' Fairweather ordered. 'Then ditch swags and horses and make speed to Herrick. No one turns back.'

Ahead, he saw Herrick dismounted, trying to hold his panicked horse; the column was buckling. Soon it would be doubled and quite in retreat. 'Swing men out,' he told Larkin. 'We need wings to fly. Skirmishing order.'

He pushed toward Herrick. Shot began to fall around, not especially deterrent. When he reached the confused head of the column, three or four men had been tumbled; others were bunched, dismounting and shouting, a target which even apprentice marksmen could not fail to strike. Herrick had lost all nerve and most voice under fire; he was standing ineffective in the pandemonium.

'Kick horses away,' Fairweather ordered. 'On your bellies if you must, but keep moving uphill.'

'We must regroup,' Herrick protested. 'We have no defence against this.'

'And we are offering none,' Fairweather said. 'We attack.'

He slapped his horse away, and proceeded higher.

'You cannot go alone,' Herrick called.

'It is rather up to you, Captain Herrick, to see I do not.'

Soon Fairweather heard men panting behind. He looked back with satisfaction upon Larkin, Mulhooly, Newman and Daniels and others of Poverty Bay. Jonah and his Maoris too. And Herrick urging along the lukewarm of Hawke's Bay.

The scrub hugged less; the wind was still stronger in his face. Exposing himself, he could observe that the firepower along the spur was modest and indifferently directed. A rearguard; a delaying action at best. Fifty yards short, tempting too much shot, he went to ground and waited on Herrick, who arrived gasping and shamed behind Larkin and Jonah. The three fell alongside Fairweather.

'We go over the spur as one,' he proposed. 'Men to fire only the one shot as we attack, and to be sure of a target. No pause to reload. Our business is done with the bayonet.'

'Have you thought,' Herrick asked, 'what might be beyond that spur?'

'I have, Captain Herrick. The answer is Kooti, to greater or lesser degree.'

'We may have a long fight to get to him. He might be miles further.'

'All the more reason, then, to make this beginning brisk.'

Larkin, peering over the scrub, had most of significance to contribute, though sparing with syllables.

'Fire,' he said.

Fairweather, lifting his own head, caught a gust of warmth. Above their position were flames fed by dry scrub and fanned by quick wind. To right and left too combustion had been encouraged. Soon the length of the spur was blazing; smoke cascaded downhill. Men stood to discharge rifles at the incendiarists beyond.

'An interesting ploy,' Herrick said.

'And very soon lethal,' Fairweather said.

He had been too headlong; any hour in Kooti's proximity could hold ingenious hazard. Whitmore again. Worse.

'Larkin?' he appealed.

'We could back off slow, sir,' Larkin said. 'And shoot as we move. They might mount an attack from behind the fire.'

'Jonah?'

'No Maori is going to back off slow,' Jonah said. 'Not when he feels that up his arse. And the Maoris from Hawke's Bay, they'll be running all the way home.'

Embers showered around them as flame drove closer; heat grew on their faces.

'We stand our ground,' Fairweather decided.

'We what?' Herrick said.

'In that, sir?' Larkin said.

'If the choice is breakneck retreat,' Fairweather said.

Scrub beside them began smouldering with falling sparks. Larkin trampled the outbreak.

'You cannot be serious,' Herrick said.

Fairweather spoke to Larkin and Jonah. 'Tell men to clear scrub around them. Then to dig as deep as they can. Assure them that the risk of cremation is slight beside that of being picked off should they scatter. You, Larkin, will give them more to think about. See the horses are gathered and guarded by the river and take up stance there. Shoot any of our number inclined to withdrawal in the heat of the moment. I trust you not to make a feast of it; one or two dropped should encourage deathless resolution.'

'You just talking of militia,' Larkin asked, 'or of Maoris too?'

'Without prejudice,' Fairweather said. 'And I shall be answerable should you kill rather than lame.'

Larkin and Jonah left, passing on the order as they moved through the lines.

'Are you not to be denied,' Herrick asked, 'whatever the cost?'

'If you wish to put it in words,' Fairweather said.

'I am trying to give you opportunity to justify yourself in full.'

'All you saw in Poverty Bay was made of two retreats before Kooti.'

'Or two vain pursuits,' Herrick argued.

'There is not to be a third. There cannot be, and will not today.'

'You can hardly deny that this expedition is no better considered than those of Whitmore and Biggs.'

'Perhaps not better considered. Better convinced. Meanwhile you might make yourself a candidate for survival.'

As heat mounted they laboured with the men around; they hacked at scrub and saplings with tomahawks and knives, and tugged out fern by the roots. Flame neared noisily; sweat flooded faces. Clearings formed, islands, archipelagoes, soon merging as a front. They began scratching, digging, trying to make impression on obstinate earth; they loosened clay with bayonets, and tore out clods with their hands. When the vanguard of the fire began spitting near, Herrick and Fairweather were resident in shallow pits; likewise men along their line.

Then it was upon them, cracking and flashing, hurling hot debris around. Coughing men tried to crush deeper into the earth; they slapped at stinging sparks.

Herrick gasped, 'Is Kooti worth this?'

'If we are,' Fairweather said.

Their eyes streamed; windpipes parched. Somewhere to their left, the line broke, men fled. Flame reached overhead and fell on fuel to their rear. They were within the blast briefly. Then it was more ample behind. With a slight change in wind, the worst raced off to the right of their line. They breathed and battered down colonies of fire. Fairweather called in singed men from the right, sent them running to the left; he also ordered them to look to their arms.

'What now?' Herrick asked.

'As before,' Fairweather said. 'We have surprise. Kooti's men must think us well cooked. The haze will help too.'

He made himself as clear to the sooty men about, and instructed that the order be passed on.

'You ask too much of them,' Herrick said.
'Kooti would not ask less.'
'Must he be your model?'
'A reliable enemy is of more use than friend. He shows a straight path.'
Herrick said, 'Then I see it may be worse than I thought.'
'Concentrate, Herrick, on seeing through the smoke as it clears. Also on the angle with which you deliver your first blow with the bayonet. It might help if you fixed it first.'
Herrick fumbled at the task; his hands were black and trembling.
'And shout,' Fairweather urged. 'It helps convince you of courage, and spurs those to your rear. Also don't dwell on what you dislodge. There will be another torso needing attention.'
'I expect we also take no prisoners.'
'Chance may provide survivors. It is not for you to intrude.'
When fire seemed sufficiently spent, Fairweather ordered advance up smouldering ground. The heat of the ash rose through the soles of boots; sputters of flame scorched trousers. Fairweather led at unsteady trot through the fog; others were shadowy on each side. There were unpersuasive shots from above, directed down valley, well over their heads. They had not yet been sighted. Luck held until the last yards. Fairweather shot down the first of Kooti's men to shout alarm, then lunged into a nest of dismayed warriors. There were other shots fired, other bayonets slashing, and streamers of blood leaping; the largest hazard was that of friendly steel. He was aware of blow after blow disembowelling, of Herrick screaming and sobbing beside him. Butts cracking into skulls silenced most of the dying, and Hawke's Bay Maoris ensured unanimity with tomahawks.
Smoke dispersed. For fifty yards on each side other engagements stuttered. To the right, Kooti's men retained the head of the spur; the rise there was too steep for the assault to make early impression. To the left it was teetering; a few militia and Maoris were still flailing forward. There was need to make the most of what was. The left had more promise. Calling to Herrick, Fairweather ran on, getting behind those of Kooti's force still giving fight; he soon rallied an enterprising ring of bayonets. They reduced a score of warriors to two disarmed and cringing. Fairweather called off the tomahawks. 'Let them bleed,' he ordered. 'We may need to talk.'
There was the right; the head of the spur. Assault from below had almost ceased. The one chance was a push along the spur itself. Mustering men again, Fairweather was aware of shot falling from elsewhere, from beyond the spur, not enough to impress. Scrub was a greater impediment as they moved up the spur; also spiny outcrops of rock and fallen fragments shifting underfoot. Fairweather slid downhill; Herrick descended to help. Fate. A volley passed over their heads. Men behind fell, fled or took cover. Fair-

weather and Herrick were left crouching in the van of the extinguished attack. From foliage they observed gun-pits with a wide field of fire at the head of the spur. Scores of Maori heads lifted; there was another intimidating volley. Scraps of vegetation flew in its path.

'There is a limit,' Herrick said. 'We can do no more for the moment. Not even you. You must accept it.'

'If we accept what we are, Herrick, we make no arrangement with what we might be.'

'I am thinking of what you might not.'

The third volley convinced Fairweather. This time the elevation was lower; shot swarmed around. He crawled off with Herrick and called on men in hiding to withdraw with wounded. By the time they had gained safer ground, Fairweather appeared redundant. Larkin had arrived; and Jonah. They were persuading men to make life less intolerable by deepening the pits and trenches they had won. More, Larkin had men swapping shot with the Maoris at the head of the spur. Fairweather was free to consider larger themes.

Forward from the spur, five or six hundred yards as shot currently flew, was a hilltop shaping as a fortress. One of modest height, but of tactical substance; it sat in the bend of a river and commanded negotiable ground in the next valley. Through binoculars he could see earth upthrown from the digging of pits, logs hauled uphill for palisades. Construction was at a standstill. The builders were engaged in mostly harmless activity with guns at long range. A hundred, perhaps. With the men at the head of the spur tallied too, only a fraction of Kooti's force was visible.

He had the two prisoners brought to him. One was middle-aged and wore recent belligerence lightly with his hands bound tight behind; the other was young and tearful. Both had been gashed with bayonets. With Herrick interpreting, they claimed no knowledge of Kooti's present location. They had been ordered to use scrub, wind and flame as Jehovah most wished.

'Ask them,' Fairweather said, 'if they served Jehovah on the plain of Poverty Bay too.'

There was lengthy questioning from Herrick. The prisoners finally grew monosyllabic, and looked at their feet.

'They claim they know nothing of that,' Herrick said. 'They say they were left behind in these hills when the attack on Matawhero and the other settlements was made.'

'Do you believe them?'

'Not especially.'

'Test them again on Kooti. Tell them my wish is to keep this painless. Is he in that fortress we view in the next valley?'

Herrick asked the question. After considering Fairweather earnestly, the two captives competed for attention, interrupting each other.

'They say,' Herrick reported, 'that Kooti has placed many of his best warriors here to detain and destroy any who give pursuit.'

'They are of his best?'

'I persuaded them to boast so. They say Kooti has gone still further into the mountains with his retinue. There, it seems, he means to devote himself to prayer and further initiatives in the name of Israel.'

'For men who claim to have been far from the last initiative, they have grown wonderfully informative.'

'They have,' Herrick said.

Fairweather turned to Larkin. 'Were horses made safe, and our supplies?'

'All I found near the river, sir,' Larkin said.

Herrick asked, 'Is there more you want of these prisoners?'

'Only that they meet death in a way more or less seemly.'

'Here?' Herrick said. 'Now?'

'Have them taken away. If Mulhooly isn't up to it, try Newman.'

As it turned out, Mulhooly and Newman took a prisoner apiece. They were miserly with ammunition. Just two shots were heard.

By the day's end they were dug along all of the spur they could make habitable. Shot still travelled in from the incomplete fortress to their front, and more exasperatingly from those entrenched at the head of the spur. Kooti's men were content to demonstrate their existence, as they might well, since there was no way for Fairweather to order a move into the next valley without chancing encirclement of his force. The spur rode across a gap between forested heights which blocked any other approach to the Urewera.

Herrick said, 'Even if you refuse to acknowledge it, we are up a blind alley. For all the blood and sweat, we have won nothing but this lump of earth. I am entitled, as brother officer, to make my view known.'

'What are you telling me?' Fairweather asked. 'That you wish to take command?'

'You know that to be unfair.'

'Or wait for Whitmore?'

Herrick was quiet.

'Well?' Fairweather said.

'One knew where one was with Whitmore,' Herrick said at last. 'Especially with you ironic beside me. There is no irony left in you. Nor proportion. Look where we are.'

'For the first time Kooti's people see men who do not back off. It may be a long march to the day of judgement; he will learn it begun.'

'I understand. Or try to. But it is not a duel.'

'My German philosopher would have it that wars of the best quality are.'

'I should have known,' Herrick said.

'With the bit between my teeth, I wish only one thing beside loyalty. Much leaner Maoris.'

Herrick said, 'I have hesitated to tell you, but there is one on the way.'

'One?'

'And his tribesmen. If sinew is what you want, Ropata should serve. More so if you want fire to fight fire.'

'You interest,' Fairweather said. 'Ropata?'

'Ropata Wahawaha. I have weighed the pros and cons of turning him loose near Poverty Bay. He loathes all Maoris of it. With reason. He is of old tribal enemies to the north, and was once enslaved after warring with Poverty Bay. The shame still bites. Any excuse for a Poverty Bay corpse is a good excuse. Fortunately for all he grudgingly accommodates the laws of the colony now. And fortunately for us is of the enlightened opinion that loyalty to the Queen is more lucrative than rebellion. Otherwise God help us. And any tribe not his own.'

'And you have uncaged him.'

'I took the liberty of sending for him after observing your mood when I arrived in Poverty Bay. I am told Ropata fights by no book, and certainly never the Bible. In short, a warrior of tried and true tradition, before missionaries confused. If our enemy postures as an Old Testament Hebrew, who better than an unreformed Maori to pay him in his own coin?'

'Herrick, I suspect you are selling an ancient bundle of bones.'

'Ropata would be all of sixty. If all I hear is true men half his age cannot keep pace when fighting begins. As for his famous ferocity, he may be a man much of your mind. Even when it comes to followers of faint heart, he is said to have relatives dragged before him and slain.'

'When,' Fairweather asked, 'can we expect this paragon?'

'Before Whitmore, desirably. Ropata may provide you with the clean sheet you want. And a duel. Certainly with landscape sufficiently reddened.'

'Then you have my provisional thanks, Herrick. Incidentally, you prove quite a tolerable killer yourself. Not that there isn't room for improvement.'

'That is sweet of you,' Herrick said.

Wounded had to be returned to the river and Surgeon Gibbs; water had to be borne uphill to thirsty men on the spur. These errands had to be managed under fire from the head of the spur; there were more casualties. Packhorses had strayed in the panic of the day; rations were short. Worse, after dark, nerveless native allies sped shot at imaginary attackers, or perhaps mountain demons. Kooti's men were not slow to reply. This made for enlarged appetites; food held in reserve was surreptitiously plundered. The dark was long, never free of truculent shouting and discharging of weapons, and sleep on short commons too. Herrick and Fairweather watched the rising of the sun through gritty eyes. The warriors at the head of the spur were undiminished in number, perhaps even reinforced. The fortress in front had solidified, with more palisades in place. Much as he reasoned with the terrain, Fairweather could make no gap appear; it was all covered by Kooti's rifles. Nor, even if he had men fit and less fretful, was there ammunition to make a path through.

'Stalemate,' Herrick said. 'And Kooti could yet use his numbers.'

Larkin did not help either; he arrived from the left of the spur with a question. 'Is it true, sir?' he said. 'I have just heard we are withdrawing.'

'We are not,' Fairweather said. 'And I should be obliged, Larkin, if you quashed any such gossip. Even if it may sound good sense to you.'

'I wasn't saying that, sir.'

'You were looking it, Larkin.'

'I'm sorry, sir.'

'As a picture of a loyal sergeant, you make a damn pious fraud. Remove yourself before I actually give vent to my feelings.'

Larkin left soundless.

'That was hardly fair,' Herrick protested. 'No man toils harder.'

'Larkin has had a lifetime of worse.'

'That is no justification.'

'Give Larkin a morsel of excuse and he may slyly suggest he has been here twice before. Twice foiled by Kooti.'

'And is that not true?'

'Not yet,' Fairweather said.

Herrick was silent. When observed, he seemed in some pain.

Morning heat grew. Sun reddened flesh, and water was again short. Fairweather ordered ammunition conserved for targets in decent proximity. They had barely enough to beat off an attack; to launch one would be madness. As for food, Maoris were crawling from entrenchments to forage for fern root and thistle. Herrick made it clear that he found conversation with Fairweather disagreeable.

'Look, Herrick,' he said finally, 'I make a proposal. Namely, for you to take command for a time.'

'And where would you be?'

'Upon a menial chore. Somewhere between here and Poverty Bay is a convoy to be hurried along. If it is slow arriving, the decision to abandon this position will soon make itself.'

'That sounds a mission more suited to Larkin.'

'I leave Larkin with you. There are old soldiers, and bold soldiers, but no old bold soldiers. Sharpen your wits on Larkin should you have to make a major decision.'

'Such as what?'

'Such as withdrawal, if I must make myself clear.'

'You would leave choice with me?'

'I should not reproach you.'

'Are you sure,' Herrick asked, 'that you are not taking the easy way out? So that retreat is not on your conscience, but mine?'

'I wish your friendship again,' Fairweather said. 'Even more, your respect. Your face is a displeasing mirror. I see futility.'

Herrick was not disposed to console. 'Very well,' he said. 'I cannot say I feel comfortable.'

'Command is not meant to be,' Fairweather said.

In the end, before Fairweather left, Herrick managed a smile.

Fairweather's penance proved more than menial. He took razed ground into the valley; faint smoke lifted from smouldering pockets of growth. At the riverside he checked on the wounded and the work of the surgeon; he directed that men too disabled be returned early to Poverty Bay. Surgeon Gibbs' battlefield technique was robust. For the most part it amounted to replacing lost blood with alcohol. 'The worst ones die happy,' he said.

Fairweather did not linger to observe symptoms of joy; he saddled a horse and took the track back toward Poverty Bay. He had ridden no more than three miles before he came on a few sorry men with packhorses. They were all that remained of the convoy. A party of Kooti's marauders had split it in two. Half was lost; and all food. The surviving half had only ammunition.

'So we sup on the bullet,' Fairweather decided.

He hastened them on. In the afternoon he shepherded them down into the valley and the prospect of more grief. On the far side he viewed the bony spur and breathed deep. It was still held; Herrick had not chosen to withdraw. But a freshening westerly had rekindled fire from furtive sparks; flame flowed down toward the riverside where wounded lay. More, it denied a safe rear to those persisting on the spur. It seemed Jehovah was making amends for yesterday's deficiencies. There was gunfire too. Herrick had an attack.

Fairweather galloped to the river. Wounded men were being rushed to the safe side of the water.

'The men up above are desperate,' Gibbs said. 'They sent messengers down for what ammunition we had left. They can't get back because of the fire.'

The survivors of the convoy began to arrive behind Fairweather.

'Lighten yourselves a little,' he ordered. 'Carry only casks of ammunition. Wrap wet sacks about anything inflammable or explosive. Then drench yourselves and your horses as we cross the river.'

'What are you asking?' a man appealed.

'To earn today's pay. The worst will be thinking about it. The rest will come easier.'

'Jesus,' the man said. 'It better.'

The men rode untidily into the river, ducking themselves, garments and horses, while Fairweather made it his business to kill doubt. Herrick had to be reached.

'There is,' he said, 'a track under that flame. The fire will burn less there. If any horse stumbles, its rider must be left to make his own peace. Two are not to perish for the price of one; nor can more ammunition be lost.'

All that remained was example. His horse had a case to state first. It reared when pointed toward the heat across the river. He dug vicious boots in its flanks, beat at its head with the butt of his revolver, until the beast lunged toward the lesser of two evils. Behind, he heard a choir of curses and whinnies as men and horses crashed up from the water.

He banged through a corridor of hell, flame storming on two sides, sparks streaming past. His face fried; he drank smoke and spluttered; his eyes seemed to melt. His left sleeve took fire, then his right; he had smouldering hair.

Then the gale diminished, died. The torment of this scorched horse did not. It continued to bolt and then, in last protest, threw him into smoking ash. He rose dizzy, beating at hair and clothes, and saw men of the convoy surface from the blast. The rest of the uphill journey to Herrick, with only spent shot dropping near, was at sober pace. He ordered horses stationed in a gully, and three to be slaughtered for food; ammunition had to be carried the rest of the distance.

A filthy Herrick was waiting. The attack had passed. Kooti's men had crawled across dead ground before charging. Corpses still clutching tomahawks lay within yards of their position.

'We held,' Herrick said. 'At the end Larkin, Jonah and I were dividing our last dozen rounds.'

'You suggest withdrawal might now be timely?'

'I tend not to suggest anything. There has to be point to this pain.'

'Good,' Fairweather said.

'Is this how you meant it to be?'

'With less drama.'

'I assure you the histrionics were shared. At least I know how you feel now.'

'Better still,' Fairweather said.

'Food? How do we hold there?'

'Horseflesh à la antipodes again. With the tang of inferno, and a garnish of thistle, it should linger long on the palate. You are of course right. There has to be point. Two trials by fire must be a message.'

'You are not talking of food now.'

'No, Herrick. Of tomorrow. If there is a point, it is not in remaining passive.'

Herrick was quiet.

'I shall send men back to Poverty Bay to establish a safer line of supply and bring up a new convoy. As for the rest, while we have ammunition there are better ways of disposing of it than sculpting rock and chipping at trees. Well?'

'I heard you,' Herrick said.

It was Fairweather's conviction that the head of the spur must be taken. Until Kooti's firepower there was stifled, retribution had no highway. He divided his force into three parties. Herrick commanded one, Jonah another, and Fairweather with Larkin a third. Herrick and Jonah would move obliquely from lower ground to divert men in the rifle pits while Fairweather's party worked up the spur.

'Nowhere does the ground favour us,' Herrick said. 'I might understand a desperate proceeding better if we had Kooti before us. But we have not.'

'See it as rehearsal,' Fairweather said. 'Desperation is better for drilling.'

He advanced his party up the spur before dawn. They met shots from pickets, then drew a single-minded volley. Most shot hummed on toward the lightening horizon; the defenders still had few visible targets.

Crouched beside Larkin, within twenty yards of enemy pits, Fairweather said, 'The first will be worst. They must divide their fire now.'

'I hope so, sir,' Larkin said.

'I know so, Larkin. Captain Herrick and Jonah should soon make an impression.'

There were cries to their right. Shots.

'Which is what I mean,' Fairweather said.

'Listen again, sir,' Larkin said.

The cries, Herrick's among them, were of panic. There were grunts and bumps from the enemy position; they heralded a rumbling repeated again and again. The sounds were soon less obscure. Herrick's party was under a rolling barrage of large rocks and logs. This recipe needed salting with very few shots. The cries were of men battered, crushed or pinned.

To their left Jonah's party began drawing fire. But the shots were few and scattered. Just one interpretation was possible. Jonah's men were few and scattered, confused in unscouted terrain.

'It seems,' Fairweather said, 'that we must force the issue.'

'Now, sir?' Larkin was doubtful.

'Now, Larkin. Now.'

He rose, urged men forward, and ran. A volley flamed in his face; it seemed to slam on and on. Fairweather took to the ground and looked for men following. There were none. He heard whimpers and groans and scuttlings in fern.

'Larkin?' he called. 'Larkin?'

It was close to noon before the last survivor crawled home to give disaster a tally. Two dozen were dead or missing, and twice as many disabled with fractures and wounds. Jonah, after trying to lead men from a baffling gully, had shot needing extraction from a shoulder; Herrick was limping with abrasions and bruises. Fairweather was merely diminished. Larkin's wound had been under his left eye before the bullet entered his brain. The badge of the obedient soldier; he had been faced to the front. A canny old workhorse of war would always have known that it would not be the enemy who was the death of him, but a lunatic commander in love with the sound of his own orders. Fairweather judged that he now had fewer than a hundred fit men to lead; whether he was fit to lead was best left unconsidered. When he had deployed them along the spur again, he slumped. It was some time before Herrick dared approach.

'I am sorry about Larkin,' Herrick said.

'I will be too,' Fairweather said.

'We may yet give his death more meaning,' Herrick cautiously proposed.

'It has meaning, Herrick. How much more does death need?'

'There is,' Herrick said, 'no need to shout.'

They held to the spur for three days more. On their fourth day they saw men spilling into the valley to their rear.

'Our convoy,' Fairweather said wearily.

It was, but only in part; there were more and more men on view. Herrick used binoculars.

'I don't know whether it is good news or bad,' he finally said.

'Whitmore?' Fairweather asked.

'Worse,' Herrick said. 'Ropata is here.'

24

A slight and leathery old Maori, with a bush of grey beard, dropped into the observation trench. There was a dusty British cap perched on his head; his eyes passed censoriously over Herrick and Fairweather. 'Well, sirs,' he said, 'what is your problem?'

He considered Kooti's men at the head of the spur, then the fortress in the valley before them.

'You cannot move them?' he asked.

A Maori ultimatum; the man was one himself.

'Not for want of trying,' Herrick said.

'And you wish me to do so?'

'If possible,' Herrick said. 'What is your feeling?'

'My feeling,' Ropata said, 'is that they are all dead.'

Later Fairweather said, 'We must arrive at an understanding.'

'Understanding?' Ropata seemed surprised.

'Of our roles,' Fairweather explained.

'My understanding, sir, is that I have work to do which you cannot.'

'That is fair summary. But I talk of command.'

'The man who does the work does it his way. Otherwise I go home. Is there more to be understood, sir?'

It seemed, on the whole, not. 'So what do you have in mind to shift Kooti's men?' Fairweather asked. 'What is your move?'

'There is only one move,' Ropata said. 'Forward.'

For most of the day he ignored Herrick and Fairweather in favour of the company of his lieutenants, a miscellaneous crew in kilts of patched tartan and trousers slashed short. Uniformity was more evident in their features; Ropata appeared to enforce brutal scars and wintry eyes. He had no patience for more than perfunctory questions from the impassive men crouched around. They assented with vigour whenever he made a point and paused to clear his throat. He turned a venomous gaze on those less audible.

'I observe no sweetness and light,' Fairweather said to Herrick. 'What does he tell them?'

'Aside from dwelling on their past deficiencies, it is mostly a matter of pouring old wine into new bottles. Though they are here for Christ and the Queen, he says, he asks them to recall the woes of their ancestors, and to remember them watching. And especially to repay past humiliations; to do as their ancestors would, or would have wished to, to Kooti and his kind.'

'That has promise.'

'Nevertheless,' Herrick said, 'we may have to take some stand if things move to excess. The banner of civilization may need unfurling. It must not be said that we are no better than Kooti.'

'Then why did you call up Ropata?'

'Expediency. Sooner or later we should have had to.'

'I think I can trifle a little with expediency,' Fairweather said. 'Even with reasonable excess.'

'What of innocents? There could be many in our path. Women and children; captives too. Ropata's men may not be of mind to distinguish.'

'The answer is surely to keep pace.'

'Or to make clear the limits of our tolerance.'

'When expedience has done its best,' Fairweather said.

Late in the afternoon Ropata disclosed his first tactic. He arrived in the observation trench and looked over the terrain, listening to his own thoughts and perhaps older voices. Then he rose wirily from the trench and walked alone toward the head of the spur. He was soon within easy gunshot of his enemy. He cupped his hands and called. All shooting ceased.

Fairweather asked Herrick, 'What now?'

'He tells them Ropata is here. He promises them their last sunset; tomorrow they will be meat for his tomahawk.'

'Thank God he is our man. I trust the colonial treasury won't stint.'

'You misunderstand, Fairweather. Ropata isn't here for mere money. Mana still interests more. Ropata's is that of the born chief. Kooti's plebeian carcass would confirm it. Kooti imperils the notion of men set above others by birth; Ropata's tribe too might be at risk.'

At pains to call up shot, Ropata lingered in his exposed position to demonstrate contempt. Then he turned his back and walked back to the observation trench without haste.

'I have words for you,' he told Fairweather and Herrick. 'Sleep well tonight that you may bear witness tomorrow.'

'Witness?' Fairweather queried.

'While we work. I say that you remain here and look on.'

'No more?'

'I wish no keepers of ill omen near. Men of defeat attack when they should not. You ignored all the signs. This I believe.'

'It is difficult to quarrel,' Fairweather said.

'My star is chosen,' Ropata said. 'Tonight it challenges the moon. Tomorrow the enemy falls. When we raise our flag you may join us. This is to be understood.'

'It will be,' Fairweather promised.

Ropata considered Fairweather with distinct reservation. 'My dream of last night warned of men with rage. They become as blind men, and evil to all.'

'Your words are strong,' Fairweather said.

'Also said. Therefore I cease on this subject.'

Ropata briskly took himself elsewhere.

'It seems,' Fairweather said, 'that we are put in our place. We are told what to do, and what not, by a wizened old ruffian with a head filled with omen and dream. That is not the worst of it. It may be fatigue, but I seem not to object.'

'It is not fatigue,' Herrick said.

In the morning Ropata's first success was visible without a shot heard. Terror had been enough to make the Maoris at the head of the spur decamp during the dark; gunpits and trenches had been emptied as they fled to join their fellows in the now sturdy fortress. Ropata's men were unmolested as they moved downhill in open order into the valley where it rose. They hurdled streams, weaved among rock and scrub, leapt from high ground to low. There was no stealth, and a strange quiet. Flanks, at Ropata's signal, were pushed forward quickly. There was no faltering when the first firearms sounded from within the earthworks of the fortress. Ropata's men pushed silently on. No imperial commander could have asked more; none could thereafter have settled for less. When men began to fall, lines tightened; there was no pause, not even pleas heard from the men abandoned. Ropata continued to hold fire. Fear was still his favoured weapon; wails from within the fortress confirmed that targets had been found. Those within were defunct for defensive purpose before Ropata unleashed marksmen. The shooting spread from the centre, with flash and smoke spurting out to the flanks as every second warrior dropped to his knees and placed shot. First from a hundred yards, then fifty. Defenders attempting escape by way of the riverside were not long on their feet. Then parties of Ropata's men with burning torches leapt over the first earthworks and fired the brushwood which reinforced the palisades of the fortress. With flame encircling the position, Ropata directed volley after volley within. Finally he raised his arm. His men were at liberty to breach the blazing palisades and lower defenders still promising fight.

Fairweather watched with Herrick and Jonah. With bullet removed and shoulder bound, Jonah had climbed back from the camp of the wounded to see offensive renewed.

Before long Ropata's flag rose above the smoking fortress.

'I have just the one thought,' Fairweather said. 'Had the enemies of Israel numbered a Ropata, we might never have heard of Moses.'

'Or the ten commandments,' Herrick said.

'I have only the one wish,' Jonah said. 'That it was not Ropata down there.'

'You hate him so much?'

'Who would love him?' Jonah said. 'You think he is fighting your war. Perhaps. Perhaps not. He is not here to avenge the killing in Poverty Bay. He has older *utu* in mind. First lives, then land.'

'The fact is that Kooti has just had his first reverse,' Fairweather argued. 'Every man walks in his own trade. I have been crawling.'

Jonah was still unhappy. 'Must I serve under Ropata?' he asked.

'It happens that I am lacking a sergeant,' Fairweather said. 'You are now mine. You answer to me, never to Ropata. Does that help?'

'If it means this Poverty Bay skull isn't split from behind.'

'They would have to demolish mine first,' Fairweather promised.

'I hope yours is thicker,' Jonah said.

The three hiked across country to the fortress. There were a few shots and cries as resistance expired. Herrick hobbled with a stick over the rough terrain. 'There is a lesson to be learned,' he said. 'This war is best now seen as civil. Between Maori and Maori. If that also means between murderous Christians and Jews, so much the worse for Kooti. What do you say?'

'That the theology of the thing may soon not matter,' Fairweather said. 'Nor how many Maori angels dance on the head of a pin.'

'But you must see my point,' Herrick protested. 'We must comprehend what we are about.'

'I thought that I had been paying more than lip service to the notion that Maoris must kill Maoris.'

'Not on so large a scale. Nor in conceding control.'

'I have no objection to civil war, Herrick, so long as it is won. What more do you want from me?'

'To see coolly,' Herrick said. 'You may need to.'

Within the fortress ugly bodies were scattered. Most of those disarmed had been too juvenile for long consideration; they were sliced down where they surrendered. In places the ground was slippery with intestine and blood. They found Ropata haranguing four captives of senior rank who had been tied and hurried before him. They did not plead for mercy, and did not expect it. One, taller and younger than his fellows, fought his bonds and talked back to Ropata.

Herrick interpreted, 'He tells Ropata that it is better for Maoris to fight and die as men before there are too many colonists. Kooti, he says, shows that it is not too late. The land must be cleansed of all of white blood and those who have taken its taint. Ropata, in turn, tells the man he is a fool. And that the wise Maori not only fights for his tribe, but joins with the tribe he cannot beat. The colonists of Britain are a tribe not to be beaten. Thus nor is he, Ropata. He says that he will be remembered as the greatest Maori fighting chief of all; that Kooti is trash and will soon be seen so.'

'Do I hear passing envy?' Fairweather asked.

'Perhaps,' Herrick said.

Ropata was given loaded rifles. With the muzzle of each he forced a captive's chin upward, until the man was obliged to stare at the sky. Then skin, bone and brain flew; a torso turned limp and fell. When it came to the fourth man, who had argued, Ropata reconsidered and ordered a fire lit. The man was toppled, tied to ropes, and dragged toward the flame.

'Perhaps it is time for you to tactfully interfere, Captain Fairweather,' Herrick said.

'You heard Ropata. His way or none. Do you want your civil war flawed?'

'Summary justice is one thing. This is another. Ropata tells the fellow that he can rehearse his disputation with the fires of the next world in the burning coals of this. He wishes it known that this will be the fate of all who give comfort to Kooti. I dare say he calculates to impress faint-hearted followers. He would give Satan second thoughts. Can you just stand there and do nothing?'

'I seem to be doing so,' Fairweather said.

Ropata had further words before launching his captive.

Looking away, Herrick said, 'He challenges the fellow to call upon Jehovah of the Jews, of Abraham, Isaac and Jacob, and see what deliverance is there.'

Slack was taken up on ropes. With a rush, the captive was tugged across the flames; the man did not cry out. Nor did he the second time and the third. There was the smell of flesh singed.

Beside Fairweather, Jonah sweated.

'Use your revolver,' Herrick pleaded. 'Put a brave man from his pain.'

On his fourth pass through the fire, the captive found Jehovah wanting; a groan bubbled. Then all spiritual obstruction departed. They heard scream after scream.

'Dear Christ,' Herrick said, staggering away.

The cries were slow to weaken. When they ceased, the body was left shrivelling in the fire; flame sputtered brighter. Ropata's men hastened the departure of fat from the flesh with sharp sticks. Then they used the ignited sticks to light the tobacco in their pipes.

'As they are no longer cannibal,' Jonah explained, 'they must make do with that.'

In the end Fairweather turned away too. To Herrick he said, 'You asked me to see coolly. I shall put it to Ropata that no one need any longer doubt his capacity to inflict hurt.'

'Please,' Herrick said.

Ropata said, 'These were men who worked defeat on your force. The memory is now banished by one more powerful. All things are equal again. War may now begin.'

He looked into Fairweather's face for reaction, and was not disappointed.

'I am not,' Ropata added, 'of mind for further delay in this matter.'

'Nor I,' Fairweather said.

'Those with quick tongues say you have reason for haste.'

'Those tongues may speak truly.'

'To strike at a woman is to humiliate a warrior, to make him more careless. We say women are as a cliff over which men fall to death.'

'I have teetered,' Fairweather confessed.

'So it is understood, then,' Ropata said. 'I do not permit you to imperil my men likewise. We fight when my signs are auspicious.'

'It is hereby agreed,' Fairweather said.

'Then I inform you that the man whose life you seek is but five miles from here. He digs defences on a peak once of the Tuhoe.'

'Kooti's best defence is fast movement in forest, with men roving and marauding to his rear. He could be safe five hundred years. A Maori Methuselah.'

'Because I am here, he must fight for mana. He must stand as a Maori, not as a Jew. Otherwise his followers must know shame.'

'And you?'

'It is necessary to show Kooti that as a Maori he is fit only to eat shit.'

'Let his appetite be large,' Fairweather said.

Horses were summoned, supplies, all men and munitions. Next morning they marched. The country grew difficult, muddled with rocky gullies and creeks among hills close packed and pyramidal. Ridges bruised. Rain drenched; weak sunlight failed to warm.

In late afternoon Fairweather and Ropata stood on a ferny escarpment and looked inland. A black brute of a mountain lifted from a swarm of heights ahead.

'There,' Ropata said. 'Ngatapa.'

Fairweather used binoculars. They disclosed the muscles of the mountain bulging beneath forest cover. Then there were sinewy ridges, ribbed slopes steep to a bald summit. In bulk Ngatapa had no rival near. 'Intriguing,' he pronounced, otherwise at a loss.

Breathless Herrick joined them. Also Jonah, careful to keep a distance from Ropata.

'Hellish,' Herrick observed.

'It is difficult to see where to get a grip,' Fairweather said. 'How to begin?'

'We listen to our feet,' Ropata said.

He spat; and considered the fallen spittle.

'Approaches seem sheer,' Fairweather objected. 'Kooti must surely defend them.'

Ropata remained more interested in the arrangement of spittle than in the topography of Ngatapa. He spat again, this time with apparently less ambiguous result.

'Tomorrow?' he said.

'Tomorrow?'

'Not today. At dawn, scout. At noon, attack.'

By campfire that night Herrick said, 'You are unusually quiet.'

'Ropata leaves me with less conversation. A burden is shed.'

'You have never been one to follow blind.'

'A man who sees his mission as moving forward has eyes enough for me.'

'To make yourself merely one of Ropata's warriors may not help anyone in the end. Least of all yourself.'

The greenwood of their fire sputtered.

'Have you more to say?' Fairweather asked.

'It seems not.'

'Good,' Fairweather said.

Ropata's scouts returned with awe in the middle of the morning. The fortress was outside their most extravagant tribal tradition. There were formidable earthworks and mazes of palisades. Rifle pits commanded approaches to the summit. On three sides the mountain was made of sheer slopes, precipice and chasm; on the fourth was a ridge from which attack might be pressed, but only at risk from Kooti's rifles. Many fires had been seen burning. They thought five hundred defenders or more.

'Then he has detained us with success,' Herrick concluded. 'He has built higher to laugh.'

'It is hardly news that Kooti does nothing by halves,' Fairweather said.

'We need an army,' Herrick said. 'Not a ragbag of militia and Maoris. And artillery might not go amiss.'

'It cannot have escaped your administrative attention, Herrick, that the imperials have gone. Or that this colony boasts self reliance. We are reliant upon Ropata for our skins. There is the joke. Your civil war is home to roost.'

'Artillery, then.'

'If you can find the elephants to haul it here. And persuade the elephants to fly.'

'Even Ropata cannot be lunatic enough to offer challenge.'

'I should expect nothing less.'

They found Ropata viewing fresh spittle.

'Two parties,' he disclosed.

'Two?' Fairweather asked.

'One of whites and all other Maoris. The other of mine. The first will present itself on the ridge of which we are told. They are to try, but not hard. Theirs is to give Kooti thought of success.'

'The second?'

'I shall attack where he thinks impossible. You have quarrel with this?'

'In only one detail,' Fairweather said. 'One white man wishes to move with your party. That man is me.'

'For what purpose?' Ropata asked.

'To see justice done. And credit given where due.'

Ropata took time to think. He asked, 'Which is your side of good fortune? Your left or your right?'

'I have never given the subject consideration,' Fairweather confessed.

'Never? As a man who fights war?'

'I admit to a wound healed in my left leg. One delivered, in a healthier campaign, by a compatriot of yours.'

'Then that is your unlucky side,' Ropata said. 'On that side, do you feel twitch or strange ache?'

'In respect of discomfort both sides suffer the same.'

'Then you may join with my party,' Ropata said.

For a time, as they tramped, unravelling ridges played with perspective; the mountain seemed to recede, to become one among others. Then forest screened it from view. When they emerged again, Ngatapa lifted lumpy above. Large earthworks could be seen, as promised, and tall palisades with fires burning beyond. The column divided, Ropata and Fairweather with one party, Herrick and Jonah with the other.

To Herrick Fairweather said, 'Every man has a breaking point. Let yours be that of your men. Hound them by all means, but not from too far in advance. There is no satisfaction in being marooned under Maori parapets. One other thing. Tell men to piss first. The Duke of Wellington's advice at Waterloo; men are still made much the same.'

They shook hands.

To Jonah he said, 'See that Captain Herrick is understood and makes himself understandable. If you feel casualties and morale leave much to be desired, you will inform Captain Herrick accordingly, and see to the respectable withdrawal which must eventually be made. Above all you are to see that he survives.'

'He will be a good white face for Kooti's guns,' Jonah acknowledged.

'Quite,' Fairweather said. 'It may not be undesirable for Kooti to think Captain Herrick is me.'

While Herrick and Jonah trudged toward the ridge they would climb, Ropata's party moved with more stealth within forest cover about the base of the mountain. There was no slope conspicuously less daunting than others. Ropata finally settled for one more tufted with scrub and tussock. Hands might find a grip where footing was slight.

They waited until they heard the first shots, Herrick's or Kooti's, from the far side of the mountain. Feint had begun.

'*Kokiri*,' Ropata ordered. Attack.

He burst across open ground and began climbing. Fairweather was at pains not to lag, nor scores of warriors around, with weapons hung on belts and slung on their backs. They clawed at rock and clay and grabbed at thin growth to haul themselves uphill. Some fell away, legs still working, dislodging others when they dropped. As the climb lengthened, there were fewer persisting. Ropata remained five yards ahead of Fairweather, feet and hands darting to right and left, a fly feeling out a wall. Finally there was a tree which Kooti's men had toppled over a cliff's edge. Ropata gripped a branch, and so soon did Fairweather; they hung there together and looked back. Perhaps a hundred had begun the climb; hardly half were still trying, and many of them faltering. The fire had grown heavier on Herrick's side of the mountain. What use that ploy now?

'We shall not have the numbers,' he told Ropata. 'Perhaps this had best be postponed.'

Gasping men began to reach them, Ropata's least attractive lieutenants, and others of moody conviction. One or two dozen men were still labouring up slowly.

'Is that, then, your wish?' Ropata asked.

'I try to talk sense,' Fairweather said.

'You do not answer my question. What is your wish?'

'I have kept it no secret.'

'And you have ammunition?'

'Of course,' Fairweather said.

'Then what is your complaint?'

Fairweather seemed not to have one of substance.

Ropata lectured his dwindled force in Maori, then swung himself the last yards to the lip of the cliff. His men launched themselves after. Fairweather was soon among them and on level ground. Forward, there were rifle pits joined by trenches, outer defences; parapets and palisades and buildings rose on the summit beyond. The few warriors left manning this angle of the fortress were recovering their wits and standing to shoot. Most could get no more than one shot delivered. The first of Ropata's men were upon them with butt and bayonet; the second wave used tomahawks to finish resistance. A few shots were fired from loopholes within the palisades. Nothing of substance; presumably Kooti was calling up fusillades on the far side of the fortress. Ropata led his men fast to dead ground under the palisades. There they attacked the slender timber with tomahawks. A minute passed in grunting and hacking. Finally they had a hole sufficient for a man to squeeze through. The first to try was blasted back again, his face ravaged at short range. His corpse was pulled clear. Ropata scrambled on to the shoulders of a pair of his burlier men until he could see over the palisades; he had one loaded rifle after another passed up to him, and fired into the fortress. This drew enough shot for men to push through the breach, Fairweather too. On the other side they found more trenches and tactically placed pits; more palisades. The fortress was a box of boxes, boxes within boxes, any one of which could be conceded without imperilling another. Smoke billowed up from rifle pits and spilled from loopholes. Fairweather dived for a trench filled with dying. Ropata joined him.

'It is no simple place,' Fairweather said.

If Ropata had a view of the matter, it was in reserve while he raised his rifle and brought down a defender. Then Kooti's men within the box mustered a charge. It met a fusillade from Ropata's men and melted, yet was menacingly renewed; the enemy seemed queerly to multiply, to rise from the ground where they should not. It took Fairweather time to deduce why.

'Tunnels,' he told Ropata. 'Kooti has his defence systems linked, and can feed men anywhere fast.'

A further deduction was possible. Kooti had men to feed through because Herrick's push up the ridge was now seen as sham. Kooti could use his numbers to wear away at Ropata, certainly to exhaust his ammunition. By afternoon that was almost the case. Trench after trench had been taken, but still no safe ground won. They were confined to a position which took fire from three sides. Carbines had grown too hot to hold, and many were jamming.

'Well?' Fairweather asked.

'Small wedges split great logs,' Ropata said.

'That may be one Maori proverb too many. Great logs also crush.'

'Would you see Kooti laugh as we leave? We have a wound from which blood flows. For each of his men dead, there will be another to doubt his mana.'

'That requires ammunition,' Fairweather said. 'I shall see what I can do.'

He scrambled along trenches, ducking under shot, back through the breached palisades to the edge of the cliff. There, with no pleasure, he found Herrick arriving with a small and tired party. Jonah was of it, and Mulhooly and Newman, and barely a dozen Maoris; they were heaving small casks of ammunition on to firm ground.

'Where are our hundreds?' Fairweather asked.

'Gone,' Herrick said. 'Our move up the ridge was unfortunate. When Kooti's men swarmed out, I was left with too few.'

'You might have rallied more to join us up here.'

Jonah said, 'Other Maoris say that if even Ropata's own men won't follow him, why should they? And Poverty Bay Maoris are having another think.'

'About Kooti?'

'And Ropata. And who is the worse.'

'Come,' Fairweather said.

'They think he wants not just to kill all Poverty Bay people with Kooti, also to get all of us against Kooti killed too. Then he will get the government to pay him with our tribal land.'

Fairweather said to Herrick, 'Is it possible?'

'I cannot exclude it,' Herrick said. 'He could also ask to be made peace-keeper in Poverty Bay. He would be difficult to shift.'

'He is still our best hope of bringing Kooti low.'

'I know that,' Jonah said. 'Or I would be gone as your sergeant.'

'Let him try to use us,' Fairweather said. 'Meanwhile we use him.'

It seemed Mulhooly, for one, was still much confused. 'Are we to defeat Kooti today, sir?' he asked.

'Is that important, Mulhooly?'

'Yes, sir. It is.'

'Then today you may help him learn that he has no lasting city. The rest will come too. Are we to get this ammunition to Ropata or not?'

Fairweather persuaded the wearied arrivals to run and crawl to Ropata's front. Herrick was aggrieved by what he saw.

'Impossible,' he said. 'No sane commander would countenance persisting here.'

'Ropata,' Fairweather explained, 'is of the view that a situation providing for enemy dead is not one for grief.'

'Your own view?'

'Under consideration,' Fairweather said.

Day became dusk, and dusk total dark. Ropata rationed ammunition among his favoured marksmen and had them fire with discrimination under the flare of Kooti's guns. 'Now,' he said to Fairweather, 'it is our turn. Yours and mine. I wish to see your worth.'

They crawled forward; they soon seemed muzzle to muzzle with Kooti's force. 'You,' Ropata whispered.

Fairweather's gun flashed, followed by that of an enemy. Ropata placed his own shot mortally at under two yards. At the next point it was Ropata who fired first, Fairweather who finished. There were soon several of Kooti's men silenced at the same range or shorter.

'You are worth further thought,' Ropata decided.

In the last hour before dawn he confessed himself baffled by the problem of food and water; there was distinctly not the ammunition for another day's fight.

'You leave first,' he told Fairweather. 'I retire my men last.'

'I should like to remain useful,' Fairweather said.

'You are best kept alive,' Ropata explained. 'I need you for next time.'

'Next time?'

'Next time I shall need every fighting Maori I can find.'

'Thank you,' Fairweather said.

The fire as they cleared the summit remained mostly irritant; Kooti appeared reluctant to risk further impairment of his mana outside his fortress. The descent took more toll. Wounded had to be lowered on ropes, dangling in anguish, with some dead at the end.

When men were grouped again under Ngatapa, and litters fashioned, Ropata elaborated on what he meant by next time. He was returning home to recruit younger and fiercer men to train in war; too many of his present warriors were aged and of bygone battles. He would return to the attack within the month of December. It was enough that Kooti could now count his dead as days left of his life.

'Enough?' Fairweather asked.

'Enough,' Ropata said with finality.

They marched seaward. Their route took them through the camp of those who had failed to climb Ngatapa or otherwise flinched. Ropata and his reddened and bandaged survivors, weapons gripped horizontally on their shoulders, looked neither right nor left, and spoke not at all; they left shame behind them and very soon fear. With Ropata departing the field, there was now nothing between the defectors and Kooti. They grabbed up weapons and possessions and hastened to follow.

Further along the track, Ropata permitted men rest. 'So there is no way to change your mind?' Fairweather asked.

'Would you wish poor omen?' Ropata said. 'A commander can retire from the enemy. Never from his word.'

'You leave Kooti to do as he will.'

'I know your need, Fairweather. I likewise know mine. Mine is to leave

Kooti to cruel dream, to waking with sweat. It is also to listen to wind, tide and ancestors and return with great quiet.'

'May I share it,' Fairweather sighed.

As they closed with the plain of Poverty Bay, in late afternoon light, there was another gauntlet to run. Colonel Whitmore had arrived, with a column of armed constabulary and militia mustered from distant parts of the colony. They were camped in summery comfort on the fringe of the forest. Whitmore surrendered the shade of his tent to make vigorous advance on Fairweather and Herrick. His late martial woes had lost him some weight, but nothing in voice. 'Have you finished the fellow?' he demanded.

'It would be immodest to suggest totally, sir,' Fairweather said.

'Then what in God's name am I looking at? Another damned rout?'

'A retirement at the request of depleted native allies, sir. Meanwhile it must be said that Kooti has been punished for the first time.'

He waited on Whitmore to take loud offence. But Whitmore, it seemed, had another canoe to paddle.

'It has been said in certain quarters that I should be held responsible for the regrettable events here; that I mischievously did my best to deny Poverty Bay protection. Would you likewise be of that view, Fairweather?'

'That could be seen as a civil view, sir. And perhaps capriciously political.'

'You beg the question. And might I remind you, Fairweather, before you make answer, that you yourself are in a most unfortunate position. I presume you have lost a number of men.'

'Humbling Jews has never been without sacrifice, sir.'

'Their deaths are at your door. You received instruction not to move against Kooti until my arrival.'

'The communication was indecipherable, sir,' Herrick said quickly. 'And the slaughter here was numbing. Angered men cannot be expected to sit and patiently interpret obscure requests.'

'Your comrade, Captain Herrick, may have much need of your charity. He has not only imperilled the prospect of a soberly conducted campaign. He has diminished the numbers at my disposal.' To Fairweather, Whitmore added, 'I can have you court martialled and ignominiously removed from this vicinity. Are we understood?'

'We might appear to be, sir.'

'You spoke of a civil view of the outrage; I await your answer on whether it is a view you also share.'

'Then my answer, sir, is that with your arrival I find it desirable to take the soldier's view. Which means keeping my head down and excluding all but the ground to be taken.'

'With grudge?'

'I should prefer politicians to have fewer sins to answer for, sir. And the plain of Poverty Bay still populated by Christian colonists in rude health. Kooti proved not to be averse to open ground; the problem was that there was nothing of martial nature to mellow him here. There may be deaths at my modest door; there is a gate wider.'

'Then I shall have your hide,' Whitmore said.

'I must protest, sir,' Herrick said.

'It is quite possible, Herrick, that you may be worth formal disgrace too. I have an open mind on the matter.'

'Colonists and Maoris might have much to say on the subject of Captain Fairweather, sir. Aside from which, at risk to himself, he would appear to have won Ropata's respect. That can be said of few others.'

'It does not accord with the evidence of my eyes. Why this slovenly retirement from the field of battle?' To Fairweather, Whitmore said, 'I suggest you swiftly prove Herrick's point. Order Ropata to turn his men around and return to the fight.'

'There seems to be some misapprehension, sir,' Fairweather said. 'Ropata does not take my orders, perhaps not even yours. He gives them.'

'Anarchy, in short,' Whitmore said.

'It is currently more to the point, sir, that his killing is conducted in tidy fashion. He is also firm that a holiday is needed to recruit fresh men; I think it unbecoming to quibble.'

'Bring the old wretch to me.'

'I should, sir, appreciate my present position made plain. Am I demoted, or currently under charge?'

'Damn you, Fairweather. Get Ropata here.'

Ropata did much to make Fairweather's standing plain. Whitmore threatened Maoris with total deduction of pay should offensive duties not be resumed.

'I think I will not speak to you,' Ropata said. 'I wish to know you no further. This is my word. I speak only to Fairweather.'

'Captain Fairweather,' Whitmore said, 'will soon not be of our company.'

'Then neither will I,' Ropata said. 'I shall make no return with new warriors. I therefore cease on this subject or any other with you. Anything more may be said through Fairweather, if Fairweather so wishes to speak.'

Whitmore was unwilling to comprehend. 'How long, Ropata, will you be? How soon can you promise to be back?'

Ropata did not reply.

'Well?' Whitmore said.

Ropata turned his back, picked his nose elaborately, and spat. This was a preliminary to even more extensive silence.

'Ask him, Fairweather,' Whitmore said with despair.

'Is that an order, sir?'

'What does it sound like, man?'

'How soon, Ropata?' Fairweather asked.

'Two weeks,' Ropata said. 'Perhaps three. You must be here.'

'Your friendship is appreciated,' Fairweather said.

'It is not friendship,' Ropata said. 'I need many men for Ngatapa. You are but one. When I return, I wish the rank of colonel also.'

'That may be difficult to arrange. The government would maintain that one colonel is more than enough for Poverty Bay.'

'Then I must be major. More than a captain. I wish you, Fairweather, to learn to say sir to me.'

'That may be less a problem.'

'We meet again,' Ropata promised. His nose pressed against Fairweather's. '*E noho ra*, captain.'

'Goodbye, sir,' Fairweather said.

25

With the port gained, Fairweather rode to the hospital with Surgeon Gibbs alongside, and wounded in train. The schoolhouse had filled with casualties of the campaign already returned; Gibbs' harassed assistant was labouring on flesh ruptured and festered, and dislocations and fractures of bone.

Meriana was gone.

The fatigued assistant reported that at first she seemed to be making recovery. In the second week she took normal food and talked, if with no great coherence. In the third some malaise became evident; she lapsed into melancholy and could not keep her food down. Food poisoning could not have been the cause; no other patient was similarly afflicted. Whitmore's surgeon had taken a poor view of her condition. Wounded beginning to arrive had made it impossible to attend to her needs. Finally she had been sent to Hawke's Bay on the vessel which conveyed Whitmore's contingent.

Gibbs steered Fairweather outside the hospital. 'It may be for best,' he said. 'You were not of comfort in the first instance.'

'We are not talking of the first instance. We are talking of now. Of nearly four weeks on.'

'I put it to you, all the same, that she will be in good hands; and still further removed from the events of which she was victim. There is a limit to what can be done.'

'Is that a professional opinion?'

'In your case,' Gibbs said.

December days limped. Summer settled, and cicadas sang thick. Dry wind blew, mud turned to dust, and dust stung the eyes. The plain of Poverty Bay remained a place of silences. Surviving colonists had no desire to return to their holdings, not with Kooti unhindered in the valleys and mountains beyond. Nor were Maoris much bolder. Armed parties went out to retrieve wandering animals; such as they found were slaughtered for those camped in the port.

Fairweather could soon count three letters written to Hawke's Bay. It was difficult to write with feeling. That presumed feelings to be felt.

'I find myself hateful,' he confessed to Herrick.

'If it is any comfort,' Herrick said, 'I am sure, at this moment, that you hate Kooti more.'

'God help me,' Fairweather finally said.

'And Kooti,' Herrick proposed.

By day Whitmore paraded men of the armed constabulary, employed to endure martial pain, across the landscape. He marched them in fours, moved them in close order and open, wheeled them and charged them, and brought them back gaunt to the port. It was his notion that Kooti could be taunted, tempted out on to open ground; Kooti was not. Whitmore was as luckless in persuading men of the volunteer militia that these excursions were needed. Whitmore, they told Fairweather, could tell his grandmother to suck eggs. Whitmore, also via Fairweather, expressed himself with feeling on the parentage of the colonists. To indicate his rage further, he moved his camp out from the port. He also ordered exercises with cohorn mortars to refurbish morale when flesh flagged. The cumbersome pieces hurled their inspirational shells into the hills; Whitmore made no secret of his desire to burst a few on the port and its population.

'This place is still not worth the saving,' he informed Fairweather and Herrick. 'Were it not for the fact that Kooti might infect more of the colony with his scurrilous scriptures, I should not be here. Meanwhile, it may be of interest for you to know of my report to the government; I have indicated that this region can now be called quiet.'

'It can what, sir?' Herrick burst out.

'You heard me, man. Quiet.'

'It is one view of the matter, sir,' Fairweather said. 'Certainly now that corpses have been decently interred.'

'There is another view of the matter,' Whitmore said. 'Having exacted his *utu*, Kooti may now feel content. After suffering a taste of Ropata, his followers might well have fallen away. He has had ample chance to show further designs on Poverty Bay; he has signally failed to disclose any. My feeling is that we may later net him at our leisure. In short, if I have my way, the campaign can be considered over.'

'You cannot be serious, sir,' Herrick protested.

'You show less surprise, Fairweather,' Whitmore noted. 'Is it fair to suppose my point has been taken?'

'It is certainly fair to suppose I am beyond surprise, sir,' Fairweather said.

They escaped Whitmore's tent and rode back to the port. There they found panic. A colonist and his son, and two Maori helpers, had been ambushed while hunting wild cattle; one of the Maoris had staggered back to report the killing of his companions.

'So much for peace,' Herrick said.

Fairweather was quiet. It was Kooti, not Whitmore, taunting and tempting. And from chosen ground.

'Well?' Herrick said. 'You look almost pleased.'

'Relieved,' Fairweather said.

'God forgive us both, then,' Herrick said. 'Which of us is to have the satisfaction of telling Whitmore?'

'Allow me,' Fairweather said.

Mustering of men began; mounted patrols were sent out. Whitmore told Fairweather, 'This time it will be done properly, or not at all. Have you quarrel with that?'

'With nothing of pugnacious nature, sir.'

'Is this tale I hear true, then? That Kooti has done you personal hurt?'

'It is a subject I should prefer to remain within the realm of rumour, sir.'

'Damn it, man, I am entitled to know.'

'Then something of the sort could well be said, sir.'

'It would have helped me in the first instance, Fairweather, if you had made this more plain. It would have gone far to explain your impetuosity of demeanour and utterance. Meanwhile you may consider yourself excused.'

'That is most benevolent of you, sir.'

'Tell me about this stronghold of Kooti's.'

'I am willing to push forward and begin investment, sir.'

'I said, Fairweather, that this will be done properly. We shall build a line of forts into the interior and man them all amply. Tracks must be widened to accommodate horse-drawn drays. Convoys will be heavily guarded and regular. Each fort will be stocked with ammunition, dry goods, and livestock for fresh meat. Creature comforts will not go lacking; there will be shelter of adequate nature. I do not again propose to sleep under trees.'

'I feel obliged to observe, sir, that those admirable plans leave Ngatapa mountain untaken.'

'It seems I have yet to make myself clear, Fairweather. Bravado has gone from this campaign. Kooti must be seen seriously. There will be no escapades of undisciplined nature. But for Ropata, it would seem, your recent enterprise would have been unmitigated disaster. Is that fair reading?'

'It is fair to say that I could not have done without Ropata, sir. It is equally fair to say no one else can. I suggest his return be speeded.'

'Would that we could.'

'Aside from posting him to the rank of major, sir, and ensuring that the commission is later confirmed, you might stress the choice nature of certain Poverty Bay land which might soon be available.'

'Land? Ropata?'

'They fight best for it, sir. As do we.'

'There could be hell to pay.'

'And hell's price worth every penny, sir.'

'There are local Maoris who take our side and yet loathe and fear Ropata. They could argue betrayal.'

'Likewise colonists eyeing the same soil, sir. Nevertheless means would handsomely serve ends. As you well know, politicians of this colony have been inclined to overlook desperate promises made to loyal Maoris in time of need; I should not let it linger on your conscience.'

'Dear God,' Whitmore said. 'Do I hear right?'

'I have tried to be lucid, sir.'

'I thought I had met ruthless men before, Fairweather. It seems I have not.'

'Thank you, sir.'

'Is there anyone you would not betray to get satisfaction?'

'I should have to think on that, sir.'

'I was right all along,' Whitmore said. 'You do have a future in this colony.'

The march to the interior was more an amble, with halts while Whitmore judged where forts and supply depots were best sited. Men sweated with axe and shovel, clearing and widening, shaping a rough road. Labouring horses and drays began to crash behind the column; and soon lamenting sheep.

'Civilization,' Herrick said, 'is a marvellous thing when it makes up its mind.'

They sat outside their bivouac with a bottle of rum and a plate of burnt mutton. In the distance Whitmore was using martial language to effect on men of the armed constabulary lately found wanting.

'This time, for the first time,' Herrick went on, 'I feel the muscle of imperial Britain pressing behind. We are pretending to be monumental at last.'

Fairweather looked inland. Sunset reddened summits; he watched a far flight of birds.

'Come,' Herrick persisted, 'I am trying to cheer. I have not heard a friendly syllable from you since we left the port. All is not gloom; we are no longer outnumbered and outgunned. True that we have Whitmore. But we also have mortars.'

'I admit to feeling lost without Larkin,' Fairweather said finally.

'Your loss is of authority,' Herrick accused. 'It all seems to be happening without you. Come on. Confess. What is the matter?'

'Nothing Ngatapa can't cure,' Fairweather said.

On the sixth day they again saw the mountain ahead. Through binoculars Fairweather observed earthworks still larger, palisades further extended; about the base of the mountain forest had been burned off to expose ravine and punishing incline. Some viewing the place for the first time ventured wonder; most remained silent. Whitmore was conspicuously thoughtful.

At length he said to Fairweather, 'You and Ropata won a foothold up there?'

'I make no pretence of total recall, sir.'

Whitmore seemed about to speak again, but did not. For a time, as they rode, he hummed a bold martial air.

With the land lifting sharply, horses had to be abandoned; a last fort and depot was established. Men now groaned uphill and downhill with more than carbines and kit; they also dragged mortars and shell.

Ngatapa mountain was not fast to move closer, nor much to diminish.

Whitmore pitched camp a thousand yards short and placed pickets. Neither telescope nor binoculars gave satisfaction; he arrived, after visible searching of soul, at an unsurprising judgement.

'It would appear that we need Ropata,' he said.

'Yes, sir,' Herrick said, solemn.

'Where in damnation is the man? I have sent the old ruffian a hundred messages if I have sent him one. He still chooses not to make an appearance.'

'In my experience, sir,' Fairweather said. 'his time is ripe when we confess impotence.'

'I have no intention of so doing,' Whitmore said. 'Tomorrow we keep men moving. Morale must not sag. We reconnoitre in strength; we push patrols around the mountain and map the ground thoroughly. We also practice the single and flying sap. And we select sites for our mortars. We shall give Kooti much to consider, with or without Ropata. If Ropata wishes only to be in at the kill, so be it. But he will not, and will never, clamber upon the backs of Britons daunted in spirits here.'

'Talking of spirits, sir,' Herrick said, 'I trust you will not take it amiss if I remind you that today is the twenty-fourth day of December. Christmas Eve, sir. Is it your intention to mark the birth of Christ in some fashion?'

'Most certainly,' Whitmore said. 'Tomorrow, with sufficient elevation, one of our mortars will give our Maori Moses a flash of Christ's enlightenment up his rectum. Do I make myself clear?'

'Altogether, sir,' Herrick said.

They watched sunset light leave Ngatapa; Kooti's fires glimmered on its summit. 'So near and so far again,' Herrick sighed. 'What do you feel?'

'As little as I can manage,' Fairweather said.

'Come on,' Herrick urged, and passed back their bottle. 'The truth cannot hurt.'

'It will not harm Kooti. By the time Whitmore has all his forts to his satisfaction, his convoys and comforts, and mapped all the ground and rehearsed his siege – not to speak of composing warlike dispatches – Kooti could be trumpeting thanks to Jehovah a hundred miles from here.'

'Can't you be content with the killing Whitmore's mortars will soon do?'

'Not especially. No.'

'In which case merry Christmas,' Herrick said, and rolled himself in a blanket.

Fairweather found Jonah distant from the campfire; he was also considering the mountain, but alone and apart, in dour native mood.

'A problem?' Fairweather asked.

'A sadness,' Jonah said.

'That is no way for a Maori warrior to talk. Think of those forefathers and their feats of arms. Don't disillusion. You aren't meant to be melancholy.'

'I may soon be better,' Jonah said.

'So what ails a sublime savage now?'

'There are times when I think Kooti might be right.'

'I see.' Fairweather was sobered.

'But not right for me,' Jonah explained. 'I like colonists' money in my pocket. The good things of life.'

'That is relief,' Fairweather said. 'I have no wish to replace and disgrace a good sergeant.'

'There were Maoris who wanted to be Jews in the beginning, when they first read the Bible, but Christ had the fine talk. They were dying of measles and of a mind for sweet things.'

'That is your sadness?'

'It is that Maoris have to be anything else. Pagan gods were not pretty, but they made sense. There was no book to set men of the same tribe to killing each other, even men of the same family. On that mountain are Poverty Bay Maoris who need never die.'

'Cousins?'

'And my father.'

Fairweather's voice, when he found it, was whispered. 'You should have said sooner.'

'It was his choice,' Jonah said. 'He thought the old chiefs too fat and greedy, and Christians poor company. He saw Kooti as the man to redeem Maori mana, and marched off with his gun.'

'All this time you have known it could be your hand which slays him?'

'Better mine than yours. The Maori house must be clean, or in Poverty Bay we will have no home at all.'

Minutes went before Fairweather spoke.

'Forgive me,' he said.

'You, captain? For what?'

'Men of religion would call it sickness of soul.'

'What would you?'

'Death of decency. Dishonour.'

'I have my problem,' Jonah said. 'You have yours.'

'Mine is Poverty Bay's. I have forgone trust.'

'I ask one thing, captain. Is it to do with Kooti being taken, this which shames you?'

'What, Jonah, is presently not?'

'Would you do it again?'

Fairweather gave thought to the question. 'Alas,' he said.

'Taking Kooti is my business too.'

'All the same, you are free to consider yourself no longer of my command.'

'I have more to consider,' Jonah said. 'It is enough if you grieve as I must.'

They sat silent as an hour of night passed.

'Thank you, Jonah,' Fairweather said.

On Christmas dawn two strong patrols moved to scout the mountain and its environs. One was commanded by Herrick, the other by Fairweather. Herrick's was largely of armed constabulary and the remnants of militia and Maoris from Hawke's Bay. Fairweather nudged Poverty Bay men into his own. He told them, without making the order especially audible, to equip with picks and shovels and fifty rounds of ammunition each.

'You are up to something again,' Herrick said.

'For the moment,' Fairweather said, 'it might be best not to ask. Ascertain where Kooti replenishes his water. Hilltop fortresses without moisture are never good for more than a few days of fight.'

'And what will you be doing?'

'If you must know, Herrick, attempting to renew old acquaintance.'

'Be it on your head, then.'

'That is the notion,' Fairweather said.

From forest edge blistered by Kooti's fire-raisers he looked up the long ridge which most tethered Ngatapa to the terrain around. It was along that ridge that Herrick's band had been routed on the last excursion here. For much of its climb it offered poor cover and uneven footing. Yet it fattened and flattened as it joined with the summit; there was some tolerably level ground left just outside Kooti's defences. Perhaps it was designed to seduce; to provide Kooti's men with rousing musketry exercise on two-legged targets. Beggars could not be choosers, though they were by nature losers; Fairweather's Christmas rendezvous could only be made there.

To Jonah he said, 'Half the men are to remain in reserve until my signal. Then push them up to join me.'

'You?' Jonah asked.

'I shall be demonstrating the virtue of the flying sap. An enterprise most efficiently conducted under some fire.'

'Even Ropata could not take Ngatapa by himself.'

'Much as I might cherish the notion of a breach into which Colonel Whitmore might fearlessly pour men, I am not here to rival Ropata's thunder.'

'Then what are you doing?'

'Sergeants, Jonah, ask no questions. They are saints among men. They know God has spoken. And they convey their commander's wish in profane forms of their choosing; I am indifferent as to how you persuade men to follow uphill. So long as they do.'

'I am not your last sergeant. This one, before he sees his bullet, wants to know why.'

'I should have known it a mistake to promote a sullen and insensitive barbarian. Can't you recognize a natural superior? Does my dulcet English mean nothing to you?'

'Not much,' Jonah said.

'If I must accommodate uncivilized impertinence, then sufficient to say that I wish to get within earshot of Kooti's defences. Which might mean much gunshot; wounds worth the risk. Does that, in the light of our conversation last evening, take on a faint glow?'

Jonah looked distinctly less stubborn. 'Just signal,' he said.

Fairweather took men forward in opportunist order; the terrain had the tactics. Once free of forest, men ran up the sides of the ridge singly, ten to twenty yards at a time, and at irregular intervals; they sheltered among rocks and in hollows until they heard the next order to scurry higher. Fairweather presented no formation on which fire could be trained; there were never more than two men visible at one time. There was some faltering when guns became relevant from beyond Kooti's parapets and palisades on the summit; on the other hand progress was improved when shot lashed close to feet. Fairweather found an eroded shoulder of earth, and there grouped his party. Some were assigned to giving Kooti's marksmen more interest in life; others began digging for their own. A sap crept into the more or less level ground Fairweather had seen; at close quarters it was rather less than more, and too often stony, with picks striking sparks, and shovels banging and rattling. With cover for more men, he signalled Jonah's reserves up the ridge; fresh hands took on the digging. By noon the casualties were light and slight, and mostly from deflected shot; no attack had been mounted from within the fortress. Perhaps Kooti was puzzling over so laboured and foolish a feint, and looking out menace elsewhere. Or he might just be intrigued, which was meant. The sun stifled in the sap as it moved forward, the clay underfoot darkened with dribbles of sweat; the heat seemed to mute even Kooti's marksmen, with fewer placing accurate shot as the afternoon moved to its middle. By then, with a twist or two, and some rifle-pits bulging off to the side, the extremity of the sap was near thirty yards from Kooti's line.

Fairweather called a halt, and ordered no fire returned. Men slumped along the sap, exchanging shovels for carbines, and sucking thirstily at canteens. He pushed to the head of the sap with Jonah.

'Shout,' he told Jonah. 'Tell them to fetch Kooti close. Tell them George Fairweather wishes *korero* here.'

Jonah waited on a break in the firing, and hailed the defenders. Shooting dwindled; a puzzled quiet lengthened. Without raising his head above the sap, Jonah gave out his message. Quiet again; they heard the call of birds circling.

'Fairweather?' A lone voice, familiar, from within the fortress.

'You hear me, Kooti?' Fairweather called. His body shook; his tongue was dry.

'Well, Fairweather. I hear you well.'

'Many must die, Kooti. In the making of death there can be no mercy.'

'Do you bring news, Fairweather, or do you just wish to talk?'

'Then I bring tidings of joy. News of Christ's birth.'

'Christ, Fairweather, lost us all. Are you here with promises?'

'I can offer no terms. I am in the canoe of war, but I neither direct nor steer. The canoe cannot stop. That is my word. Also I say that men with allegiance to Israel live short lives on heights such as this.'

'Your thought is not clear, Fairweather.'

'I speak of Masada, Kooti. A mountain much as this.'

'What,' Kooti asked, 'is this mountain to me?'

'It is a mountain of Israel, where God's chosen gathered.'

'I recall it from no scripture, Fairweather.'

'More is the pity. The prophets were dead; only people were left. Jews stood fast on Masada rather than submit to the Romans. Your stance seems akin.'

'Are you here, Fairweather, to tell me you are Roman today?'

'I am no cowed Egyptian. Nor a Canaanite baring his throat.'

'Good. So we do not submit either.'

'You hear only half the tale; the other half enlightens. The bold Jews on

Masada destroyed each other, one butchering the next, until the last slew himself. Better that than Rome's fury.'

Kooti was quiet.

'Doubtless they called on Jehovah first,' Fairweather persisted. 'Their devotion failed to move him. He made no home in this world for his heroes. That is my point.'

'I see another, Fairweather. They might be avenged.'

'This need not be another place of dry bones and grief.'

'What is this, then? You would have me live, Fairweather?'

'The gallows groans for a man who murders women and children. Not to speak of men of his own colour. The most clever of lawyers could never make that seem sane. As for Biblical injunction, even a jury of Jewish pedlars and pawnbrokers would be mystified. What Jewish warrior ever killed more of his own than the Canaanites? What Israelite rebel slew more Jews than Romans? How can this be?'

'When Jehovah wills.'

'Or when you.'

'So what is it you say, Fairweather?'

'Let your last act of war be seen as kindness, and it may be longer remembered than the killing. There are captives and converts still faint of heart. Allow them to pass through your defences and into our lines. No matter their sins I should guarantee protection.'

'What would you guarantee me?'

'Something which might pass for mana. A march to the gallows prouder in tread.'

'Then you cannot much want them to live.'

Fairweather hesitated, his voice hoarsening, his heart refusing to slow; Jonah was gently gripping his arm.

'Wait,' Kooti said. 'I ask. I see.'

There were voices raised within the fortress, then Kooti's again; and shots. Two bodies were slung over the palisades, heads and arms dangling, blood beginning to drip.

'There,' Kooti announced. 'There are two who would join you. You give them no welcome, Fairweather. They are yours now. You hear me?'

'Well,' Fairweather said.

'What if I let others live? What if I left behind all those unwilling on this mountain? Would you let me, and those still loyal, pass through you in peace?'

'Armed?'

'Armed,' Kooti said.

Fairweather was quiet.

'You do not answer, Fairweather. Would you stand aside? Or would you shoot?'

Fairweather met Jonah's eye. The grip on his arm had grown fierce. At length Fairweather had to shake his head. Jonah did not flinch, though he shifted his gaze to the ground.

'You still do not answer, Fairweather. If I walked away now, would you shoot?'

'You leave me with one great regret, Kooti.'

'What is that, Fairweather?'

'That you cannot be killed twice.'

'My respects, Fairweather. You feel much as me. What is the name of that Jewish mountain again?'

'Masada, Kooti. Your tongue may soon find it with ease.'

'This,' Kooti said, 'is Ngatapa. Let it ever be so.'

Fairweather found his question; it seethed from his throat.

'Why, Kooti?' he asked. 'Why?'

As well ask wind why the rain, earth why the sky. Anyway too late. To Fairweather's right, across a deep chasm, there was a dull shock of sound, then an overhead roar, a detonation within the fortress. Earth flew up, timbers; there were cries of surprise. The first ranging shot from Whitmore's mortars had been competently placed.

'Why?' Fairweather whispered.

Because things were. Because men. Because there were symmetries under the sun.

Kooti was gone.

Jonah's hand still held his arm. Not an intimacy Fairweather was accustomed to suffering from a sergeant; he was in no haste to lose it.

'Thank you,' Jonah said. 'You tried.'

'To take a benign view.'

'Is it true, this tale of Masada?'

'As true as man's memory.'

'There would have been Romans who thought those Jews did not need to die.'

'Along with Romans who did.'

'Why should you do better?'

'Because I might have,' Fairweather said. 'And could not.'

'You heard Kooti, captain. This is Ngatapa. What now?'

'What now, sergeant, is intelligent withdrawal while we still have our skins. We have felt for the enemy, and found him lethal of spirit. There is no more to be done here.'

But Fairweather found Poverty Bay colonists crawling forward and kneeling around him. Haggard Newman and cadaverous Daniels were among them. Mulhooly's bloodshot eyes haunted more than others.

'We got something to say,' Daniels disclosed.

'It can be of small interest here.'

'Not when you've heard it,' Daniels said.

'I remember your succinct report of a massacre. Keep this as brief.'

Mulhooly spoke through caked lips. 'It's not right, sir,' he said, and trembled.

'What isn't, Mulhooly?'

'This, sir. Dragging us up here just to do what you done. It's not right.'

'And who are you to say so, Mulhooly?'

'You know who I am, sir. And what.'

'And me,' Newman said.

'I have been at pains to give you both punitive satisfaction. It is not to be found today.'

'Mulhooly and me, others too, we couldn't believe it,' Newman said. 'We heard you telling Kooti that some of his murdering niggers could walk clean away.'

'Then hear something else,' Fairweather said. 'The word nigger will not be used in my vicinity. You will apologize to Sergeant Jonah and all Maoris within earshot. If Ropata were here, you should also be kissing his feet.'

'Maybe my tongue runs away,' Newman said. 'But we still heard what we heard.'

'If you want to know the truth,' Daniels said, 'there's some reckon you think the sun shines out of Maori arses. Nothing personal. We don't think it's right.'

'You are also of that view, Newman?' Fairweather asked.

'Because we pay them to do some fighting for us, there's no call to make so much of them. Or to make one our sergeant.'

'I see.' What Fairweather saw was soon to be ugly. To the rear of the colonists, Jonah was pushing rounds into a revolver. Fairweather might have to look to his own.

'We didn't come up here to pass the time of day with Kooti,' Daniels said. 'We thought there was more.'

'Your objections are hereby noted. And hereby dismissed. Place yourselves at Sergeant Jonah's disposal and continue preparing to withdraw. Any further communication will be with him – after, that is, you have made your apology. It has yet to be heard.'

'That's all you say?' Newman asked.

'Unless, of course, you wish to make more of it. The charge would be mutiny. In the face of the enemy the charge need not even be read.'

'We're not menacing, sir,' Mulhooly said weakly.

'That does not preclude me demonstrating it, Mulhooly. I should also require Sergeant Jonah to discharge a weapon to effect.'

'Try it,' Daniels challenged. 'There's more where we come from. And Colonel Whitmore too.'

'The colonel indeed?'

'We reckon you didn't have no authority. We reckon the colonel would be interested in what you been up to.'

'And your current proposal is to interest the colonel. Do I have the facts of this right?'

'It needn't be like that, sir,' Mulhooly soon said.

'Intrigue me, Mulhooly.'

'Not if we stay up here, sir. Not if we give Kooti a go.'

'That is your wish? To persist on this ridge?'

'That would be about right,' Newman said.

'Why in Christ's name didn't you say so?'

'You didn't ask,' Daniels said.

Fairweather felt weak. Men with a will to fight were men of whom much might be forgiven.

Jonah was of that view too. 'If they are telling you they want to kill Kooti,' he said, 'that is enough of an apology for me.'

'It is insufficient for me,' Fairweather said. 'The only fit apology is for you to take Ropata as example and fight twice as hard. Twice. Am I heard?'

'Does that mean we're staying, sir?' Mulhooly asked.

'It has to,' Fairweather said.

When Herrick stumbled up the ridge, he found Fairweather's men burrowing deeper; the sap had spread wings, with more rifle pits hollowed.

'And what am I to tell Whitmore?' he asked.

'That the scum of Poverty Bay have begun investment of Ngatapa,' Fairweather suggested.

'You cannot expect him to look kindly on this.'

'Tell him we trust that our offering will be accepted in the spirit of the season; it is a day for goodwill.'

'And you are a crazed optimist.'

'Gifts on this day are customarily reciprocal. Further food, water and ammunition would bring great rejoicing. Also reinforcement when the colonel wishes to give his numbers employment. We sit upon Kooti's one easy line of escape. That point might be made.'

'If I can get a word in edgeways,' Herrick said.

Herrick returned, just on dusk, to inform Fairweather that he had been relieved of his command. The insubordinates of Poverty Bay were to retire. Word spread along the sap; profanities were heard.

'Tell the colonel,' Fairweather said, 'that these wretches are unwilling to bestir themselves. Where are their supplies?'

'My orders are,' Herrick said, 'to withdraw your men in orderly fashion during the hours of dark. You imperil the grand design. The colonel sees the twelve days of Christmas filling with siege. Anything less might not make impression in the annals of empire; you promise to reduce a thrilling chapter to a melancholy paragraph.'

'And should clouds of glory produce a faint drizzle, he has his scapegoat in advance.'

'That is one reading.'

'Please proceed, Captain Herrick. Instruct my men in the matter of withdrawal during the hours of dark.'

'I like this less than you,' Herrick said.

'Am I to take it that you have given the order?'

'And had no response.'

'I have always said these procedures are best simplified.'

'Well,' Herrick said, 'what now?'

'Convey to the colonel that the entire colony will be bound to learn that he abandoned a party of convinced fighting men hard under Kooti's fortress. The colonial press could take a most dolorous view of the affair; likewise once compassionate politicians.'

'I shall try to suggest as much in other words,' Herrick explained.

'Don't try too hard,' Fairweather said.

No man was allowed to sleep. To make the order effective, each had to discharge one shot for every hour passing; firing was constant. Kooti, however, pressed no night attack. His triumph could have been quick.

At dawn supplies were packed uphill in grudging amount, with Herrick again ducking shot on the route.

'Do me one favour,' Herrick said. 'Make it less evident that you are enjoying all this.'

'I should enjoy reinforcement more.'

'Be grateful for small mercies. You have food. You have shot.'

'Am I still relieved of command?'

'Insofar as our colonel can make himself understood on that subject. On the other hand, he may yet bring himself to acknowledge that some form of de facto investment has begun.'

'Serenade him some more, Herrick,' Fairweather said.

Herrick's diplomacy produced nothing further to celebrate that day. It could not escape Kooti that Fairweather's challenge had more froth than flesh. Yet for much of the day martial energy amounted to Whitmore's mortars lifting shell loudly into the fortifications, with Whitmore and most of his force still standing distant ground. From Fairweather's position it was possible to deduce, from faint shouts within the defences, that Kooti was preoccupied with tunnelling deeper; the shock of the mortars might soon be small. Meanwhile Fairweather surrendered forward ground, had pits and communication saps freshly dug, checked fields of fire, and arranged men in punishing positions. In the waning afternoon, with Whitmore's mortars quiet, the attack at last came. There was a short prologue of yelling, a drawl of bugle. Kooti's men, with bayonets fixed to firearms, tomahawks flourished too, dropped over the palisades and swarmed out from apertures. Impossible to decide whether it was a quick sortie or an attack in strength. With Kooti's men sprinting, the distinction was frivolous.

When attackers were ten paces short Fairweather signalled a volley from men trenched to his right; then, on a count of three, from those to the left. As Kooti's men turned to face new fire, their backs became broad targets. Others came on. He held the volley from the centre until the range was just short of insanity. Midriffs split magically; faces splintered; bodies toppled among those entrenched. In the wavering which followed, Fairweather's men on the wings mounted second volleys. Smoke and dust gathered into yellowing fog, with men here and there warring singly with intruders. There was chopping, grunting, and soon a slime of blood underfoot. Men of Kooti's force still unshredded began running and limping back to their fortress. Fairweather had no further chance to impose form. Newman was rising, shouting to give chase. Such as Mulhooly and Daniels were not far behind.

'No,' Fairweather shouted. 'No.'

He hardly heard the order himself. Newman and others as besotted with slaughter were staggering after Kooti's men as they regained their fortress. Fairweather saw loopholes filling with carbines, muskets, fowling pieces and shotguns. The fusillade which followed was not especially disciplined. It did not need to be. Newman, for one, seemed to rise from the earth. When sound dispersed, and smoke, there was a view of men mostly lifeless. Some shivered faintly; and were still.

Jonah was at Fairweather's side. 'They will never do that again,' he observed.

'Never,' Fairweather said.

After dark, with Jonah beside him, he crawled close to Kooti's defences. Moans and whispers for water drew them to men still worth salvage. Where men were not, and still suffered, Jonah used a quick knife. Newman was not one who needed attention. Daniels had been delivered from one massacre to succumb in another. They found Mulhooly with razed scalp and tattered shoulder and tugged him back to safe ground; Fairweather tipped rum down his throat.

'We tried like you told us,' Mulhooly said feebly. 'We tried twice as hard.'

'Your apology is accepted, Mulhooly. You must also accept mine.'

'Yours, sir?'

'Mine must also be tendered to young Jimmy Newman. I did not mean to make him an orphan.'

'We tried, though, didn't we, sir?'

'Indeed, Mulhooly. That must forever be said.'

Next morning Herrick was seen moving men in large number up the ridge to join Fairweather's diminished force. Herrick, dodging from rock to rock, calling upon men similarly to keep cover, looked even more beleaguered. He dropped into a pit with a groan. 'Let it be recorded,' he said, 'that a certain innocent captain of militia was a significant casualty of this siege. If, that is, it ever happens. You and Whitmore will be named as my murderers.'

'Have we set sufficient example?' Fairweather asked. 'Is assault to be pressed?'

'Men of the armed constabulary are now to hold this position. Poverty Bay's militia is to retire.'

'To join the military picnic below?'

'Colonel Whitmore reluctantly allows that the present situation still leaves much to be desired. In short, Ropata.'

'Amen.'

'Ropata, alas, proves a bride shy of Whitmore's nuptial couch. He hove into view yesterday and camped a mile short of the colonel. And refuses to be seduced nearer. He asks why Whitmore makes no attempt on Ngatapa; he asks if he is to do all the work. I have stopped short of explaining to Ropata that our commander has been lowered by a spinal affliction earned in his last encounter with Kooti.'

'I trust he has been informed that not all have been keeping company with Kooti via binoculars.'

'Ropata says that if you were not roosting up here, he would wash his hands of Kooti and march his new men home. Weak allies are inauspicious. He still takes no orders from Whitmore.'

'Then all is not lost.'

'The fact is, Fairweather, that your notorious tact is needed. Ropata insists on communicating only with you. Whitmore tried sending me to *korero*. Ropata made it clear that I am a bumptious substitute. You seem to have a corner of the old brute's black heart. It is you or no one.'

'Thus this order to retire?'

'To join Ropata with full credit, and no recriminations. You also retain your rank. I negotiated that much for you. Whitmore can be seen intemperately inclining to the view that you and Ropata deserve each other. And, by the way, Ropata has rather ungraciously accepted his posting as a major in the colonial militia. Just to make your junior position plain.'

It took the rest of daylight and more for Fairweather to retire his men, deliver his wounded to Gibbs for renovation, and exchange careful words with Whitmore. Whitmore still saw his mortars working miracles of devastation. 'You must have observed their accuracy today,' he said.

'With respect, sir, no war is won with artillery. Especially not this.'

'Do I hear the 65th Foot? Or are you asking for scaling ladders?'

'My hope, sir, is that Kooti might soon be making that plea. And lifting them heavenward.'

'Get along with you, Fairweather,' Whitmore said.

It was near midnight before he reached Ropata's camp. Jonah was still at his side; he refused to be abandoned to Whitmore's force. Better the devil he knew, he said.

'Ropata?' Fairweather asked.

'You,' Jonah said.

They moved among three or four hundred mostly youthful warriors squatted and talking in the light of their fires; there were scores of bivouacs, and weapons in tidy stacks. Ropata himself was in conference with lieutenants, having drawn a map of Ngatapa on the ground with a stick. Marking out Kooti's likely dispositions, and lecturing on places possibly vulnerable, he was slow to note Fairweather standing near.

There was no smile of consequence. He said, 'So you are not the heron whose flight is seen only once.'

'Sir,' Fairweather said more formally. 'Captain George Fairweather reporting for duty.'

He saluted.

Ropata raised himself from the ground. There was touching of noses, sharing of breath.

'Your heart is quiet?' Ropata asked.

'And no ache afflicts right side or left.'

'Your thought?'

'Revenge is a dish best eaten cold.'

Ropata looked at Jonah. 'This man?'

'Is to be taken with trust,' Fairweather said. 'He may prove that a Poverty Bay Maori is as capable of killing Kooti as any other.'

'Of Kooti's own tribe?'

'As I say.'

'I need to think on this,' Ropata said.

Fairweather persisted, 'I must declare interest. Not only am I reluctant to part with a man who gives my thought tongue. Let it be known, from this moment forward, that this man's tribe is also to be taken as mine. We have attended each other's sorrows; we have slain side by side. Therefore it has to be so.'

'Has to be?'

'Is,' Fairweather said. 'He who takes from this man takes from me.'

Jonah stood uneasy as Ropata gazed.

'Then,' Ropata agreed, 'he must be my man also.'

'Thank you,' Fairweather said.

Ropata gave out an order; it was echoed through the camp. On clear ground between fires warriors raced to form rank after rank. They were stripped to the waist, legs bare too, and each carried firearm or tomahawk. Leaders chanted with vigour, then all took up the sound; feet began stamping. Their mass beat became louder, the tempo of voices more numbing. Sweat streamed in the flash of the fires. Muscles flexed, eyes rolled, tongues belligerently protruded. Within the lengthening ritual there was mock attack and challenge, charge and response; ranks rippled and rolled back, stiffened and stormed forward. At each climax men kicked high off the earth, legs bent back, weapons aloft. Ropata's face was impassive, though he permitted himself a nod now and then; it seemed he could detect no flaw in the fervour paraded. Certainly Fairweather could not. A tremor rose from the pit of his gut, something of the human past perhaps, and primitive; his throat tightened too.

'This,' Jonah whispered, 'is how it was in the old seasons of war. The dance is not about overcoming the enemy, for he is contemptible. Not about Ngatapa either; for that is a morsel. It is about men mastering all earth and sky. You do not like it?'

'Am I meant to?' Fairweather said.

'It makes me feel pagan again,' Jonah said. 'Not a Christian. And never a Jew.'

After an hour Ropata pronounced the performance of his hundreds impeccable; no man had faltered or fallen, none had disclosed weakness of limb or indifference of will. With all signs propitious, they were now allowed rest.

To Fairweather he said, 'We are ready.'

'I believe you,' Fairweather said.

Morning began with Whitmore's mortars working again upon the fortress crowning Ngatapa mountain. After a time Ropata's force, moving in single file, could be seen threading through forest and fern for all of a mile; they passed Whitmore's headquarters in silence. As the summit lifted above, Ropata sped parties of marksmen to knolls and neighbouring heights, wherever advantage offered, and then urged his force up inclines rising steeper. As they slowed and slid, men made pleasing targets for Kooti's guns. More and more defenders mounted palisades to get in shots, or leaned over cliff edge, exposing themselves altogether in their passion to expel Ropata. It was some time before he judged his men sufficiently blooded. Then he signalled his marksmen; a fusillade crashed overhead. Defenders spun from palisades, spilled from their cliff roosts, and here and there rolled downhill toward Ropata's tomahawks. Thereafter Kooti's men were less incautious; their volleys twitched high.

By noon Ropata was established across the front face of the mountain, in full view of Whitmore and his inert force. By dusk Ropata had shut Kooti's garrison off from all water.

'It seems I have seen war worth the name,' Fairweather told Herrick.

Ropata sent Whitmore an elegant invitation to participate in the siege of Ngatapa. He had his teeth, he said, in the breast and belly of the bird; Whitmore was welcome to partake of the rear. Insult was distinctly in the eye of the beholder; Whitmore rumbled off to his tent where, a short time later, glass was heard breaking. Then nightlong silence began.

26

Anno Domini 1869 arrived with reluctance. The dark of the old year lingered, the light of the new slow to dawn through dirty cloud. On this day of siege summer turned sour. Cold wind blew from the west, and by night rain was as bitter. The ground slimed; men in pits and trenches sank into deep mud. On the front face of the mountain Ropata had moved his force to points within ten yards of Kooti's fortress. On the rear, Whitmore arranged his men, with much attention to detail, along lower ground, other than where a tall precipice baffled robust martial planning; it slipped away into river, rocks and forest, and altogether out of command consideration. Then all became static. Mortars beat at the summit by day. By night defenders and attackers bandied defiance backed with sparkles of fire.

It seemed Whitmore now preferred time, rather than Ropata, as ally. 'Kooti is cut off from food, water, and further ammunition,' he told Herrick and Fairweather. 'I think we shall soon have surrender to contemplate. If not from Kooti himself, then from those he has misled. They will likely depose him and come to quick terms.'

'You would offer mercy, sir?' Herrick asked.

'Where fitting,' Whitmore said. 'Naturally some of his more disagreeable followers could not be allowed to go free.'

'With much respect, sir,' Fairweather said, 'if you are proposing further sojourns in the Chatham Islands, along with loss of land, then death might appear a decent option. That is where all this began. I see further Jews being fashioned. Ropata makes sense.'

'Ropata?' Whitmore bristled.

'And Kooti. They both believe in a clean sweep.'

'That is your prescription too?'

'I content myself with saying, sir, that some things make more sense than others.'

'So what happened,' Whitmore asked, 'to the scapegrace humanitarian of the 65th?'

Ropata was impatient with optimism. As the siege lengthened he sent

Fairweather to plead with Whitmore for combined assault on the mountain from front and rear. Whitmore reaffirmed his faith in the workings of chronology. 'Tomorrow is January the fourth,' he informed Fairweather. 'The year, even the month, is barely begun. Our mortars still have shell in reserve. It would be desirable not to be burdened with it all the way back to the coast. What is a day or two more?'

'A day or two more will be the fifth or sixth of January,' Fairweather said. 'I shall ensure that Major Ropata, if he carries no calendar, is thus enlightened.'

On the next day of siege despair did some killing. As damp mist lifted from the mountain, in the first light of morning, one Maori defender, then another, rose briefly on the skyline, and flew out from the summit; their bodies dropped into forest distant below. Shot from within the fortress toppled a third man attempting the same.

Perhaps not Masada, but an arresting rehearsal.

Whitmore rejoiced; Ropata saw peril, a spiritless triumph. Had he trained new men for nothing?

'Assault must begin,' he instructed Fairweather. 'Now. Today. Tell Whitmore.'

Fairweather laboured around the mountain to pass the message to Whitmore, and added, 'Major Ropata also feels, sir, that your investing lines are too loose. Kooti could still push a strong column through. Your lines would be best tightened by moving men further uphill, as Major Ropata has, regardless of terrain and the fire you call down.'

Whitmore was suspicious. 'Is this Ropata speaking, or you?'

'Let it be admitted, sir, that Major Ropata and I feel as one about the desirability of pressing attack today. Any deferment means risk of Kooti retaining some mana. If it is to be extinguished, it has to be here and now.'

'Tell me something new, Fairweather.'

'Since you ask, sir, it would be remiss not to draw your attention to the gap in your lines.'

'What gap? Where?'

'That precipice, sir. Kooti must surely observe it unguarded.'

'It is covered by fire from right and left. Damn it, man, it is almost perpendicular. Do you suggest I have men cling up there?'

'I suggest it a gap, sir. Reluctance to take it more into account presents a temptation.'

'For suicide leaps,' Whitmore said. 'And may we soon see them multiply.'

'So what is your word on assault, sir?'

'To see, Fairweather, what tomorrow might bring. A clearing of weather would gratify. Convey that to Ropata.'

'To expedite matters, sir, I can give you his reply. He will say that the climate is working to Kooti's advantage. Rain provides a little water for his garrison. The murk makes cover for determined escape.'

'No,' Whitmore announced. 'I will not have it. I will not have some unlettered old savage telling me my business. Nor his half renegade adviser. Are we understood?'

'It would seem more and more, sir,' Fairweather said.

'I know there are misguided romantics who see virtue in the primitive,' Whitmore said. 'But it is not incumbent on a Briton to stink like Ropata too.'

'You make yourself most clear, sir.'

'And furthermore, from this moment on, it concerns me not whom you choose for a bedfellow.'

'Kooti would appear to decide that, sir,' Fairweather said; and saluted; and left.

That afternoon Ropata selected his storming party. Others were assigned to push feints along the line. In the confusion of Kooti's response, Ropata's personal thrust would be made. As guns worked to right and left, and human din mounted, Fairweather hauled himself nearer Kooti's defence line. Behind him Ropata and Jonah carried a commandeered keg of powder; Fairweather had a short fuse dry under his tunic. Hands hollowed out earth under the palisade, the keg was placed, the fuse soon attached. While Ropata and Jonah retreated, Fairweather lit it with shaky fingers. Then he tumbled clear.

For a giddy moment he thought the fuse might have failed. But the blast, when it came, stunned beyond the best expectation. Debris dropped on his spine and skull. With the detonation still ringing, he rose weakly; Jonah steadied him on his feet. Ropata, with revolver, was already steering men through the smoky gap in the palisade. There were cries from those already embattled.

'Come, Fairweather,' Ropata said. 'This time we stay.'

By nightfall no resistance persisted within the outer boxes of Kooti's defence system; bayonet and tomahawk allowed few to flee beyond inner walls. Saps were moved forward to the next line of palisades. But the weather took the offensive. Wind surged, and rain; the gale stung and stifled. Saps became sludge, and powder was saturated; combat sputtered and ceased. Those defending the heart of the fortress seemed of the view that Jehovah was on their side. Between rowdy gusts of rain, singing became audible; it appeared to lack joy. Ropata's force tried to shelter from the wind, and the worst of the rain, by piling themselves under palisades. In a half covered pit, feet awash,

Fairweather lost touch with his flesh toward dawn; he dozed with his head on Jonah's shoulder. He woke imagining, or dreaming, a familiar and nervous laugh. Quite close, neighing, nagging, and then not there at all. Madness, perhaps; delirium. He could not stop shivering. The night had gone quiet; the singing too. The wind was a whisper, the rain a few flecks.

'Jonah?' he said.

'Captain?' A sleepy mumble.

'Tell men to stand to their arms.'

Fairweather crawled off to Ropata, and unwrapped the old man from a bundle of sodden warriors.

'Trouble,' he said. 'Kooti never goes quiet without reason.'

Ropata listened. Human moaning here and there; and the faint wind. 'Nothing,' he judged.

'Nothing is what I hear too.'

'An attack, Fairweather?'

'Or worse,' Fairweather said.

They moved to Kooti's inner wall, warriors rustling and whispering behind. When they pressed against the palisades, the silence was no more informative. A minute or more passed.

'As the tomb,' Fairweather said.

'I think what you think, captain,' Jonah said. 'Masada.'

To confound them still further, a lone woman's voice lifted eerily from the dark.

'Aue!' she was saying. *'Kua riro.'*

Alas. Kooti was gone.

'A trap?' Jonah asked.

'Never,' Fairweather said.

'Kua riro,' the woman wailed. *'Kua riro.'*

Gone. Gone.

'It cannot be,' Ropata mourned.

In the weak light Ropata's warriors axed through palisades, through a second wall and a third, and spread cautiously with bayonets across space they then found. They met no defiance; certainly no shot. The ground was greasy, pitted by mortar, made more hazardous with crumpled trenches, shattered timbering, and collapsed tunnels; they tripped on debris, discarded weapons and the dead. Pleading wounded were quietened with tomahawk. All left of the living, three or four score, mostly women and children, clung to each other on the high point of the summit. With Jonah hard behind, Fairweather ran for the stricken group before Ropata's men had their way. Revolver in hand, he looked into faces, and saw only fear.

'Find who they are,' he told Jonah. 'Ask what they know. And quick.'

He then turned to Ropata's men. 'No,' he said. '*Taihoa.* The killing stops here.'

He was not understood. He had to push and kick men back, all but resorting to the revolver, until Ropata arrived. Not that Ropata was much inclined to call his men off.

'A problem?' he asked.

'Of mercy,' Fairweather said.

'Kooti?'

'A little mercy might make for an answer.'

Jonah was in agitated questioning of the captives; replies were slow coming, and feeble.

'*Ngaa tane,*' Ropata ordered. The men.

Ropata's warriors surged among the captives and dragged out the few males who held tight to their women. Protests were ignored and women left mourning. The males were pushed a short distance, their legs kicked from under them, and then clubbed and stabbed. As grief mounted, Jonah found voice to report.

'They are mostly of Poverty Bay,' he said. 'Some with Kooti from the beginning, some not. They followed their men, and most now are widows, of no further use.'

'Kooti?'

'They say see for ourselves. Over the side. Over that precipice.'

'Jumped?'

'Fled. With many.'

Fairweather hurried to the point where the summit's side became a dizzy plunge. Flax fashioned into ropes, torn blankets tied together, curled over the edge and dangled down the precipice of which Whitmore had been warned. At the foot there was only dim forest. He lifted his eyes. More forest. Mountains.

Ropata and Jonah were soon standing beside him, both quite as thwarted. Kooti was not one to settle for Masada. Ngatapa was Ngatapa, and more so.

Herrick was the first of Whitmore's contingent to gain the summit.

'The mortars worked havoc,' he observed. 'Kooti must have far fewer men in arms. That must be said.'

'Tell Whitmore,' Fairweather said. 'Also that we have most energetically managed to snatch defeat from the jaws of victory.'

'Defeat? I see a great many dead.'

'And it is my impression, Herrick, that Kooti is not currently among them.'

'Will nothing less satisfy?'

'Not this side of senility,' Fairweather said.

Before Whitmore took stance on the summit Ropata sent small parties in pursuit of Kooti; he judged that Kooti's survivors would also be travelling in small groups, possibly to some highland rendezvous. Famished, and with wounds weeping, they were unlikely to move fast. Those showing resistance were to be shot down; others were to be returned to Ropata on the summit when captured.

'To die where they should have,' Ropata said.

'And Kooti, if caught?' Fairweather asked.

'To be spared.'

'For the hangman?'

'For you,' Ropata said.

Meanwhile Jonah was missing. Fairweather found him in an obscure angle of the fortress. He sat sorrowing beside a body torn by mortar shell, though the features of an elderly man were intact; a dignity too.

'My father,' Jonah said.

Fairweather knelt with a hand on his sergeant's shoulder. 'Consider your house clean,' he said finally. 'Consider yourself free to return to Poverty Bay.'

'You?' Jonah asked.

'Kooti still laughs.'

'That,' Jonah said, 'is my thought too.'

Whitmore had a mortar dragged to the summit by mutinously cursing armed constabulary; a salute was fired in celebration. When the echo of the last shot cleared, he obliged those on the summit with an impassioned summary of events. 'This time,' he said, 'let no one contest the truth that Kooti has been crushed. His prophecies have failed; so has his Jewish God. He is now no more than a fugitive, with the pathetic remains of his force. They, more than likely, will turn on him as a fraud. If he survives more than a few days, God forbid, he will never vex Christians of this colony again.'

He then announced the imminent return of his contingent to the coast.

'I cannot have heard right,' Herrick whispered. 'Is he proposing triumphal return without Kooti's head?'

'You are not being fair,' Fairweather said. 'He still has his own.'

In late afternoon Ropata had large fires lit on the summit to guide home his pursuing bands and their prisoners. At dusk, and through the first hours of dark, his men thronged back. Sometimes with three or four captives, survivors of some forest skirmish; sometimes with a score. Many of these stragglers were lacerated by bullet and shell; most were skeletal. Some were quite naked, others in fluttering rags. Women and children were set to one side. Men were examined closely, and questioned. None had even passing resemblance to such as anyone recalled of Kooti, the merchant of Poverty Bay who now marketed carrion.

'No?' Herrick said.

'No,' Fairweather said. 'Lieutenants, perhaps. Disciples. New recruits. Possibly even camp cooks. But no Kooti.'

Whitmore persisted on the summit in the hope of seeing the devil given his due. Before retiring downhill in frustration, and beginning his march out of the mountains in the morning, he made a last bid. One thousand pounds, on behalf of the colony's government, for Kooti dead or alive.

Speaking through Fairweather, Ropata wished to know why the offer had not been disclosed until now. Was Whitmore hoping to spare the colony expense or, worse, hoping to pocket the money himself?

Though with some quivering, Whitmore managed to keep himself in check. He also managed not to give any clear answer.

Ropata further asked, 'What of those prisoners already taken, and those still to be?'

'One pound per head,' Whitmore said. 'I am not empowered to go higher.'

Ropata also found this unsatisfying; it was still war on the cheap. Who, he asked, would keep count for fair claim to be made? Or would heads have to be carried back to the coast, and there carefully tallied?

'There is no need for literal heads,' Whitmore said with a wince. 'Unless, of course, Kooti's is required for positive identification. For the remainder I think you, Captain Fairweather, might be allowed to adjudicate. The task would seem to suit you more than most.'

He gazed at Fairweather with an expression calculated to wither. Otherwise he felt that terse farewells served matters best. Herrick, however, wanted a last word.

'I request permission, sir, to remain here with Captain Fairweather and Major Ropata's Maoris. I should like to see decencies observed so far as proves possible. Ensuring survival of innocents may become too large a duty for Captain Fairweather alone. And there is the matter of winning intelligence.'

'You appear to think of everything,' Whitmore said.

'One must, sir. Until, that is, we have somehow accounted for Kooti.'

'With one thousand pounds on his head, Herrick, Kooti can never feel safe.'

'Agreed, sir,' Herrick said. 'But can we?'

'Then damn you too, Herrick. Stay if you must. And do me one favour. See your friend Fairweather bathes before he returns to civilization.'

Male prisoners were bound, grouped for the night, and placed under guard. Herrick negotiated permission from Ropata for all women and children to leave the summit and journey home without hindrance. Often the women protested, while being urged away, and looked back with rising laments on their men.

'I must say I feel ill about this,' Herrick confessed. 'Fields of glory promise to become pastures of cold blood.'

'What is your wish?' Fairweather asked.

'That history could be kinder,' Herrick said.

It resumed with as little compassion at dawn. Cool summer sunlight allowed Ropata to hurry his bands further into the territory beyond Ngatapa. This time, with no excuses acceptable, they were to fetch back Kooti. For purposes of remuneration bags were passed out to collect heads when fugitives refused surrender. Kooti, however, was still to be returned intact for identification.

'Perhaps we should arrange a modest wager,' Fairweather said. 'One thousand pounds to one pound that we shall not see Kooti on Ngatapa again.'

'You still display great respect.'

'And you, Herrick, will never grow rich.'

On the second day of the hunt, another fifty captives were harvested, half of them women and children; and Jonah had news.

'We have a wife,' he said.

'You? Me?' Fairweather said. 'Astound me no further.'

'One of Kooti's wives,' Jonah insisted. 'Come and see.'

Fairweather walked with Jonah to a group of women currently being herded apart from men. The woman was short, fat and dark. Also the owner of quick eyes and an unattractively crooked smile.

'Her?' Fairweather said.

'Mata Te Owai,' Jonah said, 'She was his first.'

The woman gazed at Fairweather, her head on sly tilt, as Fairweather pushed questions through Jonah.

Yes, she agreed, she had become Kooti's *wahine* during his exile. When he walked tall as prophet, and told Maoris their destiny, he took her to bed. Since then Kooti had been able to pick and choose among many female followers; she, Mata Te Owai, had suffered neglect. More, in the flight from Ngatapa, Kooti seemed determined to leave her behind. She followed from old grievance, yet was not altogether dismayed to be caught.

'And how does she feel about Kooti now?' Fairweather asked. 'Is he, to her, a good man or bad?'

'*Ka Kino*,' Mata Te Owai said. '*He porangi*.'

'She thinks he is not only bad,' Jonah interpreted. 'Also mad.'

'She is bitter, then?'

'*Pouri*,' she confirmed, and spat; her smile grew more serene.

Fairweather found fresh breath. 'Was she present during the events in Poverty Bay? The time of the many murders?'

The woman grew animated. Finally Jonah disclosed, 'She says yes. She saw the killing of Biggs, also of others. She saw houses burn.'

'And was it all on Kooti's order? Not merely the wildness of his men?'

'She says all was as Jehovah wished.'

'Keep her to one side,' Fairweather said. 'We may need her testimony at some future time. Explain so to her.'

The woman listened to Jonah, more and more impressed, and then began to babble. Jonah found it difficult to call stop.

'She says,' he explained, 'that you make her feel important again. She will say whatever you wish her to say.'

'That was not quite my point. But no matter.'

'She also,' Jonah went on, 'asks if you wish to bed with her here.'

'Get her away,' Fairweather said. Then, 'No. Yes. One other thing. Ask where she resided in the time of the killings.'

Jonah finally interpreted, 'She says with Kooti and his brides of war, in the Smith house where he camped and gave orders. She says she will tell you all you wish about what happened there.'

There was a pause in which Fairweather fought disgust.

'Get the creature out of my sight,' he told Jonah. 'Get her a long way from here.'

This required no translation. Mata Te Owai looked Fairweather over with scorn. Finally he felt her spittle; sudden fingernails tore at his face too. Jonah caught at the woman's arms and bundled her away.

Making enemies was nothing new for Fairweather. It was all, so to speak, in a day's work. Nevertheless he walked downhill, found water, and washed.

On the eve of the fourth day Ropata conceded failure. In the light of the fires burning on the summit, more captives were brought in, and none of them Kooti. Essentials could not be delayed. Kooti might have rewritten Masada; Ropata was of a mind to revise Ngatapa. He might not have Kooti, but he had considerably more than one hundred of Kooti's surviving fighters as spoils. He ordered his lieutenants to begin placing prisoners along the lip of the precipice in tight groups of ten; he also selected execution squads.

'I do not suppose,' Herrick said, 'that there is point in pleading that this might yet be handled in a more Christian way.'

'What is it you want?' Fairweather said. 'The bullets blessed too?'

Ropata's men bustled back and forward with prisoners; ammunition was passed out. The grouped men were phlegmatic. Some had been waiting without illusion for three days already. Herrick found urgent concerns elsewhere. Fairweather remained with Jonah while the first prisoners were paraded to the precipice edge.

A voice rustled somewhere among them. 'Sir?' this voice said.

'This is one who knows you,' Jonah observed.

In the confusion of faces was one too vivid to be forgotten. A face wrinkled, mostly toothless, densely tattooed, and framed with white locks. Nama, warrior chief of the Tuhoe, was now shambling and thin; his hands were bound behind his back. He pushed clear of his captors to touch noses with Fairweather; he sighed and spoke through Jonah.

Jonah said, 'He wishes to remind you that he was your host in the high mountains of the Urewera. That he once laughed with you, and gave a cloak of fine feathers.'

'True,' was all Fairweather found to say.

'He says he knows you to be a good man. One of much mana.'

'And one who fights Kooti.'

Nama understood that without translation. Yet managed a smile.

Jonah said, 'He tells me that he knows that also. He says he has now twice been your enemy, twice felt your hurt.'

'Ask him what madness made him leave his lake and go killing for Kooti.'

'He says you should know. The tribe of the Tuhoe must prove themselves fearless or their mountains will be no more. He says that though Kooti promises much, he, Nama, still prefers many gods speaking through lightning and storm.'

'Then ask what he wants of me. If mercy, explain that it is not in my power. These next minutes are between Maori and Maori.'

Nama's reply came at some length. Behind him, other prisoners overdue for execution banked up.

Jonah said, 'He hopes to die as fits a Tuhoe. He has but the one wish. To die by your hand. He would deem it great privilege.'

'He cannot ask this,' Fairweather protested.

'He reminds you again of his gift. He now sees the meaning. Your gift is foretold.'

Impatience grew elsewhere, with Ropata questioning the delay.

'Please,' Jonah whispered. 'You have to be quick.'

Fairweather took grip on his revolver; and discovered it heavy. 'Ask Nama this one thing,' he said. 'Ask him whether Kooti is *tika* or not. Right or wrong?'

Nama himself obliged with the answer. '*Tika,*' he said.

Fairweather trained his revolver between Nama's interested eyes. The next seconds were dream. Then not. The shot was of this world; likewise the flesh at his feet.

It served as a signal. Prisoners were rushed to the precipice, and group after group shot. Firing parties never paused. While one party replenished carbines, another was shooting. In the red light of Ropata's fires the victims jerked, twisted, and teetered from view. A second volley was never necessary; the drop over the precipice made coup de grâce redundant. There were no cries, no pleas. Just the fumes and din of the shooting, and fires burning high.

It seemed never to finish. For Fairweather it refused to. As he made to move away, with enough groups of ten tallied, a feeble voice slowed his feet. He heard, 'Hori? Hori Fair Weather?'

Never. No.

Again he heard it, this time muffled by a blow. 'Hori? Hori Fair Weather?'

It had to be. Was.

He pushed back into the muddle of slaughter. There, eyes bright with terror, and with freshly scarred face, was Hamiora Pere bound and beaten, and ready for killing.

'You,' Fairweather said.

'Very bloody goodbye,' Hamiora said.

'How? Why?'

'I been a big bloody bugger. Kooti took me.'

'Took?'

'Or I die.'

Fairweather grabbed at Hamiora's thin shoulders. Together they were bumped right and left by other prisoners; they bobbed in the tide which pushed to the precipice.

'Stop,' Fairweather called, with indifferent authority.

In the shadowy commotion he was in hazard himself from Ropata's men prodding prisoners with bayonets.

'Stop,' he managed again, this time producing a pause.

From the pause Ropata appeared. An overseer irritated by another impediment. 'Yes?' he asked.

'This one, this boy, is to live,' Fairweather said.

'Live, Fairweather?'

'As my friend.'

'Any man spared,' Ropata said, 'may mean that Kooti lives also.'

'Damn your omens. This one lives. Or you also shoot me.'

'This is your true meaning, Fairweather?'

'This is my word.'

'And you hear mine also, that Kooti may live?'

'You will hear me. But for this boy I might have been meat for the eels of the river. He once wished to serve against Kooti; I refused him a gun.'

Ropata was not impressed. 'Did he swim with Kooti's fish,' he asked, 'or did he swim with ours?'

'You ask a Maori question. I give you English answer. If this boy must be sacrifice to Kooti's capture, then I say no. No. He must not. Better that Kooti suffocate in his own righteous stink. This boy does not die.'

Ropata considered. The shooting had halted. He eyed Fairweather with despair.

'One day,' he said, 'you may live to curse mercy.'

Ropata then turned away and gave out a command. Prisoners were hurried on again; executions resumed.

Hamiora shuddered as Fairweather sliced away his bonds. 'You are a good bugger, Hori,' he said.

'Don't count on it,' Fairweather said. 'Count the days of your life. Each is now a gift.'

'Gift, Hori?'

'*Koha,*' Fairweather translated.

Hamiora stood free, flexing cramped muscles. Still with disbelief, he breathed deep and sighed.

'Your *koha* is good,' he judged.

'May it long be so,' Fairweather said.

To Jonah he said, 'We must keep the boy close at all times. Ropata could arrange a quick accident.'

'I understand,' Jonah said.

'Do you believe it too? That sparing one small life means Kooti likewise escapes?'

Jonah shrugged. 'Maoris are Maoris. You *pakeha* believe in queer things too. Or pretend to.'

'Like what?'

'Like justice,' Jonah said.

They were quietened by nearby gunfire; the last prisoners were set on the precipice.

Fairweather said, 'You call it *utu*. We call it just deserts. Currently, aside from this hiccup, there is a meeting of minds.'

The hiccup stood between them, listening to everything said, and slow to understand. 'I am very all right, Hori?' Hamiora asked.

'Very bloody all right,' Fairweather argued, and cuffed the boy's ear.

'*E tika,* Hori? True?'

'My life on it,' Fairweather said.

The last volley left a dwindling echo, a silence which seemed a sigh. Sound on the summit became merely the crackling of fires and the rustling of men. With the day's meadow mown, Ropata's executioners cleaned and oiled their cooling weapons. Ropata remained at a distance from Fairweather; his fury had still to be weathered. As the quiet lengthened Herrick made subdued return. He found Fairweather sprawled and smoking between Hamiora and Jonah.

'If ever asked,' Herrick said, 'I should like to explain that all this happened, so to speak, on the far edge of my perception. And that, when my attention was finally drawn to it, I endeavoured to ameliorate the more unfortunate features of the affair. I should, by the way, also speak highly of your difficult role, Fairweather.'

'In keeping tally of heads?'

'In the preservation of innocents. When word reaches London, the Colonial Office may not take kindly to this. Or to bounties offered. Church authorities too can be relied on to make sanctimonious sounds. As usual they have no real appreciation of local circumstances. Always the good colonist's excuse.'

'Must you become a miserable administrator again, Herrick? And so soon?'

'I cannot wait. Desk, pen and paper; a dedicated quill driver at work. I write, you must know, most elegant reports. If obliged to produce one on Ngatapa, it will be a model of its kind. My story, will be entirely consistent with the facts of the matter; and have not one word of truth.' At last Herrick began to break; and then shake. 'God in heaven, Fairweather. Is this what we have come to?'

'You may have,' Fairweather said. 'I was already there.'

Herrick refused comfort.

'Do sit down,' Fairweather said. 'You are making an unimpressive spectacle. At least pretend to have earned a pipeful of tobacco.'

'How can you do it, Fairweather? How just recline there as if this had not been?'

'I relax because it has,' Fairweather said. 'And because I am at my ease, under the stars of this summer night, with two good friends. Jonah requires no introduction. Hamiora, on the other hand, does.'

'Hamiora?' Herrick said vaguely.

'Hamiora Pere, no less. The only member of Kooti's force neither defeated nor dead. Show him, Hamiora. Speak. This is Captain Robert Herrick, another big bloody bugger. Amuse him. He is much in need of your smile.'

'Very damn hello, Captain Robert,' Hamiora said.

Hamiora spoke further through Jonah. On the evening of November the ninth Kooti had the people of Patutahi dragged from their beds to pray for the success of the night's work. All were then pronounced children of Israel. Older men still under missionary influence had been tomahawked when they protested Christ's love. The young men were obliged to serve Jehovah or similarly perish. Certainly Hamiora did not have to think long. The gun he was given made him feel big and brave. He rode with Kooti's men fierce on each side, not knowing where, until the dwellings of Matawhero climbed from the dark. Even then nothing was clear until shooting started and burning houses cast light. Hamiora did not much like to talk about it now.

'Tell him we are agreed,' Fairweather said.

Hamiora had gone with Kooti's men back into the mountains. He wished he had not. Other boys of his village tried to escape, or pretended to weary; he had not been as bold.

'Tell him we buried them,' Fairweather said.

All then became a fever of fighting and dying; of mortars, hunger, and thirst. Kooti's great canoe was splitting and sinking. Hamiora remembered flax rope burning his hands as he slid down the precipice before he began running. He sucked forest berries, sought wild honey; always there were the cries of Ropata's hunters behind. He began tripping and falling and thinking it sweeter to die.

Having finished in Maori, Hamiora found his flawed English more pungent. 'But I very bloody have not,' he said. He rolled his eyes in mock wonder, and wolfed down some tired mutton with relish. 'I think many things now, Hori. The thing I think most is life is better. Life is more *komutu.*'

'Surprising,' Jonah translated. 'He says life is more surprising.'

'We must keep it so,' Fairweather said. 'What do you say, Captain Herrick?'

'Yes,' Hamiora said. 'What do you bloody think, Captain Robert?'

'Intriguing company you keep, Fairweather,' Herrick said. 'Are there more of him?'

27

Forest and river formed the only challenge on the hot journey home to Poverty Bay. They no longer had to brace for ambush or encirclement, one fruit of victory safe to taste. Fairweather's estimate was that Kooti might still be adrift in the mountains with two hundred fellow survivors. Many would be festering with wounds and fear; some surely sickening with suspicion. Jehovah had been seen lacking; perhaps Kooti too. He might need more than eloquence to deploy them serviceably again. Psalms were no substitute for food, nor prayers for powder and shot. Forest pilgrimage, and absence of illuminating function, could reduce Kooti's numbers still more. Boredom and desertion might thin his men better than Whitmore's mortars.

'Is the spirit of vengeance dimmed?' Herrick asked.

'Only in the proxy sense,' Fairweather said.

There was silence as they rode.

'So it is not over,' Herrick said.

Fairweather could think of no useful reply.

Herrick and Fairweather rode at the centre of Ropata's long column, with Hamiora between them; Jonah remained at their rear. Ropata's disgust was still vocal; one of his men might be inspired to make Hamiora's back a target. Hamiora was inclined to offer no provocation. He looked neither right nor left, and seldom spoke.

Finally the land lost its grip; they gained open ground and wide sky. They travelled downhill to the Poverty Bay plain, the Pacific filling the horizon.

'The date?' Fairweather asked. 'What is the damned date?'

'January the tenth,' Herrick said.

'Two months to the day since killing began in earnest,' Fairweather said. 'Only one thought appalls more. Very soon I shall have been in Poverty Bay one year. Thus do grosser humours confound. A soldier again; I was once something else.'

'Fatigue is talking,' Herrick said.

The plain allowed Ropata's mounted men to canter and spread. Untidy

Turanga came into view. Murky tidal rivers, and timber dwellings of the township salted with tents.

'I feel the shades of the prison house growing around,' Fairweather said. 'Also a powerful urge to hurl myself aboard the deck of a departing schooner.'

'Of course,' Herrick said with sympathy.

'Hori is leaving?' Hamiora asked. He was even more apprehensive with Ropata's men galloping around.

'No, Hamiora,' Herrick said. 'I think Captain Fairweather is not.'

'Not?' Hamiora was still anxious.

'Not,' Herrick said. 'Captain Fairweather, you see, is a man of much honour.'

'That will be enough, Herrick,' Fairweather said. 'You put wild ideas in the boy's head.'

'What is honour?' Hamiora asked. 'Mana?'

'More,' Herrick said.

'More? More than mana?' Hamiora refused to believe it.

'Honour,' Herrick explained, 'means trying to do that which is right. A man of honour must sometimes forget mana.'

Hamiora was powerfully amazed. 'Forget?' he said. 'Forget mana?'

'Quite so, Hamiora.'

'Why?'

'To feel better, perhaps,' Herrick said. 'That is the most important thing about a man of honour. He must feel good about himself.'

'Then I am a man of honour too,' Hamiora decided. 'I feel good about myself. *E tika*. True.'

Herrick laughed. 'Here endeth this lesson. In confusion again.'

The plain was as silent as they had left it. Tall grass and weeds greened the ash and debris of dwellings; climbing plants tangled up through skeletal timbers still standing. Tidal rivers, on closer acquaintance, stank of decay.

'Well,' Herrick said to Fairweather, 'what now, traveller?'

'I expect we wait,' Fairweather said. 'Or I shall.'

'For what?'

'To see what fate thinks of next.'

'And you, I take it, will ensure that fate lacks no food for further thought.'

Fairweather was quiet.

'If you are talking of Kooti,' Herrick went on, 'no man could have done more. He has been thrashed within an inch of his life.'

'It is the last inch I find fascinating.'

'Come,' Herrick said. 'You have more on your mind now.'

'When I know its nature,' Fairweather agreed.

The last of the journey, into Turanga itself, could not have been quieter. Sight of Ropata's armed men persuaded Poverty Bay Maoris to move indoors. Pale inhabitants of the port, Trader Read among them, made no welcome party either. Whitmore, on his way through, had pronounced peace at hand, and Kooti probably dead. Never disposed to feed pessimism, Whitmore had not even mounted a guard on the port before voyaging off to feats of arms elsewhere.

Read was still reddened and bloated from celebration. 'Is it true?' he asked. 'Is Kooti dead?'

'Like another dissident Jew,' Fairweather said, 'he seems to have survived crucifixion. When we rolled the rock from his tomb, there was neither hide nor hair left.'

'You mean the bugger's got us beat again?'

'Not beaten, Trader. Baffled.'

'That's not what Whitmore said.'

'If you prefer a good night's sleep, Trader, then Colonel Whitmore is your man. Speaking for myself, I think it best to let you down lightly. There is still a Kooti. He would still like your head. But if it is any consolation, he might now prefer Ropata's.'

'So we still need protection.'

'I am not going to quarrel.'

'I'm talking about providing it. You.'

'I trust the colonial authorities, unless again of pacifist mind, will take your need into account. Once bitten they should be twice shy of Whitmore's claim of conquest.'

'They'd better be. I'll call a bloody meeting in the port.'

'By all means, Trader. I see Kooti cringing.'

But Read's gaze had shifted to bruised and subdued Hamiora.

'Who's this ruffian?' he asked. 'He one of Kooti's?'

Hamiora pushed his horse closer to Fairweather's. His eyes remained low.

'He is one of mine,' Fairweather said. 'And I shall trust you to remember it, Trader. And anyone else hereabouts.'

'You don't answer my question,' Read said. 'Was he one of Kooti's or not?'

'Spoils of war, Trader. I permit myself one memento.'

'I thought them buggers was all killed. Why wasn't he?'

'Because I willed it,' Fairweather said. 'I shall continue to will it. Do I make myself understood?'

'Not much,' Read said with grievance.

'Come,' Fairweather said to Hamiora.

They dismounted, left their horses with Jonah, and went on foot toward the hospital. Hamiora looked fretfully over his shoulder. Ropata was terror enough; now he wasn't safe near colonists.

'They must not concern you,' Fairweather said. 'The man who looks behind finds a bayonet in his belly.'

Hamiora said in hoarse voice, 'I didn't mean to, Hori. I was made.'

'Mean to what? Made to do what?'

'Kill,' Hamiora said.

Fairweather was slow finding voice. 'Kill?' With further difficulty, he added, 'Kill who? Maoris or colonists?'

'All. Kooti said shoot and I shoot.'

Fairweather swallowed. 'I do not want to know, Hamiora. Nor do I need to. Nor anyone else. Understand?'

'I must not talk of this?'

'Never. So bail out your damn Maori mouth. You saw nothing, did nothing. It was all confusion and wild talk with Kooti, and you were just a boy to fetch and carry. True?'

'*Pono,*' Hamiora said with thought.

'And,' Fairweather said, 'make it more true every day.'

They arrived at the hospital. Surgeon Gibbs was attending wounded and ill earlier brought in from the mountains. Mulhooly was among them. When he saw Fairweather he sat up with a difficult smile; he also offered a weak hand to be shaken.

'It's all right, sir,' Mulhooly said. 'You mustn't blame yourself still. I did what I did for myself, sir.'

'Young Jimmy Newman?'

'He comes here to talk. I tell him how his father died. I say there was no better soldier ever seen.'

'And I shall confirm that for him,' Fairweather said. 'I hope to do rather more.'

With Hamiora following, he walked on to Gibbs. 'What word?' he asked.

'As you see,' Gibbs said, 'she has not yet been returned from Hawke's Bay. They are holding patients back until it is clear that the situation is settled here; it is no use burdening us further with the halt and the lame.'

'But no information?'

'I get none unless in the event of decease. You can take it she lives.'

'Small mercies.'

'It is possible she is still in need of great care. Her condition could not have been more appalling. Were I to guess, it might be a six month before she resembles her former self. We are talking of two.'

Fairweather slumped into the first chair he had seen in weeks. The world still lacked no firepower. A sympathetic hand came to rest on his shoulder. Hamiora's; he had almost forgotten the boy.

'While I think of it,' Gibbs went on, 'I seem to have a letter here for you. It could curb your impatience if it is from the woman in question.'

Gibbs shambled about his improvized surgery, fiddling among potions, papers, sharp tools of trade. Finally he lifted an envelope in triumph. 'Perhaps,' he said, 'you would prefer privacy to read it.'

'There is no need,' Fairweather said. He watched his hand shake as he reached for the letter.

'I see a man who might at least use a drink,' Gibbs diagnosed.

'I am willing to make that an order,' Fairweather said. 'Also something of less spirituous nature for my friend.'

'Friend?' Gibbs asked, gazing at unkempt Hamiora. 'I saw a new patient.'

'Friend,' Fairweather said. 'I shall explain when I can.'

Glass in hand, Fairweather considered the letter. The female handwriting on the envelope disclosed no more than his own name; he took breath and leapt. Inside was a single sheet of paper with very few lines. They required much reading, also a second drink.

Dear Fairweather, she wrote. *You must not worry for me. All is as could have been expected. I am also as can be expected. Sometimes I think I am ill, sometimes I think I am not. But that is not important. What is important is that there are things of which I cannot think. I am sorry I cannot write further. I can hear Matiu saying I must, but that too is past. Arohanui, Meriana Smith.*

Fairweather found his third drink more convincing. Gibbs and Hamiora kept a tactful silence while he read and then ceased to.

'Trouble?' Gibbs asked.

'Difficulty.'

'Women,' Gibbs observed, 'mostly never mean what they say.'

'This one does. And says nothing.'

Gibbs said, 'The woman might never forget. Nor perhaps you.'

'Are you tendering a professional opinion again, Surgeon Gibbs?'

'A sympathetic one. Human in nature.'

'Then I should prefer you confining opinions to the ills of the flesh.'

'If you insist,' Gibbs said warily.

'I heard you say that in a six month she might somewhat resemble her former self.'

'In a manner of speaking.'

'That, then, may well suffice, for most human purposes, may it not?'

'Your point is unclear,' Gibbs said.

'It may become so,' Fairweather said. 'Especially when we are all more on talking terms with our former selves.'

'I see,' Gibbs said.

He did not, of course. Could not. Even Fairweather groped.

'Meanwhile there are matters of more urgent concern. This boy, for example. Might I enquire, first, into your own position here?'

'The authorities have asked me to continue giving what help I can to Poverty Bay. With all the uproar about the place having been ill served in recent months, not to speak of the possibility of more casualties, it is seen fitting that I maintain a presence.'

'An interesting price for a surgeon. One hundred corpses. Think of what two hundred might buy. An apothecary too.'

'Bitterness brews no cure for Kooti.'

'Nor,' Fairweather said, 'does it do much for this boy. I trust you can use help here.'

Hamiora stood shy and uncertain.

'I can always find employment for a pair of hands,' Gibbs said. 'But him?'

'With soap and water and a white shirt, he should soon present a more plausible aspect. I want him out of harm's way. Ten paces from this hospital and he is fit only for the coroner.'

'He was with Kooti?'

'And plucked up before Ropata's broom swept Ngatapa. It has occasioned resentment. Not only from Ropata; here too.'

'November the tenth is a wound slow to heal. I trust you read the colony's newspapers.'

'Not if I can help it. No.'

'They say Kooti's savages must be exterminated like wild beasts lest they make colonization of the country impossible.'

'We are talking of a boy,' Fairweather said. 'Before trouble began he was of much use to me. His help might even have spared Poverty Bay. He showed me the track Kooti would use. It did not suit Biggs to think so.'

'Yet he served Kooti. And you ask trust.'

'He is as much a casualty as any of your current patients; and his condition could be terminal. Keep him busy. And indoors. I presume you have a revolver on hand. It might only be necessary to flourish it in imaginative fashion and fire a shot skyward. That is, if some colonists find enough courage in a bottle to play judge, jury and executioner.'

'You place me in a difficult position,' Gibbs said. 'If I say no, I am seen to be lacking in compassion.'

'In short,' Fairweather said.

'I am also a Christian.'

'Even more to the good.'

'You misunderstand, Fairweather. I am trying to restore ravaged Christians of this colony. This boy's hands, for all I know, may be red with their blood.'

'Come, Surgeon Gibbs. This is rather excitable. Hamiora? Hold out your hands. Hands. Very damn quick.'

Understanding only that he was the subject of contention, Hamiora cautiously did as told; he looked at Gibbs and quickly back to Fairweather.

'There,' Fairweather said. 'As hands go, they are of nondescript native hue. And anatomically sound.'

'It would help,' Gibbs said, 'if he made it clear that he had forsworn his recent activity, and his associates.'

'What do you want? A thousand word essay on the terrors associated with Biblical tribesmen? Or an oath of allegiance to the Queen?'

'The latter would certainly be desirable.'

'Hamiora,' Fairweather asked, 'who is the Queen?'

'Keen?' Hamiora said, distinctly vague.

'Queen.'

'Ah,' Hamiora said, and tried to look knowledgeable.

'Come,' Fairweather said. 'The Queen, Hamiora. Queen Victoria. Who is she, and what?'

'I think I do not know, Hori,' Hamiora confessed.

'Then let me tell you. She is a great lady, Hamiora, who dwells in a land far from here. *Kuini Wikitoria* has more mana than anyone else of this world. She rules half of it. Poverty Bay too.'

'Rules? She?'

'She tells you, me, and Surgeon Gibbs here, what we must do. She tells us on whom we must make war, and on whom we must not.'

Hamiora was even more bemused.

'I want you,' Fairweather went on, 'to say that you will serve her true. *Pono*. Like me. Understand?'

'I will be like you, Hori,' Hamiora promised.

'Swear, Hamiora. Swear true.'

'Swear?' Hamiora remained uncertain.

'Very damn true. Quick. Now.'

Hamiora said, 'Bloody. Bastard. Bugger.'

'There,' Fairweather told Gibbs. 'The wording may not be of the authorized formula, but there is inspired innovation. Come, sir. Show me a smile. Tell me we need press this no further.'

Gibbs relented. A Scot, after all. And of a profession built on benevolence. 'Damn you, Fairweather,' he said. 'You may leave the boy here. I shall certainly see him unharmed.'

'And you, Surgeon Gibbs, shall have a box seat in heaven. Should he prove too insufferable, threaten a rendezvous with Ropata.' To Hamiora he added, 'You are to be good. Very good here.'

'I be bloody good,' Hamiora vowed. 'You soon see, Hori.'

'And not wander too far.' Fairweather drew the edge of his hand across his throat. If any man is bad to you – any man *kino* – you are to tell him that Captain Fairweather, no less, will rain the wrath of hell on his head.'

'Wrath?' Hamiora asked. 'Hell?'
'Ngatapa,' Fairweather translated.

Elsewhere in the port he found Jimmy Newman. The boy was playing with Maori children on the bank of the river, busy shaping small boats from flax and floating them out on the tide. The game did not entirely preoccupy. When he looked up at Fairweather, his smile had a sad twist.

'I should like you to walk with me, Jimmy,' Fairweather said.

'It's all right,' Jimmy said. 'I been told my Dad's dead.'

'And you are a brave boy, Jimmy. It would not hurt, though, sometimes to cry.'

'I done that, sir. I done that at night, in my bed.'

'Of course. I am only saying that you may cry, if you wish, with me.'

'Thank you, sir,' Jimmy said, but did not.

They walked the riverside, past driftwood and shells and pungent seaweed.

'I cried for my Mum longer,' Jimmy confided. 'My Dad was a soldier like you. Soldiers get killed. They don't like people to cry.'

'Who cares for you now, Jimmy?'

'People,' Jimmy said. 'They all look after me, and see I am fed.'

'I should like to look after you too, Jimmy.'

'You, sir?'

'You heard.'

'You don't have to, sir. You're busy killing Kooti. Everyone says.'

'I mean, Jimmy,' Fairweather persisted, 'that I should like to look after you in a more special way.'

'Special, sir? How do you mean?'

'That I may be able to do some of the things your Dad did, and would have. Do you see?'

'No,' Jimmy said. 'Why?'

'Because I wish to, Jimmy. Perhaps it is not yet time to talk of this.'

'You mean, sir, you want to be my Dad now?'

Fairweather was marooned in a silence of growing duration.

'I may be saying something like that,' he finally agreed. 'Yes, then. I am.'

'True?'

'True, Jimmy. So what do you think?'

They stopped walking where the mouth of the river met sea. There was a sigh of muddied water leaving the land. Jimmy looked up at Fairweather; Fairweather looked back. Jimmy's small face had a frown, a smile, and again a frown. His lips began to shape words, then found others to suit. Fairweather knew he had missed his last tide; he felt himself beach.

'I think I would like that,' Jimmy decided. 'Yes, sir. Yes, please.'

'So be it, then,' Fairweather said.

'So be it? What's that mean, sir?'

'That whatever we are, or think we might be, the world still has its way; and sometimes yes is the one word to say.'

'I still don't understand, sir.'

'You will,' Fairweather said.

'Will you do something, sir?'

'What is that, Jimmy?'

'Bend down, sir. For me.'

Fairweather knelt. Small arms tried to crush him; he felt a wet kiss.

'There,' Jimmy said. 'Why do you shake so much, sir?'

'Because, you young brute, you are half murdering me.' When Fairweather stood again, the world was intriguingly steady. 'Now, Jimmy, I want you to do me a great favour. I know you go often to the hospital to see Mr Mulhooly. I want you to go there now. I have a friend who is helping Surgeon Gibbs; I wish you to be his friend too. To talk to him so that he learns better English and swears rather less.'

'He must be a Maori,' Jimmy concluded.

'Of a cheeky sort,' Fairweather said. 'I am going to get him to look after you when I cannot be about. I shall arrange with Surgeon Gibbs to give you a bed until I can find you a home. Is that understood?'

'I reckon,' Jimmy said.

Fairweather rejoined Herrick at the hotel, which again served as headquarters; Ropata, meanwhile, had camped his men outside the port to await pay and proposals to renew fighting.

'News?' Herrick said.

'To be wondered at,' Fairweather said. 'The word from Hawke's Bay is indifferent. Perhaps indifference. I have no means of knowing. She lives; she can write in fair hand. Otherwise, nothing.'

'So what else is to be wondered at?' Herrick asked. 'You seem unusually agitated.'

'As you might be, Herrick, had you been careless enough to acquire, between one minute and the next, far short of the desirable nine months, a son in full bloom.'

Much of the day was given to untangling communications from the authorities, and to composing replies. Whitmore's reports of triumph had to be tempered; the need for protection of Poverty Bay stressed. Ropata and most of his men should be paid to remain in the vicinity. The messages were signed by Fairweather, with Herrick's name added for weight.

'One day a killer,' Fairweather said. 'The next a damn clerk.'

He rode out of the port and found Ropata. 'Will you stay?' he asked.

'With refreshments,' Ropata said. 'Also a promise. That we will soon again go after Kooti. This must be.'

'It is not a promise for me to make.'

'He is weak now. He can be finished.'

'If found. Many men are needed to cover that territory. I do not have them. Neither do you.'

'Must we wait on Kooti to make war again?'

'That might be helpful,' Fairweather said. 'Speaking of promises, Kooti's words surely still tell of a land pledged. Why not take his word as true?'

Not that Ropata was placated. He spat, but did not consider how his spittle fell.

Toward the end of the day Fairweather rode across the plain. There was no urgency this time, though still dread. Cicadas rattled in the heat as he neared the Smith homestead. He tethered his horse and argued himself inside. The despoiled rooms echoed with his slow footfall. Broken windows had allowed storm to savage the building still more; shreds of curtain shifted in faint breeze. He stopped to pick up a trodden chessman from the floor, a whisper of an unfinished contest with Pita; a playing card insisted on an unpaid poker debt to Matiu. Stench persisted too.

He finished in the upstairs room, overlooking the river, which Matiu told him to call his own. For reasons best known to Kooti it had suffered less; perhaps it had been kept for Kooti's personal use. That thought was not to be dwelled on. The bedding was soiled.

Cupboards still held the same contents. Possibly paints, brushes and palettes had been thought poor plunder. Paintings too. Wrapping had been torn away here and there; they seemed to have provoked no great curiosity. Perhaps judgement. His own could be cooler. Ruskin? A far bell tolling too; it might soon be still fainter.

Though of two minds, something not unfamiliar, he let his mission run its course. He packaged few things for removal to the port; the rest could be left to time and chance. It might be months before any place beyond Turanga could be called secure. All the same, he tramped downstairs again, located shovel and broom, and began to skirmish with debris and dirt.

28

January was lost in labour. Stockades soon enclosed the port; a blockhouse and barracks rose, and a watch tower of substance. Saps were dug between buildings to cover movement of men in the event of attack. A compound was made for the discarded wives and widows of Kooti's force, and they were there guarded to prevent intelligence being passed out. Pickets were strong, and patrols rode daily toward the mountains, watching for fires. Others paddled up rivers and checked banks. Ammunition was expended on suspicion of ambush, and many wild sheep brought low. The port never lacked industry or alarms. Read arranged gatherings of colonists, and more angry pleas went to government. Fairweather insisted on daily parades and practice with firearms. He ordered that no man was to move outside the stockade alone or unarmed. He conformed to his own ruling. When he rode out on the plain, it was seldom without Jonah. Jonah showed some ingenuity as carpenter in repair of the Smith homestead. A platoon of armed constabulary was eventually at Fairweather's disposal. Money arrived in niggardly sum; hardly enough to retain Ropata's men on half pay. Ropata threatened to depart.

'It cannot be long,' Fairweather promised. 'Each passing day must diminish Kooti in the eyes of all men. If he is ever to strike again, it must be soon.'

'Then?' Ropata asked.

'We shall have him, of course.'

Fairweather had a plan for the day Kooti reappeared on the plain. Kooti's scouts would be allowed to pass unmolested; Ropata would move fast into the hills, cutting off escape routes, while Fairweather distracted Kooti with vigorous defence of the port. The hope was encirclement of Kooti's force; the plan was fashioned from the assumption that Kooti would never again have the numbers. Also from the proposition of Fairweather's preferred philosopher that the best battle plan invited the enemy to participate in his own destruction.

'It is we who should strike,' Ropata said. 'We who should say when.'

'I agree. But I am one man alone.'

'Not with me,' Ropata said.

In another matter Fairweather was as powerless. From Meriana he had only one further communication. The letter, even briefer than the last, said she was out of medical care and now living with distant relatives in Hawke's Bay. Then nothing; the silence could not have been more complete.

Early in suffocating February Herrick announced that he was leaving for Hawke's Bay to spruce up his personal affairs, dust out his house, and ensure that his desk was not interred under correspondence; he promised to be back soon.

'Find her,' Fairweather asked. 'Talk to her. Tell me the worst, if you must. Any word must be better than this.'

'Do you wish me to talk of your feats in restoring her home?'

'Not if it distresses.'

'Then what, in respect of yourself, do you most want me to tell her?'

'That I am here.'

'Is that to be taken as an expression of feeling?'

'As an expression of me,' Fairweather said.

As Gibbs' hospital emptied of battle casualties, to be replaced by conventionally infirm, Jimmy Newman and Hamiora had the place more to themselves. Outdoors, they fished together, with Jonah or Fairweather watching; swam; fired slingshots at seagulls; and otherwise provided mischief for tolerant Gibbs. Jimmy had a friend when Fairweather was absent; Hamiora was usefully employed, with a less perverse grip on the language of *Kuini Wikitoria.* It was Jimmy who now did the swearing. Fairweather, fearing the worst, eavesdropped on the most perilous conversation between the pair.

'Why,' Jimmy asked, 'don't you ever come with me to bloody old Trader Read's store?'

'Because better not,' Hamiora said.

'You steal from Trader Read? I done that too.'

'I haven't stole,' Hamiora said.

'Then you can come with me.'

'I must not. No.' Hamiora was firm.

'Why not? Why?'

'Because Trader Read is a man with a gun.'

'He doesn't shoot at me.'

'He might at me.'

'Why?'

'It is better not to tell.'

'You must of done something very bloody bad,' Jimmy decided.

Hamiora was quiet.

Jimmy said, 'I think you must of been with bloody Kooti.'

Hamiora still didn't speak.

'True, isn't it,' Jimmy said. 'See? I know now.'

Fairweather was about to intervene, but thought better. Sooner or later it had to be said, and Jimmy was not long in saying it.

'You might,' he judged, 'have been one of the buggers who shot my Dad.'

'Yes,' Hamiora said miserably.

Jimmy thought about that, and continued to think; Fairweather braced.

'Well,' Jimmy said finally, 'so what do you want me to steal you from Trader Read's store?'

Herrick returned from Hawke's Bay with sober face and a reluctance to speak until he sat Fairweather down with a glass of respectable brandy in hand. Then he overturned Fairweather and emptied him too.

'I did all you requested,' he said. 'I met with the woman more than once. Our talk was enlightening. I can see she is, or has been, all you suggest.'

'Well?' Fairweather said, impatient.

'I also met with the physician who treated her. I can give you swift reassurance on two scores. She is mostly restored in mind, though some grief is still natural. Also splendidly sound of limb and feature. She could be said to have made total recovery.'

Herrick poured more brandy.

'Could be?' Fairweather asked.

Herrick held his glass to the light, as if to see sediment. 'Does it occur to you, Fairweather, that Kooti might be more than just a rebel crazed with religion?'

'What are you talking about?' Fairweather said.

'Of a curse. On our kind, and not just in this country. Trample such a curse here, and it takes fire there. I see more like Kooti to come with terror and a text. If not flourishing the words of one testament, then those of another. There will always be a Biggs to kindle the fuel; always a Whitmore to stoke it. And others, such as yourself, to suffer the blaze.'

'Talk to the point.'

'I am,' Herrick said, quickly the worse for drink. 'I think I am talking original sin.'

'To the wrong man. You either have news or you have not.'

'I had no wish to play messenger,' Herrick said. 'I told her she should write. It seems she has tried, several times, but the pen faltered on paper. The physician confirms it; it explains her precarious internal condition when she was sent south to Hawke's Bay for care. There is no doubt at all.'

'You leave my mind a muddle,' Fairweather said. 'Doubt of what?'

'That she is, quite simply, with child.'

This time Fairweather reached for the brandy. He heard his voice at an absurd distance. 'Quite simply?'

'In a manner of speaking. Her condition is by no means advanced. It can hardly have run a third of its term.'

'Why this reticence about telling? The thought that I might feel entrapped?'

'Quite,' Herrick said.

'Then I do not,' Fairweather decided.

'For God's sake, man, think on what I have said. Think.'

'I am thinking most transparently. Or has your sight frayed?'

'Three months, man. Three months. Hardly more. When did you last see her as she once was? When did she last share your bed?'

Fairweather shrugged. 'Late October; early November. A night's break from patrolling.'

'So you are talking of little more than one week before Kooti struck?'

'Give or take some comfortless days.'

'That makes it worse,' Herrick said. He looked at Fairweather, looked away, but found no place of rest for his eyes. 'It is now February. Three months. Who is to say?'

This time Fairweather neither raised his glass nor reached for the bottle. He asked, 'Who is to say what, Herrick? And when?'

'Then I must, and now. The child could be Kooti's.'

After a time Fairweather lit his pipe.

'Well?' Herrick asked. 'It seems to me that you are in an intolerable position. And she.'

'You excite yourself, Herrick. Recent experience suggests there is only one intolerable position. Prone, and riddled with shot, outside a Maori fortress. The rest is the fun of the fair.'

'What are you telling me? That you might yet make this woman your wife?'

'It depends much on her.'

'There is nothing to say it is your child.'

'There is nothing, Herrick, to say it is not.'

'Dear God,' Herrick said. 'Is this what you want?'

'It is what I have,' Fairweather said.

'There is no need to push virtue so far. She would not expect it.'

'I wish to like myself more, Herrick. Might it help, on the other hand, if you saw avarice? Fertile acres and a homestead?'

'I would not believe you.'

'It may be desirable to try.'

'An antipodean farmer? You?'

'Land is a legacy in turn to be passed on. Flesh and spirit too for that matter. Much asks for shape.'

'Even if the flesh is not of your making? Or the spirit?'

'It can be seen as sparing of further carnal labour; I have done my fair share.

Nor should I have been the first to have been cuckolded before reaching the altar.'

'But few with full knowledge. Still fewer in circumstances so hateful.'

'Then it can be said I am making sense of folly. Jimmy Newman's parentage is not in doubt. He lacks a home. It could be argued that I am getting off lightly. Paying two dues, so to speak, in one.'

'Is that really all there is to be said?'

'Quite possibly, Herrick. Yes.'

'I do not understand you.'

'Then we have that in common,' Fairweather said.

That afternoon Mulhooly reported fit for duty. On whim Fairweather made him a corporal and assigned him ten men to take on patrol. Jonah was given a more strenuous task. He was requested to travel to Hawke's Bay, on the boat which brought Herrick, and bring Meriana Smith home to Poverty Bay.

'As a personal favour to me,' Fairweather said. 'I cannot make this an order.'

'What,' Jonah asked, 'if she refuses?'

'Then you make it an order to her.'

'And if she does not accept it?'

'You drag her back. Otherwise I shall be looking for a sergeant with more muscle than fat.'

'Don't worry,' Jonah said. 'A fat smile works wonders with ladies. They smile back. They can't see the harm.'

'I wouldn't wager on this woman.'

'You watch me,' Jonah said.

The day had one disfiguring flaw. Passing the compound where the female survivors of Ngatapa were guarded, he saw a face he preferred not to see. Mata Te Owai; Kooti's castoff wife. Food and safety had done little to temper her unholy stare.

'You,' she called boldly.

He halted, and wished he had not.

'You,' she said. 'We know of you.'

One of Ropata's guards placed himself between Fairweather and the woman; the butt of his rifle was raised.

'You are cruel,' she told Fairweather.

'Complaints,' Fairweather said, 'can be tendered to the man in charge of the guard. He may then see fit to inform me.'

'I am kept with these other women as an animal,' she protested. 'I have said I would help. I have said I would say all you wish about Kooti.'

'There is nothing which currently needs saying. And, think on this, you may have a longer life here than elsewhere. Some secret friend of Kooti's might like to tear the tongue from a woman wishing to betray her former man.'

'Your boy walks free,' she said. 'Your boy. The Maori. Yet he was a soldier for Kooti.'

'He is but one,' Fairweather said. 'And wholesomely employed in the hospital. He is hardly to be kept here with women.'

'We know why,' she said. Lewd accusation became apparent. 'We know of you.'

'Then you are welcome to that knowledge,' he said, and began turning away.

It did not deter; her derision grew in pitch. 'We know of English, missionaries too, who have boys as women. Men who never know what is between woman's legs. Men who are not. We know of you.'

Her tirade was calculated to make an impression on the port; it could not fail. Further strident sound followed Fairweather as he walked on to the hospital.

Hamiora waited at the hospital door, eyes bright. He had heard all that was significant.

'That woman,' he told Fairweather, 'is bad. Worse. I cannot say it in English. Maoris say *whiro*.'

'I think evil is the word you want.'

'Evil, Hori?'

'We all have our share. But she more than most.'

'I saw her tell Kooti to kill,' Hamiora said. 'If she did not like someone, she tell Kooti to kill.'

'Then hear this, Hamiora. Keep your face far from her sight. She has no liking for you.'

'She says things untrue. You know I am not as a woman for you.'

'No,' Fairweather said. 'I am just your good friend.'

'And Captain Robert is my good friend too.'

Fairweather thought about that, and Herrick, and declined to wonder further. 'Tell me about girls, Hamiora. Girls. *Wahine*. You must have known more than a few.'

Hamiora was silent.

'Come,' Fairweather urged.

'I think I am too *whakama*, Hori.'

'*Whakama*? Shy?'

'I am just funny boy. I make them laugh. I make funny faces so they think I am not *whakama*.'

'But why shy, Hamiora?'

'Because,' Hamiora said, 'I am not much.'

'You speak wrong, Hamiora. A nuisance you may be, a nothing you are not. A *tutua*, never. Understand?'

Hamiora tried to.

'No men are much,' Fairweather said. 'Some hide it better. Men make masks.'

'Masks, Hori?'

'As the face tattoo of a Maori. Behind it a man can seem strong. Yet they are still as small children with fear of the dark. That is their true bravery, that they are not brave. And have but their mask.'

Hamiora had to think.

'Never mind,' Fairweather said. 'You will find yours. A mask more than a funny face. Some *wahine* will be lucky.'

'They need a man with land to be lucky, Hori. My uncle says I am lazy. His land is never for me.'

'Then I make this promise,' Fairweather said. 'When all this is over, and may it be soon, I shall have you work for me.'

'I will not be lazy for you, Hori.'

'You damn well will not be. My tongue will be worse than a tomahawk. On the other hand, your money will soon buy you a fine suit of clothes; no *wahine* will laugh at handsome Hamiora.'

'True, Hori?'

'True. When all this is over. When Kooti is gone.'

Herrick came riding into the port, after checking on pickets, and found Fairweather and Hamiora still at the hospital door.

'I hear of some altercation,' he said as he dismounted.

'Woman trouble,' Fairweather said. 'As with most woman trouble, grievances flung far and wide. Kooti's ejected witch sees injustice in her situation. She is given no respect, and has small chance to stir a depraved brew. She would like Hamiora as ingredient.'

'Never,' Herrick said. He reached out protectively for Hamiora's head. His hand lingered in Hamiora's wild hair a shade too affectionately for Fairweather's comfort. Even the most virile male mask could have aberrant rift.

'Why Hamiora?' Herrick asked. 'What does the woman say?'

'Nothing to detain the mind for a moment,' Fairweather said.

But his own refused to move on. Scatter dung and it stuck.

Jonah returned from Hawke's Bay after a week. Meriana Smith could be seen beside him, on the deck of a schooner making slow progress into the river. She appeared indifferent to familiar surroundings; she was not quick to look up and observe Fairweather waiting on the riverside. She also seemed to reconsider raising her hand to greet him; and about joining Jonah in a dinghy which he then rowed to shore. It was as if she were yet another female captive for the port compound. Fairweather found her hand limp as he helped her from the dinghy. Her eyes were wary, unwilling to meet his. He knew that nothing was over, nor could be; Kooti might never be gone.

'I counted days,' he said. 'One more and I should have sailed to fetch you myself. You had a calm voyage?'

'Quiet,' she said.

'I hope Jonah made an agreeable companion.'

'Jonah did all you said.'

Jonah, meanwhile, pushed past them with her belongings; they were left alone on the shore.

'Much has passed here,' he said, beginning to labour.

'I have heard. Where do you want me to go?'

Perhaps a beginning.

'There is a room in Read's hotel. Your room neighbours mine. That means only as much as you wish. It can be a noisy place, with men coming and going, but at least it is safe; I shall ensure greater quiet.'

'Thank you,' she said.

At the hotel she followed him silently up stairs and along a creaking passage. He led her into a small room furnished with bed, chair and wash-stand. Jonah had already deposited her belongings and tactfully gone. From a window there was a view of river and uninhabited plain. She chose not to consider it. The room might have been a cell; she looked at the floor.

'It is the best I could arrange,' he said.

'Yes. I am sure.'

He closed the door against eavesdroppers.

'You must wonder about your own home.'

'Do I?' she said. 'I think not.'

'Jonah told you nothing?'

'I did not ask.'

'We have cleaned and repaired. The place could soon almost be as you knew it. As you might gather, it cannot yet be called safe; nowhere outside the port is. Perhaps we might ride out there together one day.'

'If you wish,' she said.

'It is what you wish. You.'

'Very well,' she agreed.

'Please,' he said. 'We must try.'

'Try?' she asked.

'It would seem more than necessary now.'

She stiffened; her eyes found his. 'Fairweather,' she said, 'what is it you want?'

'Perhaps best not to ask.'

'You want all as before.'

'And marriage.'

'Why now?'

'A soldier can fight himself into a corner. No way out, no way back. Things are. I know where I am. Here.'

'You say this to make it easier for me.'

'And for me.'

'The child may not be your own.'

At least it was said.

'So Captain Herrick has told me.'

'And you still say the same?'

'I have been saying it all. Must I again?'

She sat limp on the edge of the bed.

'Very well,' he said. 'Believe this instead. An ageing itinerant must find somewhere to camp. Meaning land. Perhaps Matiu, all along, knew his man. A bargain between an acquisitive man and a woman in need. How does that sound?'

'Better,' she said.

'Credible?'

'You are good at making things so.'

'Can I,' he pleaded, 'say nothing right?'

She was slow making answer. He heard cicadas beyond the window, and bees. There was hammering and sawing somewhere near, as the port's defences were further reinforced. Then hoofbeats as an early morning patrol rode back in; harsh male voices. He would soon have to hear their report.

'You try too hard,' she told him. 'Sit quiet beside me. I might know my mind better. You too.'

He took a chair, placed it cautiously near her, and sat. After some minutes he said, 'If I can manage it, we shall ride out to the homestead tomorrow.'

'Of course,' she agreed.

29

In late February summer cooled. More so in March. To replenish foodstuffs Fairweather sent parties across the plain to forage for pumpkins, melons and potatoes growing wild. It was not a season for harvest thanksgiving. Once weekly, so long as her condition allowed, Meriana rode with Fairweather out to the Smith homestead to perform lighter rites of exorcism. Fairweather always ensured that there was a patrol within sound of a shot. Tension might persist, but at least ghosts were laid; she attended the grave of Matiu and Pita with fewer tears. Empty at night, and for most days of the week, the homestead waited on life. It was some time before high spirits were heard. This came on a March day when there was a picnic beside the brimming river with Hamiora and Jimmy Newman paroled from hospital.

'This place is all right,' Jimmy announced.

'I live here too?' Hamiora said, more awed.

'If it is your wish,' Fairweather said. 'There is room for all four of us. Even for five.'

'Five?' Hamiora puzzled.

'With the one to come,' Fairweather explained.

He watched Meriana's face. It still told too little.

The youth and the boy skidded in and around the place like a pair of apprentice demons; they selected rooms and then dived naked into the river and swam to the far bank. Hamiora rose upon it first, faster by more than a length, until Jimmy grabbed his ankle and toppled him back into the water. Death threats were audible as Hamiora surfaced, spitting out tide. Fairweather heard an unfamiliar flutter of breath beside him. The sound was that of a woman beginning to laugh.

Fairweather's strategy was redundant by the time March had half gone; Kooti refused the invitation to test it. Instead, with three hundred men, perhaps even four, he surprised sunny settlements a hundred miles north; settlements against which he had no known grievance. It seemed the point was purely to leave dread; his butchery this time, especially of his own kind, exceeded his best past performance. The daughter of an obstinately Christian chief, known for her beauty, and who might have made Kooti a useful wife, was dissected and fed to her pet pigs. The quickly widowed Maori wife of a French colonist had to submit to execution by coerced relatives, with her sister holding her hands. Maori dwellings were plundered and fired when the killing was finished.

'So much for Whitmore's feeble fugitive,' Fairweather said.

It seemed Kooti's escape from Ngatapa sang louder than Ropata's guns. Aside from surviving veterans, he had scores of recent recruits, mostly mountain tribesmen of the Tuhoe. In weeks these men were further seasoned in slaughter. With a flourish of energy a Napoleon or Wellington might envy, he marched his men south, under cover of forest, bypassing Poverty Bay, and into fresh fields. Hawke's Bay had its turn. Again there were corpses, communities left blazing. Maoris protesting love of Christ the redeemer were penned in a barn and battered and stabbed before the barn was burned; babies were tossed from bayonet to bayonet. Kooti was not of a mind to settle for one massacre if three were there for the making.

April; autumn. A month of molten sunsets and migrant birds. They were skies such as Fairweather might have painted, and perhaps seen serenity. In this season they were skies under which Fairweather, Ropata and Herrick rode again to war.

Whitmore, returned from undistinguished campaigning in the west, yet far from wearied of belligerence, was again the herald; he had instructions from the authorities, who felt matters out of hand and migration to the colony altogether imperilled. Colonist protest at past martial enterprise had placed political reputations at risk; men in government had to make harsher sound than malicious rivals.

'Let there be no mistake,' Whitmore told his assembled force. 'This time we do the thing well.'

'When have we not?' Herrick whispered to Fairweather.

'When Kooti is better,' Fairweather said.

'There is only one sound military policy,' Whitmore said. 'No quarter.'

'Meaning Ropata again,' Herrick muttered.

'Do I hear voices?' Whitmore asked.

Herrick was quiet. Whitmore did not.

'The Tuhoe tribe of the Urewera,' Whitmore said confidentially, 'can no longer be left to make free with this colony's laws. If they allow themselves to be duped by Kooti, the piper has to be paid. Their mountains make a sanctuary from which Kooti can strike at will. No one knows better than I what those mountains mean.'

'Indeed and amen,' Fairweather said sotto voce to Herrick.

'This time we grasp the nettle,' Whitmore went on. 'We march into the mountains in three columns. We lay waste to villages; we destroy crops. We leave no comforts for Kooti. If that means leaving the Urewera uninhabited, that is surely how God meant those wretched mountains to be. Ours is the task of cleansing the colony and placing posterity in our debt. Am I clear?'

Fairweather was moved to ask, 'Are we to take it, sir, that in this crusade the Tuhoe is to be expunged as a tribe?'

'Other than as a zoo piece, perhaps,' Whitmore said. 'If we fail to collect live specimens, we may have to content ourselves with a few hides stuffed for museums. Have you some quibble, Fairweather? On recent experience I should have thought that right up your street.'

'Ngatapa can be seen as a place of atonement in the tried manner of war, sir,' Fairweather said. 'You appear to be talking of more.'

'Kooti must be forced from hiding. Harried and starved.'

'At the price of a people, sir? That is my question.'

'What is your problem, Fairweather? A melting of resolve?'

'Not in respect of Kooti, sir.'

'Excellent,' Whitmore said. 'Consider the subject closed.'

Before he left, Fairweather said to Meriana, 'This is not much to my taste. I am glad you took me into the mountains, among those people. It may soon be a lost world.'

'I have no wish to recall it,' she said. 'There are other worlds lost.'

'Yes,' he agreed.

The subject was closed there too. Her silence spoke with less pity than Whitmore.

To Gibbs he said, 'It must now be five months. I should be grateful if you kept a close watch.'

'My life on it,' Gibbs said.

Gibbs had cried off this expedition, feeling his age; he would wait at Turanga for casualties to be borne back.

'As for Hamiora and Jimmy,' he added, 'I shall see the devil finds no idle hands.'

'You will be long, Hori?' Hamiora asked unhappily.

'What is your trouble?' Fairweather said.

'I do not like it that you and Captain Robert leave me here.'

'Take my word. You will be safe.'

'I could go with you, Hori.'

'I shall have enough on my mind without your nonsense too.'

Herrick was listening. He said, 'It would not be impossible to arrange.

Hamiora could come with me. He might be a nuisance to you, but I should find his good spirits no burden.'

Fairweather gazed briefly at Herrick. Herrick's eyes did not quite meet his.

'No,' Fairweather decided. 'Hamiora stays here.'

Whitmore's column moved to the north, Ropata's and Fairweather's to the centre, Herrick's to the south. Whitmore aspired to sweep Kooti's men toward a net spread by Fairweather and Ropata. Those slipping the mesh were to be left lifeless by Herrick patrolling Urewera lakeside. With autumnal Poverty Bay gone, they met winter in tumbling walls of mountain sleet. Beyond were rivers and winds groaning down canyons, saturating trees with their tops lost in mist. Ropata soon had his first satisfying omen. A slight figure, brief on the skyline, was brought down by a fusillade.

'He might have provided intelligence,' Fairweather said, turning the corpse with his boot. 'He might even have been friendly.'

'The flying fish,' Ropata said, 'must always be slain. The first man to cross the path of war.'

'Always?' The corpse was young.

'Even if my brother,' Ropata said. 'Even if you.'

He moved parties on. Harassing fire sputtered here and there from hilltops. If a sniper proved persistent, men were sent to locate him and bring in a head. Others were left to report that Ropata was abroad.

They came to their first village. Fairweather arrived only minutes after the massacre. Bodies of male tribesmen, sometimes spent firearms alongside, lay outside dwellings beginning to burn; there were cries from wounded within. To pacify Fairweather, women and children had been spared and turned loose to test themselves against the forest and the long mountain winter. Gardens were trampled, animals butchered, food stores plundered. Ropata did not tire of telling Fairweather that mercy was misplaced.

There were more villages fired, if few skirmishes fit to report, before Ropata and Fairweather made rendezvous with Whitmore in the heart of the mountains. Herrick was still lost somewhere to the south. Limping Whitmore had his own narrative of destruction.

'Let them offer hospitality to Kooti now,' he said.

They were camped in an extensive and cleared valley, with villages still smouldering; the inhabitants had been caught in converging volleys.

'But Kooti, sir?' Fairweather asked.

'He is overdue for a showing,' Whitmore said. 'If this is his kingdom, he cannot lose countenance. He must be tempted out.'

Days passed, mostly in thunder and gale; tents sailed fifty yards. Kooti might have reservations about contesting Whitmore's claim on the mountains, but the storm god of Urewera was palpably less diffident. It was Whitmore who literally lost countenance; his face daily shrivelled. First he sickened with dysentery; his voice became a whisper as his bowels drained him thinner. Then rheumatism pressed home an attack. Fairweather was called to the sickbed.

'I think I am finished, Fairweather,' the colonel confessed. 'One campaign too many, perhaps. Reassure me on one score. Can this be counted as triumph?'

'In respect of most desired objectives, sir. His allies, such as survive, must surely think twice.'

'We have not always agreed, Fairweather.'

'You put it tactfully, sir.'

'But I daresay you would agree that these mountains could be my death. I have the feeling that I shall never live to see Kooti hung, Fairweather. Never.'

'This is no circumstance for pessimism, sir.'

'There is mystery here, Fairweather. How were good soldiers of the Queen foxed by a Bible-banging Maori? Tales will be told.'

'Perhaps, sir. And perhaps we can still whip up one or two more.'

'Not me.' Whitmore seemed to weaken still more. He wheezed, 'And I tell you my fear, Fairweather. We shall be forgotten. Our hardships, our pains, even our dead. But that black wretch will be remembered. Some will see romance in this squalor; in him.'

'There is no accounting for fancy, sir.'

'If only I once had him in my sights. Once, Fairweather. Once.'

'Your feeling is shared, sir. And I did.'

Whitmore extended a hand; Fairweather shook it. 'A sheathing of swords?' the colonel asked.

'We are as our world makes us, sir. You, me; even Kooti.'

'God damn it, then,' Whitmore said. 'God damn the world.'

That day he retired from martial history on a stretcher. Ropata and Fairweather, before they marched in Herrick's direction, watched the colonel's column toil up a hillside and drop out of sight.

'We have the war now, Fairweather,' Ropata said. 'We.'

'It is all yours,' Fairweather argued.

As prophecy, that proved fair.

Pressing toward Herrick, Fairweather scouted the track with Jonah; Ropata was never far to their rear. They passed through defiles, blundered through rivers, and zig-zagged up cliff faces. Climbing an exposed ridge, their path was cut by a gully eroded perhaps thirty feet deep; it was spanned by a felled tree across which one man at a time might wobble.

'I go,' Jonah said.

'I think today is my turn to be first,' Fairweather said.

The log had been polished by passing feet; there were dead limbs to grip. With revolver held, he made modest steps forward. Part way across, he caught peril in the corner of his eye. A figure with a firearm had risen from behind a stump on the far side of the gully. There was nowhere for Fairweather to go. He made a pretence of aiming his revolver, which might have disconcerted the other interested party, for the fellow's shot muttered past. Fairweather discharged his own weapon with passion; Jonah fired too. Then a throng of armed men disclosed themselves on the far side of the gully. Behind him, Ropata's men were arriving on the run, and kneeling to shoot. Marooned on the log bridge, Fairweather was likely to be sliced by shot from both sides. The slippery log delivered him from speculation. It ceased to exist underfoot; he flew outward, sighed, and fell. The floor of the gully lifted brutally; a rock connected with his skull as coup de grâce. As he groped mistily into the world again, he understood that an engagement of some dimension was banging away overhead, and that he had no part in it, nor could have; his left leg had again failed to survive. There was little to choose between the moat of a Maori fortress, when the New Zealand wars had more style, and this muddy mountain gully; he was back where he began, abandoned, defunct, letting others shorten their lives.

The back of his head stung. It seemed he was shot after all. He felt for the wound, and instead found an oily rag burning; bullet wrapping had fallen from high and left his hair smoking. He flung it away and slapped down the sparks.

He also calculated that his left leg had been broken in two places and possibly three; he was due to make ignoble retirement from the battle for the Urewera. When he tried to take peace from his pipe, he found that snapped too. Pebbles, chips of wood, clay and spent shot rained upon him as men fought above. Let it be, he decided; let it all be.

It all would.

Ropata soon dominated the ridge and log bridge. His disappointing and now dead opponents had proved to be no more than a lost band of Tuhoe adventurers looking for trouble while Kooti's main force loped away into forest and mist.

Jonah scrambled down into the gully. He eased Fairweather on to a litter and strapped splints on his afflicted limb. He also furnished Fairweather with a serviceable pipe, dry tobacco, and an extravagant ration of rum. It took ten men to heave Fairweather up from the gully; six carried him as the long march continued.

Herrick was sighted three days later. With incredulity and much Maori hilarity, they observed him bobbing in a flotilla of small craft across the great lake of the Urewera.

'Boats?' Fairweather said.

'We built them,' Herrick bragged. 'We couldn't find our way round the lake to join you. There was only one thing for it.'

'A shipyard,' Fairweather said with wonder.

'Quite,' Herrick said. 'What do you want us to do now?'

'Sink them,' Fairweather said.

Turanga was first seen as a far and faint glimmer in a chilly dusk. The next morning they approached the port across sunlit plain. 'Has it really been no more than a month?' Herrick asked.

Young Jimmy Newman was the first identifiable face. He trotted out from the stockade, calling out, failing to make himself heard, and presently sprinting. He pushed breathless among Ropata's Maoris and arrived at Fairweather's litter.

'They came,' he said. 'They came and took him away.'

'Took who, Jimmy? Slow down.'

'Took Hamiora. They took him away.'

Fairweather felt apprehension bite. 'Who did, Jimmy? Who?'

'Men,' Jimmy said.

30

'I do a fine line in fractured legs,' Gibbs said. 'I try not to amputate more than two out of three.'

He stripped Jonah's splints, tore away some of Fairweather's trousers, and looked appalled as he felt for breaks in the bone. Fairweather cried out, found breath and said, 'Talk to the point. Who came, and why?'

'Constabulary on a special mission. Much has changed in your month in the mountains. The government fell; the colony has a new Premier. Fox. William Fox.'

'I know that name,' Fairweather said. 'A middling sort of artist, as I recall. A dab hand for vacant landscapes with a few miserably picturesque Maori huts seen in a corner. Fine propaganda for aspirant colonists.'

'He now shows some artistry as a politician. He promises that the colony will no longer be trifled with by mad Maori rebels. There have been too many churchmen and humanitarians preaching patience. He says the time for patience is past.'

'I thought we had just been demonstrating as much in the mountains. But no matter.'

'Fox's point is that the Queen's authority must now be seen in full cry. Fire-eating stuff. Talk bound to suit colonists and win even more votes. But you know how politicians come to power with promises. They soon cut their cloth to suit the needs of the day.'

Fairweather groaned as Gibbs again put pressure on his leg. He managed to say, 'But Hamiora?'

'You aren't going to like this,' Gibbs said.

'My leg, or Hamiora?'

'Either.' Gibbs applied fresh pressure.

This time Fairweather's cry was full throated.

'It might,' Gibbs said, 'be mercy to bring out my saw now.'

'It's no joke,' Fairweather said.

'Your leg, what survives of it, most certainly is not.'

'Come on, man. Explain. What has political waltzing to do with Hamiora?'

'Examples of native dissidence are being sought. The new government has to show its outrage sufficiently.'

'Outrage was keenly expressed on Ngatapa. Near enough to one hundred and fifty of Kooti's men informally executed.'

'A pity,' Gibbs said. 'Had you spared a few, matters might have been simpler. Look. If you are going to wriggle like this, I am going to fetch Ropata to stun with a rifle butt.'

'Spared a few? Simpler? Make yourself clear.'

'Still, man. Still. It's going to be worse before it gets better. Understand this. The constabulary couldn't go home to Wellington empty handed. They needed prisoners. Survivors of Kooti's force. They found that wretched wife of Kooti's, whatever her name is.'

'Mata Te Owai. Her?'

'They considered her a prize. She complained to the inspector of constabulary that she had not been treated as important; she had been waiting for someone to talk to.'

Fairweather felt nausea, and not just to do with his leg.

'The woman obliged them in every respect,' Gibbs said. 'That is, before they took her away too.'

'Good riddance. Every respect?'

'She led them out across the plain to places where a few bolder Maoris are going about their business again. She pointed out sympathizers of Kooti's, spies; and one or two wearing recent scars. Anyone, in fact, whose face she didn't like. They were taken away also, though chiefs hereabouts have been kicking up an unholy row.'

'Hamiora?'

'An especially dangerous individual, she said.'

'This is absurd. Hamiora? On her say so?'

'Read did his best to confirm it. You know how he laments the injustice of any of Kooti's crew left living. He assured the inspector that Mata what's-her-name was the soul of integrity. Anyway it wasn't Read's identification they wanted, but hers. And she, I might add, has a vivid tongue.'

'I should have cut it out,' Fairweather said. 'Or fed her to Ropata.' He clamped his teeth together as Gibbs went about more painful business. 'What did Hamiora say? Do?'

'Protested, of course.'

'What did you?'

'Did my best to give credence to his tale. About his having been made captive by Kooti and forced to fight. I also made much of the help he has given me here. The inspector was deafened by Kooti's madwoman spitting fire. At all events the manacles were soon out.'

'Manacles?' Fairweather felt a chill gust through his innards.

'And they led him away. The pity of the thing is that you weren't here. You might have asserted authority.'

'I might also have felled one or two idiot representatives of law and order.'

'Then let me tell you,' Gibbs said, completing examination, 'that you won't be felling more than a hospital flea for some time to come. You'll be on your back two months or more. Then if you're lucky, and forswear strong liquor, I'll let you have crutches. You have much mending to do.'

'What do they want with Hamiora?'

'God alone knows. And even He may be mystified.'

Herrick arrived at the door with Meriana. She moved toward Fairweather with speed. 'You are all right?' she asked.

'Aside from Gibbs wishing to do more hurt than Kooti.'

'I have yet to begin,' Gibbs said. 'It is not just a matter of setting bone, but of breaking again and resetting. I shall silence him with an opium pill and drown him in chloroform.'

'Poor Fairweather,' she said. She knelt and took his head in her arms. It was the closest he had known her in more than half a year. There was sweetness; there was also lost carnal sting. Her figure was fuller. Some women became finer and fresher of feature with motherhood upon them. Emily Biggs had been one; he now saw another.

'Leave us,' he told Herrick and Gibbs.

The two men withdrew.

'Did you miss me?' he asked.

'Of course,' she said.

'And I you. What is your wish?'

'Mine?'

'The time to talk is now. I make the claim on pity.'

'It is for you to speak first. And not to say what an Englishman ought to feel. To say what he does.'

'Then I feel you might kiss me decently, at least. You will find my mouth on the way through these new whiskers. Should they prove too impenetrable, you can shave me with Gibbs' razor.'

'Later,' she said, but otherwise found his proposition acceptable. Then they whispered.

'Yes?' he asked.

'Yes,' she said.

'So you had best find a man of religion. It should be done quick, before your girth gets too embarrassing.'

'Not for me. It is mostly the Maori way. It proves the man has a good bargain.'

'Or is a fool not to have seen sooner. How did you manage that kiss again.'
'You,' she mocked. 'You.'

'Herrick,' he called after a minute.
Herrick returned, with Gibbs close behind.
'What is this about Hamiora?' Fairweather asked.
'Meriana told me,' Herrick said. 'I cannot make head nor tail of it. Damned officious morons. A boy.'
'I went down to the boat,' Meriana said. 'The men taking him told me to go about my own business. Hamiora was chained along with the others. And weeping.'
'Find out what is happening,' Fairweather told Herrick. 'Get a dispatch off damn quick. If Hamiora was spared, it was for good reason. It isn't for uniformed ninnies to question the judgement of men in the field.'
'I shall pour buckets of scorn,' Herrick said.
'Ordure, Herrick, indecently fresh.'
'I know it unfair to say so,' Herrick observed, 'but Hamiora would have had a happier time of it had you allowed me to take him with my column. He could have helped build my boats.'
'Don't remind me,' Fairweather said. 'And please make that a promise.'
'Very well,' Herrick said.
'On the healthy side of the ledger, it seems I have an urgent favour to ask of you. Namely to be my best man.'
Herrick looked at Fairweather, then at Meriana. 'With delight,' he said.
'And Gibbs,' Fairweather went on, 'since the bridegroom may be fainting away after your attentions, it might be as well to keep a surgeon close to hand. As groomsman and witness, say. And for purposes of making the event painless.'
'I shall keep a hammer near,' Gibbs promised.
'There is one lack,' Fairweather told Meriana. 'I am thinking of the role which should have been played by Matiu. We need a man of substance to give the bride away.'
'He is easy to choose.'
'Jonah?' he asked.
'Of course,' she said.

The bonding of George Fairweather and Meriana Smith was celebrated at the hospital on a bright midwinter day. People pushed past Fairweather's bed to press congratulations. Corporal Mulhooly was one of the first. Meriana, for the most part, stood off to one side.
'How,' Herrick asked, 'does it feel to be a colonist now?'

'The subject is best considered with thirst eased,' Fairweather said. 'Loss of locomotion doesn't mean I need no fuel.'

Ropata approached the bed. He wore new militia uniform, that of a major; a sword swung to one side. Noses touched; breath mingled.

'I should,' Ropata said, 'have preferred to see you wed one of my tribe. But I can now call you brother.'

'One minute a colonist, the next I am Maori,' Fairweather complained. 'I have small chance to feel whole.'

'Then make us more one,' Ropata said. 'For you, and for her, we will yet finish Kooti.'

'Thank you, sir. But it would be better not to let Kooti colour this day.' With Meriana near, Fairweather had no wish to be explicit.

'Things must be said, Fairweather. As brother.'

'Or father. I am more comfortable with that.'

'My gift,' Ropata said, 'must be *utu*. The vengeance of Ropata. Until that day, from one warrior to another, there is this.' He presented Fairweather with an ancestral Maori walking stick, elaborately chiselled: nicks and notches swam into whorls of wood where phantom figures floated with taunting tongues. 'It will give strength when you stand again. And when you walk and talk one day with the sons of your sons; and tell of old battles.'

'Thank you,' Fairweather said. 'When I grip it, and walk with them, I will tell much of the finest warrior I ever saw. This world has no greater than the Maori; the Maori no greater than Ropata.'

The tribute seemed sufficient to Ropata; he turned to Meriana. 'Some things are meant,' he said. 'I read Fairweather's omens when he was not so inclined.'

'Thank you,' she said.

'I read one for him now. He will live long and well. And guard you with care.'

'For that I am grateful.'

'Be grateful for more,' Ropata said. 'I think his fighting done.'

'For that too,' she said.

The most cautious guest to arrive at the bedside was Jimmy Newman. He was well scrubbed, and for once respectably dressed in white shirt, tie, and shiny shoes. He gazed for a time at Fairweather, then as carefully at Meriana. A juvenile question was hovering.

'Well, Jimmy?' Fairweather urged.

'It's like this,' Jimmy said. 'Can I still call you Dad?'

'Why not?' Fairweather said.

There was a puzzled pause. 'All right,' Jimmy said, considering Meriana again, 'but what do I bloody call her?'

'When you watch your language, Jimmy, a matter becoming more urgent, you might call her what you feel best.'

'You mean Mum?'

'If you are happy with that.'

'Of course I'm bloody happy with that,' Jimmy said. 'You been a bugger not telling me.'

Jonah, for his part, collared a bottle of fine French brandy to sustain Fairweather for the rest of the day. Fairweather took it in a firm grip before Meriana, or perhaps Gibbs, confiscated it in his own interest.

'The best cure for bedsores,' he said. 'The patient has rights.'

'You might fall from your bed,' she protested, 'and undo Gibbs' good.'

'Understand this,' he said. 'Surgeons have their place. So, for that matter, do wives. But an officer never forgets that his sergeant knows best. An army can fight without generals or colonels. Never without sergeants. Stand to attention, Jonah, and salute a superior.'

'Sir,' Jonah said, and did roughly as ordered.

'See?' Fairweather said. 'He's even got the hang of that, for the first and last time. So to hell with it, Jonah. We'll sink together. Empty that glass.'

'Fairweather,' Meriana pleaded.

'This is man to man,' he said. He freshened Jonah's glass. 'A toast to absent friends. One in particular.'

'To Larkin,' Jonah said.

The day promised to pass without flaw. Then a steamer arrived in late afternoon. Herrick, though having imbibed too freely to be safe with oars, rowed out to the vessel to collect dispatches from the skipper; and was slow to return. His face was distinctly sober as he pushed through celebrants to Fairweather with documents in hand.

'I don't know where to begin,' he said.

'The Queen is dead,' Fairweather decided.

'Perhaps I should save telling you until tomorrow.'

'The second coming, then,' Fairweather said. 'Is it in Bethlehem again, or where?'

'It is,' Herrick said, 'about Hamiora.'

Fairweather was not of a mind to take much seriously. 'Well?' he said. 'Are they packing him back bag and baggage? If so, not before time.'

Herrick was quiet.

'Come on, man,' Fairweather said. 'I still have drinking to do.'

'Brace yourself,' Herrick said.

'Consider me uncommonly fortified.'

'Hamiora has been brought before court.'

'For what? Offensive language to his guards? Urinating in his cell?'

'Listen,' Herrick pleaded.

'I am endeavouring to do so. You still have too little to say.'

'He has been formally charged,' Herrick said, in growing pain.

'With what, man? With what?'

'High treason,' Herrick said.

Fairweather's world was less misted. 'Say that again,' he suggested.

'You heard me the first time,' Herrick said. 'He is being held for trial with a handful of others gathered up here. They all face the same charge.'

'High treason? Hamiora? This has the makings of farce.'

'Plainly you have never been in a court at its most solemn moment of climax. When the judge, that is, wears the black cap on his wig.'

'Come on, man. This is not real. Not Hamiora.'

'By all means, if it suits you to think so today.'

'And what do you think?'

'Today or tomorrow?'

'Now.'

'I don't know if there is a heaven for us, Fairweather, but there is surely a hell.'

31

Fairweather chafed. May was gone, soon most of June. 'I have to go to Wellington,' he told Gibbs, 'and put an end to this lunacy.'

'You are going nowhere,' Gibbs said. 'Let Herrick.'

'Herrick is technically in charge of this garrison. A casualty can be considered a free man. By my reckoning a discharge from the militia is due.'

'You are not discharged from me. I can have you strapped to your bed. Let me also remind you that your wife requires your presence. And most urgently, in a few weeks.'

'All the same,' Fairweather said.

He and Herrick had composed reports, gathered statements, offered themselves as witnesses to the authorities in the capital. They had heard nothing in return. Hamiora was still held.

'The birth of this child is no light matter,' Gibbs said. 'Not for you, I trust, and most certainly not for her.'

'You tell me nothing,' Fairweather said.

In the third week of June news came from another quarter. The mountain campaign against Kooti had produced some result. With the Urewera bare of amenities, his Tuhoe hosts thinned, Kooti had pushed into the open volcanic territory of tussock and lake to the west. The signal of this was ten patrolling troopers slain. Kooti was attempting to impress formerly rebellious inland tribesmen with martial bravado and the majesty of Jehovah; and interest them in renewing war through the colony. He killed those who failed his doctrinal expectations, and left villages aflame, which did not necessarily win allies. Influential chiefs were bound to ask with whom Kooti was warring.

For Fairweather the intelligence meant that menace had passed from Poverty Bay, at least for a time; Herrick was now free to travel to Wellington and fetch Hamiora home.

'Don't expect an overnight miracle,' Herrick said. 'He is one of a dozen or more being held. Chiefs are speaking up for the others. I might be in the midst of a babble, trying to make myself heard.'

'Shout,' Fairweather said. 'Stamp your feet. Kick at chairs. Forget that you are a damned civil servant. Sit, and say you are not to be shifted until you have Hamiora by the ear.'

'Sit where?'

'In Fox's office, if necessary.'

'I cannot go directly to the Premier. Keep some perspective. Hamiora is one native boy. Fox has the entire colony to steer.'

'If he cannot concern himself with dim underlings, Herrick, this colony's skipper is already on the rocks.'

'I shall do all I can,' Herrick said. 'Don't ask for more.'

'Wait and see,' Fairweather said.

In early July Herrick boarded a steamer bound for Wellington. It was a cold month, with snow tipping the peaks of the interior and frost stealing down slopes to the plain. A few colonists and many more Maoris were warily reoccupying their land. Among the Maoris were faces unseen for months; Trader Read protested that they had been in service to Kooti. 'Let sleeping dogs lie,' Fairweather said.

'All very well for you to say,' Read grumbled.

'It is,' Fairweather agreed. 'And I say it again.'

Patrols were still desirable, and scouts watching for movement in the hills; Jonah, and more and more Mulhooly, could be relied on in that respect. Fairweather administered matters from his bed when not learning to stagger about on crutches. Later Ropata's Maori walking stick proved sturdily sufficient. Meriana, less supple herself, took his arm and helped him out into winter sunlight when it warmed; they sat on a sand dune and watched waves rise from the sea.

'You are,' she said, 'almost as I first met you in Auckland. Hobbling about with a stick.'

And a garrulous Maori named Coates, he remembered, but spared her the thought. 'Look,' he began.

'I listen,' she said.

'I have wished to say this before. But I have wished to say it with calm.'

'Say what, Fairweather?'

'This child, your child, also is mine. Is that understood?'

'I am to believe this?'

'You are never to doubt.'

'I hear you,' she said.

'Hear this too,' he said. 'In the Maori belief the earth is the mother of all, the sky the great father. I much prefer that to the petty tale of Adam and Eve. For one thing the Maori saga suggests that the coupling of which men with which women is a matter of small moment. In the end the immortal parents of mankind prevail. We are their children, as our children will be. Let that faith be ours.'

She was slow to lift her head. 'This is not from pity?'

'It is from me.'

'You have not yet spoken of love,' she said.

'No,' he said. 'I may learn.'

She was quiet again.

'Let us be clear on one thing,' he said. 'All may not be easy for us, as with many who marry. As this child rises taller, I may lust elsewhere. You may likewise be tempted. Even without that, we could bicker and fight. Unkind things could be said. But never, most never, of this. Of this child. Do I make myself clear? And have you forgotten the brandy again?'

'How could I? My Yankee father, when he started his next bottle, told me I must not dream of marrying a drunkard. Here. And your glass.'

'Be it on your head, then.'

'There is more in it than on it, Fairweather. We will grow old together. And die.'

'Me first,' he said. 'Widows have more dignity than bereaved men. I speak as one who has made many.'

Her face was expressive; it should not have been said. He sped on, 'I seem to have lost my last chance for a soldier's death. Better with boots off, in a deep feather bed, in a time of spring blossom. I would wish to know that I feed the earth, and that earth feeds those flowers. That I am but a phrase, perhaps just a beat, in the world's music. And proud.'

'You have not spoken of this before,' she said. 'Or like this.'

'It is the company I keep,' he said.

With July ebbed, August begun, Herrick was still missing. What was the man up to, why so long in Wellington? There were only so many government offices in which Herrick could sit stubbornly; a puny colonial capital lacked the labyrinths of Whitehall. Somewhere, surely, there sat a servant of justice with considerate face. One who would free Hamiora with never a thought more.

Herrick was forgotten, Hamiora too, when the child filling Meriana's belly twisted and shifted and looked for escape. Under a sky filled with frosty stars Fairweather and Jonah raced her from the hotel to Gibbs' hospital. Sleepy Gibbs pronounced waters burst. On the other hand, after intimate inspection, he forecast a long labour.

'The child is not small,' he said. 'There could be battle ahead.'

'What does that mean?' Fairweather said.

'In brief, perhaps a keen knife.'

'And I could kill you, Gibbs, if so minded.'

'Jonah?' Gibbs said. 'Remove Captain Fairweather. Dispose of him fast.'

Outside there was pale dawn in the east.

'Does it,' Fairweather dared ask Jonah, 'mean she may die?'

'I think Gibbs knows his business. He saved many wounded.'

'I remember those buried.'

'Then trust in God,' Jonah said.

'Whose? This, you know well, is no ordinary birth.'

'There is no strange star in the sky. Nor men bearing gifts. The child will be as we. A good sergeant knows when not to say more.'

'Say it.'

'Whether your child, or Kooti's, it will be of good fighting stock.'

'That is no consolation.'

'You asked,' Jonah said. 'And I spoke.'

'That suggests a son. What of a daughter?'

'Worse,' Jonah said. 'I grieve for her husbands. She will bury them all.'

Jonah had Fairweather tight by the arm; he was steering him to the hotel and then down steps to the cellar. As sergeant, ministering to the thirsts of his men, Jonah had his own key.

'Where do you think you are taking me?' Fairweather said.

'To the next best thing to chloroform,' Jonah said. 'A bottle might not be enough. I may need a barrel.'

Fairweather woke to afternoon sun through a window. He was on his own bed, altogether clothed, and in boots. Bleary Jonah stood above him, also haggard Gibbs. He swam upwards through fear.

'She lives,' Gibbs was saying. 'Also the child.'

Fairweather sighed.

'A boy,' Jonah said.

'When last seen,' Gibbs said, 'he appeared to be bawling for sight of a father.'

Fairweather's thoughts turned, tangled; he located words. 'Jonah? Could you leave me alone, for a moment, with Surgeon Gibbs?'

Jonah withdrew; the bedroom door closed.

'There is,' Fairweather told Gibbs, 'a question I thought never to ask. It seems I still must.'

'Yes?' Gibbs said; the man seemed to know what was coming.

'This child. This boy. Does he tend, would you say, toward the dark or the fair?'

'That is something you can very soon see.'

'Prepare me, at least. She will be watching. Whatever my face says, the moment will last. It might blight a lifetime. Not one lifetime. Three.'

'I should be hardened by now,' Gibbs said. 'I have seen hundreds into this world. But I still feel the awe. Still shed a tear. This crusty Scot. True, Fairweather. True.'

'The shade?' Fairweather asked.

'Once blood had begun mingling, colour is a mystery to all but our Maker. She had a pale father; even Kooti could have a castaway sailor in his ancestral closet. I have met half castes who could pass for Cornishmen, even for Scots, with brothers and sisters black Maori. If you think colour tells you much, or more than you wish to, then you are mistaken.'

'Thank you,' Fairweather said.

'For your information,' Gibbs said, 'your son's shade is a passable coffee. Your wife waits too. Are you ready?'

'As I will ever be,' Fairweather said.

Meriana rested in a bed from which bloody sheets had still to be taken; she held the child in her arms. Her smile might have been weak; her eyes were still vivid.

Things had to be said. Were.

'We are not agreed on a name,' he said. 'If a daughter, I had thought Emily, perhaps.'

'My mind empties too,' she said.

'Then Matiu,' he said, 'or Matthew. The spelling is of small moment. Either way it has a strong sound.'

'So does Pita,' she argued, 'or Peter.'

'Then Matiu Peter he shall be. Or Matthew Pita. He can arrange the names to his satisfaction as he grows.'

'Thank you,' she said.

'In one week, I promise, you shall be in your own home.'

'You have not taken him yet. Lift him in your arms at least.'

Fairweather stepped forward, and took the child to himself; it was too tiny to convince. Its eyes opened slowly. There was a small wail.

'Yours,' she said.

'Mine,' he agreed.

Fairweather knew all he needed to know; he lived where earth and sky met.

The day before the move to the Smith homestead, a surprise schooner brought Herrick. Aboard also were several Maoris once with Kooti and now released from custody; Hamiora was not among them.

'Why, in God's name?' Fairweather said.

Herrick was harassed and drawn; it had not been a comfortable voyage. 'The boy is still held,' he said.

'That seems more than plain.' Fairweather's sarcasm was heavy. 'You are telling me you failed.'

'Not for want of words. I mustered every argument. I met faces much as his prison wall.'

'But these?' Fairweather asked, of the former prisoners hastening ashore. They did not mean to linger in the port, with colonists like Read barely leashed; they would find safety further out on the plain.

'They are to be seen as special cases,' Herrick said.

'Special? How? As stumbling by chance into sympathy with Kooti?'

'They come into the category of those with influential relatives; chiefs with mana and tracts of good pasture.'

'Land.'

'Quite,' Herrick said.

'Can colonists still learn no other language?'

'You have lately been speaking it yourself.'

'For convenience.'

'The government could say the same. Fresh migrants from Britain arrive almost daily. They have to be settled somewhere. Where suitable land hasn't been confiscated, then it will have to be purchased from chiefs willing to part with it at reasonable price.'

'The release of these will ensure reasonable price?'

'Certainly less bitterness. The government does not wish to inflame responsible Maori opinion; not with Kooti still loose and trying to tempt retired rebels into the fray. It is seen as undesirable to put too many captives on trial for their misdeeds. A token number, perhaps, to pacify colonists. Promises have been made. Poverty Bay's massacre cannot go unpunished.'

'Is this what Wellington does to you, Herrick? You are speaking like them. We are talking of Hamiora. You saw him?'

'I wish I had not.'

'Come on, man. Come on.'

'At least an animal roams within its cage. He sits in a corner of his cell under a blanket. I left feeling sick. He seemed not to comprehend the situation, nor even want to, when I explained.'

'Explained what? High treason? As doing or designing anything which might do damage to the Queen within her realm?'

'You are becoming insufferable,' Herrick said. 'I tried to tell him that we, you and I, had been trying to tidy up this unfortunate affair; that we were trying to prevent his being brought to trial. Most certainly not on the charge brought against him, which seems less than just. I might as well have been talking Chinese.'

'To my ears it has a not dissimilar sound. God knows how you must have confused him. There is one word which Hamiora understands well. *Kino.*

Bad. Even more so *whiro*. Evil. It is that about which we are talking. The bad of men. The evil. Greed. And gross appetite.'

'The trial,' Herrick said, 'has been set down for late September. How many will stand in the dock beside him is still obscure.'

'This cannot go further.'

'The machine has been set in motion. People due to confront the machine in its majesty cannot be plucked from its path.'

'Some have been.'

'Because the evidence against them has been found slight.'

'When land resides discreetly on the scales of justice?'

'Fairweather, this has not been easy for me. Try not to make it worse.'

'You were talking of evidence.'

'There is the grief. Mata Te Owai, in short. Kooti's enraged spouse will be principal crown witness. She is especially damning of Hamiora. She claims she saw him bearing arms; that he was often in the vanguard of Kooti's murderers.'

'Even if true, he was forced.'

'That, it would seem, is no defence in law.'

'His other choice was death.'

'Nor that, it would seem.'

'What world is this?'

'Ours,' Herrick said.

'Did you try to see Fox?'

'As a menial servant of the crown from an outlying place I couldn't pass muster for an audience. Secretaries blocked my way. Mr Fox has the urgent raising of loan monies for roads and railways on his mind. Not to speak of the outlawing of liquor. He sees the purification of the colony as desirable; not just pacification. Consumption of strong drink may soon be treasonable too.'

'Secretaries exist to be pushed aside, Herrick. And shut doors to be battered down.'

'Easy for you to say.'

'Has Hamiora a lawyer?'

'One kindly contributed by the crown. I talked to the man at length. Insofar as he was willing to be enlightened, he lent half an ear. The law is the law, he said, and ignorance of it no excuse. Hamiora is as much a subject of the Queen as we.'

'Even if he had not, until late, heard of the Queen?'

'Even if. And if adherence to the Queen's enemies is proven, all may not go well. The judge must wear the black cap and pass the most severe sentence in law. It cannot be other.'

Fairweather located his voice. 'I'm damned if he will,' he said.

'Make yourself clear.'
'I have, Herrick. I am on my way to Wellington.'

Meriana accepted his explanation; she had to. 'I may be about to live with you,' he said. 'I also have myself to live with.'
Child in arms, she said, 'You tell me to return to the homestead alone? To start again without you?'
'This cannot be allowed to happen. Nor begin to.'
He could not see how to soften her dismay.
'You will have young Jimmy to distract you,' he added. 'Also I have asked Jonah, whom I shall discharge from militia duty, to help you settle back in. Gibbs promises to be a regular visitor.'
'It will not be the same,' she said.
'Nothing is,' he said.

Nothing. Fretting into sleep that night he heard Ropata among Ngatapa's fires. 'One day you may live to curse mercy,' Ropata said.
Kooti evergreen; elsewhere the black cap and coiled hemp. The day was at hand, certainly the curse.
Fairweather damned Ropata, Whitmore, Kooti and mostly himself; he damned all men of death.

Next day a second schooner called and discharged prisoners taken with Hamiora and now, for the greater good of the colony, permitted to return home. If Fairweather calculated right, only Hamiora was left to stand trial. There was another calculation evident; legal extravagance. The court would not be inconveniently crowded with noisy and baffled Maoris. Colonists could see politicians flexing punitive muscles at moderate price and minimum risk.
'The flying fish,' he said to Herrick.
'What flying fish?' Herrick said.
'Ropata's expression for the first to be felled on an expedition. When the government went on the warpath, Hamiora was the first to cross it.'
'And the least,' Herrick said.
'Rather the point, surely,' Fairweather said.

The schooner brought instructions to Ropata and Herrick. Since Kooti was still exposing himself in the centre of the island, a move had to be made while he was still vulnerable and before he further seduced impressionable Maoris. Columns were to march against Kooti from east and west and surround him before he retreated again into forest. Ropata and Herrick were to lead the column from the east; a token garrison could be left to look after Poverty Bay.

The message asked Herrick to prevail upon Fairweather, in view of his physical infirmity, to serve as civil administrator in Poverty Bay.

'No,' Fairweather told Herrick. 'I shall serve no one and nothing of this colony. And you know the reason.'

'Come,' Herrick said. 'You might be in a position to make a more potent appeal on Hamiora's behalf.'

'I might also be muffled. I should have to remain here.'

'Would it not make more sense to wait for the trial? Sane jurymen might well see the charge of treason as ludicrous; it may literally be laughed out of court. Against Kooti, perhaps. Against a conscript boy, no.'

'You have said nothing to suggest sanity so far.'

'Then consider this. If the trial went the wrong way, you could make yourself heard tactically. On practical rather than compassionate grounds. You could argue that the death penalty could imperil relations with sober Maoris. Your name is known in the colony now. Even Whitmore has had to pay credit where due.'

'You would have me lie, Herrick?'

'I do not quite follow,' Herrick said.

'There has been too much death here for Hamiora's to be lamented. Or would you have me invent some landed relatives likely to sell?'

'It might not hurt to stretch truth just a little. The end surely justifies the means.'

'No.'

'Why so stubborn?'

'Because I believe in vengeance. A courtroom carnival is vengeance debased.'

'In which case,' Herrick said, 'you set yourself against the government. More, against every colonist too. The fact is that Hamiora followed Kooti, and there is someone to say so. Believe me, you cannot head off the trial. Wait.'

'No.'

'You would be there?'

'If it cannot be prevented.'

'It cannot.'

'In which case, Hamiora will have one friend.'

'His eyes haunt me too,' Herrick said.

Fairweather remained in Poverty Bay long enough to move Meriana and small Matiu into the rejuvenated homestead; Jimmy and Jonah too. He shook hands with Herrick, and pressed noses with Ropata, both ready to ride after Kooti again. He wished for a mission as intelligible.

Then he sailed for Wellington. From the rumbling deck of a schooner he watched familiar land subside beneath unruly September sea.

32

Wellington had grown no more pleasing a colonial capital in the eighteen months since Fairweather passed through. It was still an unconvincing overture to civilization sketched under the summits of the island's stormy southern tip. Saloons filled the breezy seafront, where moored and mostly rigged vessels bucked on the tides. Inelegant government buildings had multiplied, and official residences crankily rococo in character climbed bleak hillsides; here and there a Union Jack was tugged by the wind. The half-drained streets stank of refuse and horses and were untidy with touts, pimps and whores. Fairweather limped into the least repellent hotel he could find. He was fatigued and salty, but neither bed nor bath interested. With the address Herrick had given him, he set out to see Hamiora's advocate. The building where the man dispensed his legal energy sat in that part of the settlement with pretensions, closest to courts, colonial Parliament, and offices of the crown. Fairweather mounted stairs, taking each with care on Ropata's stick, yet still with twinges of flesh and bone. Along a polished passage he met frosted glass embellished with names and legal degrees; the name he needed was in minor placing. He forced the doors apart with his stick; they swung open to disclose a startled grey clerk at a desk burdened with documents, all doubtless testifying to colonial woe. Wellington, perhaps, was no more than Poverty Bay writ larger.

'Mr Allen,' Fairweather said.

'You have an appointment?'

'I certainly have business to state.'

The clerk recognized urgency. He bustled ahead of Fairweather, around dim corners, past nameplates on doors. He knocked on a door with a nameplate newer than most; there was a mumble within. The clerk opened the door and had time to say, 'A client, it would seem, sir.' Then Fairweather pushed past.

Mr Allen, half rising, was young and fair, rather sweet in a willowy way. Fairweather took abrupt stance in the modest office, leaning on his stick.

'Concerning Hamiora Pere,' he began.

'I'm sorry?' Allen said, quite baffled.

'Concerning Hamiora Pere. My name is Fairweather. Captain, to some.'

'Ah,' Allen groped. 'Captain George Fairweather. Of course.'

He waved the clerk away and pushed out a shy hand; Fairweather shook it briefly.

'Please sit,' Allen said. 'Please.'

Fairweather located the room's one leather chair. 'My business should be plain,' he said. 'It seems this boy must face trial.'

'Regrettably,' Allen said.

'High treason? The thing is rank lunacy.'

'I find it disproportionate too, sir. It is thus that I shall argue.'

'It should never get that far.'

'It has,' Allen said. 'To be frank, Captain Fairweather, I am surprised to find you also bursting in on me. I have already had dealings with your colleague Captain Herrick; he was quite as precipitate in approach.'

'And I trust as commonsensical.'

'Captain Herrick was apprised, and with much patience, of the situation as it stands.'

'That the law is the law? And that the law is in motion?'

'If that is how he reported our lengthy discussion, he is not far astray.'

'There appear to be prodigious exertions to speed the law on its journey.'

'The government is determined that these native disturbances must end.'

'They are best ended down a gun barrel.'

'I appreciate the soldier's viewpoint, Captain Fairweather. But no war is conducted outside the confines of political need. I am all for arbitrary justice myself, even if it might tend to put me out of a job. But ritual is necessary, especially for rebels. Think of India. That continent might fall apart without the blessings of British law. Even the most miserable dissident can still have his day in court. Suitably chastened, some have even been known to go free.'

'With a good advocate.'

'I cannot pretend to vast experience in this area, Captain Fairweather. What lawyer has, of high treason? But I assure you that I do not want to see that boy suffer. Some colleagues have begun looking askance. What, they ask, is another dead rebel here or there? Most colonists, of course, would sooner no ceremony at all.'

'That is the best you can tell me?' Fairweather said.

'My present wish is that my client were more pleasing of countenance. He has the aspect of a young ruffian, which is bound not to impress judge or jury. Perhaps you might persuade him to look less sullen and sly.'

'As I understand it,' Fairweather said, 'arguments rather than appearances decide the day.'

'Appearances assist. More so here. The prosecution has a powerful witness.'

'As I am aware.'

'This woman will swear on all the Bibles in the colony that she saw Hamiora Pere bearing arms. That is the crux. It cannot be denied that he did. Nor will he.'

'There is much to be said in mitigation.'

'Not to useful effect. No, Captain Fairweather. I have tested the wind and found the best tack to take. As you may be aware, colonists' feelings run strongly against churchmen. Especially against those of the cloth who speak out against land confiscation and like injustices suffered by the Maori. I can safely assume that most of the jury will have small sympathy for the missionaries. Even less, say, than for rebel Maoris. That is where I hope to drive my wedge. At the least I shall give them something to think about.'

'You fail to give me much to think about, sir. Or to reassure.'

'Unable to contest that he served Kooti, I shall make the point that Hamiora Pere was just a boy confused by Kooti's Old Testament claptrap. The blame should fall fairly on the missionaries. I shall argue that the whole affair demonstrates the folly of placing the Bible in savage and superstitious hands.'

'Then you set yourself against eighteen centuries, Allen. A ragged Jew named Peter began the business when he set out to convert superstitious Romans.'

'The Romans were men of civilization. They had the wheel; they had the written word. We are talking of South Sea savages. Hamiora is best portrayed as a pathetic result of missionary stupidity.'

'The same plea might be made on Kooti's behalf. You could be seen as justifying him too.'

'Perhaps.' Allen was thoughtful.

'No jury, with Kooti in mind, could embrace that tale. Nor, for that matter, can I.'

'I understand from Captain Herrick that you are in no position to take a dispassioned view of Kooti.'

'It is fair to say that I have observed his progress from victim to villain. It has not been without grief.'

'Interesting,' Allen said. 'It seems to me that you might, after all, make a useful character witness. Your appearance would give the lie to suspicions that I am endeavouring to acquit Kooti of crimes. From Captain Herrick I also gathered that you had some acquaintance with the boy before the events for which he is to be tried.'

'I can certainly testify that he was harmless. And helpful.'

'Excellent,' Allen said. 'Another string to my bow.'

'I hope that it can be persuaded to play an acceptable tune.'

'You doubt my capacities, Captain Fairweather.'

'Your argument. Better to urge that the first loyalty of Maoris is to land;

land for which they have been fighting for nearly ten years. Hamiora, as one who bore arms, cannot in reason be called subject of a Queen of whom he knew nothing. Whatever Kooti's vices, he is the last of a long line of Maoris demanding loyalty to land. He was also sane enough to see that the New Testament muffled Maori firepower; that there was muscle in the Old. Hamiora was in service to a man resisting alien encroachment. Treason? I think not.'

'As newcomer to the colony,' Allen said, 'I find little to my taste here. Especially the lack of plain speaking, the humbug, the hypocrisy. Do we dare? I mean, Captain Fairweather, that we should literally be taking treason by the horns and turning it round.'

'And slapping its rump.'

'There are risks.'

'Either way. There is still mitigation. You might ask if the boy before the court makes a sufficiently splendid substitute for Kooti. It must be seen as absurd.'

'There we differ,' Allen said. 'Wherever I look in this colony, and especially in a political direction, I see absurdity enthroned.'

'Fox?'

'Especially the Premier.'

'His paintings, as I remember them, were not altogether ludicrous. His hand knew what he wanted.'

'His right hand, perhaps. Not his left. He is incapable of consistency. One minute he poses as a friend of the natives. The next he says that it is bad for their character to be possessed of too much land. There is just one explanation for his jerks and twists. Powerful speculators and merchants are pulling strings from the shadows; he is their vain puppet.'

'So what are you telling me?' Fairweather said.

'That we can hope for little from Fox. He will lean on the law and at the same time seem not to be doing so. He cannot denounce the foolish compassion of past administrations and yet have nothing to show. His Attorney General, a devious monster named Prendergast, is taking the case. Prendergast will make the trial his next step up the ladder to the post of Chief Justice. He knows what Fox needs.'

Through the window of Allen's office Fairweather watched native trees, spartan of form, bending to the wind.

Allen went on, 'Perhaps I should not be telling you all this. Within certain establishments in Wellington, where all but the abstemious Fox drink, the thing is common knowledge.'

'I understand Herrick better,' Fairweather said at last. 'And his frustration.'

Allen rose, walked around his desk, and gripped Fairweather by the shoulder. 'All is far from lost,' he said. 'You have given me a clue as to how I might best fling treason back in their teeth. And your own testimony cannot fail to impress.'

'The trial?'

'In three days. I asked for an adjournment, to look more widely for evidence, but it wasn't to be. Nevertheless we can still make a fight of it.'

'I should prefer talk of winning.'

'Of course. Meanwhile I imagine you might want to meet and reassure the party concerned. Your friend Herrick was none too successful. I wish you more luck. Shall we say tomorrow morning?'

'Now,' Fairweather said.

The prison rambled along a steep ridge above the town, perhaps the one Wellington building proof against gale and earthquake; its walls were of convict-hewn stone, its windows few, meagre and barred; there were turrets and watch towers, and armed guards apparent as Fairweather toiled uphill with Allen toward the entrance.

'Additional precautions have been taken,' Allen explained. 'Treason is treason.'

'Do they expect Kooti to raid this far south, to rescue the boy?'

'A little drama never goes amiss in a dull colonial capital.'

'What if it were Kooti himself? He would need a castle, no less. And most of a regiment.'

'And still get away?' Allen asked.

'Perhaps,' Fairweather said.

'He must,' Allen mused, 'be a remarkable fellow.'

'If you care for carnage. Fortunately for us he now seems most concerned with engineering the extinction of unenlightened fellow Maoris. A species of purification, perhaps.'

'It could be put to Fox that Kooti is best encouraged, meantime.'

'He has been,' Fairweather said.

'I mean to clear the ground for colonists.'

'I heard you,' Fairweather said.

The prison entrance rose above them; a slit banged open, and half a bearded face appeared. Allen's credentials were passed in, inspected, handed back. There was rattling and crashing of metal and the groan of a heavy door swinging inward to admit them and then slamming shut behind. Fairweather and Allen stood in a much trodden yard.

'Exercise is conducted here,' Allen said. 'Also other functions less instrumental to health.'

A triangle for flogging of prisoners was visible; arrangements more punitive were left to the imagination and knowledgeable carpenters. A guard led them into a long and dim building where eyes had to search for the doors of separate cells; there was the stench of excreta awaiting disposal. Fairweather's stick scraped on the stone floor.

'Here,' the guard said. Keys; a lock turning. 'Be long, sir?'

'I think not,' Allen said.

'I'll be standing out here, sir,' the guard said. 'Just shout if the black bugger gets up to nonsense.' He kicked the door open.

Hamiora still sat as pictured by Herrick, blanketed and huddled in the corner of his cell. There was a small window above, a patch of colourless sky beyond bars.

'I have,' Allen said, 'brought you a visitor. A friend.'

Hamiora did not look up; did not even stir.

'Very bloody hello,' Fairweather said.

'Hori?' the boy shivered. He lifted his eyes; his lips found a wan smile. 'Hori Fair Weather?'

'Me, Hamiora.'

'You came,' Hamiora said. 'Now I know all will be well.'

Fairweather found reply difficult.

'There is a man of Christ who visits this place,' Hamiora said. 'He teaches me prayer. I prayed for you, Hori. For you to take me home. But you just sent Captain Robert; and he did not.'

'He could not. Captain Herrick came because I was prisoner in Gibbs' hospital.' Fairweather lifted his walking stick to explain. 'We had to find where you were. What had happened to you.'

Hamiora thought on that. 'What has happened to me, Hori? Why am I here?'

Allen whispered, 'He still won't take it in.'

'It is all confounded difficult,' Fairweather told Hamiora. 'They think here that you are someone you are not. Someone like Kooti. Perhaps Kooti himself.'

'I am not Kooti, Hori.'

'You served him. Took orders. That is the problem. And the Queen is highly displeased; or her people in this place.'

'The Queen?'

'*Kuini Wikitoria.* The lady I told you of, in a land far away.'

'Then I tell her I am sorry,' Hamiora said. 'You write her for me.'

'It is not so simple. And too far for a letter. What you are supposed to have done is something called treason. The worst sort of wrong.'

Hamiora's eyes widened. 'Worse than killing?'

'Much. And for this there must be *utu.* That is why you are shut within here.'

'I think it is enough *utu* now,' Hamiora said.

'I agree,' Fairweather said.

'And you take me home now, Hori?'

Fairweather looked at Allen, and Allen at Fairweather. 'Not today, Hamiora,' he said.

'Tomorrow?' Hamiora asked.

'Nor tomorrow.'

'When, Hori? When?'

'There has to be *korero*. The matter must be discussed. Mr Allen here will speak for you. He will sing as a bird in the trees of the forest. He will be singing, Hamiora, for you. Understand?'

'Will the *korero* be long?'

'Many will have much to say.'

'And then I go home with you, Hori?'

'We will be together,' Fairweather promised.

'You will not leave me lonely again?'

'I shall not. I shall see you each day until all is over.'

'Captain Robert just came and touch me,' Hamiora said with grievance. 'He touch me and go.'

'Touched you?' Fairweather would sooner not ask.

'And kiss me,' Hamiora said. 'He tell me not to fear. He *tangi*. Weep, Hori. I do not know why he kiss me and weep.'

'Because he felt for you in this cold place, so far from Poverty Bay,' Fairweather said. 'And because he wished you with him on our last expedition. I did not permit it. And now you are here.'

Better buggery than this, Fairweather thought bleakly. Herrick's affection for Hamiora could have been harmless enough. And buggery never broke necks.

'You look sad, Hori.'

'Because I must leave you here. I must get some sleep.'

'You will come tomorrow?'

'And the next day, and the next.'

'It is very bloody all right, then,' Hamiora judged. 'I have fear no more of this place. Gone, Hori. Gone. Soon I see Poverty Bay again.'

'Think on all that is good,' Fairweather said. 'Think on all that is you.'

Outside the prison Fairweather sagged and found support, for a time, on Allen's young shoulder.

'Even visiting the worst criminal here,' Allen said sympathetically, 'I still feel the horror.'

'But him.'

'Just so,' Allen said.

'And the machine grinds on.'

'It never lacks lubrication. Law is all oily words.'

'Yet you practise it. You twist truth. You connive. You play with men's lives as if it were cricket.'

'I know this to be no game,' Allen said. 'Whatever happens, win or lose, there may be no future for me in this colony.'

'Is that your own thought?'

'It has been suggested to me what I should say in Pere's defence, and what I should not.'

'And what should you say?'

'Sufficient for appearances.'

'Men can perish for appearances. Not least in this colony.'

'Exactly, Captain Fairweather. That would seem to be the notion.'

'Am I encouraging you to say what you should not?'

'I was trying to anyway. Not that it matters.'

'But it does,' Fairweather said. 'A convinced advocate is what Hamiora most needs. It gives us a chance.'

They began the walk downhill to the town.

'God is best placed to give us that,' Allen said.

33

The trial of Hamiora Pere, on charge of high treason, began on all but the last day of September. Justice became a bustle of wigs and black gowns; Hamiora viewed the preliminaries in a suit of approximate fit which Fairweather had hastily purchased. The boy's hair had been tidied, but his facial scars could not be made more acceptable. Allen had told Hamiora, rather unnecessarily, to affect solemn wonderment so long as the *korero* lasted. The courtroom rearing around was only a few years built of pale New Zealand timbers. It filled with echoes as jurymen were summoned, selected, sat in two rows. Allen made few challenges. He preferred a shopkeeper to a landowner; a bank clerk to a retired army major. A Mr Justice Johnston, with jowly face under long wig, oversaw proceedings. Retired from obscure English assizes, he was not one to miss his chance in the colonies, nor make light of his task in a trial of promising dimension. The business before the court was unfamiliar to most, he said, and thus he would be failing in his duty if he did not take the unusual step of making jurymen more intimate with their responsibilities before the trial proper began. The day was given over to his voice as he enlightened all present on the long history of high treason. The definition of high treason, he said, had served the British race well for five hundred years. Neither race nor location of the crime was relevant.

'High treason,' he summed up, late in the afternoon, 'consists for the greater part in doing or designing anything which would lead to the death, bodily harm or restraint of the Queen; levying war against Her Majesty within the realm, or adhering to her enemies within or without.'

He took breath and considered notes, then the faces of the jurymen. Fairweather saw worse coming.

'It will not be your task,' Mr Justice Johnston said, 'to consider whether others might have committed the same crime and escaped being charged here. Nor will it be your task to compare the offences of the prisoner, should they be proven against him, to the crimes committed by that rebel leader best known as Kooti. Treason knows no better name. You must do your duty not only as the law instructs; you also have an awesome responsibility to this vexed colony. Trials for high treason have been few and far between in our beloved mother country for hundreds of years. Here, however, we may well have a unique chance to remind ourself of the gravity of the crime, and to stress our abhorrence. You, gentlemen, have history sitting with you. May you prove fit company.'

Allen, gathering up notes as the court emptied, looked dismal. 'I had not expected that,' he said. 'Nor history's siren song.'

'Sing a better,' Fairweather said. 'What is, here and now.'

'Then pray for me.'

'If necessary,' Fairweather said.

With his stick, he edged toward Hamiora before the boy was taken away between guards; they permitted Fairweather a minute.

'That judge man liked talking,' Hamiora said.

'He surely did,' Fairweather said.

'Is he the boss of the *korero*? Like God?'

'Within these walls, one might say. That is why he sits highest of all.'

'I did not understand what he was saying,' Hamiora confessed. 'I did not hear him say anything about me. What was he telling those men, Hori?'

'Too much,' Fairweather said.

'That,' Hamiora said, 'is what I think too. English *utu* is long. I see you tomorrow, Hori?'

'Rely on it,' Fairweather said.

In the morning Attorney General Prendergast commanded the court's attention; his youthful face suggested disdain for the business on hand, and his voice professional impatience. Content with quick lightning after Justice Johnston's zealous thunder, he did not burden the jury with a long outline of his case; he called Mata Te Owai as his first witness. There was shuffle of interest as Kooti's wife took the stand and gave oath on the Bible. She was sleeker than Fairweather remembered, better fed, better dressed, altogether prospering with eminence. Her eyes wandered about the court, in search of approval, until they found Fairweather. There was no humour in them. Nor lenience.

Yes, she agreed through an interpreter, she had married Kooti in a ceremony of his own devising at the time of exile in the Chatham Islands; and had escaped with Kooti from confinement there. In breach of old custom, but at her own insistence, she had often been at her husband's side while he fought. She knew most of his fighting men, those whom he trusted, those he did not.

Did she recognize the man accused, Hamiora Pere, as one of Kooti's fighting men?

She did.

Trusted?

Most certainly. Those who were not trustworthy Kooti soon killed.

She had seen the accused, Hamiora Pere, with gun in hand?

With gun in hand. And firing it too.

At the time of the hideous atrocities in Poverty Bay?

He had been there, most certainly. She could remember too well.

Rather surprisingly, and tantalizingly, Prendergast seemed to weary. After some deliberation, and with the faintest of smiles, he left his witness.

Allen stood to cross-examine. He consulted notes nervously and suddenly asked, 'How many fighting men would Kooti have had in your time, Mrs Te Owai – or should it not be Mrs Kooti? How many? Be quick.'

Four hundred, she said. Perhaps five.

'Among them,' Allen suggested, 'there would have been many mature men, most tall and sturdy?'

Many, she agreed.

'Among such a muscular throng,' Allen asked, 'is it not remarkable that you recall one trivial boy?'

It was not remarkable, she said. She recalled faces well. This one, Hamiora Pere, was cheeky. He rolled his eyes wide when Kooti spoke; he sometimes cursed in an English way.

'If your recall is so splendid,' Allen persisted, 'perhaps you also remember Kooti invading the Poverty Bay village of Patutahi on the night of November the ninth last year, on the eve of the massacre?'

She did, she said. She recalled Patutahi.

'And,' Allen said, 'was it not the case that some older men of the village were murdered in the name of Jehovah?'

It was, she thought.

'And the young men of the village forced to watch?'

She could not say for certain. Perhaps.

'Was it not also the case that these young men of the village, Pere among them, were given the choice of serving Kooti or meeting death?'

She had not been witness to all of that which took place at Patutahi. Anything could be true of Kooti. Perhaps.

'Nevertheless,' Allen said, 'Kooti's ranks were swollen on the eve of the massacre?'

There seemed to be more, she said. There were always more when killing was near.

'In this case, increased by the young of Poverty Bay villages, and particularly Patutahi?'

Possibly, she said.

'Now,' Allen said, 'let us consider the massacre itself. Is it not true that it was, for the most part, conducted in the hours before dawn of that very same night?'

It was.

'In the dark, in short?'

In the dark. Until houses burned.

'There must have been hundreds milling around. Much shouting, stamping, and many hoofbeats. Not to speak of the axing and shooting. Or the screams of those dying.'

She could never forget, she said.

'It must have been truly terrible confusion?'

It was, she agreed, and lowered her eyes.

'Let me put it to you,' Allen said with sudden vehemence, 'that you were party to that event. You, Mata Te Owai.'

Never. She just happened to be there.

'At Kooti's side?'

Never far, she said. She was his wife.

'One wife among many, as I understand,' Allen said. 'And later a woman scorned. Is that why you stand witness today?'

It was not. She served Christ again, not Kooti. Christ, the true saviour.

'Then,' Allen said quickly, 'tell me more of services rendered Kooti outside your marriage bed. Did you serve him well that night? Did you give strength? Did you encourage him in his deadly work for Jehovah?'

Never. Jehovah confided only in Kooti. Only Kooti was intimate with Jehovah's true wish. She would not presume.

'Let us say, at the least, that you did nothing to discourage Kooti that night? Or to spare lives?'

Prendergast had risen elsewhere in the court. 'Mata Te Owai,' he objected, 'is not here on trial.'

Mr Justice Johnston considered the objection. 'Mr Allen?' he asked.

'I am concerned, your honour,' Allen explained, 'to establish the reliability or otherwise of the witness. If in passing she reveals herself more culpable of the crimes wildly attributed to my client, I am not one to complain or to phrase questions more delicately.'

Mr Justice Johnston's ruling went against Allen; he must not persist in his present questioning. Allen did not appear greatly frustrated. He had pushed the witness as far as he might.

'So,' he said amiably, 'let us think again of that night of the massacre. Of the great storm, with the fangs of Kooti and Jehovah, raging murderously out of the dark.'

He paused. Even Mata Te Owai seemed awed. Fairweather felt unease. A lawyer turned poet was alway a risk.

'In all that vast and fatal commotion,' Allen asked, 'is it not rather wonderful that what you seem to remember best of that night is one puny boy called Hamiora Pere, only hours conscripted by Kooti?'

The witness decided she did not understand the question.

Allen tried again for an answer; he would live long regretting it. 'How is it,' he challenged, 'that you manage to save so clear a memory of Hamiora Pere from so confused a night?'

Mata Te Owai looked much better pleased. That question she could answer. Before Christ she could. While the houses were burning, she had asked Hamiora Pere to hold her horse. He was armed. She remembered that especially, because his weapon was not one familiar to her, nor to him; he had been trying to make it function with cartridges too large. The weapon had certainly been loot from a colonist's home, perhaps that of Major Biggs.

The corner of Allen's mouth twitched. Fairweather saw the offensive against Mata Te Owai become rout.

'Thank you,' was all Allen had left to utter; and Mata Te Owai, beginning to beam, left the stand. She gave Fairweather a triumphal stare. Kooti might pick liars for wives; he did not pick fools.

There was a charitable adjournment. Allen raised his wig and mopped his brow. 'It isn't all over,' he told Fairweather. 'We have never contested that Hamiora served Kooti. And will not.'

'All the same,' Fairweather said.

'I know,' Allen said bitterly. 'One question too many. Prendergast shrewdly left it for me to ask. I walked into the trap; it was sprung.'

'Cricket,' Fairweather said. 'A game.'

'I am sorry,' Allen said. 'I know how you feel. Instinct should have told me just to leave passing doubt. Greed took over. Power.'

'Come. We are all in hazard there.'

'Thank you,' Allen said. 'You could not be kinder, considering.'

'I have to be. Hamiora has no one else to bat for him here.'

'I shall try not to disappoint you again, Captain Fairweather. I still have the thrust of my attack. And you.'

'Then I must regroup,' Fairweather said.

The prosecution had one further witness. Colonel George Stoddard Whitmore, late commander of military expeditions against Kooti, took the stand and gripped the Bible with conspicuous fervour. He also contrived to consider Fairweather with a cheerless eye; and then, after thought, decided to consider Fairweather no more. Whitmore was distinctly thinner, his voice still a croak, as much a ruin as his reputation; Kooti had ravaged more than villages. It was like wheeling in an obsolete cannon to aim at an ant. Fairweather looked at Hamiora. The ant was more mystified than ever.

What Prendergast wanted from Whitmore was what the colony knew. Kooti's escape from the Chathams; the pursuit; the atrocities. And finally the subduing of Kooti's garrison on Ngatapa mountain. For some inscrutable legal reason it had all to be placed on record, though Whitmore, at certain fragile points in his testimony, would clearly have preferred not; he was even more at pains to avoid Fairweather's eye.

Prendergast said, 'It was on or near Ngatapa mountain, was it not, that the man accused was made captive?'

'As I understand,' Whitmore said.

'And this after many stern days of siege?'

'Most taxing days,' Whitmore confirmed.

'You were facing most determined opponents, united in their desire to defy British arms? Determined and united in levying war within the Queen's realm?'

'That would be true,' Whitmore said. 'Most determined. Most united.'

'Thank you, Colonel Whitmore.'

Allen had a slight smile as he rose to cross-examine.

'Colonel Whitmore, sir,' he asked, 'would it be true to say that many of Kooti's men were made captive in the storming of Ngatapa mountain, and in the days following?'

'It would be true to say so,' Whitmore agreed.

'What happened, may I ask, to the majority of those prisoners?'

Whitmore felt obliged to acknowledge Fairweather's presence in the court again; and then found comfort in lifting his gaze to the ceiling of the court.

'The handling of prisoners,' he finally answered, 'was not directly within my compass.'

'But you were overall commander, sir, were you not?'

'I delegated responsibility for the prisoners to my Maori allies, and to officers of mine closely associated with the same allies.'

'You could hardly have been unaware, sir, that the fate of those prisoners was to be shot down by Ropata and his men?'

'I am aware of traditional Maori custom in this respect,' Whitmore conceded.

'Might you be more specific about that, sir?'

'There is generally no quarter. Ropata, as an old warrior, still fights according to custom. I did not feel it incumbent upon me to interfere, not after the massacre in which all or most of the captives participated; they got as good as they gave. Nonetheless I instructed that retribution be tempered with mercy.'

'Instructed whom, sir?' Allen asked.

'My officers. Those who remained with Ropata after I had stormed Ngatapa mountain.'

'And what were those instructions, in brief?'

'To the effect that innocents be spared.'

'Innocents, sir?'

'Women, children, and the like. Those defenceless.'

'Among whom was Mata Te Owai, Kooti's abandoned wife, from whom this court has just heard.'

'As I understand it,' Whitmore said with unease.

'She could hardly be classed as innocent. A woman who had doggedly followed Kooti, perhaps killed for him, from the first?'

'She was a woman nonetheless. Who would wish to see captive women shot down?'

'Your point is taken, sir. My point is that, during the period of retribution, others were spared.'

'Thanks to my officers exercising Christian compassion.'

'These officers, then, were men of experience and virtue?'

'To the best of my knowledge.'

'Would you mind naming them for the court?'

Whitmore plainly did mind. 'Principally,' he said, 'there were two. Captain Robert Herrick of the Hawke's Bay militia. Captain George Fairweather, late of the imperial army, now of the Poverty Bay militia.'

'Reliable men, sir? Sensitive to those wishes you have described to the court?'

'I should trust so.'

'And men of fair judgement?'

Whitmore was slow answering.

'Come, sir,' Allen persisted. 'Yes or no?'

'I like to think of myself as a good judge of character,' Whitmore said.

'That is not quite the answer I sought, sir. I am talking of those to whom you delegated responsibility. Did you consider those officers equally astute?'

'In the circumstances,' Whitmore said.

And was caught. Allen, as spider to fly, was fast down the web.

'Then,' Allen said, 'I should draw your attention to the fact that the individual currently accused in this court was considered by your officers as innocent and worthy of sparing. Does that surprise?'

'No officer is infallible,' Whitmore said wearily.

'But surely, sir, there is something remarkable in this? That a youth judged a misguided innocent on the summit of Ngatapa, by your very own officers, should here be facing a charge of high treason?'

'It is not for me, as I understand the matter, to pass judgement on the business of this court,' Whitmore said; and looked up to the bench for support.

Mr Justice Johnston ruled so too. Had Mr Allen more to ask of Colonel Whitmore?

'I think not, your honour,' Allen said. 'Unless the distinguished Colonel Whitmore wishes, with hindsight, to voice criticism of the officers he left to dispense mercy on Ngatapa mountain. If this is the case he should be allowed, here, opportunity to do so. Sir?'

Whitmore shifted comfortlessly in the witness stand, permitting himself to look long and hard at Fairweather; Fairweather looked longer and harder at Whitmore.

'I have no such criticism to voice,' Whitmore eventually disclosed.

'Thank you, Colonel Whitmore,' Allen said with genuine gratitude.

There was another adjournment. 'Splendid,' Fairweather said to Allen. 'The way you guided Whitmore must make impression. I saw second thoughts even on obstinate jury faces.'

'It is not thoughts we want,' Allen said, 'but acquittal. Speaking of which, I have decided against placing Hamiora in the stand. He is too naive to see that honesty can hurt in this *korero*. One unfortunate admission and Prendergast would club him to the floor in cross-examination. Perhaps make him seem the worst of Kooti's killers. No. I must gamble on you.'

'Alone?'

'Until I make my final plea. The enfilade fire may be difficult. Prendergast won't forgive my persuading Whitmore to collapse on the witness stand. He must make you look worse.'

'A grubby duel,' Fairweather protested.

'Nothing can make this less squalid,' Allen said. 'So long as Kooti still rampages, there seems much at stake. That is why Prendergast must cut a dash as Attorney General in this court. If only we had word that Kooti had been captured or killed, the climate would be different. But it is not. And we are not.'

'Nor Hamiora,' Fairweather said, watching guards bring their prisoner back into the court.

'No one,' Allen said.

After being sworn, Fairweather was led through his narrative by Allen. The first encounter with artless Hamiora Pere on his painting expedition. The request to join Fairweather in the militia; Hamiora's amiable help in locating the old and forsaken trail which Kooti was eventually to use in the raid on Poverty Bay. Answering Allen, Fairweather said he was aware that before, during and after the raid young Maoris had been forcibly recruited by Kooti; and that those not coming up to Kooti's requirements had been killed. He had seen the bodies of many so executed. It had been most natural to save Pere from Ropata's guns on Ngatapa mountain; he could not have done otherwise, and would still do so today.

'So this trial comes as a surprise to you?' Allen asked.

'Altogether,' Fairweather told the court, 'and especially the charge faced by my former prisoner. Until I attempted some explanation, which I am not sure he even now comprehends, he had not even heard of the Queen, let alone known that he resided within her vast realm. These proceedings affront reason.'

'That will be enough,' Mr Justice Johnston said tersely, and then reprimanded Allen. 'It is not for your witness to give vent to opinions on the business occupying this court. You will desist from inviting such opinions, Mr Allen.'

'As you please, your honour,' Allen said. 'But before leaving my witness I feel it my duty to observe that, unlike some, Captain Fairweather has served with distinction in the campaign against Kooti; and that mercy has not been a feature of that campaigning. It is also to the point that Kooti has struck at Captain Fairweather personally; he is no friend of the Queen's real and overt enemies. And would not be here unless he felt high treason was a nonsensical charge to bring. A charge with the gravest consequence in law.'

'I am now obliged to warn you, Mr Allen,' Mr Justice Johnston said.

Fairweather felt a flutter of gut as he awaited Prendergast's cross-examination. He had never stood witness before, other than in minor courts martial, rites often ended with laughter at the cunning of some thieving soldier, and a few dozen lashes. His present position did not provide for laughter; it would for a lashing. After some pursing of lips and rearrangement of gown, along with a little footwork, Prendergast struck; his first question was meant to draw blood.

'Captain Fairweather, I wonder if you might enlighten this court as to the manner of your departure from the imperial army? From Her Majesty's 65th Foot Regiment?'

Prendergast was well briefed, probably by Whitmore.

'It was a confused affair,' Fairweather said. 'And had much to do with undisciplined drinking, not uncommon among soldiery after surviving a distinctive battle.'

'Would it be true to say, Captain Fairweather, that your departure also had not a little to do with sympathy for your Maori foe?'

'A sympathy much shared, sir. Even, I might add, by my general. As is well known.'

'You would have had something to do, no doubt, with a certain – and some might say infamous – memorial placed to fallen Maoris by officers and men of your regiment before its departure from these islands.'

'A spade is a spade, sir; heroes are heroes. It is my view that the officers and men of the 65th did nothing to discredit their uniform.'

'So your sympathies were with the Maoris then? That is fair reading.'

'As an officer, sir, my sympathies were first with my men. I had no wish to see their lives lost in questionable cause.'

'Questionable cause, Captain Fairweather? The pacification of this colony?'

'At the least, sir. It seemed to many that the Maori might best be left alone with his land; that colonists manufactured excuses to fight. We attacked territory where piety and peace prevailed, and left such territory bloodied desert.'

Careful, he told himself. Too late.

'Might it not be true to say, Captain Fairweather, that your sympathies are still similarly coloured? And have much to do with your presence in this court today?'

'My answer is simple, sir. I have killed more Maoris than you.'

'An interesting reply, Captain Fairweather. But not to my question. Which was, are your sympathies still engaged with the native inhabitants of this colony?'

'Discriminatingly, sir. I number some as friends; others as enemies.'

'Might you not, Captain Fairweather, be seen to have been singularly naive? Now that you know more of the savagery of which Maoris are capable?'

'Had justice been served, sir, this colony might never have heard of Kooti.'

'The fact is, Captain Fairweather, that this colony now has. Hundreds of graves now testify to his eminence. Is that not so?'

Allen was on his feet in objection. 'I have already made the point,' he protested to the bench, 'that no one has been more personally committed to pursuit of Kooti than Captain Fairweather. He is not to be discredited as a mere Maori lover.'

Mr Justice Johnston wavered for a time, then ruled for Allen. Prendergast was not dismayed; his damage was plain.

'To turn to the man accused before this court,' Prendergast said. 'You have sketched your dealings with him prior to the massacre. It is known, is it not, that Kooti had many sympathizers, and spies, in Poverty Bay?'

'Prior to the massacre, sir?'

'Prior to the massacre. And perhaps still.'

'It is reasonable to say so. Some have given to his cause actively, others less so.'

'Quite, Captain Fairweather. Sympathizers. Spies. Gleaners of intelligence. Planters of false clues.'

'I fail to take your drift, sir.'

'My drift, Captain Fairweather, is that you might well have been, and perhaps certainly were, deceived by the individual before this court. I put it to you that he was in Kooti's service from the beginning.'

Helpless, Fairweather looked in appeal to Allen. But Allen was shaken too. It seemed Prendergast was not one to rely on the letter of the law to win a conviction; his triumph had to be made of more than the intricacies of treason.

'I find that absurd,' Fairweather said.

Prendergast hardly troubled to hear the reply; he was looking at notes. 'Hamiora Pere, if I heard your earlier evidence right, seems to have been endeavouring to ingratiate himself with you, in ways large and small, prior to the massacre. Should that not have struck you as suspicious?'

'Never, sir. Not of a Maori. They make something of a feast of strangers.'

'In times past quite a literal feast,' Prendergast said, never at a loss in milking the last drop of prejudice. 'The most delectable portions of the human anatomy were, as I understand, reserved for the chiefs.'

Fairweather chose silence while Prendergast looked for smiles in the jury and found some to satisfy. He persisted, 'So it never occurred to you, Captain Fairweather, that when Hamiora Pere came to you, especially with a request to join you in the militia, that he might be trying to further Kooti's ends? And gather information about the defence of Poverty Bay useful to Kooti?'

'It did not,' Fairweather said.

'On the face of things, however, it is quite possible?'

'It is also possible that the world will see no dawn tomorrow. The boy was no more than a genial nuisance at worst. And at best a useful companion.'

'Plausible, in short.'

'Credible, sir. Just another naturally inquisitive young Maori. A shade more winning than most.'

'Too winning, perhaps. You would not quibble, I take it, with the proposition that even the best soldier can be taken off guard?'

'We are only men, sir.'

'You used the word inquisitive. Inquisitive about what?'

'About my transactions with Poverty Bay's woods and waterfalls in the first instance. He failed to see point in my depicting them when the woods and waterfalls were already plain to the eye; Maori art is less disposed to fuss with the world as we see it. He nevertheless proved a good guide.'

'You anticipate my next question. There was another occasion, was there not, when he served you as guide?'

'There was, sir.' Fairweather sensed swamp seeping underfoot.

'He took you to an overgrown Maori track into Poverty Bay. A track which, as things turned out, Kooti was later to use in his cruel raid. You were, at that time, leading Poverty Bay's scouts.'

'And checking all possible approaches to the region,' Fairweather agreed.

'You were deceived, were you not, about the route Kooti took?'

'I have not had a day to forget it, sir.'

'I put it to you, Captain Fairweather, that the person accused before this court played an active part in that deception.'

Fairweather felt a heave within. 'I put it to you, sir, that I am not a damned fool.'

There was a short silence. Prendergast's face was rich in satisfaction. Mr Justice Johnston had a reprimand. 'You are not among rude and licentious soldiery here, Captain Fairweather,' he said.

Prendergast resumed slowly, with a mere glimpse of menace. 'I put it to you again, Captain Fairweather, that Pere took you to that track precisely to demonstrate its overgrown and disused nature, while at the same time knowing that it was the track Kooti proposed to take. I put it to you that by demonstrating the track overgrown and disused Pere, working on Kooti's behalf, wished you to ignore it in your calculations for the protection of Poverty Bay.'

'Nonsense,' Fairweather began, and then tried to swallow the word; nothing was nonsense here.

'Really, Captain Fairweather? It appears to me most logical that he might thus have misled you.'

'Directly I saw that track,' Fairweather said, 'I reported back to Major Biggs. I urged that it be watched. Major Biggs chose only to mark its existence on a map; he thought we had not the scouts spare to keep watch there. Since the track was a tangle, and seemingly little known even to local Maoris, he considered any risk from that quarter could be discounted.'

'Major Biggs, alas, is no longer with us to confirm that story.'

'He is not,' Fairweather agreed. 'Had he heard my plea that day there might have been no massacre. We should not be having this trial.'

'But we are, Captain Fairweather. And essentially you appear to be telling me that the ruse worked. If not with you altogether, then with Major Biggs. Suspicion was allayed concerning use of that track.'

'I must repeat, sir, that neither Major Biggs nor I knew of that old track until Pere disclosed its existence; the knowledge I won of it was virtually chance.'

'But it would seem Pere rather went out of his way to show you that track. Chance, Captain Fairweather?'

'I used a casual encounter to collect further intelligence of the region I was scouting. To that end I used anyone.'

'Consider it possible, Captain Fairweather, that Pere was under instruction from Kooti. Kooti likes to taunt, does he not?'

'When he can afford to.'

'How better to taunt you, then, with knowledge of the actual route he would use – knowing full well that it would not be taken too seriously.'

'As tactician Kooti isn't stupid. Taunting is one thing. Giving away his game is another.'

'Let me put it another way,' Prendergast said. 'I suggest that Kooti was concerned that you might, sooner or later, become aware of that track. In which case he might have thought it best that your attention be drawn to it, and that it be seen as an improbable route.'

Fairweather was silent. Prendergast's quick brush strokes were merging. The best to be hoped for was honourable retirement; something short of a débâcle.

'Well, sir?' Prendergast asked.

'Your proposition is ingenious,' Fairweather said.

'And is not Kooti himself?'

'Within limits.'

'What limits, Captain Fairweather?'

'Those of religion and race, sir. He fell upon Poverty Bay as a vengeful Jew. He took stance on Ngatapa mountain as a vainglorious Maori. Both postures will prove – if they have not already – to have undone his cause. If, that is, he has one beyond the intoxications of power.'

'But you would hardly differ when I say that it has been sufficiently demonstrated that Kooti is a man of much cunning? And has had many willing human tools in the manufacture of slaughter?'

Prendergast was no longer looking at Fairweather; his gaze was now lethally on Hamiora. The eyes of jurors had to follow.

Ache grew in Fairweather's leg; nor was that in his bowels inclined to diminish. It was not over yet. Prendergast plainly had more.

'I take it, Captain Fairweather, that you questioned Pere when he was made captive consequent upon the siege of Ngatapa?'

'I did, sir.'

'Closely?'

'In winning intelligence. Yes.'

'Was he forthcoming?'

'To an admirable degree. He was relieved to be alive.'

'I trust that he was also forthcoming about his personal role in Kooti's service.'

'He was frank,' Fairweather said. He was up to his knees in swamp now, still sinking.

'Did he speak of trying to escape Kooti's command?'

'He spoke of others who had tried. And perished.'

'But he made no such attempt?'

'It seemed he was sufficiently intimidated.'

'Your reply, I take it, is that he made no attempt to escape.'

'My reply, sir, took intimidation into account.'

'Did you not have the reasonable suspicion, Captain Fairweather, that he might have made no attempt to escape because he had, in fact, entered into the fiendish spirit of the thing?'

'There were no grounds for such suspicion, sir.'

'If he had indeed entered into the spirit of the thing, he would not of course have admitted so. You would accept that, Captain Fairweather?'

'You are asking me to accept conjecture.'

'Let me be blunter. Did he speak of bearing arms for Kooti?'

Fairweather hesitated. Truth? At the edge of his vision he saw Allen's small, despairing nod.

'Well, Captain Fairweather? Did he so speak or did he not?'

'Yes,' Fairweather sighed. 'He spoke rather ingenuously of bearing arms for Kooti.'

'Of killing for Kooti?'

'He spoke, sir, of taking Kooti's orders to shoot.'

'To kill?'

'Killing is the consequence of a tidy shot. Not all find their mark.'

'It is my impression – and I should willingly be corrected, Captain Fairweather – that much of Kooti's murderous shooting has been at remarkably short range. A range which does not permit any consequence other than death.'

'On occasion, sir.'

'On too many occasions, Captain Fairweather.'

'If you say so.'

Prendergast paused, smiled, and said in soft voice, 'But I wish to hear you say so, Captain Fairweather. I wish to hear you agree that the man accused in this court was never more, and certainly never less, than one of Kooti's foul and treasonous killers.'

There was always an end. Had to be. Fairweather made it his own.

'In hell you will, sir,' he shouted.

The court was quiet, even Mr Justice Johnston. Prendergast, with compassion apparent for the first time, permitted Fairweather to leave the witness stand. After all, Prendergast had more than he needed; he had merely allowed Fairweather liberty to arrange the rope.

In the adjournment Fairweather fretted beside Allen; he would accept no comforting word. 'Ropata was right,' he told Allen.

'Ropata?' Allen asked.

'Mercy was a mistake. Not because of omens. Because better a quick shot than a long march to the gallows.' He avoided Hamiora's puzzled face.

'You need a large drink,' Allen suggested.

'I need a distillery,' Fairweather said.

Prendergast, as if fatigued by truths too familiar, made a passionless summary of the crown case. It had been proved, and confirmed by the one distinguished defence witness, that Pere had served Kooti. There was testimony suggestive that his allegiance had been to Kooti even before the massacre; it could not be contested that he was a participant in that massacre. Thereafter he had also borne arms in Kooti's battles. Pere, in short, had levied war against the Queen within her realm. Given the facts, the jury could only find Pere guilty of high treason, as charged. Any other finding would fly in the face of long established English law.

Allen stood to plead, not one to fly in the face of anything, rather to navigate gracefully among the perils of prejudice and law. He asked the jury to assume, for a moment, the contentious notion that Hamiora Pere had willingly served Kooti. If so, might not the act be understandable? Poverty Bay was a far from civilized corner of the colony; Maoris there were often still much as they were. As they were, Maoris had recognized only one form of authority. The chief. Their chief. For better or worse they looked up to their chief with reverence, and were obedient to his dictates. If that chief had confirmed his hereditary rank with deeds of daring then his influence was virtually irresistible. Kooti might not have been a hereditary chief, but his deeds had made him the equal of any, not to speak of his wayward intellect, and his power to bewitch with words. Simple Hamiora Pere could be forgiven for having been in thrall. He might also be seen as just another Maori whose first loyalty was not to a remote Queen, but to native soil; and who had been joined with others in resisting intrusion on that soil. High treason hardly fitted his case.

Allen was too elaborate by far. Jury faces were shut. Then Allen's nerve seemed to go. He stopped, coughed, shuffled paper; and to the bewilderment of most in court began again.

Now it was the argument that Fairweather had heard, and dismissed, in Allen's office on their first meeting; it sounded no better in desperation here. The true culprits in this affair, Allen said, were those naive men of religion who had placed the Bible prematurely in pagan hands; who had left much of it open to misinterpretation; who had irresponsibly permitted Maoris to identify themselves as warring Israelites. Would not selected excerpts from the New Testament have been sufficient to convert Maoris to Christ? Or, better still, just a few general prayers? Hamiora Pere, like many others, had best be seen as an innocent victim of missionary folly.

Fairweather looked up at the jury. Faces were interested now. Interested. Not convinced.

'In the name of all reason,' Allen pleaded, 'this young man before the court cannot be considered as having given grave offence to a Queen of whom he knows little or nothing. Forget the atrocities of which you have heard. Consider this hapless young Maori alone. Can you, in good conscience, convict him of the most serious crime in English law? Can you, in your hearts, see fit to deprive him not only of freedom, but of life? I think not.'

Fairweather, watching the jurors as Allen came to rest, thought otherwise. Allen sat with head lowered and looked at his limp hands.

Mr Justice Johnston, before summing up, nevertheless congratulated Allen on his eloquence; as an advocate he had left no stone unturned, even if matters hitherto unmentionable in respect of missionary practice had been brought to light. It could never be said, therefore, that his client had not received a fair trial.

Then Johnston turned to the jury. 'Mr Allen has spoken of reason,' he said. 'I am here to instruct you in law. The two may not amount to the same thing. Were the world made of reason, we should not need law. I shall now – lest all this verbiage has confused you – talk of the statutes concerning treason again.'

Fairweather knew the trial as good as over, though Johnston wandered fastidiously around his theme for more than an hour; when he found no further vantage points from which to observe treason, and appendages thereof, the jury retired.

'There is still hope,' Allen told Fairweather. 'One or two sane men may hold out.'

They could not look at each other. Fairweather, heavy on his stick, eased his way across the court to Hamiora before the boy was removed from the dock.

'Is the *korero* finish now?' he asked.

'For the moment,' Fairweather said. 'There will be a little more.'

'I cannot go with you, Hori?'

'Not yet. No. Hamiora, I ask of you one thing. Whatever you hear said, I wish you to be as brave and proud of your ancestors when they battled Ropata's tribe in times gone. Understand?'

'Brave?'

'And proud. What you hear said may not be meant. May not happen. Must not. And will not. The way of the English is not Kooti's. We talk much, but often do nothing.'

Hamiora did not understand. It was enough that he was asked to be brave and proud. 'For you, Hori,' he said.

'No,' Fairweather said. 'For you.'

The men of the jury found fifteen minutes sufficient to consider five hundred years of English law, and all relevant precedent; they returned to the court, with Mr Justice Johnston presiding again, to pronounce Hamiora Pere guilty of high treason.

Johnston, with risen interest in proceedings, then asked, through an interpreter, if the prisoner could say why sentence of death should not now be passed upon him, according to law.

'*Kia mate ai?*' Hamiora asked.

'*Kia mate ai,*' the interpreter confirmed.

He was still slow to comprehend. He looked toward Fairweather and then found his promise. His body stiffened; his face too.

'I was taken by Kooti,' he replied through the interpreter, 'and made to do all Kooti said. The evil is not mine. The evil is Kooti's. Hear this always as true.'

His voice shook only at the end.

The black cap already resided on Johnston's wig. He bent benignly toward Hamiora and said, 'You, Hamiora Pere, must consider yourself a most fortunate young man. Yes. You must. The crime of which you stand here convicted is judged, in well governed and peaceable communities, the greatest of all crimes; a crime which has been punished with death of a degrading, lengthy and terrible kind. Men were cut down while still kicking on the gallows rope and then slowly disembowelled, their heads severed, their bodies sliced into small portions. Only in that fashion, it was believed, could a truly Christian community express its horror of treason. Until a short time ago such a fate would have been yours. The law has now changed, some might say for the worse, to make the punishment more trivial. It could not be more providential for you. You will merely be returned to the place from whence you came and there hanged by the neck until you are dead. May God have mercy on your soul.'

As he heard Johnston through the interpreter, Hamiora managed to remain motionless. Johnston hastened from the court with a flourish of gown. Fairweather sped to Hamiora.

'It is true, Hori?' he asked. 'Will they do that to me? It is true?'

'Not yet,' Fairweather said.

Tears arrived; and terror. Fairweather pushed guards aside and took the boy in his arms.

34

With only a week of October gone, and while Allen and Fairweather worked on a petition for clemency, an electric telegraph message said that Kooti had been surrounded in volcanic desert to the north. Kooti improvized a fort on a long ridge overlooked by steaming mountains. Militia, armed constabulary and Queen's Maoris advanced from three sides, shooting down Kooti's skirmishers and storming parapets and trenches; his warriors succumbed by the dozen, some drowning in their own gore. It was a triumph with a familiar imperfection. The fourth side of the fort was never credibly invested. As din and smoke rose, Kooti abandoned his dead and doomed and fled with a few wives and disciples through fern. The message said he was still being hunted; there were hopes of early capture.

'Anyway,' Allen said, 'it appears to have been devastating. He is now a general with no army. His menace has gone; his capture a matter of time.'

'With a little imagination,' Fairweather said.

'At least the disaffected tribes he was trying to interest in rebellion will now give him short shrift. He will win no allies. Nor converts. He has failed.'

Fairweather tried to locate something within himself suggesting jubilance. 'When a ton of stone sits on Kooti's grave,' he said, 'we can call him finished. I should prefer two ton for safety.'

'Come,' Allen said. 'It makes our task easier. With no fear of an extensive uprising spread by Kooti, things must look different in the capital. We are entitled to a moderate stance from the government; a reprieve.'

'Kooti would appear to have won one for himself. Or are there more to go around?'

'I fail to follow you,' Allen said.

'I mean I should have been there,' Fairweather said.

Three days later another message said there had been no sighting of Kooti, though a party of seasoned men, under Major Ropata and Captain Herrick, was continuing pursuit. The message said it was understood there were still grounds for optimism.

'Try, Ropata,' he urged silently. 'Try, Herrick.'

'Churchmen are making their own appeal for clemency,' Allen said. 'That should add weight to our own.'
Fairweather could not bring himself to speak.
'Why so despondent?' Allen asked.
'Christian virtue is notoriously not on the winning side, Allen. It even celebrates an execution, if I recall right.'
'There is more to your mood,' Allen said.
'Perhaps I fought too long beside Ropata. Portents. Omens. Twitches of flesh. Stars in the sky.'
'You seem all but a Maori.'
'Which may be better than nothing,' Fairweather said.

Letters arrived from Meriana. The spring had been warm. Jonah had been ploughing and sowing seed for a crop of corn. Young Jimmy ensured there were no silences in the house; the boy was a feast of commotion, but otherwise useful. As for their son Matiu, he prospered too. Gibbs, when he rode out to the homestead, said he had never seen a baby more spirited. Another who called often was a young man called Mulhooly, with his recent Maori wife. He talked with respect of Fairweather, and offered himself for work Meriana wished done. Everyone asked the same question: When would Fairweather be home with Hamiora?

The weeks in Wellington grew no shorter, nor days of those weeks; not with numbing visits to the prison, a daily climb and daily descent best obliterated by liquor. As a condemned inmate of the institution Hamiora had been established in a more substantial cell; he had wooden table and chairs as well as iron bed. There was a large spy hole in the door, a guard always on duty.
'This isn't forever,' Fairweather said. 'I promise.'
'That judge,' Hamiora said, 'promised too. He promised I must hang by the neck forever.'
'I promise Poverty Bay again. Think on it more.'
'I think it is gone, Hori. I think I have forgot.'
'Then let me remind you. A fair plain with rivers which flow to bright sea. Trees with plump pigeon and waters with fat fish.'
Hamiora shook his head. 'I see only this place,' he said. 'I see men look and go. Why they look at me, Hori? Why they look long?'
Fairweather said carefully, 'Because you are important. *Take nui.* There is much talk of you. Much interest.'
'Because the judge wishes me hanged by the neck?'
'And because some wish not. There is much argument. Much *korero.*'
'About me?' Hamiora was impressed.
'All about you. Every day.'

That required further thought. 'So I am *he take nui.*' Hamiora said.

'Very. You see.'

'You know what I see, Hori? I see I never been damn important before. I see that.'

'True,' Fairweather said with pain.

There was another letter from Meriana. Was it true, this news Jonah brought from Turanga, that Hamiora had been sentenced to hang? Fairweather, she said, must write and reassure her; it could not be true. If there were a God in heaven, it could not be true.

Fairweather emptied a bottle and attacked a second to compose respectable answer. What could he say? That there was no God in heaven, and for that matter no heaven?

Telegraph messages from the centre of the island became sparse. There had been skirmishes, a few of Kooti's stragglers shot. This far, however, no one had seen so much as a footprint which might be identified as Kooti's; the land seemed to have opened up and swallowed him down. October was ended; November nudged into place.

'Soon one year since the massacre,' Fairweather told Allen. 'The government must have something to show.'

'Meaning?'

'The bird in the hand.'

Allen was quiet, but not long. 'You think so?'

'I am going to see Fox.'

'The pleas for clemency are still moving along the regular route; they might not have arrived on the Premier's desk. Or they may be making him dither. To arouse ire might produce uncongenial result.'

'November the tenth is arriving too fast. Old wounds will be open. Our hope was that Kooti's death or capture might make for an absent-minded fit of compassion. It cannot be counted on.'

'Compassion?'

'History. I should have believed Ropata. Legend and magic. If we spared one, he said, Kooti would survive. Kooti has, or seems to.'

'You cannot take blame for Kooti. You are too harsh on yourself.'

'You have yet to hear me on that subject.'

'At all events you cannot have it both ways. The fact is that you spared Hamiora.'

'For Fox, his judiciary and government, to make good that flaw?'

'Go to see him, then,' Allen said. 'Or try to. Meanwhile I shall consult a map of the empire; I shall look for a colony where I might have less of a past and more of a future.'

'You have a past?' Fairweather asked.

'By the time you have finished with Fox,' Allen said.

The Premier's staff had never been imposed on by a recuperating militia captain with carved Maori walking stick brutal in hand. Resistance collapsed and took cover. Fairweather rapped briskly on Fox's closed door, breathed deep, and turned a handle. Within was no beefy ape of a colonist. Instead a small, bald and white-bearded man of perhaps sixty, with pen in pale fingers, was bent to documents on his desk. He looked up at Fairweather mildly.

'I make no apology for this intrusion,' Fairweather said.

'I have yet to ask for one,' Fox observed.

'Captain George Fairweather, sir.'

'Ah,' Fox said. Then, 'Do you mean to close the door behind you, or must I?'

Fairweather kicked the door shut with the better of his two legs.

'And do you intend just to stand there?' Fox asked. 'Please take a chair.'

Reluctant to give away high ground, Fairweather lowered himself into a padded item of furniture; the pain in his leg eased.

'Now,' Fox suggested, 'explanation is due.'

'You shall have it,' Fairweather said. 'I shall also be asking one of you.'

Fox was in no haste to hear. He smiled agreeably and said, 'Don't think, by the way, that your name is unknown in this office. I am familiar with it twice over, in truth. Quite recently, in the establishment of a southern friend, I was admiring one or two of your prettier little paintings; I could not fault the draughtsmanship, only the lack of discrimination. You overdo things so, Fairweather. Work more within your means. As a soldier, as most prefer to know you, your virtuosity also seems to keep company with imprudence. Nonetheless, my government is appreciative of the pains you have been to over the past year to quell Kooti; your endeavours will not go unrewarded. Do I make myself clear?'

'Then I can come quick to the point, sir. I should be most rewarded by an affirmative answer to the pleas for clemency on behalf of the convicted Maori Hamiora Pere; they should by now have come to your notice.'

'Indeed they have,' Fox said. 'I disposed of them this morning.'

'I presume your response, sir, is not to remain a state secret.'

'Smoke, if you feel so inclined, Captain Fairweather. Relax. I have no objections to the fumes of a pleasing tobacco. My distaste resides elsewhere. Perhaps a little tea too?'

'The response of your government, sir?'

'This matter, as you must know, has become excessively complicated. Are there times in your life, Captain Fairweather, when you wish the world away?'

'One Maori, sir? Complicated?'

'When all viewpoints are taken into account. How fortunate we are as painters, Fairweather. We have only the one viewpoint. Our own. And if we are persuasive with the brush, we make others share it.'

'You still beg my question, sir.'

'Then my answer is that politics is a horse of another colour, Fairweather. Yet the beast must be ridden.'

'Are you telling me decision is not yours?' Fairweather asked. 'Or not made? Postponed?'

'We have had a decade of war with the Maori, Captain Fairweather. For the greater part, from good Christian motive, we treated the Maori fairly as foe. We took prisoners and freed them again. We took their land, never their lives. That, I suggest, was mistaken. Perhaps even pernicious. It kept the pot boiling. It encouraged belated rebels like Kooti to chance their arm. Had we been firm from the start, there might have been no massacre in Poverty Bay.'

'And perhaps no Maoris either.'

'To take the extreme view.'

'The extreme view is currently all I have, sir.'

'Let me put it this way, Captain Fairweather. A Maori feels no shame for death in battle, by the gun or by bayonet. Some appear to revel in the prospect. What we have most lamentably failed to do as colonists, I suggest, is fill the Maoris with wholesome dread.'

'Wholesome, sir?' Fairweather was baffled.

'Quite so. There is no glory in swinging by the neck from a gallows. There could be no misinterpreting that message; every aspirant rebel must take heed.'

'You would seem to be talking of your decision, sir.'

'It has not been postponed,' Fox said. 'Nothing is changed. It has all been decently considered. The prisoner will hang.'

Fairweather heard paper rustle, a clock tick.

'We may need only the one,' Fox added.

'And it doesn't matter which?' Fairweather heard himself ask.

'No expense has been spared. Legal ceremony, as you must know, does not come cheap. The colony's purse is not bottomless. You would surely not have it done all over again?'

'So the merits of clemency go for nothing?'

'Politics, Captain Fairweather, is all fraught decisions. Yet this prisoner can be seen as a godsend. With one potent example we may guarantee the lives of colonists and law-abiding Maoris.'

'And you have a political promise.'

'Our wish for stern measures is shared by the populace. To the extent that it is judicious, we must be seen to be stringent.'

'And to the extent that you have a *tutua,* perhaps. A landless nobody, sir. A prisoner presenting no problem.'

'There has been fair trial and a spirited defence. Kooti himself could not demand more, had he been captured. When will he be, Fairweather? When?'

'I share your wonder, sir. But I am talking of Pere.'

'And I am no longer. Thank you for so frank an expression of your concern, Captain Fairweather. There is no more to be said. Though it may surprise you, I am not without melancholy myself.'

'Sir,' Fairweather began.

'I think it in your own interest to press this no further, Fairweather. I am willing to overlook your unruly intrusion. I am even willing to put it down to extravagant consumption of liquor. But only up to a point. That point appears to have passed.'

'The date?' Fairweather asked as he levered himself to his feet.

'It should come as no surprise to you.'

'November the tenth.'

'Exactly one year. Sometimes I think that such as ourselves – men of affairs, yet also of art – are set on this earth to impose shapely form on human endeavour. What do you say?'

'Nothing, it would seem, Mr Fox.'

'Make yourself useful to the colony, man. Waste my time and your talents no more.'

Fairweather, as he went to the door, heard Fox's voice behind.

'Would it help, Captain Fairweather, if I instructed prison authorities to allow you full and unimpeded access to the prisoner between now and the due time? I think I can rely on you not to abuse the privilege. More to the point, you might have some calming effect.'

'That is most thoughtful of you, sir.'

'It is the least a Christian can do,' Fox said.

'Who is to tell Hamiora?' Allen said.

'Me,' Fairweather said. His mind was less on Allen than on the particulars of mercy. To smuggle a revolver into the prison would be no great feat. Presenting it suddenly to the rear of Hamiora's head might involve a ploy of more ingenuity. The outrage would be greater than that of a financially deprived hangman; there would be the colony to pay out with a prison sentence of salutary dimension. On the other hand, if Ropata had it right, a shot might herald the end of Kooti. Allen could plead at Fairweather's trial that things Maori had begun to prey on his distinguished client's mind; that there was ample mitigation.

'Only three days more,' Allen said. 'You will tell him today?'

'I shall sleep on it tonight,' Fairweather said. 'That will shorten his wait to two.'

'By tomorrow they will be erecting the gallows. One day to raise it, another to test.'

'Then I shall drink a bottle less than warranted,' Fairweather proposed, 'and visit very early.'

'I note that you pass no opinion on Fox,' Allen said. 'Nor on his species.'

Fairweather, embarked on oblivion, found time to spit.

'I think India may suit me more,' Allen decided. 'If we are to rule, let it be with style. Not as unkempt colonists; as kings of creation.'

Fairweather woke with inflamed brain and despoiled gut. As nightmare lifted he was left with one worse. All the same, he was not long in arranging the revolver under his tunic, and hiding it still further under a bulky coat. Metal pressed uncomfortably against his ribs as he paused at the prison entrance; he knew himself too late. There was the sound of hammer and saw, of men at work with timber of the sturdiest kind. The commotion would be heard in Hamiora's cell, its meaning unmistakable. Fairweather did not linger in the prison yard or view the tradesmen employed there this bright November morning. He proceeded fast to the cell, but was late there too. Hamiora sat in converse with a man of the cloth Fairweather had not seen before. A substantial representative of his sort, perhaps in his fifties; rather sharp nose, and severe lips, but with eyes not unkind.

'It is all right, Hori,' Hamiora said. 'You do not have to tell me. Mr Hadfield has told.'

He did not speak quite without tremble; his eyes were still bruised with grief.

'Hadfield?' was all Fairweather managed.

'Octavius Hadfield.' The cleric stood, a little breathless, with an asthmatic wheeze. 'Archdeacon of the Wellington diocese. You, I take it, are Captain Fairweather, of whom I have heard much. Not least from our mutual friend Hamiora.'

'Archdeacon? Does the church bring out artillery at first sniff of a Maori soul to be plucked from the gallows?'

Hadfield remained calm; he did not mean provocation to reach him here. 'I have worked for clemency also, Captain Fairweather. This morning I likewise feel bitter. Better that I came personally, I thought. I have worked thirty years among Maoris, and nursed many woes, but never have I seen a day more degrading. That shallow man Fox and his cronies are set on their course. They do not pause to consider how God might view them. Or even what history will say.'

'If anything,' Fairweather said. 'And of God's likely ruling I have even less competence to speak. Hamiora?'

Hamiora looked up. There was a slow tear.

'Are you brave today, Hamiora?'

Hamiora had to think. Hadfield said, 'In the past hour he has swiftly proved himself so. He is reconciling himself to the thought that God's ways are not for our judgement.'

'I hold no brief for the Almighty,' Fairweather said, 'but He must be acquitted of part in this.'

'As you please, Captain Fairweather, but I insist that His deliverance is here.'

Deliverance of less protracted sort was available under Fairweather's jacket. Two buttons to undo, a butt to grip. Then quick. Hamiora would have no time for prayer. To hell with Hadfield.

'God is a good man,' Hamiora said quietly. 'He waits for me, Hori. My Father. I understand now.'

Hadfield said, 'And Hamiora also understands that, unlike many, he has forty-eight hours to prepare himself for that divine meeting. Forty-eight hours to grow calm. He now knows that to be his good fortune.'

Hadfield gazed lengthily at Fairweather. It was as if he saw into Fairweather, knew of the revolver.

Meanwhile Fairweather's moment was gone. The sound of hammer and saw seemed to grow louder.

'Shall we all three pray together for guidance?' Hadfield asked.

'Me?' Fairweather said.

'We,' Hadfield said. 'All three.'

'You too, Hori,' Hamiora said. 'You must help.'

Hadfield and Hamiora knelt. So presently did Fairweather.

35

Cloud swarmed up from the cold south; rain flicked on the prison roof for most of Hamiora Pere's last night. He had been transferred to the debtors' cell, with more space for callers, also with a shorter walk to the gallows, desirable if a condemned man dragged his feet. Hadfield and Fairweather sat with Hamiora while he ate a large supper. Well before midnight he drooped and slept. Hadfield prayed briefly. Fairweather was quiet.

'You should take rest,' Hadfield argued.

'You also,' Fairweather said. 'Yours is the largest task in the morning. You paint God on his golden throne well. I almost envy Hamiora his journey.'

'Don't mock,' Hadfield said. 'What can you give the boy?'

Fairweather found no reply.

'You see,' Hadfield said.

'I shall see out the night here,' Fairweather said. 'You go home and have yourself woken at five. I have a flask for company; it can be depended on to help me doze. I also have some small matters to attend to.'

'Small matters, Captain Fairweather?'

'In the eyes of God, shall we say.'

'Your cynicism does not convince, sir. Redemption waits upon you too.'

'Get out, Hadfield. Go home. If Hamiora should wake early, I shall have him mouth the right prayers until you arrive.'

'These small matters you speak of. You mean nothing drastic?'

Hadfield, it seemed, still had suspicions.

'It is not my intention to interfere with formalities,' Fairweather promised. 'God will still have His exit line. I am more concerned that Hamiora is sped off reliably. You look to the spiritual, Hadfield; I shall care for the physical. I have been known for my dedication to the extinguishing of life.'

'Of course,' Hadfield murmured, and went.

Fairweather considered Hamiora; the boy slept with mouth open, snoring, apparently dreamless. The hours could soon pass. He left Hamiora to a guard, and limped off to the warden of the prison, a gaunt man with something of the pallor of those he kept in confinement, by name of Prince.

'I came to talk of tomorrow,' Fairweather said.

'The arrangements are excellent,' Prince said.

'Even so, you do not have much of this here.'

'It is a law abiding community. Three in ten years.'

'That suggests lack of experience.'

'Today's rehearsals were most satisfactory. We have even effected an improvement in the manner of the drop, one which might well be adopted elsewhere. Generally it is worked by a screw. One of our more inspired tradesmen has come up with a mechanism worked by a lever. It will make the drop speedy once signal is given. There will be no agonized pause.'

'The hangman?'

'He has performed the office in Sydney. We have been holding him here for minor crimes. In return for his duties tomorrow, he goes free.'

'A Sydney criminal?'

'Of the sort who see pickings here. He appeared most proficient in rehearsal. The remuneration offered attracted no other useful candidates. Besides, this fellow has a reputation to uphold. He even insists on wearing no disguise. He wants to be recognized and remembered; he hopes for further employment if native problems persist.'

'Might I meet this ambitious man?'

'To what end, Captain Fairweather?'

'To satisfy myself of his talent, sir.'

'Isn't my word sufficient?'

'To be frank,' Fairweather said, 'it is not.'

'It is in the middle of the night,' Prince said, 'and all most unnecessary. I am not even sure I have the authority. Your access is to the prisoner; not the executioner.'

'I require only an informal minute, sir. If I find him lacking, or a liar about past performance, I shall report to you accordingly; and volunteer my own services.'

'Surely not.' Prince was shocked.

'And furthermore with no remuneration other than a warming glass at the end.'

'What troubles you, Captain Fairweather? And at this late hour?'

'Thought of a job botched. My interview with the man might serve your interest too. There will be journalists present tomorrow. As critics judging the most theatrical of civilized procedures, they make it their business not only to record every tremor of the man expiring; also every flaw in the performance.'

That gave Prince thought. 'Very well,' he said finally. 'You may have your minute or two with the man. No more; I insist.'

'A few seconds may be enough to stomach,' Fairweather said.

Prince called a guard. 'Take Captain Fairweather to Bird's cell,' he ordered.

Bird the hangman was also sleeping well, possibly in a dream of the first tavern en route to the town tomorrow. He woke with complaint when Fairweather touched his shoulder; a fleshy, foul-smelling man heaved up from blankets. 'Has there been a bloody reprieve?' he said. 'Who the hell are you?'

'There is no reprieve,' Fairweather said. 'And I am a friend of your client.'

'So what do you want?' Bird asked.

'To offer inducement. Ten pounds, in short, to excel.'

'Of course I'll do a good bloody job. But if you got money to throw around, I'll take it. My oath.'

Fairweather sat on the edge of Bird's bunk and looked over his shoulder. The guard was out of earshot, in conversation with another. Fairweather lifted a small vial from his pocket and passed it to Bird. 'This,' he said, 'goes with the sum mentioned.'

'What is it?' Bird asked. 'Poison?'

'Quiet,' Fairweather said.

'Well?' Bird was hoarse, afraid, but still counting pounds up to ten.

'Chloroform. To be sprinkled discreetly within the hood before you cover his face for the more sensitive spectators.'

'The bugger might go to sleep on me.'

'Not with moderation. Just a few drops. You do not draw the hood over the face until the last moment. Then press it into his mouth and nose; press hard.'

'You'll get me hung too,' Bird said. 'I couldn't get away with it. The stuff stinks.'

'Where everything reeks, a small whiff of chloroform will command small attention. Anyone near will likely think he imagined it; and put it down to nerves. And other odours are notoriously attendant upon hanging, are they not?'

Bird shook his head. 'I don't like it,' he said. 'Why you doing this anyway? The sod will soon be gone one way or the other.'

'I wish to ensure he goes the one way. In calm.'

'You must want it something bad.'

'Just so,' Fairweather said. 'Twenty pounds, then. And the best possible lawyer to represent you should this be detected. I should assume primary responsibility and say I menaced you. Not bribed.'

'Twenty?'

'My limit.'

'I got away with worse in my time,' Bird decided.

'I'm sure,' Fairweather said.

He returned to the warden. 'Well?' Prince asked. 'Do you find Bird adequate?'

'He doesn't go out of his way to be lovable,' Fairweather reported, 'but my impression is that he may have feeling for the work.'

'My thought too, Captain Fairweather. Mind you, when all is said and done, it is the clean crack of the neck that is important. If we don't get that, then we are in trouble.'

'We?' Fairweather said.

He took his place in the debtors' cell for what was left of the night. Hamiora still slept under the eye of his lacklustre guard. One candle fluttered. Shadows were tall.

'Have a piss,' Fairweather told the guard. 'Take a long walk; brew some tea. I shall keep him quite safe.'

'You sure, sir?'

'I am a man given to meditation, which is what I most require now. Otherwise I shall ensure that the prisoner remains intact for the morning's festival. I wouldn't wish to disappoint anyone, the prisoner included. Lock us in as you go.'

'I'll look in now and then,' the guard promised. 'And bring breakfast at five thirty.'

'Breakfast too?'

'They go off better on a full stomach. Gives them more heart, so to speak.'

Fairweather sat immobile after the guard left. At length he found his flask, his pipe and tobacco; other comfort was lacking. Toward morning he dozed. He patrolled serene landscape with Larkin in summer light. Nothing had ended. Nothing begun. It was not yet November the tenth.

It was; and again. Hamiora had woken. It was just after five. He tugged at Fairweather and said, 'Where is Mr Hadfield?'

'He will be along soon,' Fairweather said sleepily, and then quite awake.

'Hori, I think I need him much now.'

Hamiora stood shivering in his prison nightshirt, barefoot on the stone floor.

'Dress yourself,' Fairweather ordered. 'Wash. Give yourself things to do. Mr Hadfield would tell you that you can't go to heaven unscrubbed. You must look your best.'

Hamiora made shaky use of the pot beneath his bed and asked, 'Hori, tell me more of heaven.'

Fairweather wished bitterly for Hadfield. 'I am no authority,' he said. 'All I have heard of heaven is from men who have thought on the subject. I have not been afforded a glimpse.'

'But you believe?'
'Today and our yesterdays might hardly be worth living if heaven were not.'
'I think I do not understand,' Hamiora said.
'I am not sure I do either,' Fairweather said. Hurry, Hadfield. Hurry.
Hamiora pulled on a clean shirt, with collar cut off so not to impede the noose; trousers with legs slit so his limbs might be bound easier. 'Tell me how you think it is, Hori. Tell me now.'
'As I told you to think of Poverty Bay. All things fruitful. All things fair.'
'Birds too?'
'And fish.'
'Trees?'
'In light everlasting. Perhaps waterfalls too.'
'But you will not be with me, Hori.'
'Then I shall be at pains to be a candidate also. Meanwhile you will find it all most familiar. Your soul will lack nothing of joy.'
'True, Hori?' the boy asked.
'As true as I can tell,' Fairweather said.

The guard arrived with Hamiora's breakfast and, more mercifully, with Hadfield. The breakfast was fried liver, bacon and a brown mess of potato. Hadfield said grace before Hamiora began on it hungrily. While he ate, Hadfield said, 'Thank you, captain, for your vigil. It seems it has been an easy night.'
'I have made it worthwhile,' Fairweather said. He could hardly say more; or that he had less faith in Christ than chloroform.
When Hamiora had finished, and noisily gulped down tea, Hadfield began prayers. Fairweather felt it tactful to excuse himself; Hamiora could now be given more reliable intelligence of heaven. His flask had been emptied too fast; he took his pipe and tobacco out into a prison walkway. He saw the first colour of day in bleak sky beyond bars. Rain still fell. Less than three hours left; soon only two. He heard the rise and fall of Hadfield's voice, sometimes Hamiora's in unison.

Less than two hours; suddenly one. Propped against a stout wall, Fairweather was lighting his pipe again when a hand gripped his shoulder. He swung about as fast as his damaged leg allowed and saw, so help him, Herrick. A Herrick thinner, weathered, and drawn.
'How?' Fairweather asked. 'When?'
'Last night,' Herrick said, breathless. 'The steamer hovered out in the harbour and didn't berth until first light. I went to your hotel first, to locate

you, and then hurried here. I had not realized there was so little time left. It cannot be true. Cannot be happening.'

'You don't have to depend on my word. The law is as vehement. One pound of flesh; one Maori morsel.'

'Then we are all damned.'

'A man with a fine sense of vocation is currently convincing Hamiora that he certainly is not. Keep your voice lower.'

'Is this what we have been hunting Kooti for? What kind of colony are we trying to make safe?'

'The one there will be,' Fairweather said.

'Better Kooti's barbarism.'

'What happened this time? You had a sitting duck.'

'Commanders again; like Whitmore again. Quarrels. Loss of nerve. But it was only in respect of Kooti we failed.'

'Only,' Fairweather mocked.

'He has to be finished. Everything suggests that he is stumbling here, staggering there, among tribes who refuse to make him welcome or to hear of Jehovah. He doesn't know where to go or what to do. He may push back into the Urewera mountains and find sanctuary among Tuhoe still willing to listen. Even there we will get him.'

'Too late.'

'Don't you care?'

'Not especially, Herrick. Not after eight this morning.'

'Is memory so short?'

'It promises to be.'

'Meriana sends love. Jonah and Jimmy too. The house is a picture, the land also. When I left Poverty Bay, it was still their thought that you would save Hamiora.'

'Hadfield in there is saving what can be. The battle is his.'

'Yes; and there is this,' Herrick said. He gave Fairweather a long envelope. Embossed, sealed, official. 'It was at your hotel. I thought it might be important, so I brought it along.'

'Only a reprieve would be important. We should have heard of it by now.'

Fairweather cut open the envelope. A page slid out and fell to the floor. Herrick bent to retrieve it.

'Read it to me too,' Fairweather said. 'The essence; no more.'

Herrick scanned the page. 'It could be worse,' he said.

'I take it I am not to be court martialled and deported for activities unbecoming a killer.'

'On the contrary. A grateful government, in recognition of your recent services to the colony, hereby presents you with five hundred acres of Poverty Bay. They don't stint. The best of the land to be confiscated.'

'Sugar to sweeten a sour tongue.'

'It is not to be spurned. Or will you make more of this?'

'To what end? Nothing has raised the dead these last eighteen hundred years.'

'Then you will take the land.'

'Did I say that?'

'No one could argue it unearned. Not even Kooti.'

'Herrick, I weary. You drain me still more.'

'Of course you must take it,' Herrick decided. 'It is your duty to yourself. You owe it to offspring. Your landholding will be more than marital; you will be a colonist of substance.

'Please, Herrick.'

'By all means,' Herrick said. 'Your answer is plain.'

There was silence in the debtors' cell.

'Your moment is here,' Fairweather told Herrick. 'Go and say your goodbye. Remember he is already dwelling elsewhere. Be tender. Don't break the spell.'

'You can rely on me,' Herrick said.

'I know,' Fairweather said. 'Kiss him sweetly for me too.'

At ten minutes to eight all were in company with Hamiora: Hadfield, Herrick, Allen and Fairweather. Allen was last to arrive, still penitent about legal failure, and now physically scarred too; he wore bruises and grazes from a drunken attempt to break down Premier Fox's residential door the night before. The constabulary had arrived and been at pains to subdue him.

'Let us kneel with our brother in Christ,' Hadfield said.

Fairweather knelt with an arm around Hamiora. The boy began to shiver; the shivering mounted when the sheriff entered the cell and requested the body of Hamiora Pere in compliance with law. Hangman Bird arrived too, no more attractive in daylight, cord dangling in hand. He bore down swiftly on Hamiora, jerked him into standing position, and bound his wrists behind him. Hamiora whimpered; the sound became a powerful moan.

'Your prayers,' Hadfield pleaded. 'Remember your prayers.'

Hamiora, eyes stricken, moan rising, was deaf.

It had to be Fairweather. 'Listen,' he said ferociously to Hamiora. 'Listen to me.'

Hamiora quietened while Bird tied knots.

'One day,' Fairweather said, 'men will want to know more of this. You may be even more important than now. Your manner of leaving this world will be recalled. Understand? We all can be forgotten. Captain Robert, Mr Allen, me; even Mr Hadfield. All. But never you.'

Hamiora was impressed. Even Bird was given pause.

'So be seen as a man,' Fairweather said. 'Let it be known, and forever, that never did a Maori win more mana in departing this life. That never was there a Maori – not Kooti, not even Ropata – with more mana seen. Understand?'

Hamiora gazed at Fairweather; he seemed to be finding a path through his anguish. Passing seconds ballooned to grotesque size.

'I understand,' Hamiora said. 'I remember mana.'

'All the way,' Fairweather said. 'You are no more a *tutua*. Never, never a nothing.'

'Very bloody goodbye, Hori. And you never mind. You never mind nothing no more.'

'Thank you, Hamiora. I may very well not. Remember your prayers, and go well.'

They pressed noses; Fairweather felt Hamiora's cooled tears drip on his face.

Hadfield headed the procession to the scaffold, reciting firmly from his book of prayer. Hamiora followed, head erect, with Bird and the sheriff. Then came Prince and other servants of justice, followed by Fairweather, Allen and Herrick with official spectators and journalists.

Hamiora's step did not falter when they met the rain and greasy earth of the prison yard. Soon he appeared to be leading, rather than Hadfield. The scaffold arrived, the noose, the open coffin below; Hamiora had no difficulty finding the steps up to the platform. Hadfield's voice rose above the whispers, the shuffles, the more resonant preliminaries. Hamiora moved to the noose without guidance; and stood. Bird, who seemed the more nervous, bound the boy's legs and adjusted the rope about his neck.

'Your prayers,' Hadfield urged.

Hamiora repeated them quite audibly until Bird presented the hood and pulled it over the boy's face.

Now press, Fairweather said silently. Press.

From below the gallows he could not see.

Bird leapt almost in fright to the lever which colonial enterprise had provided; and had to wait until Hadfield was finished. Hamiora's hooded shape hovered in the thin rain, quite still, quite alone; surely a vision Fairweather would never shift.

'In the name of the Father, the Son and the Holy Ghost,' Hadfield ended, raising his hand as signal. 'Amen.'

Bird grappled with the lever, which stuttered. With another tug it fell; the drop too. Fairweather shut his eyes and saw symmetry seethe in darkness; within the crash he heard worlds collide, suns, moons, and stars. Finally he was numb and knew nothing.

He heard Herrick say, 'Dear Christ. He's not dead.'

His eyes opened. Hamiora twitched and heaved on a rope which swung right and left. The chloroform had been no help, nor could be now. Bird, hurrying down steps, gazed baffled at his indifferent handiwork; and did no more than continue to gaze. Others seemed equally unwilling to do other than witness slow strangulation, though there were utterances of horror, with some fascinated, others turning aside.

Fairweather hobbled free of the crowd, bumping Bird to one side, casting away Ropata's stick, and launched himself with momentum at Hamiora's legs. Something seemed to tear in the boy's neck or spine, but Fairweather hung on, his own feet swinging short of the earth, until he was certain of life relinquishing the slight limbs. Then he fell. Herrick and Allen raised him from the slimy ground. Something more potent than mud oozed down his face and seeped into his shirt. Excrement, tears perhaps; and certainly the substance of Hamiora's lost manhood expelled in his spasms. Allen steadied Fairweather on his feet; Herrick held Ropata's stick ready. Fairweather declined to grip the fiercely carved wood.

'It seems to have served its purpose,' he argued. 'As I have mine.'

He swayed, slow to command equilibrium, until his eyes met Hadfield's.

'Pray, sir,' he asked. 'Pray that my room in hell is made trim.' More loudly, for others assembled, he said, 'I pronounce Hamiora Pere hung by the neck until he is thoroughly dead. Vengeance is ours. May you fry forever too.'

Even Hadfield flinched.

They waited until the prison physician confirmed death, until men delivered Hamiora's flesh to its coffin.

'Come,' Herrick said. He walked Fairweather away. 'You did all you could. The shame, the stain, is never to be lost now.'

Hadfield walked with them. 'We are all guilty,' he whispered. 'All.'

Fairweather raised his face higher. The rain had lifted. Beyond the prison yard his eyes found bird and cloud, but mostly mountains heaped on hills; a horizon of land. He tried to live his future. It refused to begin.

To Hadfield he said, 'Until doomsday, then, sir.'

'Doomsday, Captain Fairweather?'

'The day when, so word has it, we see whose arse is blackest.'

Fairweather's war was done, not to be won; he went on.

Fact and further:

HAMIORA PERE, after execution for high treason in November 1869, was buried within the precincts of the now demolished Terrace prison in Wellington; his bones have not been rattled in more than a century. Neither his name nor his trial is mentioned in formal histories of New Zealand; his name is not even familiar where it might most be expected to persist, among the Maoris of Poverty Bay whose ancestors fought both for and against Te Kooti Rikirangi (see below). His unmarked grave, under weeds in a pocket of urban waste ground, once neighboured the residence of this narrator, who would thus like to imagine the story haunted into existence.

KOOTI, or Te Kooti Rikirangi as he became better known, was probably born about 1830, and died in 1893. Though two or three times wounded, he was never apprehended. Time and again, for another two years after 1869, more than four years in all, he evaded entrapment in the New Zealand forest. He continued to win followers and raid settlements, leaving many more Maoris dead in the attempt to remodel his race much as Cambodians of the Khmer Rouge were to winnow their own people in the late 20th century. When both he and his pursuers were wearied, some close to death, he was given sanctuary by other still dissident but quiescent Maoris in the North Island interior. He was officially pardoned in 1883, eleven years after the last shot had been fired in his direction, but was blocked, by a muster of armed colonists and aggrieved Maoris, when he tried to make peaceful return to Poverty Bay in 1889; he was detained, briefly imprisoned, and celebrated by colonial society upon his release. He gave his last years to the founding of the Ringatu Church, an institution based largely on his reading of Old Testament texts, but cautiously taking Christ into account, which still has several thousand Maori adherents today. Te Kooti Rikirangi practised faith healing, sometimes with apparent success, and was revered by his followers; it was even rumoured that he could walk on water. No reliable portrait and certainly no photograph of the man exists; he refused to turn his face toward posterity. He prophesied an accidental death for himself, and so it was, after the iron-shod wheels of a runaway cart passed over his body. A memorial beside the harbour where he passed his last years claims that he was 79 years old when he died; on balance the age of 63 years seems more likely. To prevent desecration of his remains by those who still loathed him even in death, the site of his grave was kept secret by the four loyal disciples who toiled to dig it, in darkness, by the light of an oil lamp; that secret perished with the four and his resting place is still as much a mystery as the man.

WHITMORE, or Major-General the Honourable Sir George Stoddard Whitmore, KCMG, MLC, remained prominent in New Zealand as soldier, politician and affluent landowner until the end of his life in 1903. In 1902, with time's chariot waiting, he braced himself for departure by publishing a book called *The Last Maori War in New Zealand.* Age had not wearied him, nor the years condemned; the book is as lusty a compilation of lies as any to grace military history.

TRADER READ, or Captain Read as he was also known, was born in 1815 and died after an apoplectic argument with a fellow colonist in 1878. The verdict at his inquest was 'Died by the visitation of God, and not by any violent means whatsoever'. Turanga, the port where he prospered as pioneer trader, was renamed Gisborne at the beginning of the 1870s when it was formalized as a town; in 1986 it was a modest city of 33,000 people. The only visible trace of the former trader is a riverside road called Read's Quay.

BIGGS, or Major Reginald Newton Biggs, was 38 years old when, with his 19-year-old wife Emily, and new born son George, he died in the Poverty Bay massacre; a darkly weathered memorial records their names, and those of other victims, in a small cemetery just outside the city of Gisborne. In the vicinity, with Te Kooti Rikirangi and his violent life and times now romanticized, and racial matters sensitive, the event has lately and tactfully been renamed 'the Poverty Bay incident'. Other than for amnesiacs, however, the massacre remains a massacre; nor is there any name sweeter for that which transpired on Ngatapa's summit, beneath which human remnants are still found, or on the sites of those vanished Urewera villages where only bird and wind now reside.

ROPATA, or Major Ropata Wahawaha, was born about 1807 and died in 1897. His tribe, the Ngati Porou, powerfully survived the colonial era, and is still influential today; Ropata encouraged farming and education, and lived to see the beginning of an impressive revival of Maori spirit after the depletions of war. In recognition of his service in the campaigns against Te Kooti Rikirangi he was awarded a government pension and, along with many of the tribesmen he led, a comfortable acreage of Poverty Bay land; in his case with a cottage. He later sold land and cottage profitably. He also received a New Zealand Cross, the colonial equivalent of a Victoria Cross, from *Kuini Wikitoria,* and a sword of honour. Ropata became a member of the colony's Legislative Council, and on his death, at or near the age of 90, he had a spectacularly thronged martial and Maori burial.

ROBERT HERRICK, like George Fairweather, is another story. Herrick, not to be confused with a colonel of the same surname who likewise fought in the New Zealand wars, was born in 1843. He published a small and undistinguished book of verse, *On The March,* consequent upon his martial adventures; and after leaving government employ was for a time a freelance journalist and then an editor of prudently liberal persuasion. Twice elected to Parliament, he had a short and patchy political career, flawed by a cavalier stance toward the colonial electorate. Much about his later decline is mysterious, and even the date of his death is difficult to establish. Excessive dependence on drink has been suggested as one cause; sexual irregularity another. A last sighting, in 1898, had him down at heel and selling newspapers in a Wellington street. He would then have been 55 years old.

FAIRWEATHER? A composite character in these pages, yet still far from fictional, he was born in 1824 and died in 1901. From the time he took up land in Poverty Bay at the end of 1869 he seldom moved outside the region; he played no further prominent role in local or colonial affairs. In accord with his instruction, there was no military tribute paid at his funeral, which took Maori form. His wife predeceased him in 1890. There were three children of the union, and an adopted son, James Newman. Fairweather was known as a somewhat reclusive colonist, an apparently conscientious husband and father, and infrequent churchgoer; otherwise he appears to have been a workaday farmer and Sunday painter. A memoir of the man, published after his death by a sometime fellow militiaman named Michael Mulhooly, records that on occasion Fairweather went into alcoholic retreat with an old Maori associate, Jonah Whakaari; and that these retreats began in proximity to November the tenth of each passing year. Some of George Fairweather's watercolours of early colonial life, and especially of Maori life in the mountainous Urewera before European intrusion, have begun to fetch respectable prices in auction rooms. Two of his dependents were also soldiers. Captain Matiu Fairweather, his first child, was killed in the foothills of Turkey's Sari Bair range while leading a silent night attack with bayonet by the New Zealand Maori contingent on the Gallipoli peninsula during World War I. Hours later on the same day, August 8, 1915, his adoptive brother James Newman, with the rank of sergeant in the Wellington Infantry Battalion, was killed by defective British salvo while attempting to hold the summit of Chunuk Bair against

Turks in huge number. By then there were few left with first-hand memories of the cruel season when Te Kooti Rikirangi led his Israelite warriors from the wilderness; a more extensive and durable season of slaughter had begun. (Fairweather, after his twopence worth of the 20th century, concluded that it was going to be no improvement on the last. As understatements go, that is one worth recording.)

One anecdote must be added. In the autumn of 1891, soon after his wife's death, Fairweather no longer felt bound by a promise he had once made her. He took his first substantial excursion outside Poverty Bay in two decades. Coach, steamer and hired horse – a journey lasting four days – carried him to the small coastal community where Te Kooti Rikirangi had been given land by the colonial government on which to dwell with his devout entourage and entertain visiting congregations of faithful. In his baggage, and then in his saddle bag, Fairweather had a revolver, often oiled and tested, which had served him usefully more than twenty years earlier. Among the many prophecies made by Te Kooti Rikirangi was one with personal pertinence. 'When I meet again with Fairweather,' he was recorded as saying, 'then I know death to be near.' In the event he had a bonus of another two years, before the wheels of an untended cart began rolling. Fairweather found a grey, lean, and volubly holy old Maori still much addicted to rum; a figure asking pity rather than venom. Fairweather's weapon remained in his saddle bag. When they were at last face to face, the two ageing men gazed at each other for some time. No hand was extended; no noses pressed. At length Kooti ended tension by offering a revised prophecy. 'Perhaps,' he speculated, 'we both die now.' Much as men mortally enfeebled, survivors of a long voyage with an elusive landfall at last seen, they sighed and toppled into each other's arms. An afternoon passed without unseemly incident. They drank more than was desirable for men of their years, talked often with vehemence, laughed sometimes, and grieved. They lurched on to sensitive ground when Fairweather asked Kooti if he might consider posing a second time for a portrait. After a time Kooti laughed loudly; the neighing no longer left a chill. Then he held up an open hand. The portrait was mentioned no more.

Toward night, after a temperate hour or two of rest, and when Kooti had conducted a tolerably sober prayer service for visitors, the two men walked a sandy shore. They had, after all, little to say to each other. Then Kooti halted; Fairweather paused too.

'You forgive me,' Kooti said. Not a question; a statement.

Fairweather agreed that this appeared to be the case; it also appeared to be the case that Kooti had forgiven him.

'That is so,' Kooti acknowledged.

'In which case,' Fairweather said, 'may Hamiora Pere, wherever now residing, find leniency in his heart too.'

'Hamiora Pere?' Kooti was puzzled. 'Who is he? Who was he?'

'Quite,' Fairweather said. 'Nothing. No one. Never mind.'

They walked on again. As day cooled and dusk grew, Fairweather confessed himself baffled by the world. Kooti, letting his pious face slip, confided that he likewise was often perplexed. Then, and for some time, the two men were quiet. They stood together, as stars brightened above, and looked out on dark sea.